THE FARBER
LEGACY

GEORGE ENCIZO

Copyright © 2015 George Encizo
All rights reserved, including the right to reproduce this book or portions thereof in any form whatsoever.
ISBN: 1507649274
ISBN 13: 9781507649275

Printed in the United States of America

To family and friends, thanks for all the great memories

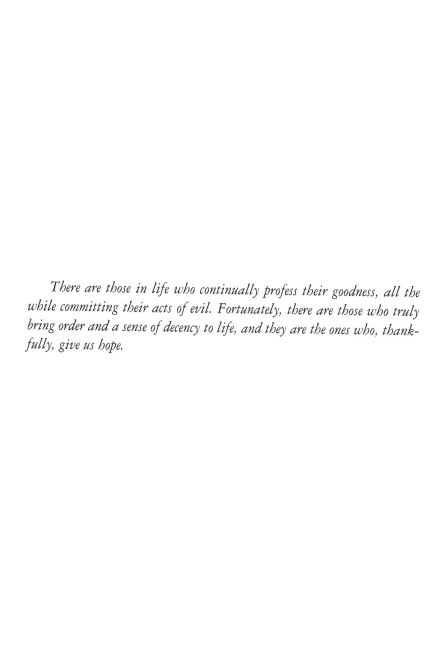

There are those in life who continually profess their goodness, all the while committing their acts of evil. Fortunately, there are those who truly bring order and a sense of decency to life, and they are the ones who, thankfully, give us hope.

THE FARBER
LEGACY

PROLOGUE

North Florida—1927

On a late Friday afternoon in mid-October, Sylus Farber harnessed his horse, Gertie, to the wagon after collecting his weekly wages as manager of a pecan farm inside the Florida-Georgia line. He had a three-hour trip south ahead of him to his small farm in White Springs. Sylus had been making this trip for several years. His wife, Myrtle; son, Sylus Junior; and their dog, Banter, would be waiting for him at home. He could have found employment in Lake City, but working the pecan farm paid more than the meager $2.32 per day from the few jobs available. As the manager, Sylus earned four times that amount and a bonus if the harvest came in on time. The country had gone through a mild depression in the early 1920s, and there were rumblings of another, possibly worse, coming.

Sylus didn't have to rely on his farm as a means of income, unlike many farmers who, unfortunately, were experiencing foreclosure. His farm was primarily for family needs. The crop supplied the necessities for their dining room table, as did the chickens and hogs he raised. Myrtle and his son look after the farm during the week while Sylus worked at the pecan farm. Sylus was up at four thirty every Monday morning, and after doing what chores were required of him, he began his trip. Since he couldn't afford an automobile, he had to make the trip either by horseback or by horse and wagon.

Sylus was halfway into his three-hour ride on the lonely dirt road. Late afternoons and evenings in North Florida were still warm but comfortable. The sound of cicadas could still be heard, and the fields still displayed an array of wild flowers. Except for the wild flowers, the terrain is mostly barren. The land is mostly flat with a few oak trees and an occasional deserted barn. When the wind blows, the dust makes it difficult for a traveler to breathe. This is pecan country, and it's also harvest time, when the farmers pick their crop. Further north, in Georgia, is peanut country.

It has been a long week for Sylus Farber, and he is anxious to get home to his wife and son.

"Hope we get home by dinnertime, Gertie, 'cause I'm gettin' hungry."

Sylus normally arrives home around eight o'clock, and Myrtle always has dinner waiting for him. When he gets home, he likes to play with his son after dinner. They play catch and afterward play fetch with their dog, Banter. Later, Sylus and Junior tend to their chores. Sylus has to clean out the stalls for their mule and for Gertie. He is in bed by ten o'clock.

So far the weather has been good to him, and he is always grateful for clear skies, but conditions are about to change. Suddenly the temperature dropped, the wind picked up, and the sky darkened. In the distance, he saw dark clouds and a storm heading his way. Sylus may have to bring Gertie to a gallop and hope they make it to one of the old barns up ahead.

"Come on, Gertie, we gotta beat that storm before it gets to us."

He gave her a light slap with the reins, and Gertie took off at an easy gallop, hopefully quick enough to avoid the storm. Sylus saw a flash of lightning in the distance and heard the ensuing clap of thunder. Judging by the sound of the thunder, he felt certain that they had time to reach shelter.

Another flash of lightning lit up the sky and struck Sylus, knocking him off the wagon. Gertie took off, leaving Sylus lying on the ground unconscious. Time stood still as he lay there with his hat nearby. When he finally regained consciousness, the weather had dramatically improved. Clear skies greeted him, but Sylus had no idea as to what had happened or how long he had been on the ground. Sylus didn't own a pocket watch, so to him, time meant nothing. He judged time by the sun and shadows. No-see-ums nipped at his face. Sylus held his hand up to shield his eyes from the sun and looked around for Gertie and the wagon, but they were nowhere in sight.

Sylus swatted some no-see-ums and then walked over, picked up his hat, rubbed the back of his head, put the hat on, and started walking home. He hoped to eventually find Gertie and the wagon, unless she went on home. Minutes later, Sylus saw Gertie and the wagon in a field. She was feeding on the tall grass, and the wagon was still harnessed to her. Sylus whistled, and Gertie's head perked up. She turned toward Sylus and then trotted over to him.

"Good girl, Gertie." He climbed onto the wagon, grabbed the reins, and gently snapped Gertie's rear. "Come on, girl, let's get on home. Don't know what the hell happened, but I seem to have lost track of time. Gonna be real late when we get home."

Gertie obeyed his command, and they got back on the trail. Sylus suddenly realized that it was no longer evening but midafternoon.

"How the hell could it be midafternoon now, when I left the farm late in the afternoon? Somethin's definitely not right."

Two hours later, Sylus arrived home. His wife, son, and dog were waiting to greet him, and all had worried looks on their faces.

Myrtle's concern appeared obvious by the tone of her voice. "Sylus, where have you been? We've been worried about you."

"No need to be worried, Myrtle. I'm just a little late. There was a lightning storm, and I was thrown off the wagon. I'm all right, though."

"Sylus, do you know what day this is?"

"Sure, woman, it's Friday. Why you askin'?"

"No, Sylus, today is Sunday. Are you confused?"

Sylus's eyes squinted, and then he scratched the back of his neck and asked, "What do you mean Sunday? Are you daffy, woman?"

"Sylus, it most definitely is Sunday, and we've been concerned where you've been all this time. Do you think I'd make something like that up?"

He wondered what really happened out on the trail. Sylus knew that he had found himself on the ground and his horse and wagon gone, but how could it have been for almost two days? Then he remembered the lightning. Could he have been struck by lightning and knocked unconscious? he wondered.

"Damn, Myrtle, the last thing I remember was a bolt of lightning. Maybe it hit me and knocked me unconscious, 'cause as far as I know, it's still Friday. You better take a look and see if I got any burns or bruises after I put Gertie away."

Sylus unhitched Gertie from the wagon and put her in the barn, and then Sylus, Myrtle and Sylus Junior went into the house. He sat, removed his shirt, and Myrtle looked him over. If he had been struck by lightning, he should show some visible signs.

"You do have a little burn on the top of your head, Sylus, and some hair is missing, but it doesn't look serious. You say you don't remember anything after the lightning struck?"

"Nope. Maybe it knocked me unconscious and I was out for almost two days, but that's a hell of a thing."

"Sylus, watch your language around Junior."

"Sorry, but this has me concerned. I'm gonna have to go see Doc Peters. Maybe he can explain it."

Doc Peters lived a mile from their home, and they would have to take the carriage. The carriage could only accommodate the three of them, so Banter had to stay home, and he wasn't happy.

Doc Peters was nearly seventy years old and had been practicing medicine in White Springs for about forty-five years. Everyone went to see Doc Peters when they had a medical issue. He could handle simple matters right there in the office located in his residence, but anything major meant a trip to Lake City, Tallahassee, or Jacksonville. The doctor's office had its own entrance, and the doc's wife served as his nurse, although she wasn't an actual nurse. She was all he could afford. Folks didn't have much in the way of paying the doctor for his services, so he had to do what he could to cut costs.

When they arrived at Doc Peters's office, he greeted them and showed them to his examining room.

"So, what seems to be the problem, folks?"

Sylus explained about the lightning and the loss of time. He also told the doc about waking up on the ground and how the last thing he remembered was it being Friday evening. Doc Peters listened carefully and then checked Sylus's head.

"Sylus, my guess is you were definitely struck by lightning and knocked unconscious. It's a wonder you weren't killed. Do you have a headache or any pain?"

"Nope. I feel just fine except for the loss of time. You mean I really was out for almost two days?"

"Yep. It's known to happen occasionally. You definitely are lucky. There's nothing I can do for you, but if you get any headaches or experience any strange sensations, you come back and see me."

"Thanks, Doc. I'll do that. Come on, Myrtle, let's get on home. I'm hungry, and seeing as how it's been two days since I et, I'm gonna want a dagum big dinner."

"You always eat a big dinner, so you must be okay because your appetite's fine."

Assured that he was all right, Sylus took his family back home. Myrtle prepared him a feast, which he devoured, making up for two days of lost meals. The next morning, Sylus got up early as usual for a Monday, and after a good breakfast, he and Gertie were off to the pecan farm.

CHAPTER 1

Lake City, Florida—1989

Sarah Carter and her family embarked upon their annual trip from Tallahassee to Lake City on Interstate 98 to visit her mother. Sarah was the last child of Myrtle and Sylus Farber. When Sarah was just a child, her mother worried that she might grow up and inherit her father's memory lapses. Joining her on the trip were Sarah's husband John, her son John Junior, his wife Emily and their five year old daughter Jessica. Myrtle was ninety-six and was approaching her final days. Myrtle and her husband, Sylus, moved to Lake City after their son, Sylus Junior, passed at the early age of twenty-nine. She had been living in an assisted-living facility for fifteen years.

For a woman of her age, Myrtle still had lots of spunk and a great sense of humor. John Junior loved to visit her and listen to stories about his grandparents and his mother. Myrtle always delighted in seeing her great-granddaughter when she came with her parents. Although Jessica was named after her maternal grandmother, she looked a lot like Myrtle did when she was a child.

Myrtle was lying in bed resting and asked if she could speak to John Junior alone. She had never requested that before, and everyone thought it strange but honored her request. After everyone but John left, Myrtle asked him to come close, as she had something of importance to tell him. At first John thought it may be another story about his mother, or possibly about an inheritance. He was about to find out that neither of those was the reason.

When John stood by her side, Myrtle asked him to put another pillow under her head so she could better speak to him. Myrtle lifted herself on her frail elbows, and then John got a pillow and placed it under her head.

"Is this okay, Grandma?"

"Yes, thank you. Come closer."

John grabbed a chair and sat close to her bed, and then leaned in so she could speak without raising her voice.

"John, I have something to tell you and a question for you."

He listened carefully as she told him about the time when his grandfather was struck by lightning. She told him the entire story, including his loss of time and other occasions when he would be gone for short periods and would have no recollection of where he had been.

"John, have you ever experienced anything like that?"

He measured his words before telling her.

"Yes, Grandma, I have. A few times I would experience a day or two when I couldn't remember where I was or what I'd been doing. I thought it strange."

Myrtle put a hand on his cheek and said, "John, you may have inherited it from your grandfather, and you should ask your mother if she has experienced anything."

"I will, Grandma, and I'll also watch for anything similar with Jessica. I asked my doctor about the memory loss. At the time, he could offer no explanation for it."

"Keep this a secret between the two of us, okay, John?"

"Yes, it will be our secret. I better go join the rest of the family. Bye, Grandma."

"Bye, John."

John then went to join his wife, daughter, and parents.

Six months later, Myrtle passed in her sleep, and the entire Carter family returned to Lake City for her funeral and burial. She was laid to rest next to her husband and son.

After the burial service, John called his mother aside, and while they were alone, he asked her the question his grandmother had suggested he ask.

"Mom, have you ever experienced periods when you couldn't explain where you were, and did you experience any memory loss?"

Sarah contemplated her words carefully before responding, but she had an idea that her mother had prompted his question.

"Yes, John, I have, but only a few times. When they happened, I shrugged it off as either due to childbirth, menopause, or old age." She smiled, put a hand on his arm, and said, "Why are you asking, John?" She didn't mention that when she experienced memory lapses she sometimes projected into the future.

"I was just curious, Mom." He failed to mention the conversation with his grandmother.

Five years later, John Carter Senior died from an aneurysm at the age of sixty-eight. John Junior became visibly upset over the loss of his father. He made a promise to himself that he would take care of his health and his body. John joined a gym and was there three times a week at six in the morning for two hours before going to the office. He also cut down on red meat and alcohol consumption.

Three years later, John experienced another memory loss. He visited his doctor and they decided to do a brain scan. The scan proved negative and his doctor told him not to worry about it, so he decided to let the matter rest.

CHAPTER 2

Randall County, Florida—2001

ecky Larson and Jennifer Williams, former college room-mates who had each been the other's maid of honor, were embarking on a journey that would take them away from their past. They met in the afternoon at the same house where they had previously discussed the idea of leaving Florida. The house belonged to some special friends and allowed them privacy to discuss how both could get away from their husbands. It was Jennifer who knew the specifics as to how it could be accomplished. There were going to be three of them originally, but the other woman changed her mind at the last minute. Jennifer gave Becky a special cell phone to give to the woman. She had to memorize the number to call and would have only one chance to use the phone. After that the number would be disconnected and the phone would no longer be in service. Becky wished the woman well and hoped someday she would change her mind.

Jennifer made a call and was told to drive to a secret location. Becky drove, and once they were there, she abandoned her vehicle and they were given another one for the first leg of their trip north. Jennifer made another call and was told where their next stop would be.

"They said we should drive to Atlanta. I have the address. We'll get further instructions there, Beck."

"This is so clandestine, Jenn, like in the movies."

"Yeah, we're like Thelma and Louise."

They giggled, and Becky got on County Road 373 heading north.

Jennifer turned the radio on and found a country music station. When Alan Jackson started singing, Jennifer played air guitar and chimed in, "It's five o'clock somewhere." Becky joined her.

"Feels like going on spring break, Beck."

"We sure partied then."

"We did some amazing things together too, Beck."

Becky turned, and they smiled at each other.

They were still singing when Becky glanced in the rearview mirror and saw the front end of a truck closing in on them. Before she could say something, a Chevy pickup truck rear-ended them. Both women were jerked forward.

"What the hell was that all about?"

"I don't know, Jenn, but they're still behind us and coming back. What can we do?"

The truck slammed into them again, and Becky struggled to maintain control. She checked the mirror again and noticed that the truck was now coming alongside them. The truck's passenger rolled down the window and tossed the rest of his orange Slurpee on the road.

"We can't call the sheriff because we're not allowed to. Maybe it was just some kids playing a prank, Beck."

"Some prank, Jenn."

Becky checked the outside mirror and noticed the truck was practically beside them.

"Jenn, they're coming alongside us."

"Hold on to the wheel, Beck, just in case. Maybe if we're lucky they'll go on by."

Today wasn't their lucky day. When the truck came alongside them, the passenger had the window rolled down and his arm extended holding a pistol. The truck bumped them hard as he fired the pistol. Becky lurched forward, and the bullet missed her but hit Jennifer in the shoulder.

Their vehicle careened to the right. Becky tried to stay in control, but her attempt was futile as their car sped toward the edge of the road.

"Jenn, I'm losing control!"

Jennifer touched her shoulder and quickly removed her hand. When she saw the blood, she panicked.

"Beck, I'm bleeding!"

Both were extremely worried as Becky lost control of the vehicle. She hit the brakes, and the tires screeched as the car careened off the road and landed front end down in a roadside ditch. Their airbags failed to open. Becky's body slammed into the steering wheel, and her rib cage cracked. Her head hit the dashboard and cracked her skull. Jennifer was thrown face first into the windshield and suffered a serious blow to her head.

They screamed just before impact, but no one heard their cries. Their pretty faces were a bloody mess of bone and tissue, and the inside of their vehicle was splattered with blood. They had both escaped abusive husbands, but bleeding to death in a car lying in an open ditch on the side of a Florida highway wasn't part of their plans.

The truck slowed, the passenger looked back at the wreck, and then it sped off as he rolled the window back up.

"Damn, that was fun, Jake."

"Why did you do that, Nate? That's not what I wanted to happen. What good is she now?"

Nate extended his arms with palms up and replied, "That's life, cuz."

Two hundred yards south, two teenagers were just turning onto 373. They saw the accident and watched in horror as it unfolded. The girl in the pickup truck screamed, and the boy reached for his cell phone as the girl buried her face in her hands and cried. As she sobbed, the boy dialed 911 and reported the accident but refused to give the operator his name.

CHAPTER 3

Tallahassee, Florida

John Carter just returned from lunch at the Back Porch. He entered Carter and Associates, LLC, and greeted his legal assistant, Jayne Burrows. Jayne had been with him for fifteen years, and he couldn't have asked for a more loyal employee. An attractive single mom with two teenagers, she always dressed in business attire, and her appearance was a pleasant distraction for Carter from the daily legal routine. Jayne always had a smile on her face. She resided in Northeast Tallahassee, unlike John, who lived in Dodson County.

Jayne was in Carter's office gathering some files off his desk. Smartly dressed, and with her coiffed light ash-brown hair, she looked exceptional to Carter.

"Good afternoon, Jayne. You look nice."

Jayne smiled and blushed. "Why, thank you, John, and good afternoon to you." She walked out of his office, turned and asked, "How was lunch?"

"Not bad. Maybe I'll tell you about it later, but for now I just want to relax and catch up on some paperwork before my doctor's appointment."

"Close the door, John—that way I won't disturb you."

As usual, she always thought of his well-being.

"Thanks, I'll do that."

Carter went to his office and closed the door. After placing his briefcase on the chair in front of his desk, he took his jacket off and put it over the briefcase, and then sat down behind the desk and pushed his chair back. He felt an urge to close his eyes, so he did as he stretched out with his feet up on the desk. Forty-five minutes later, Jayne tapped on the door then opened it. She noticed him napping and would have left him there, but he had to leave for his appointment with the doctor.

"John, wake up—it's time to leave."

Carter opened his eyes, rubbed them, and replied, "Sorry, Jayne, guess I was tired. What time is it?"

She looked down at her watch and said, "It's two thirty, and your appointment is at three fifteen, so get a move on."

"Okay already, I'm going."

He got up, grabbed his jacket and briefcase, and left.

A week prior, Carter had visited his doctor and requested another brain scan since lately he'd been having more episodes. Today he was to get the results.

Carter sat in the doctor's office patiently waiting for the results of the scan. He watched for signs on the doctor's face to determine whether the news would be good or bad, but all he saw was a blank expression. As an attorney, Carter had to be patient, but the waiting was wearing on him. Impatiently, he switched legs, crossing the left over the right then right over left. In the courtroom, judges and juries rarely rendered a quick decision, and Carter had to watch the faces of witnesses and jurors for signs of what they were thinking. Like juror number three, who constantly chewed on the arm of her glasses, and juror number eight, who would rub his jaw during testimony. And there's the witness who pulled on his tie before responding to a question. Would his answer be truthful or would it be a falsehood?

In all the years that Carter had known Dr. Jacobson, he never noticed the tell the doctor had that would reveal what his thoughts were. He always kept a blank look on his face. He must be a hell of a poker player. Dr. Jacobson kept perusing the two sets of scans, and Carter became more impatient. Finally, the doctor put down the scans, scribbled something on a pad, and then pushed back from his desk and looked straight at Carter. Carter hoped that whatever he'd written wasn't a prescription for him.

Dr. Jacobson rendered what for him could be construed as a smile and said, "So, John, you want the good news or the bad news?"

Carter could never read that smile. Was he being sarcastic or serious? Dr. Jacobson was a practicing neurologist in his sixties and had been practicing for over twenty years. He was known to give his patients honest medical opinions with his peculiar smile, whether good or bad.

"Give me the good news first. I've been so busy lately that I've been feeling a little stressful." Carter just wanted the news and now, whatever the outcome. Apprehensive, Carter waited hoping for good news.

Dr. Jacobson stood up, held the scans in front of him, put them on the lighted board for Carter to see them, and then turned to address him. Carter looked at the scans; however, he had no idea what he was looking at. He tried to discern what the doctor saw in the scans, but they only reminded him of his last vacation by rail and motor coach through the Canadian Rockies. He saw snowcapped mountains with peaks sometimes blurred by dense cloud cover. Carter recalled stepping out onto the Columbia Icefields in Brewster and seeing acres of snow and ice with no visible signs of vegetation. That was what the scans looked like to him.

"John, I'm going to be honest with you. There's nothing in this new scan that tells us anything. That's the good news, but I still don't have an answer for what you're experiencing."

Carter felt grateful for good news. However, he still had no explanation for what caused the episodes.

"Doc, that's good news. It's also bad news, because you still have no answer for me as to the cause. I've been wondering if I've been hallucinating, and the thought of schizophrenia entered my mind. It's not that, is it, Doc?" Just the idea of it really concerned Carter.

Dr. Jacobson looked at Carter, shook his head, and then answered, "John, where did you get that from? No, you're not schizophrenic. Your brain scan would have shown something, and it doesn't seem to be an everyday occurrence with you. It's probably caused by stress." Then he recalled their last meeting. "Didn't you once tell me that your mother experienced the same thing?"

Carter felt relieved that he didn't have schizophrenia.

"Thanks for saying that, Doc. I feel better, and yes, I did tell you that my mother also experienced them. She apparently inherited them from my grandfather. His doctor said it was nothing to worry about and not uncommon. Does that help explain any of it?"

The doctor pondered Carter's explanation, picked up his pen, and responded, "That's a hell of a legacy, John, and that doctor may have been right. There's nothing in my medical books that truly explains what you're experiencing. If you're not getting headaches and they're not affecting your lifestyle, then I suggest you don't worry about them. They're not doing that in any way, are they, John?"

"Not at all, Doc, I'm at the gym weekday mornings at six, unless I have to be in court early. I eat healthy except for the occasional business luncheon." He grinned and followed with, "They haven't affected my sex life either, in case you were going to ask."

Dr. Jacobson picked up the pad that he had scribbled on, nervously turned it in his hand, and Carter could see what he had written.

His tell sign, but who the hell expects to beat himself at tick-tack-toe? Carter said to himself.

"A little too much information, John, but yes, I intended to ask. If there's nothing else, my recommendation is to enjoy your life. One more question. Do you have any recollection from these episodes after you wake up?"

Carter scratched his chin and rubbed the back of his head then answered, "Actually I do get little bits of things. They're not much, a name or something. I remember once something about a Randall County and a sheriff. Does that mean anything?"

The doctor crossed his arms, looked up, and replied, "John, whenever you remember something, no matter how miniscule, write it down. You may even want to put it in a diary with the date and the time. What do you think?"

"I think that's a good idea. I can't believe I'm going to be keeping a diary."

Dr. Jacobson shook his head and grinned. "Just think of it as getting in touch with your feminine side, John."

Carter's head jerked back, and he held on tight to the arms of the chair. "Damn, did you have to make that last remark about getting in touch with my feminine side, Doc?"

The doctor again rendered his peculiar grin and said, "I'm just trying to be helpful, John. I guess we're all done here unless there's something else you want to talk about."

Carter smiled, got up from his seat, and extended his hand as a gesture of goodwill.

"Nope. I'm good, Doc, thanks. Hope I don't see you too soon." Carter paused then said, "Wait! You never told me the bad news, Doc."

"The bad news is you still have to see me for your annual physical and a digital rectal exam, John."

Carter stiffened and replied, "Shit, Doc, do you have to?"

"Yes, John, somebody has to."

Carter nodded his head then left the doctor's office. Since it was late in the afternoon, he decided to go home and take a nap.

CHAPTER 4

Creek City, Florida

Sheriff John Carter was sitting in his usual booth at Leroy's Diner having lunch and oblivious to his surroundings when Leroy Jones, who owned the diner, shouted from behind the counter for the fifth time.

"Hey. Are you the Randall County sheriff or not?" Each time Leroy shouted, he got no answer.

Leroy stood six foot five and weighed two hundred and fifty pounds of solid muscle, same as he did when he played running back for the Randall County High School football team. John Carter was the quarterback. The Cougars won the state championship in their senior year, and Leroy received a scholarship to the University of Central Florida, where he made All-American. He was later drafted by the Tampa Bay Buccaneers and played five years of pro ball before retiring after he hurt his knee. With his pro earnings, he purchased the diner and renamed it Leroy's Diner.

It had been successful ever since because of Leroy's personality, Cougar fame, and the diner's specialty—Friday rib night.

John Carter received a scholarship to Florida State, where he played only one year before an injury ended his college career. He graduated and went on to law school at Jacksonville State, and then went into law enforcement.

Having finally lost his patience, Leroy grabbed a copy of the morning newspaper, folded it, came from around the counter, and walked over beside Sheriff Carter. He slapped the folded paper hard on the counter in front of the sheriff, hoping to get his attention, but unfortunately he didn't. He did get the attention of everyone else in the diner, though. He slapped the counter again.

"Dammit, man, are you deaf or what?"

John Carter was deep in concentration, wondering who could be talking to him and where he was. He'd never heard of Randall County and had no clue as to who was the sheriff. John Carter lived in Dodson County, not Randall County, and was a lawyer, not a sheriff. Suddenly he snapped out of his trance and responded to Leroy.

"Hey, you don't have to shout, dammit. I'm not deaf."

"Then why didn't you answer me the first time? Your deputy has been calling you. Something about an accident out on 373. You best call her back, right away."

"Sorry, Leroy. I was lost in thought, and my brain kinda shut down."

"You've been doing that a few times lately, John. You sure you're all right?"

"I'm fine—it's nothing. I best call Amy before she gets worried."

Carter started to wonder what was happening to him. This wasn't the first time he'd had a temporary blackout and lost track of time and his location during a specific time frame. He might have to see his doctor and ask him about it, but for now he had business to take care of. Amy Tucker had been one of his deputies for almost six years, and she worried about Carter. She treated him like a son, even though she was just three years older than him. He dialed her number and knew she would answer immediately.

"Amy, it's Sheriff Carter. What's up?"

When Amy answered, he could hear the annoyance in her voice.

"John, where have you been? Have you had another one of your blackouts again?"

Amy had known about his blackouts for some time now. He'd confided in her several years ago. They both agreed that it would be their secret as long as it didn't interfere with his duties.

"It's nothing, Amy, I was just distracted." He hoped she believed him. "What have you got?"

She decided to wave off his response since she had urgent matters to deal with.

"There's been an accident on County Road 373. It's not a pretty sight, John. I'm here now, and we need you."

"I'm on my way. Be there in about twenty minutes or less."

"Best make it less, John," she snapped.

"Okay, I'll try."

Amy was aggravated because she'd been waiting in the heat for some time now before he finally answered her plea to Leroy.

Sheriff Carter left the diner and got in his car. He switched on the flashers and siren, and then drove to the accident scene. Fifteen minutes later, he was on CR 373. When he neared the accident, he turned to his left and smiled when he saw the dirt turn-off road and recalled fond memories of it.

As he drove past the turn-off road, he smiled and said, "Damn! What a great make-out spot that was. I bet it probably still is."

He slowed down as he approached the accident scene. Carter pulled over to the side of the road behind Amy's car and parked.

He turned the ignition off, turned in his seat, and almost put his foot on the ground until he noticed a soggy mess.

"Shit. Damn litterbugs." It was the last of an unfinished orange Slurpee.

Carter restarted the car and backed it up a few yards, and then got ready to exit the vehicle but checked the road first. Seeing nothing but pavement, he got out and walked toward the scene.

The sun blistered on his head, and heat radiated from the paved road. Were it not for his sunglasses, he would have been blinded by the bright sunlight. As he approached the accident, he saw two sheriff's cruisers, an EMS vehicle, and a fire truck. Then he noticed the Toyota Camry lying with its front end down in the roadside ditch. Carter could almost imagine what the passenger or passengers must look like in that mess.

The firemen had the doors pried open, and the EMS personnel had two bodies out and on the ground. The victims' heads were covered in blood. Both skulls appeared to be smashed, and there was no possible chance of survival.

He stepped closer and approached the scene carefully.

Amy stood there wearing sunglasses to shade her eyes and holding a pad and pen. Her streaked, dirty-blond hair was tied in a ponytail. Her hair color differed from Carter's dark brown with a hint of gray. She had a nice figure, although not quite the shape of a fashion model, but dressed in her uniform, she made quite an impression.

"What does it look like we got here, Amy?"

"First glance, it looks like a freak accident, but the front driver's-side window appears to have a small hole in it. I'd say it's not a freak accident but an intentional one."

"How did you find out about the accident?"

Amy gave him a frustrated look, as he should have known better than to ask.

"An anonymous nine-one-one call, but we'll get the name of the caller eventually."

Carter walked over, looked inside the vehicle, and then asked, "Didn't their airbags open?"

"Apparently not. Maybe they malfunctioned."

"So, this may be a crime scene. We'll have to wait before making that decision. Could you identify either of the bodies?"

Amy checked her notes and replied, "Two females. One is a Jennifer Williams, and the other is Becky Larson. Williams is from Orlando, and Larson is from Waterton. They may have been on their way to Georgia—otherwise, there's no reason to be headed this way."

County Road 373 West was an old paved road that took you past the state parks and eventually to I-75. It was bordered on both sides by palmetto bushes, occasional palms, and old water oaks that here and there provided a canopy. Where the Camry lay, there was no canopy and the surrounding roadway blistered hot from the overhead sun. There were two things you could be certain of in Florida: heat and mosquitoes. There was no shortage of either of them today.

Carter swatted a mosquito away, and then wiped his brow with his shirt sleeve.

"Maybe they were going to one of the springs, Amy. This time of year a lot of people go to one of them. Not much there, except some swimming spots." He turned his head and glanced the opposite way. "Or maybe they were on their way back from Georgia. Hard to tell which way they were heading by the position of the vehicle."

"Except that there are skid marks pointing north, so they weren't on their way to Waterton, John. Why weren't they taking I-75? What were they doing out this way?"

Carter mulled it over but still wanted to wait until they had more clarification. He swatted another mosquito. Amy did the same.

"I see your point, Amy. Let's find out if either of them has any family in Waterton. You know, the Waterton mayor's last name is Larson. Could be they're related somehow."

"Already checked. Becky Larson's husband is Peter Larson, the mayor. Jennifer Williams is also married, to a Sam Williams, or she might be divorced. We've already contacted people in Waterton and are waiting to hear back. We haven't checked Orlando yet."

"Good job. Let's get this mess cleaned up. Has Doc Warren cleared the bodies for transport?"

"He did, and then left, something about a family situation."

Doc Warren wasn't actually the medical examiner but often helped out at accident scenes; however, generally never at a homicide. They were left for the medical examiner, Marge Davids. Doc Warren was the chief medical examiner before he retired and Marge replaced him, which was why he was sometimes asked to act as the coroner on accident scenes such as this one. Randall County's small forensic department handled all autopsies in the county, whether from accidents, crimes, or natural causes. The department issued all death certificates, regardless of the cause of death.

Carter again wiped his brow on his shirt sleeve and said, "Damn, it's hot out here, Amy. It's probably his teenage granddaughter. She's been giving her parents a rough time lately. Who's towing the car?"

She stretched the corners of her mouth and said, "We all did, John. Bucky's Towing should be here any minute."

"Have him take it to the garage so the techs can look it over." He reached behind him, grabbed the handkerchief from his pocket and wiped his sweaty brow. His shirt sleeves were already soaked. "Come on, let's get back to the office and do some work from there. It's hot in this damn sun."

They walked over to their vehicles, and just before she got in her vehicle, Amy pulled Carter aside and asked him if he really felt okay. She also said that she worried about him. Carter told her not to worry about him and not to fuss over him.

"John, we need to have another talk soon."

Carter shook his head, got in his vehicle, and left for Creek City and the Randall County Sheriff's Office. Amy got in her car and followed him.

The Randall County Sheriff's Office was located in a one-story building in downtown Creek City. The back of the building housed a locker room with a row of lockers and a pair of restrooms. The sheriff's office was located at the rear near the three cells: one for the men, one for the women, and one for juveniles. An interrogation room, a small conference room, and a squad room with desks for the deputies were located toward the front of the building. Amy Tucker had her own desk, and none of the other deputies dared use it.

When they arrived at the sheriff's office, Amy got a call from someone at the Waterton mayor's office. The city of Waterton was inside Randall County, so Sheriff Carter's office was the official law-enforcement agency for the city. Waterton was a much smaller city than Creek City, with a population of approximately 4,500. The mayor had tried repeatedly to convince the city council to employ its own police force. Every time the subject came up, the council voted it down. They were satisfied with being under the jurisdiction of the sheriff's office.

The man who called said that his name was Peter Larson, and he wanted to know why Amy had called about his wife, Becky. Amy tried to be as delicate as she could as she told him the bad news.

"I'll be in Creek City and want to see my wife. Was she alone in the car, Deputy?" he asked.

"There was another female, sir, but we can't disclose her name at this time," she replied.

"Was it Jennifer Williams, Deputy?"

"Sorry, Mr. Larson, I'm not at liberty to discuss that information with you."

"I knew something bad would happen. I told Becky to stay away from Jennifer. If it was her, you best check her out. That's all I have to say." He hung up abruptly.

Amy practically slammed the phone down because of Larson's attitude and his abrupt hang-up.

"What was that all about, Amy?" asked Sheriff Carter.

"That was the Larson woman's husband, John." She crossed her arms, and her lips flattened as she tightened her expression. "Rude son of a gun. He wanted to know if Jennifer Williams was in the vehicle. He also said to check her out, as he told his wife to stay away from her. Then he hung up on me."

"Well then, let's do just that, but don't tell him anything more for now, and don't mention the hole in the window."

She grinned and gave him a thumbs-up. "Okay, John. I'll get Billy on the background check of both women."

Amy gave the information to Billy Thompston, told him what she wanted, and to keep the information confined to her and the sheriff. Billy said he would get right on it.

CHAPTER 5

Jacksonville—1991

Becky Johnson and Jennifer Brown had been roommates the entire four years at Jacksonville College of Art. This was going to be their last spring break before having to enter the real world after graduating. They were both art majors and weren't sure what they were going to do after college—perhaps a trip to Europe before seeking full-time employment.

The two met at freshman orientation and formed a special bond. They both decided to become dorm-mates in their freshman year. In their sophomore year, they found an apartment together and had been roommates until graduation. Both liked to party, so being roommates was convenient, since they kept late hours on weekends and often during the week. Neither had any interest in joining a sorority but participated in rush week just for the fun. They were each selected for a different sorority, but both declined.

Becky and Jennifer were going to spend the week in the Keys and had their reservations at one of the hotels frequented by the college crowd. For this trip, they each bought the skimpiest of bikinis and a good supply of T-shirts. They planned on participating in every wet T-shirt contest, showing off their plush breasts. Before finishing packing, they took time to model their bikinis for each other.

"Holly shit, Becky, you sure look hot in that thing, even though there isn't much of it."

Becky wiggled her ass and smiled. "I know, and all the guys are going to get a good show because I plan on showing off as much as I can." She looked Jennifer up and down then exclaimed, "Speaking of hot, you look great too. We are going to have fun, fun, fun, girlfriend!"

Jennifer wiggled her hips, cupped her breasts, and pushed them up. "Oh yeah!"

They finished packing, put their bags in Becky's Honda Civic, and were off to the Keys. It took them all of twelve hours to make the trip from Jacksonville. When they arrived at the Hotel DiMarco, they immediately took a nap after unpacking. Partying would have to wait a few hours, as they were too tired.

After a good nap, both girls were ready to party. They slipped on shorts and T-shirts without bras and headed for the nearest bar. The Tiki Bar was already filled with the college crowd, and the music and liquor were flowing. Jennifer managed to get them each a Jose Cuervo margarita in red solar cups, and then they found a place to sit and watch the crowd. It wasn't long before they were both asked to dance by two guys. The four got out on the dance floor, and the two girls let their bodies mingle with the others. After a few dances, the two guys bought them all a round of drinks, and then they danced some more.

Since this was their first night of partying and after a long drive, they decided to call it quits for the night. The two guys they had met were disappointed but said that they would see them again. Becky and Jennifer went to their room, stripped to their boxer shorts, and got in bed together. The room came with only one bed, so they had to share it, which was fine with them.

In the morning, they showered, headed out for breakfast, and then off to check out the crowds. For lunch, they went to a bar that was packed with other students on spring break. The sign by the entrance said, *Wet T-shirt Contest Today.*

"Becky, this place looks like fun. Let's hang out here."

"You're right, Jenn. Look at this crowd."

Everyone was getting really excited in anticipation of the contest. The announcer called for all participants to register and join him on the stage. Becky and Jennifer wasted no time signing up and getting up on the stage. When the crowd saw them, they started whooping and hollering. The two girls loved the attention and were prepared to give everyone their money's worth.

When the announcer called out their names, Becky and Jennifer took their positions, ready for the dowsing. Both were drenched, and their T-shirts clung to their bodies, revealing the shapes of their beautiful nipples. The jam-packed crowd screamed as Becky and Jennifer stood there shaking their booty for them. When their turn was over, they smiled at each other and laughed. It was why they came here.

The announcer shouted, "And the winners are, Becky and Jennifer."

To the amazement of both him and the crowd, both girls stepped up and took off their T-shirts. The place went crazy, and the announcer told them to cover up before the police arrested them. They obliged and accepted their award of two hundred dollars each. That night, they partied some more, and for the next three days did the same thing over and over. By the end of five days, they each had one thousand dollars, enough to pay for almost their entire trip.

On the last day, Becky met a guy from the University of Florida named Peter Larson. The two hit it off and spent most of the day together. Becky had to meet up with Jennifer in the evening for a last night's round of partying, so she said good-bye to Peter and gave him her telephone number.

"Call me sometime, Peter." She didn't expect he would.

After a night of partying, Becky and Jennifer retired to their room, but this time they stripped completely. They got in bed and enjoyed a night of pleasure. After several orgasms, the two fell asleep. In the morning they showered, dressed and went for breakfast. Jennifer paid the bill, and they left for Jacksonville.

Six months later, Peter Larson called Becky and the two started dating on weekends.

After graduation, Becky and Jennifer took a six-week vacation backpacking across Europe. When the vacation was over, they spent one long last night of pleasure together before going their separate ways.

Becky continued dating Peter Larson. After a year, he proposed and they were married. They moved to Peter's hometown of Waterton, where Peter got involved in local politics. He was elected mayor, and Becky taught art at the gallery where she worked.

Jennifer moved to Orlando and a year later met Sam Williams. They dated for a year, and then Sam proposed to her. A year later, they were married. Sam was a building contractor, and Jennifer ran an art gallery.

Both Becky and Jennifer's marriages went smoothly until three years later. Jennifer's marriage started to fall apart after Sam lost his contractor's license due to a faulty construction project on which someone was injured. He was considered at fault, and his license was revoked. Not long after that, he started drinking heavily and began hitting Jennifer. She eventually got a restraining order, followed by a bitter divorce.

Soon Becky's marriage began falling apart also when Peter Larson started hitting her, verbally abusing her, and having affairs. Since Larson was the mayor and a hometown favorite, there wasn't anything she could do to protect herself. Fortunately, one day Jennifer contacted her. It had been seven years since they had last seen each other, but their friendship never ended. The two of them met for lunch, and Jennifer told Becky her story, which gave Becky the courage to tell hers.

CHAPTER 6

Randall County—2001

Sheriff's Deputy Billy Thompston had just completed his search on Jennifer Williams and was about to give the information to Amy when Peter Larson entered the sheriff's office demanding to see his wife. Larson became extremely annoying, shouting and demanding to see the sheriff. Amy tried her best to placate him, but he just ignored her and shouted even louder.

"I don't want some imbecilic deputy talking to me," he shouted. "I demand to see the sheriff, and right now!" He slammed his fist on a desk and screamed, "My wife is dead, and I want to see her and want to know what happened, you imbecile."

The "imbecilic" remark really pissed Amy off, and she would just love to put this idiot in jail. She understood that he was grieving the loss of his wife, but there was still no call for that remark.

John Carter got up from his desk and stepped out of the office as soon as he heard the shouting. Visibly annoyed at Larson's comments, he would have said something about them but decided to ignore them, thinking it was grief causing Larson to act like a complete asshole.

"Mr. Larson, sorry for your loss," Carter said sympathetically. "Why don't you come into my office and we can talk."

"I'm not interested in talking, and don't give me any bull-shit, Carter." Larson pointed his finger at the sheriff and yelled, "Where's my wife, Carter? What happened to her?"

The sheriff put his hands on his hips and replied, "You're not gonna get any answers with an attitude like that. And if you keep it up, you're gonna find yourself sitting in a cell until you cool down."

"Don't threaten me, Carter," shouted Larson. "I've been threatened by bigger fish than you, so just give me what I want."

Sheriff Carter had had just about enough of the idiot standing in front of him. Grief or not, he wasn't going to put up with this any longer and would make sure that Larson clearly understood him. He'd been down that road before and understood what was happening, but sometimes it's the ones who scream and protest the most that have something to hide.

Carter crossed his arms and calmly said, "You can keep acting like an asshole, Larson, but I'm not the least bit intimidated. If you want some answers, you're going to have to act civilized or get the hell out of here before I do something that you'll regret but I won't."

That was enough to take the wind out of Larson's sails, because he calmed down some, offered a half-hearted apology, and then followed Carter into his office. Carter offered him a seat and asked if he wanted coffee or water. Larson declined both.

There was nothing pretentious about John Carter, and his office reflected it. It was a plain and simple office, just a desk, two chairs, and a water cooler. Carter didn't show off any medals, awards, or pictures. He was a no-nonsense law-enforcement officer.

When Larson finally calmed down, Sheriff Carter tried to have a decent conversation with him.

"Mr. Larson, I know you would like to see your wife, but I'm going to be honest with you. I think it best you didn't for now. The accident was pretty bad, and I can tell you that she doesn't look pretty, so you may want to wait awhile. At least until we're finished processing her remains."

"What do you mean 'finished processing her remains'? I don't understand."

"I can't say any more, except there is a question as to the cause of the accident and we have to process everything." Larson frowned, obviously a bit taken back by Carter's comment. "Can I ask you a question, Mr. Larson?"

Larson's demeanor changed somewhat. "Sure. What is it you want to know?"

"Did your wife have any enemies that you know of?"

Larson's head jerked back in surprise at Carter's question.

"Enemies—what are you talking about? No, Becky was well liked by everyone who knew her. What's this all about, Sheriff?"

"Look, I really can't say any more. We're trying to do our job here, and as soon as we know more, we'll let you know. Can you go with that for now?"

"Do I have any choice, Carter?"

"I'm sorry, but no, you don't."

"Well, then, I guess I'll have to do things my way, Sheriff." Larson's attitude shifted to negative. "You'll definitely be hearing from my attorneys and some people I know."

Now it was Carter who was surprised.

"What's that mean, Larson?" Carter purposefully dropped the title.

"You'll find out soon enough, Sheriff."

With that, Peter Larson left. Carter called Amy and Billy into his office. He wasn't happy with Larson's remarks and figured he needed to get on top of this right away. He may have to talk to some people he knew.

When Amy and Billy entered the office, he asked, "Do we have anything new on this, Amy?"

"Billy finished the background check on Jennifer Williams. Why don't we let Billy tell what he found?"

Carter glanced at Billy and said, "Billy, the floor is all yours."

Billy Thompston was twenty-eight and had been a deputy for almost five years, right out of college. He had a psych degree that did nothing for him career wise. Billy turned to law enforcement and Sheriff Carter gave him a chance by taking him on as a junior deputy. Now, he was a full-fledged deputy and an eager one too.

Billy looked at his laptop and read his notes.

"Jennifer Williams is from Orlando. She's married to Sam Williams, a construction contractor. Jennifer manages an art gallery and is a successful artist in her own right. The Williams's have been married for about six years. I haven't checked with Orlando as to any criminal records, but they both appear to be clean. Jennifer graduated from Jacksonville College of Art, with an art degree, according to her bio."

Billy beamed with satisfaction at his presentation so far. He checked his laptop again and continued.

"It's worth noting that Becky Larson also graduated from the same college with an art degree. Jennifer's last name was Brown, and the Larson woman's maiden name was Johnson. I'll keep digging for more. Do you want me to call Orlando, or do you want to, Sheriff?"

Sheriff Carter scratched his chin and considered Billy's request. "Why don't I contact Orlando, Billy? I might be able to get more information. Amy, you check with the medical examiner. See if she has anything yet. Also, see if the crime-scene investigators have anything more on the vehicle, especially that hole in the window."

"I'll get right on it, Sheriff," Billy responded. "What are you going to do about Larson? Sounds like he's going to make trouble. You know what they say about he who protests the loudest? They're usually the guiltiest."

Carter nodded his head in agreement. "I'm thinking the same thing, Billy. While you're at it, do some checking quietly on Larson. Let's keep all this between the three of us. The other deputies have enough for now."

With that settled for the time being, Carter decided to drive over to Leroy's for some good cooking and maybe even a beer. After all that had happened, he could use one. Carter also had to decide how he was going to communicate with Orlando, and with whom.

At the diner, Leroy was busy cooking and talking with customers. As soon as he saw Carter, he took a break and came over to talk with him. The diner wasn't that busy, and therefore Leroy could let his fry cook take care of the cooking.

"So, John Carter, what happened out on 373? Was it bad?"

"I can't tell you much, Leroy, except that it was really bad. We got two corpses, and I got one angry husband." Carter pointed a finger at Leroy and said, "But, you can open me a bottle of beer and fix me a plate of whatever the special is. I don't care as long as it's not tripe."

"John, you know I would never feed you tripe." Leroy's cheekbones rose up when he smiled and quipped, "At least not that you would know I did."

"You son of a bitch...Is that what I had the other night? I thought we were friends."

Leroy's eyes danced as he smiled. "I'm just kidding, John. Geez, don't get your nuts in a knot. It was cow's gut what I gave you."

"Dammit, Leroy, that's what tripe is."

Leroy burst out laughing, and so did everyone else in the diner, mostly members of the Cougar football team and their girlfriends. Sheriff Carter gave them all a stern look. They turned their heads but continued giggling.

"You guys keep laughing and I'm gonna show you what a real football player can do. Ain't you guys got a game or practice to go to?"

Jimmy Cochran, the quarterback, responded. "Tonight's a bye week, and practice was this afternoon. Don't get offended, Sheriff. We're just ribbing you."

"I know, but today hasn't been a good day, and my mood ain't too good. Sorry, guys."

Carter's concern went back to tripe and whether Leroy had tricked him into eating it.

"It's okay, Sheriff. Does it have anything to do with what happened on 373?" Jimmy asked.

The sheriff's head turned toward the counter and Cochran. He thought about the anonymous 911 caller.

"What do you know about what happened out there, Jimmy?"

"I know there was a bad accident, because I'm the one who called it in."

Hearing that, Carter became extremely interested in what Jimmy had to say and beckoned to him.

"You better come over here and let's have a little chat. Don't worry, you're not in any kind of trouble, but I'd like to hear what you know."

Jimmy started to walk toward the sheriff, but not before his girlfriend, Tanya Miller, gave him a tug on the arm and a "don't you dare" look. The sheriff noticed the look. He'd seen it before from his wife.

Tommy placed his hand on hers and whispered, "It's okay, Tanya, I won't mention us." He walked over and sat down in the booth with Carter.

"Jimmy, tell me what you know and don't leave anything out, and I mean anything."

Jimmy leaned over the table, the sheriff leaned over too, and Jimmy told the sheriff it had to be in confidence. He didn't want anything coming back to him. Carter knew right away that it had something to do with him and Tanya. They were probably parked and doing something that Tanya's old man wouldn't be happy about.

"Okay, Jimmy, this is between you and me. No one else will know." Carter glanced at Tanya. "I take it you don't want anyone to know that you were with Tanya. Am I right?"

Jimmy's expression registered relief. "Thanks, Sheriff. Her old man would kill me if he knew. We were parked at that spot off 373 and were just turning onto the highway when all of a sudden we heard this noise that sounded like a gun firing. Then we looked to our left and saw a truck broadside a car. I got out of my truck to look, and that's when I saw the pickup truck speeding off. Next thing, the car swerved and landed in the ditch. We knew right away whoever was inside had no chance. I called nine-one-one and told them what happened." Tommy leaned closer, put his hand near his mouth, and whispered, "We left because, well, you know, Tanya and me."

Carter leaned back and grinned. They were using the make-out spot just like he used to when he was in high school. He leaned forward and replied, "Jimmy, did you happen to notice the license plate or color of the pickup?"

"Didn't notice the license plate number, Sheriff. It was too far away, but it wasn't a Florida plate, and the color of the pickup was either black or a dark blue." Jimmy sat straight and asked, "We cool, Sheriff?"

"Yeah, Jimmy, we're cool. Have a good season. I like your throwing mechanics. Any schools looking at you?"

Jimmy beamed. "Thanks, Sheriff. A few. I'm considering FSU. With Fisher becoming the head coach, I think the Seminoles have a good future ahead of them, finally."

Carter pointed his finger up, smiled, and said, "Wise choice, Jimmy."

Then Jimmy went back to his friends and his girlfriend. Tanya punched him in the shoulder, and it was obvious that she wanted to know what he said. Carter could tell that Jimmy told her that he hadn't mentioned her at all.

Leroy came over, opened a beer for John, and then fixed him a plate of fried chicken, corn, and mashed potatoes. For dessert, he gave him a big slice of apple pie with a scoop of vanilla ice cream. He asked Carter if he learned anything from the Cochran kid. Carter replied in the affirmative but couldn't say any more. Now he had to go talk with Amy about what he'd learned. With an eye-witness, this was definitely no accident.

CHAPTER 7

Tallahassee—2001

When Jessica Carter returned from her morning practice session, she decided to go to her room and take a nap before lunch. She had already put her damp swim clothes in the washing machine after entering the house. Her mother noticed her when she came in from the laundry room.

"Hey, honey, you're back early. Did you have a good practice?" Emily Carter always asked Jessica about her practice sessions since she had a keen interest in Jessica's swimming.

Jessica stopped, turned, and smiled. "Yes, Mom, I did but I'm exhausted. I'm going to lie down, maybe take a nap before lunch."

"Go ahead. I'll wake you when it's time."

Jessica turned, went to her bedroom, and changed into a pair of comfortable shorts before lying down. Immediately after reclining on the bed, she dozed off into a deep sleep.

In Louisville, Kentucky, the 2003 Duke women's swimming and diving team experienced their best season in school history and had reached the final four of the NCAA Championship. Anchored by two sophomores, Jessica Carter and Kristen English, competing in the 200-meter individual medley, 200-meter backstroke, 500-meter freestyle, and 1,000-meter relay, the Blue Devils were assured a victory in at least three of the events and possibly a record time in at least one.

Carter's specialty events were the backstroke and the individual medley. English's specialty event was the freestyle. Carter would most likely score a record time in the backstroke, and the team could possibly score one in the relay event. Members of the team were excited, and anticipation covered their faces like billboards.

John and Emily Carter watched in anticipation, as did George and Karen English. They traveled together in Carter's SUV. The excitement heightened as each minute passed before the first event, the 200-meter backstroke. When the starter's gun fired, Jessica was in the water first, with Kristen right after her.

"Go, Blue Devils!" the Duke crowd roared.

The two swimmers led the field through the entire event, and Jessica finished in record time, with Kristen seconds behind her. In the next event, the freestyle, Jessica also finished first.

Kristen was the only Blue Devil participating in the 500-meter freestyle. She landed first in the water at the start and paced herself throughout the event, saving her energy for the final laps. At the turn for the final two laps, she had a slight lead, but her extra lung power kicked in and she took a commanding lead, finishing in record time. Jessica waited at poolside to offer a congratulatory hug.

"Yay, Kristen! Way to go, girl," she shouted.

Kristen's face lit as she asked, "I got a record, didn't I, Jess?"

"You sure did. Let's get one in the relay."

The final event that would put the Blue Devils in the championship meet was the 1,000-meter relay. Each swimmer covered 250 meters. Melanie Parker led off, followed by Amanda Timmons, English, and Carter at anchor because the two hundred was her specialty. The team finished victorious and in record time.

What a day for the Duke Blue Devils! They were headed to the championship for the first time in school history. Carter's and English's parents were so proud of their daughters and glad they had made the trip. John Carter had hoped that his daughter would choose FSU over Duke; however, when she announced that she wanted to become a doctor and chose Duke because of their medical school, he was proud to become a Blue Devil parent.

Jessica woke from her nap and realized that she had lost all track of time and missed lunch. She hadn't realized she napped almost the entire afternoon since coming home from her Saturday morning practice.

Jessica yawned, stretched her arms up high, and said, "I hope I was just tired and didn't have another one of those episodes. I remember there was something about Duke, however."

She got off the bed, went to the bathroom, splashed water on her face, and then went to find her parents. When she entered the kitchen, her mother had just finished setting the table for dinner.

"Hey there. You must have been tired, because you slept right through lunch. I was going to wake you, but you looked too comfortable sleeping. I hope you're hungry."

Jessica rubbed her eyes, and then glanced at the pot roast on the stove and smiled.

"It was a tough practice. I have that big meet on Monday." She sniffed the air and rubbed her stomach. "I am hungry, and that pot roast looks good. Where's Dad?"

"Working in his office. Go get him. Dinner is about ready."

Jessica turned and went to get her father so they could all enjoy dinner together, and then maybe after watch some television.

Sunday evening before Jessica Carter was to compete in the Leon County Invitational representing the Sinclair Academy High School women's swimming and diving team, she noticed her father working in his home office reviewing an active case. She knew the current case he was working on because she was the one who got him involved in it from the beginning.

Jessica knew of this girl who was on another high school's swim team and often competed against her. The girl also volunteered at the library as a literacy tutor on the same days and time as Jessica. Rachel hadn't been coming to recent meets and wasn't at the library either for the past few weeks. At the last meet Jessica asked Rachel's coach about her. The coach implied that Rachel had a personal issue and had to drop off the team. The coach also gave no further explanation, but Jessica felt there was more. Jessica asked the librarian about Rachel, and she told her the same thing.

One of the girl's teammates overheard Jessica's conversation with the coach and approached her. She told Jessica that one day she saw Rachel's father talking to the coach, and whatever he told her made the coach upset. That's when Rachel dropped off the team. The same girl said there had been rumors about several boys taking advantage of girls, and she wondered if that was what might have happened to Rachel. She also offered that Rachel had once mentioned another girl, whom the teammate didn't know, invited Rachel to a party, and soon after, Rachel stopped coming to practice.

"Jessica, the rumors are that the boys were taking advantage of girls to prove their manhood, and most likely they were assaulting them. None of the girls had pressed charges for fear of reprisal," the girl told Jessica.

"That's awful. Thanks for telling me."

"Don't tell anyone that I told you, okay?" she whispered.

"I won't. It will be our secret." Jessica crossed her hands over her heart, lowered her voice, and said, "I feel awful for Rachel."

"Me too. See ya—I got to go."

Partly due to feeling sorry for the girl and partly feeling that she should do the right thing, Jessica told her father about what she learned and asked if he would talk to the girl and perhaps her parents. Carter was proud of his daughter for bringing the information to him.

"Jessica, I'm not really sure I can do anything. Maybe I should stay out of it."

She looked him square in the eyes and replied, "Dad, what if it was me and not Rachel—would you then do something?"

He touched her arm and smiled. "You've got guts, Jessica. I'll see what I can do. However, whatever I learn will be confidential and I won't be able to tell you anything."

She put a hand on his and responded, "Thanks, Dad."

"You're a heck of a negotiator, Jessica." He shook his head and lifted the corners of his mouth. "You should consider going to law school someday."

"I can't answer that, counselor. It's confidential."

They laughed, and Jessica left him to his case.

CHAPTER 8

Rachel Whatley had already told her parents what had happened and asked them not to go to the authorities for fear of reprisal, but Mr. Whatley insisted on it. The girl begged him not to, and finally he agreed to temporarily refrain from doing so.

On Saturday morning, John Carter decided to take a drive by the Whatley house, hoping to catch Mr. Whatley out working in his yard. The Whatleys lived in a middle-class neighborhood featuring one-story homes pleasantly landscaped with nicely manicured lawns. The home reflected the loving care given to the front landscape. Roger Whatley happened to be working on some flower beds in the front yard when Carter drove up. Wearing shorts and sandals to look casual, he approached the man cautiously, with his outstretched hand offering an introduction. Mr. Whatley stood up and eyed Carter apprehensively.

"Mr. Whatley, my name is John Carter. I'm an attorney. Do you have a minute?"

Whatley's eyes registered suspicion, but he removed his glove and shook Carter's hand.

"I'm Roger Whatley. What can I do for you?"

Carter attempted to delicately explain his reason for being there.

"I'm not sure how to go about this since I've never had to do it." He paused to think then continued, "I have information about your daughter and what happened to her. I'd like to offer my help." Carter waited for a response from Whatley, but he remained stoic. "I have a daughter about the same age as yours, and if anything like what happened to your daughter happened to mine, I'd be devastated. Please, I really would like to help."

Whatley seemed surprised by Carter's offer and wondered just how much he knew.

He removed the other glove and held them in his hand as he replied, "What makes you think something happened to my daughter, and if anything did, what help can you offer?"

Carter had no intention of revealing his source and would rather discuss the matter privately in Whatley's house.

"I know that something happened with a boy." He searched Whatley's eyes for a response then said, "I won't say how I know, but I believe I can help you resolve the matter legally." Carter then appealed to the man's sense of privacy. "Please, can we go inside to discuss it?"

Again Whatley appeared surprised, but being at his wits' end, he decided to listen to what Carter had to say. He pointed toward the front entrance.

"I'm willing to listen, but I'm not sure Mrs. Whatley will. Let's go inside—it's hot out here."

Carter followed Whatley into the house, where Whatley introduced him to his wife, Rebecca, who had been watching them through the front window.

"Rebecca, this is John Carter. He's a lawyer and wants to offer to help us with Rachel."

Mrs. Whatley's face turned white, and she exclaimed, "Roger, what have you told him? This is not for public disclosure."

"He already knows about Rachel's plight, and he assured me that he wanted to help us." Whatley extended his arms and waved his hands. "He didn't say how he knew, but I'm interested in hearing what he has to say."

"I'm not so sure, Roger," she replied. "What about Rachel?"

Neither was aware that Rachel was standing nearby and overheard the conversation between her parents and Carter.

Rachel tentatively approached them and said, "I know who you are. You're Jessica's dad. I've seen you at swim meets and once at the library. Did Jessica send you here? I didn't think she knew anything."

Carter felt that he had to be honest with the girl if he was going to help her.

"She didn't actually send me here, but she influenced me to come. She doesn't know what really happened to you but is worried about rumors she heard. Not necessarily about you. I really want to help you, Rachel," he replied, and then paused for effect. "I wouldn't like something like this to happen to Jessica, and I would do everything in my power to help and protect her, just as I would like to do for you, if you will let me."

Rachel studied Carter's expression and saw the sincerity in his eyes. "Seeing as how Jessica goes to Sinclair, I'm guessing you're an expensive lawyer, and I don't want to burden my parents."

"Jessica, you won't be burdening us, and I don't care what Mr. Carter charges. We just want to help you," Mr. Whatley interrupted.

Carter appreciated Whatley's comment and hoped that the girl would accept his offer to help.

"Yes, I am expensive, Rachel." Then he smiled and said, "However, my fee for your case will be one hundred dollars as a retainer and maybe a charge for expenses. I'm not sure on that." He crossed his arms and looked directly at her. "That's my bottom dollar if you accept."

Rachel looked to her parents for guidance. Still uncertain, Mrs. Whatley offered some assurance. "It's up to you, honey. You have our utmost support."

Carter explained that they had two choices: go to the district attorney and request an investigation, or pursue a civil suit using Jane Doe as the plaintiff, which could result in a criminal trial. He wasn't sure exactly how he would go about it, but he had a very good friend who could advise him on the best procedure. The civil suit would shield Rachel's identity until it was absolutely necessary for her to be made known, and even then she wouldn't necessarily be in the public record. Carter's explanation still had some unanswered loopholes to it, but the way he explained it to Rachel in a very understanding and sympathetic manner, as though he were talking to his own daughter, seemed to convince her and her parents.

"Mr. Carter, since you're Jessica's dad, I would like you to help me." She turned to her mother and father and pleaded, "Mom, Dad, please say yes."

"Okay, honey, if you want us to, then we will. Mr. Carter, we'd like your help."

"Thank you, Mrs. Whatley."

Rachel, Roger, and Rebecca Whatley agreed to let Carter file the civil suit but insisted on paying him. Carter argued against it but eventually relented and agreed to expenses and the one hundred dollars. He told them that he wasn't going to file the suit until he talked to his friend.

"Does your friend have any influence, John?"

Carter and Roger were now on a first-name basis since Roger initiated it.

"Roger, my friend is very influential and a very good friend of mine, so confidentiality isn't a concern."

"Then we're satisfied, John. Thank you." He extended his hand and they shook hands.

"Yes, thank you, Mr. Carter," said Rachel.

"You're welcome, Rachel. Mrs. Whatley, it was nice meeting you. I'll get back to you all soon." Satisfied with their acceptance, Carter left.

When he arrived home, before pulling into the garage, he made note of how more elaborate the landscape was than at the Whatleys'. Unlike Roger Whatley, Carter had a gardener who took care of it. After parking in the garage, he entered the house where Jessica was waiting for him.

"Where were you, Dad?" she asked.

"I visited the Whatleys."

She stood on tiptoes and shrieked, "You did? And what happened?" Jessica leaned forward, put her hands together as though praying, and pleaded, "Come on, Dad, tell me, please!"

Carter extended his arms, waved his fingers at her, and smiled. "Calm down, Jess. I can only tell you that we talked and I'm going to represent Rachel." Trying to calm an excited teenager is like trying to calm a raging bull as it charges toward you. Even matadors know better than to try. "I can't say any more because it would violate client-attorney privilege. Sorry, Jess."

She gave him a hug that almost squeezed the life out of him.

The next day, Jessica won the Leon County Invitational in both of her events. Fifteen schools from five different counties competed, and the next week she won again at another meet against another private school. She didn't tell her parents about her temporary loss of time and memory that occurred on Saturday morning. She attributed it to oversleeping.

CHAPTER 9

Monday morning, John Carter sat in his office perusing case files when his legal assistant, Jayne Burrows, tapped on his door. He had a slightly heavier caseload then he normally had. If Jayne had another case for him, he'd have to turn it down, especially after talking with the Whatley girl.

He looked up and smiled. "Yes, Jayne, what is it?"

"There's a Marge Davis to see you, Mr. Carter." Jayne turned her head slightly in the direction of her desk. "She said the attorney general sent her. Should I show her in?"

Carter leaned back in his chair and lowered his eyebrows. "Yes, please—but Jayne, before you send her in, would you do me a favor?"

"Sure, what is it?"

"Could you do that gaggle thing you do?"

Jayne interrupted him before he could say more. "It's Google, John."

"Whatever. Gaggle or Google, just please do me this favor."

She shook her head and noticed the legal pad on his desk with his writing on it.

"John, is your laptop on?"

Carter sheepishly looked at her. Busted, he replied, "No, it's not. I can't use that key thing because the letters are so small."

Jayne stifled a laugh. "I can get you a separate keyboard, John, like mine, but will you use it?"

He contemplated her suggestion and knew that if he didn't say yes, she would only badger him.

"Okay, but about that favor. Would you also do that thing and look up Bensmille, North Carolina, for me?"

"Certainly, John, but what's it for?"

Carter had no idea except he had written the words down after his last episode.

"Just something I wrote down and don't know why. Now, send that woman in, and thank you, Jayne. By the way, I thought we gave up standing on ceremony and agreed you would address me as John. We've known each long enough."

"I know; however, when she said the attorney general sent her, I figured formality was necessary, John! I'll send her in and then go do that favor for you."

She punctuated the word *John*, so he knew she was right. Carter said nothing, just smiled, and she smiled back. Jayne escorted Marge Davis to his office and introduced them. Not knowing if she was married or not, Carter chose to address her as Mrs. Davis.

After his conversation with the Whatleys, Carter had called his friend the attorney general for advice. Without mentioning the girl's name, he explained Rachel's case and asked if it was possible and if it had ever been done before. The attorney general said she wasn't certain but wanted to check on it and would get back to him expeditiously. He guessed that this must be what she meant about getting back to him.

"Mrs. Davis, it's nice to meet you. How is Patricia? She's not looking for another campaign donation, is she?" Carter extended his hand.

"It's Ms. Davis, and the attorney general said you would ask that question." She accepted his handshake and followed with, "The attorney general sends her regards and best wishes to your wife and daughter."

"That's nice of her, thanks. Please have a seat. What can I do for you, Ms. Davis?"

"If you don't mind, could you call me Marge?" Then she sat down. "I'm not one for standing on ceremony, especially when I'm not on official business."

Her comment about not being on official business intrigued him. Why had the attorney general sent her if this was an unofficial business matter?

"I'm not sure what you mean by unofficial business. Please explain. And if I'm going to call you by your first name, then you have to call me John. Okay with you, Marge?"

"Yes, thanks, John. Patricia sent me here to offer my personal assistance in a case you're considering involving a potential Jane Doe. I happen to be familiar with cases of that nature and would really like to help. You can call Patricia and ask her if she sent me. I'm sure she'll explain why, but I'd rather do it myself, if it's all right with you?"

Carter wondered how she knew about the Jane Doe case, but his friend had sent her, so he decided to hear her out. He decided there may be more as to why Marge was offering her services.

"I think I'd like to hear what you have to say, Marge. Tell me, why are you unofficially offering your services?"

"The attorney general is aware of my background and what your case most likely is about. I was once a Jane Doe myself, so I suspect, as does Patricia, that your case has to do with a teenage rape." She looked him square in the eyes and asked, "Am I close to the facts, John?"

Carter had a good relationship with the attorney general, and he knew she wouldn't have sent someone to him who didn't have knowledge of the facts surrounding his case. Marge's revelation that she was once a Jane Doe suggested that his friend was offering him some much-needed help.

"Without confirming anything, I'll just say you're within the ballpark. I'd like to hear more before I say anything else, Marge."

She sat straight in her chair, laced her fingers, swallowed, and then responded. "Let me start with a little of my background. I'm a licensed private investigator and occasionally have been asked to assist on sensitive cases, like yours. I was raped in my senior year of high school, and my parents chose to go the civil trial route with me as a Jane Doe."

Carter leaned forward and put his elbows on his desk as she continued.

"Unfortunately, we lost the case and the boy who raped me got away with it. He tried it again when he was in college; however, he paid a price for his actions, and he no longer has the ability to have sex with any woman. The girl had some influential friends, and that's all I can say." She paused for effect like Carter did in the courtroom. "I'm here to offer my help if you would like it. Unofficially, of course, but you can hire me as your PI." She raised the corners of her mouth and followed with, "I'm cheap, and for this case my fee is twenty dollars."

Carter smiled and stood, reaching out to offer her another handshake.

"You're hired, Marge, and I could really use your help. I'm at a loss right now and don't have much time."

She shook his hand and replied, "Well, your job just got a little easier, John, because I'm very good at what I do, especially in these types of cases. Was I right about a teenage girl's rape?"

"As a matter of fact, you were; however, I can't tell you her name just yet." He hit the desk with a fist and said, "Welcome aboard, Marge, and your fee is insufficient. We'll work that out. I'm a tough negotiator."

"So am I, John."

"One more thing. You seem to be on a first-name basis with the attorney general. Why is that?"

"Her father was my attorney, and his fee was twenty dollars too."

They both laughed, and then Carter introduced her to Jayne, who showed Marge to a small vacant office and set her up with whatever she needed. Marge thanked Jayne and went right to work, starting with reviewing John's meager case file. She also wanted to talk with Carter's daughter, Jessica. John said he would make her available when it was convenient for Jessica.

As Carter walked back to his office, he inquired of Jayne if she had done that favor he asked for.

"Jayne, did you gag—"

"It's Google, John. Say it—Google."

"Whatever, Google, Gaggle, did you do it?"

She laughed. "See, you can say it. Yes, I did, and there's no such place. Anything else?"

"Wait." Carter stepped into his office, glanced at the pad on his desk, and turned toward Jayne. "Could you do Randall County?"

"Yes, John, I'll go do it."

"Thanks, Jayne."

Jayne went back to her desk, sat at her laptop, and Googled Randall County. The response was negative, so she got up to tell Carter what she found.

Carter scribbled something in a small book when she entered his office.

"John, just like that other place, there was nothing on Randall County. Anything else you want me to search for?"

"No, but I'll let you know. Thanks, Jayne."

"Anytime. You really need to learn to use your laptop and get a real phone, one that I can text you on and you can do your own Google searches."

"I'm still a dinosaur, Jayne, and Emily and Jessica have one, so why do I need one? Mine works just fine for me."

Raising her eyes and throwing her hands up in defeat, Jayne turned and left.

Carter marked the result next to the notation about Bensmille in his diary.

Two days later, Marge met with Jessica and obtained the name of the girl who first told Jessica about Jane Doe's situation. She promised Jessica that neither girl's name would ever be mentioned. Jessica said that if it was ever necessary, she wouldn't mind, but Marge said she would have to talk with her further first.

After talking to the other girl, Marge managed to get more particulars. The girl slipped and mentioned Rachel's name. Marge acted like she didn't hear it and told the girl that everything they discussed was in confidence. No names would ever be revealed. The girl was very sympathetic toward Rachel and glad to help.

"Just as a precaution, don't say anything to anyone, promise?" Marge told the girl.

"I swear, and thanks for trying to help Rachel," she replied.

Marge was reasonably certain the girl wouldn't say anything. She had good instincts when it came to teenage girls.

CHAPTER 10

Marge Davis sat behind the desk in the small office Carter had provided her pondering her conversation with Carter's daughter. She reviewed her notes then completed a search on her laptop. Marge already had the name of the girl who'd told Jessica about Rachel Whatley. Marge had also interviewed her, and the information she'd gleaned from her was very promising. Although she didn't have the name of the other girl, she felt certain that Rachel might.

She decided to have a discussion with Rachel, but not before getting permission from Carter and the girl's parents. Marge had a feeling the girl hadn't told her parents everything about the night of the rape, and she wanted to ask the girl some questions. She wanted to do it one-on-one as she didn't want Carter or the parents present. Marge knew that it was going to be a challenge, but she needed it to be her way.

Carter happened to be in his office when she approached, so Marge decided to broach her idea with him and hoped that he would be receptive to it. When she reached Carter's office and tapped on the door, he seemed to be lost in thought. She knocked lightly. Still no response, so she called out his name.

"John. Earth to John—are you there?"

Carter suddenly realized she was there. He raised his head and responded.

"Sorry, Marge. I was lost in thought and didn't hear you. Come in. What's up—anything new?"

She stepped into his office and said, "John, I've finished talking to Jessica and the two girls she overheard. I want to talk to Rachel, and I'm going to need your help."

He leaned forward, frowned, and asked, "Why do you need to talk to her? Is it really necessary, Marge?"

"Yes. Because I honestly believe she hasn't told her parents everything about the rape and is holding something back. John, it's probably important." She sat down then said, "Can you trust me on this, John?"

He lowered his head and rubbed his hand through his hair, considering her request. Carter trusted Marge's instincts and decided to let her.

"Okay, Marge, I'll arrange it; however, I'm going with you. That's not negotiable."

"No problem, but if you and her parents let me talk to her alone, I believe I'll have better results. I promise I won't do anything to upset her."

Knowing Marge's background, Carter felt comfortable agreeing with her plan. He called the Whatleys and arranged the meeting, but they wanted it at their house. Carter agreed, and he and Marge made the drive together.

At the Whatley house, Carter rang the bell, and Mr. Whatley answered then invited them in. After a pleasant greeting, he escorted them to the living room, where Mrs. Whatley and Rachel waited. Mrs. Whatley was reluctant to put her daughter through any more questioning; however, she agreed to her husband's request.

"I don't want anything to further upset my daughter, Mr. Carter."

"I understand, Mrs. Whatley, and we won't do or say anything that will upset her. You have my word. Ms. Davis just wants to ask her a few questions."

Marge wondered how she would get the Whatleys and Rachel to agree to her talking to the girl alone, but she needed to do it her way, so she asked, "If it's all right with Rachel and you two, I'd like to talk to her alone?"

"I'm not sure I can agree to that, Ms. Davis," answered Mrs. Whatley.

Sensing that Marge respected her privacy, Rachel decided to put her mother at ease. She had some things to say, and they weren't for her parents' confidence.

"It's okay, Mom. I'd like to talk to Ms. Davis alone, if you don't mind? Please trust me on this."

Mrs. Whatley put a hand on Rachel's arm and said, "Are you sure, Rachel?"

Mr. and Mrs. Whatley looked at each other and then at Rachel.

"Absolutely, Mom."

"Okay, Rachel. Ms. Davis, you have our permission and we're placing our trust in you."

"You have my word, Mrs. Whatley. I won't do or say anything that would hurt Rachel."

Marge had already decided that the house was not the place to have the conversation with Rachel. She wanted someplace where Rachel would feel more comfortable and maybe more willing to answer questions.

"Rachel, would you like to take a walk with me? It's a nice day, and we can enjoy the outdoors. Is that all right with you?"

"I think I'd like that. Don't worry, Mom, I'll be okay."

The Whatleys nodded and watched Marge and Rachel leave the house. Carter knew that Marge was doing the right thing by having their conversation away from Rachel's parents. He was also glad that Marge was on his team.

As Marge and Rachel walked, a cool breeze offered a pleasant scent of fresh-mowed lawns. A squirrel crossed their path then scampered up a tree. At first it startled Rachel, but then she giggled as the squirrel climbed the tree. Marge smiled but sensed Rachel's nervousness.

During their walk, Rachel became more at ease and seemed ready to answer Marge's questions. Marge delicately asked for more details about the night of the rape. Rachel started by telling her that she had gone to a party with a friend of hers—at least she thought the girl was a friend. Later she learned that was a misconception on her part.

"Marge, at the party, this so-called friend introduced me to two boys. The four of us shared some conversation for a while, and then one of them suggested we all go to his house. His parents were away, and we could have a party of our own." Rachel fidgeted, looked right, and then continued. "At first I declined, but the other girl assured me it would be fun, so I agreed. The four of us left for this boy's house. He lived in a nice neighborhood. The other girl and I followed in her car."

Marge interrupted her. "Rachel, can you tell me their names?"

Rachel hesitated as she contemplated her answer.

"The girl's name is Debbie Lakes, and the boys' names are Andy and Dave."

The rest of the story was difficult for Rachel. She told Marge that the home had an outdoor pool, and they all decided to take a dip. At first Rachel was reluctant because she didn't have a bathing suit. Neither did the others. When the boys and the girl stripped down to their underwear and jumped in the pool, Rachel foolishly joined them. They played several games of "sea-horse riding" with the girls on the boys' shoulders trying to knock the other one off.

After the games ended, the four separated into couples. Rachel went with Andy, and Debbie went with Dave to separate bedrooms. Rachel and Andy went to the master bedroom and began making out. Rachel had kissed and made out with other boys, so she was okay with the situation. She also wanted to make out with Andy and felt that he was kind of cute.

"Marge, Andy started fondling my breasts. I didn't stop him and actually enjoyed it, but when his hand moved to third base, I said no. He persisted, and I protested, saying no over and over again."

Rachel's tone of voice changed to fear, and she told Marge that she started to push him away, but Andy grabbed her hands and arms and raised them above her head. She sensed another presence, and before she knew it, Dave forcefully restrained her on the bed. Andy took off Rachel's underwear then took off his own.

"I shouted, 'Please, no. I'm a virgin.' But he ignored my protest and said 'that's extra points.'" The rest was difficult for her, but she continued, "He mounted me while I continued to try to get loose. Dave was much too strong for me, and as much as I tried to get free, the tighter he held on to me." Tears formed on her face when she said, "Andy penetrated me and took away my virginity."

Marge glanced toward the street and saw a man and a woman dressed in athletic shirts, shorts, and footwear jogging toward them. They both waved and Marge waved back. Rachel lowered her head, and Marge assumed she felt ashamed. Marge and Rachel continued to walk only in silence.

"Take your time, Rachel. I know this is difficult; it was for me too," she said softly.

Rachel turned toward Marge and had a look of disgrace on her face. Marge put her arm around Rachel's to reassure her, and then Rachel continued her story.

"When it was over, I just lay there sobbing, feeling at last it was over. Unfortunately, it wasn't, because the boys switched places and Dave took his turn. When they were finally done, they got up and left me alone. The awful part is that Debbie watched everything."

Heavy tears rolled down Rachel's cheeks. Marge took out her handkerchief and gave it to Rachel. She wiped the tears then began to tremble as she spoke.

"I stayed there for quite a while crying and then finally got up and put on my wet underwear and left the bedroom to get my clothes by the pool. As I approached the pool, I overheard the three of them talking. Andy and Dave told Debbie that she did good, and they'd reward her later." Rachel wiped more tears then continued. "They didn't notice I was listening. When they saw me, Debbie walked up to me, handed me my clothes, and told me I'd be more popular now."

She looked toward Marge for acceptance. Marge reached down and took Rachel's hand and said, "It's okay, Rachel. You don't have to say any more."

"But I want to, Marge. I grabbed my clothes, started dressing, and yelled at her to take me home, right now. Then I shouted, 'I don't care about being popular.'"

Rachel told Marge what happened after they left the house. On the drive home, Debbie told Rachel not to say anything as those boys could make life miserable for her. Rachel remained quiet during the drive, and when they arrived at her house, she got out of the car, slammed the door, and then went into her house.

The following day she told her parents about the rape but didn't mention the pool party or the make-out session. She also said that she didn't know the name of the boy who raped her and had never seen him before that night. Her parents didn't question her any further, and the subject didn't really come up after that, until Carter approached her and her parents.

"It that all, Rachel?" Marge asked.

"Yes, Marge, but please don't tell my parents. I feel so ashamed, and I'm afraid of what they'll think of me."

Marge understood Rachel's pain, so she confided in the girl about her own rape and what she went through. Marge said that she told her parents every detail about the rape.

"Rachel, the smartest thing I did was telling my parents everything. However, if you want to do the same as I did, the decision is up to you."

"Thanks, Marge, for sharing. I'll think about it."

"Rachel, what kind of car does Debbie drive?"

"I don't know, but I know it's a yellow one. Does that help?"

"Yes. Thanks, Rachel."

On the way back to the Whatleys', Rachel decided that she would do as Marge had done and tell her parents everything.

"Marge, I'm going to tell my parents everything, but would you be there with me when I do it?"

"Absolutely. I'm happy you decided to, Rachel."

When they got back to the Whatley house, Rachel told her parents and Carter the whole story. The Whatleys broke down in tears, grabbed Rachel, and practically hugged the daylights out of her. Carter looked at Marge and mouthed "good job" to her. Marge mouthed "thank you" back. She now had the so-called friend's name and the first names of the two boys.

Mr. and Mrs. Whatley thanked them both, especially Marge, and then Carter and Marge left for his office. As they were leaving the Whatley neighborhood, Carter told Marge that she was good, really good, and he understood why the attorney sent her to him.

"Thanks, John. I'll tell you what I learned tomorrow after I do some more investigating."

Marge had more to work with, and the first thing she planned on doing was to interview the so-called friend, Debbie Lakes, and get the last names of the two boys. Marge planned on showing the girl no mercy. This was getting personal with Marge, but she would manage to keep things in perspective.

"Okay, Marge. Let me know what you learn."

Feeling good after the day's events, Carter called Emily and asked if she was up for dinner at a nice restaurant. She said absolutely and asked if he felt good about being a lawyer.

"Without a doubt, and if I weren't married to you, I'd ask the attorney general to marry me."

Emily laughed and said, "What would her husband say if you did?"

They both laughed, and Carter said he would see her later.

CHAPTER 11

The following afternoon at Dodson County High School, Marge Davis canvassed the school's student parking lot. She had a particular vehicle she was looking for. Rachel had described the color and appearance but didn't know the make and model. Marge didn't expect there would be too many bright yellow cars in the parking lot, and fortunately there was only one.

"How stupid can a teenage girl be selecting a bright yellow car color?" When Marge was a teenager, she wouldn't have been caught dead in one.

She pulled up behind the car and copied down the license plate. Next she called a friend and asked her to run the plate. Within minutes, Marge had the owner's name and address, but the car was registered in the girl's mother's name. She decided to hang around awhile, hoping to get a glimpse of the girl when she came to get her car. Marge had only a short wait, because Debbie was walking toward the car talking on her cell phone. Marge would later find a way to get the cell phone records.

When Debbie backed out of her parking space, Marge followed her. Oblivious to Marge's tail, Debbie drove off. A while later, she drove into an upscale neighborhood, turned into a driveway, got out, and entered the house without ringing the doorbell or knocking.

Marge copied down the name and address on the mailbox—Zane. Then she parked several houses down to avoid being conspicuous. If any of the neighbors called in a suspicious vehicle, she had her identification from the attorney general's office and could say she was on a confidential assignment. It had worked before.

Thirty minutes later, Debbie and the two boys exited the house and went to her car. One of the boys was white, the other was black. They both kissed the girl on the mouth, and then she backed out of the driveway and drove off. Marge waited until the boys went into the house before following the girl. This time the girl drove home. She lived in a nice neighborhood, but not even close in appearance to the upscale neighborhood she had just came from. Marge decided she had enough for one day and would wait until tomorrow to follow Debbie again, so she went home.

The next day, Marge was back at the high school waiting for Debbie Lakes. After Debbie left school, she got in her car and headed east. Marge followed at a safe distance, knowing that it would be easy to spot the yellow car if she fell too far behind. It started to rain, which impaired Marge's visibility, but the yellow car could still be seen. Afternoon showers were a normal occurrence in Dodson County this time of the year.

Debbie headed toward Tallahassee via the main highway. An hour after leaving Dodson County, she went south on Monroe past the old capitol building and continued south until she turned left into a small industrial complex consisting of attached mini-warehouses. Debbie pulled up to one of the warehouses and exited her car. She knocked on the door and was granted entry. Marge drove by the warehouse, copied down the address, and then drove around the complex. She returned to a spot where she could see the yellow car without being spotted.

A half hour later, Debbie Lakes and a man in his late twenties or early thirties exited the warehouse carrying several boxes. Debbie put the box she was carrying on the roof of the car, and then got in and popped the trunk. They put the remainder of the boxes in the trunk, and then Debbie closed it. The man took Debbie in his arms and kissed her on the mouth. She seemed to enjoy it because she returned his kiss. When they finished kissing, Debbie got in her car and drove off.

Marge followed the yellow car back to Dodson County and eventually to the girl's home. Debbie backed into the driveway, put the garage door up, got out of her car, looked around, and then put the boxes in the garage, except for one. She got back in her car and drove away from the house. Marge followed at a safe distance. Debbie drove to the same upscale neighborhood and pulled into the Zane's driveway.

She gave a light beep on the horn and waited. The same two boys exited the house and walked up to her car. Debbie popped the trunk, and then the black one retrieved the box from it. The white boy passed an envelope through the window to her, and then the boys went back into the house. Debbie backed out of the driveway and drove home. Marge's travels for the day were over, so she decided to go to John's office and see if he was still there.

Fortunately, he was still there and so was Jayne. When Marge approached Jayne's desk, she said, "Putting in a long day, Jayne?"

"Every day is a long day with John Carter. Are you putting in a long day too? Did you get wet out there today, Marge?"

"Actually, I never got out of my car, and it looks like I'm going to be putting in more long days. I've got a lot to talk to John about."

"How's the case going so far—anything new?"

"Yes, there is. Wish I could talk to you about it. I could use another woman's perspective, Jayne."

"That bad, huh? If it's okay with John, I'd be glad to help, and I can stick around awhile longer if you two need me."

"Thanks. First I have something to do; then we can see what John says."

Marge could use another woman's perspective, especially after what she'd learned so far. She planned on asking Carter if Jayne could sit in on some of their conversation, but only what he allowed.

She went to her office and called a friend who did background checks for her. Her friend learned that Betty Lakes was a single mom employed by an accounting firm. Marge thanked her friend for the information and said good-bye.

Marge approached Carter's office and tapped on the door. He looked up and beckoned her in. "Marge, I didn't expect you back. Are you putting in a long day too?"

"Yes, John. I need to have a conversation with you, and I don't have good news."

"You're going to spoil my day, aren't you, Marge? Okay, bring it on."

"Do you think Jayne could sit in with us? You can decide what she can or can't hear. However, I'd like another woman's perspective on this."

Carter frowned then said, "Is it that bad? Okay, let's call Jayne in."

Jayne, on alert as usual in case she was needed, overheard John's last comment.

"I'm right here, John—no need to call."

"You're so efficient, Jayne. Come on in. Marge wants your perspective on something with this case. If I don't think it's something you should be privy to, I'll ask you to excuse yourself. You know the drill."

"Sure, John, I understand. Marge already told me she could use another woman's view on the case. Maybe I can be of help."

"Okay, Marge, we're all yours."

Satisfied with the arrangement, Marge proceeded to tell them about Debbie Lakes, saving Rachel for last. When she finished telling them about Debbie Lakes, she waited for comment from John or Jayne. Neither of them spoke, but they were obviously surprised. Then she told them about her discussion with Rachel and what the girl hadn't told her parents. It took a while for both of them to absorb what she told them, but finally John commented.

"Damn, Marge, this doesn't help our case, and it certainly puts a different light on it. I don't know what we do now, and I'm guessing you have more surprises for me."

Marge hesitated because of Jayne.

Before Marge could respond, Jayne said, "John, I'm guessing Marge may not want me to hear what else she has to say, so if you want, I'll step out. First let me comment on what we know so far. Somehow Rachel got herself involved with this Debbie Lakes." Jayne paused for a response from Carter or Marge. Since neither of them said anything, she continued on. "Rachel willingly went to the boy's house with Debbie and participated in the games as well as the make-out session. That means she was not completely innocent of what happened, and a defense attorney will surely use that against her. We don't know if the boys used protection, so there's a possibility of another problem. Am I right so far, Marge?"

Marge was surprised at Jayne's understanding of the situation. So far she was right on the mark, except for Rachel being a virgin at the time. She wasn't sure she should bring that issue up, but John trusted her, so she owed it to him to tell him everything.

Carter remained silent and was about to get the worst of the situation.

"You're very intuitive, Jayne. Also right on the mark," answered Marge. "Yes, there is something else, but maybe John and I should talk alone."

He was still in shock over what he'd heard so far. What more did Marge have for him? There wasn't much he held back from Jayne as he valued her judgment and confidence.

He glanced at Jayne, who was about to leave. "Wait, Jayne. Marge, whatever you have to say, Jayne might as well hear it. She's going to find out anyway."

Marge straightened in her seat, looked at Jayne then at Carter, and said, "But, John, I gave Rachel my word."

"I understand, Marge, but we're a team here, and Jayne is as much a part of this team. So whatever it is, you can rest assured Jayne will keep it in the strictest of confidence."

Marge threw her hands up in defeat and replied, "John, Rachel was a virgin at the time of the rape, and if they didn't use protection, she could be pregnant."

Carter leaned back in his chair, looked up at the ceiling, and exclaimed, "Aw, damn, that's the worst thing we need now. I'm not sure what we do with this. If either of you have a suggestion, let's hear it, because this is all new for me."

Since she was being included, Jayne weighed in, "John and Marge, I don't think we should get too upset with what we've learned regarding Rachel. Look, she may not be pregnant, so let's not focus on that aspect. When you two started on this case, you knew it wasn't going to be easy. Rape cases never are, so get over it and focus on what needs to be done. I believe we should focus on the other girl and what she was actually doing. Maybe we can get enough that we can get her to turn on the boys. What do you think, Marge?"

It put the ball back in Marge's court, where Jayne was sure Marge wanted it. Carter knew that Jayne was right and felt foolish about his comment. Before he could say anything, Marge jumped in.

"I think Jayne is right, John. I'm going to start taking pictures and see what I can get that will intimidate her and maybe help us. She comes from a single-parent home, and I'm willing to bet she doesn't want her mother to know what's going on. As far as the contraband is concerned, she's the ringleader there.

"She may also be enticing other girls to the boy's house. If I can get proof, then we have something to work on. John, are you willing to bring in the sheriff's office on this? Your friend can always pave the way."

He scratched his chin, rubbed the back of his head and answered, "I may not have much choice, Marge, but first let's see what you come up with. You know, I'm really glad you two are on my side. I took this case to please my daughter, but I didn't expect to get involved with something like this. Eventually, Rachel is going to have to talk to her parents and, Marge, that's where your expertise comes in. Thanks, Jayne, for setting me straight. You always do."

Carter didn't want Jayne to know about Marge's background, so he concluded the meeting in respect of her privacy. If Marge wanted to tell Jayne, it was her decision.

The three of them decided that it had been a long day, so they all went home. Fortunately for Marge, tonight she had someone coming to visit, because she needed a respite.

CHAPTER 12

Jennifer Brown was happy with her life in Orlando. As the manager of the Mastertson Art Gallery, she received a nice salary and benefits. The owners were philanthropic and liked to sponsor emerging artists. They often sent Jennifer to Europe, or other parts of the United States, to check out unknown artists and their work. If Jennifer liked their work, she would arrange for a gallery showing. She was very good at selecting artists whose works sold and made good commissions for the gallery.

For a girl who grew up in Bensmille, North Carolina, the adopted daughter of Edward and Edith Brown, Jennifer had done well for herself. Her childhood wasn't spectacular, since the Browns were extremely religious and forbade her from dating and attending high school functions. Jennifer rebelled and was often punished harshly. The more they restricted her, the more she rebelled.

In high school, Jennifer excelled at art and was fortunate to have an excellent art teacher. Mrs. Worthington, the art teacher, took a liking to Jennifer, and sensed that there was something troubling the girl. Jennifer confided in Mrs. Worthington and asked her not to say anything. Mrs. Worthington became her mentor and confidant. The two spent hours talking and reviewing Jennifer's artwork. She encouraged the girl to apply to college and helped with the applications.

Deborah Worthington was a graduate of the Jacksonville College of Art and the Savannah College of Art and Design. She had a good friend who was dean of admissions at Jacksonville College. Mrs. Worthington called her about Jennifer's application. It was her influence that got Jennifer accepted, but it was Jennifer's portfolio that enabled her to get a scholarship. Jennifer was so grateful to her art teacher for all she did for her. Mrs. Worthington also helped Jennifer get through the awkward stages of puberty.

Jennifer had decided that Friday night she was going to enjoy herself. She selected a sexy outfit from her wardrobe that contoured her body, revealing just enough cleavage to tease. Her plan was to visit the Roof Top Lounge, a trendy place that the post-college yuppies frequented to hook up and dance. This wasn't her first time at the lounge. She'd been there several times, and had even dated a couple of guys she met there. Jennifer was satisfied with how she looked and set out for a night of fun.

When Jennifer arrived at the Roof Top Lounge, it was around nine o'clock, and the place was already crowded. She managed to find a place at the bar, ordered a bottle of beer, sat and enjoyed the music, while checking the crowd.

Sam Williams, a construction contractor, entered the bar with his buddies, who along with him were beginning a night of bar hopping, hoping to get lucky. Sam's eyes immediately noticed Jennifer sitting at the bar. The first things his eyes took notice of were her nice cleavage and her pleasant ass. He told the guys he was on to something and would catch up with them after a while. Sam wandered over to the bar next to Jennifer. He introduced himself and asked if he could buy her a drink.

Her head tilted to one side, expressing interest, she smiled and said, "What, no cute pickup line? Just hello, can I buy you a drink?"

He hunched his shoulders and replied, "That's the best I got, unless you want me to make something up. I promise, it will sound lame."

"Well, at least you're honest. Sure, why not." She offered her and said, "My name is Jennifer. Nice to meet you, Sam."

Jennifer was used to lame pickup lines and getting hit on, but for some reason the guy's honesty intrigued her. Maybe this was his pickup line, but she liked it.

He accepted her gentle handshake and replied, "Nice to meet you, Jennifer."

Sam ordered each of them a beer, and they engaged in conversation for a while before he asked her to dance. They danced several numbers until she said she needed a break. Both were fortunate to grab an empty table, and when the waitress came by, Sam ordered two more beers. Sam and Jennifer continued their conversation, and Sam ordered more beers. They seemed to be enjoying each other's company.

Sam's buddies came over and said that they were ready to move on to someplace else, so it was time to say good night to his lady friend because Sam didn't have his own transportation.

Jennifer felt an attraction with Sam and didn't want him to leave yet. She looked at his buddies and then at Sam, winked, and said, "I can give you a ride home if you want to stay awhile, Sam."

Sam's buddies gave him that look that said, "Man, you scored."

"If you don't mind, Jennifer, I would like to stay awhile longer. Just so, you know, I'm also harmless, regardless of what these guys might say."

"Yeah, he's harmless all right, but you may be disappointed, girl."

Jennifer tilted her head and responded, "It's okay. Besides, I think he's kind of cute. Don't you?"

"All right, that's enough. We're out of here. See you, buddy."

Sam's friends left, and he wondered if he had done the right thing. .Jennifer had a certain effect on him. He put his hand on her arm, smiled, and said, "Well, I guess I'm at your mercy for the rest of the evening. Just be kind to me, Jennifer."

She put a hand on his, tilted her head, and replied, "I like your sense of humor, Sam, but why don't we get out of here?"

"Sure, but if you think I'm going to say 'my place or yours,' you'll be disappointed."

She sipped the last of her drink, winked, and said, "That's okay, because we're going to my place."

Sam settled the tab, and they left for Jennifer's apartment. When they arrived, she unlocked the door and invited him in. As soon as they were inside, they locked in an embrace, and Sam pushed her up against the wall. Their tongues explored each other's mouth like it was their first time. Sam's hands were then all over her breasts. Next he removed her top and bra, played with her nipples, and then reached for the zipper on her jeans. Jennifer reached for Sam's belt, unbuckled it, and unzipped his jeans.

Their hands went immediately to each other's crotch and grabbed whatever they could put them on. Next, they started sliding off each other's jeans. When they were both naked, Jennifer told Sam to follow her. She ran to the bedroom and leaped onto the bed. Sam joined her. Their tongues once again ravaged each other's mouth. Sam played with her breasts, and then his mouth slid down her body until it was between her legs. He gave her pleasure until she shouted that she wanted him inside her. She spread her legs, and then Sam mounted her, plunging deep inside her, moving like a jackhammer.

The two of them worked in unison until neither could control themselves, and they both gave way to a climax at the same time.

Jennifer had her arms wrapped tightly around him, but she let go and started slapping her palms on the bed shouting, "Oh my God."

Sam stayed on top of Jennifer for a short time, and then rolled off and lay beside her. Both were wet from perspiration. They lay there in silence for a while with hearts beating rapidly. It was something neither had experienced before.

Sam let out a deep breath and said, "I'm sorry. I would have used protection, but the mood was too much to break up."

She gently patted his thigh. "No problem. I don't have to worry, unless you got something I can catch?"

He turned his head, grinned, and said, "What's your name, again?"

"It's Alice, and yours is Robert, right?"

"I'm not sure." He rolled over on his side, kissed her on the lips, and replied, "Nice to meet you, Alice. Want to try again?"

"First I got to pee. Be right back."

Their little name game amused them and actually increased their attraction for each other. Jennifer got up and ran to the bathroom. Sam watched and enjoyed the site of her beautiful ass. When she returned, he couldn't take his eyes off her beautiful tits and that triangle below her belly button that he had enjoyed.

She lowered her head, spread her legs, winked and asked, "Enjoying the view, cowboy?"

"Just admiring it, that's all. It's certainly a nice view, officer."

"Yes, it is." She glanced at his midsection, raised her eyebrows, and said, "Are you going to use that thing, or let it go to waste?"

"Get on your back, officer, and I'll show you what I can do."

She climbed onto the bed, kissed him on the mouth, and then rolled over on her back. "You already have, but why don't you show me again?"

He mounted her, and they went through a repeat performance. When they were done, Sam felt it was kind of late for her to drive him home, plus he didn't want to leave.

"It's a little late for you to take me home, and I'd be worried about you driving back here. Any chance I can stay for breakfast?

"Only if you like pancakes and bacon. That's all I cook."

"Are you kidding? I love pancakes and bacon, especially buckwheat pancakes."

"That's all I have, so I guess you're mine for the rest of the night, cowboy."

Sam gave her the biggest grin, and his eyes almost popped out. "I forgot. What did you say your name was?"

"It's Patricia, and don't you forget it."

"What happened to Alice?"

"She went home after the first round."

"You mean there were three of us? Did I miss something?"

"Nope, you were here for it all, and you were very good. I think I like you, cowboy."

"I like you too, officer."

In the morning, they had breakfast together, and then Jennifer took Sam home. They started dating the following weekend, and within weeks they were exclusive. Nine months later, Sam proposed marriage one Saturday night while they were out to dinner. Jennifer accepted, and they were married six months later. They were so deeply in love with each other, and their playful name exchanges continued.

It was a happy marriage until Sam's business took a downfall. Sam started drinking and doing a little carousing during the week. Jennifer tried her best to build up his confidence, but he became more miserable each day. Even his buddies tried to perk him up, but they too were unsuccessful.

CHAPTER 13

Becky Johnson grew up in Live Oak, where her alcoholic father raised her. He started drinking heavily after the death of Becky's mother. Before that, he was an all-American dad and treated Becky like she was still his little girl. Fortunately, he never abused her, but living with an alcoholic father was almost like being abused. She never knew what to expect, which was why she didn't have many friends. Slumber parties at her house were a forgotten thought.

In high school, she only had two close friends. Both came from troubled homes, so the three were sort of kindred spirits. Becky excelled at art and was constantly encouraged by her art teacher to consider art school. Because money was an issue, art school wasn't possible. Her art teacher suggested that she apply to colleges that offered art majors. She even offered to help with the applications and with Becky's portfolio.

Thanks to her art teacher's help, Becky was accepted at Jacksonville College of Art and offered a scholarship due to her impressive portfolio. She enrolled at Jacksonville College, where she met another scholarship art student named Jennifer Brown. The two bonded at orientation and chose to be roommates. They roomed together for all four years, and after graduation they took a trip to Europe together.

Becky met her future husband during her last spring break in college. They later became engaged then married. Her father managed to stay sober for a week to attend the wedding ceremony and gave Becky away, but he didn't stay for the reception because the Larsons were paying for the entire affair. Embarrassed, he went home, but before he left, Becky told him thanks for giving her away and that she loved him. He left sad but grateful for Becky's words. He knew that he didn't deserve them.

Becky and Peter bought a home in Waterton with the help of his parents. Peter worked in his father's law firm but became itchy for something else. He decided to enter politics and ran for the mayor's office at the next election. The Larsons were well known in Waterton, and Peter's father had connections in Tallahassee. He was thinking governor eventually for his son.

It was a bitter campaign. Peter's father had no reservations about dragging mud out on his son's opponent. They took every opportunity to discredit the man and his family. After the election, the family moved to Lake City to spare their young son further embarrassment. All that took place, and her husband and father-in-law's actions, surprised Becky. It was a whole different side of the Larson family dynamic.

A year after the election, Becky started to notice more changes in Peter. She thought that he was a bit too friendly with some of his staff, especially the females. Becky was starting to question if he was being unfaithful to her. They didn't have any children, because Peter didn't want a child to get in the way of his ambitions. In a way, Becky was grateful, because she didn't want to raise a child in the Larson family environment.

Becky had a nice job at a local art gallery where she also taught several art classes. She used her talent to enter some online shows and actually won several awards. What money she received, she kept for herself, hidden from Peter. Becky didn't care if it would become a tax issue. She was tired of asking Peter for money. She also kept her salary. It gave her a sense of independence.

She hadn't touched base with her friend Jennifer since the wedding, when Jennifer was her maid of honor. Becky often considered calling her to catch up on events in her life. She missed her friend and the friendship they had, all of it. One of these days she was going to call Jennifer and make plans to get together.

CHAPTER 14

Randall County

John Carter was engrossed in a dream about playing football for the Cougars and throwing the winning touchdown pass when he felt the punch on his arm. He also heard a ringing but had no idea where it was coming from. He rolled over and noticed the sumptuous women next to him lying naked on her back. His eyes were focused on her lovely breasts and the clean-shaven triangle just above her shapely legs.

He remembered how enjoyable it was last night with her. Carter had the pleasure of making love to Marge Davids, the Randall County medical examiner and his wife of ten years. When they first met, she did everything she could to ward off his advances, but eventually he wore her down and they started see-ing each other occasionally, and then exclusively. She almost had a stroke when he romantically proposed to her.

Romance wasn't one of Carter's better qualities. Marge had since taught him well, but the only romance was with her. Good thing, because she had great surgical skills to go along with her great body.

"Are you ogling my tits, Sheriff?"

"I sure am, Madame Examiner."

"You call me madame again, and you'll never see these puppies ever again, quarterback."

"Geez! Sorry, Ms. Davids. Can I at least kiss my wife? That's legal, isn't it?"

"You can do more than kiss her, but first she's gotta pee."

"I can wait. Just hurry."

She got out of bed, glanced back at him, and said, "I will since that hard-on of yours seems like it can't wait. Be right back. Keep that thing straight."

When she returned, they did more than kiss. Their bedroom antics were like two honeymooners on their first night. They had just finished when Carter's phone rang, again.

"You better answer that, quarterback."

"Where the hell is it?"

"How should I know? Maybe it's up your ass. Just find it and answer it."

Carter rummaged around and finally found the phone on the floor under the bed. They must have had some heavy sex last night, because his phone was usually on the nightstand. When he got it, he hit receive and answered.

"Sheriff Carter." It was Amy Tucker, his deputy, calling. "Hey, Amy, what's up? Why are you calling me on Saturday morning? Can't whatever it is wait until Monday?"

"Sheriff, you better get down here. Larson's attorney is here with a court order for his wife's body, and he's not being pleasant. I told him the medical examiner has her body and she has to release it first, but that's not satisfying him."

"Okay, Amy. I'm on my way, and so is the medical examiner. See you in about thirty minutes."

Marge slapped him on the shoulder, and her eyes registered annoyance. "What the hell do you mean 'so is the medical examiner'? What was that all about?"

Carter flinched from the slap. "Ouch. Damn, Marge. We got trouble. Larson's lawyer is at the sheriff's office with a court order for his wife's body. With what the Cochran kid told me, this is a homicide, and I want that body with us."

Marge gave him a pleasant smile. "Don't worry, John. He can't have the body until I'm finished with it. Homicide evidence trumps his court order, but to be sure, you'd better wake up Judge Henry and get a restraining order. Tell him I have the body, and it is evidence. I have to take a shower first."

"So do I, but can we take one together to hasten things up?"

She shook her head and bit her lip. "Only if you can keep your hands to yourself, quarterback. Remember what I said about my surgical skills."

"Dammit, Marge, you're no fun."

"This isn't any time for fun, John. We got a problem to solve."

They showered together, and John kept his hands to himself, partly out of fear, and because Marge was right. They had a problem. When he finished showering and was dressed, Carter called Judge Willard Henry, who was pissed at being disturbed on the golf course. The judge agreed to issue the restraining order and told Carter that he would call his clerk, have her draft the order, and bring it to him for his signature. The judge's clerk would deliver it to Carter after he signed it, but Carter suggested that she deliver it to the medical examiner, since she had the body.

"Sheriff, find out who the judge was that signed the order, since nobody called me about it and I'm the chief judge of the county. Something like that should have gone through me first."

"Okay, Judge, and thanks."

Carter then called Amy and said that he was on his way and so was a restraining order. Next, he told Marge about his conversation with the judge and that he would see her later at the morgue.

"I told you, John, that a homicide trumps a domestic case." She gave his shoulder a light smack and followed with, "Next time listen to your medical examiner, okay, quarterback?"

"Go ahead, rub it in. You love that, don't you? Okay, you're still my favorite wide receiver."

They laughed, kissed, and said good-bye. Carter wasn't happy about the situation, and now he really disliked Peter Larson, especially that damn Gator tie tack he wore. Carter was a true Seminole, even though he'd only played one year for them.

When Carter arrived at the sheriff's office, Amy greeted him and introduced him to the lawyer.

"Sheriff Carter, this is Mr. Goodwin. Mr. Goodwin, Sheriff Carter. You want me to stay or leave, Sheriff?"

She started to walk away, but he put his hand up and answered, "Stay, Amy. I'd like you to witness this conversation. Mr. Goodwin, it's a pleasure to meet you."

Carter extended his hand, but Goodwin refused to take it, which annoyed Carter, though he kept his cool. John also noticed that same Gator tie tack on the lawyer.

He turned his palm then pulled his hand back. "Suit yourself. Amy, would you mind getting me a cup of coffee and put it in my Seminole cup, please."

Amy smiled and said she was glad to. She knew what he was doing. Neither of them offered the lawyer a cup of coffee. If he asked for one, Amy planned on telling him they were all out after Carter's cup.

Goodwin opened his briefcase, took out a sheet of paper, and said, "Sheriff, let's get down to business. I have an order requesting that you turn over Mrs. Larson's body to her husband and restrain from an autopsy. It's all here signed by a judge."

He gave Carter the order, and Carter made like he was perusing it. He was mostly interested in the judge's name. After looking it over, he asked Amy to make a copy so they would have an extra one on file. Amy made the copy and gave it to the sheriff.

"Well, Mr. Goodwin, I don't think I'm going to be able to do that."

The attorney stepped back, gave him an icy stare and said, "Why not, Sheriff?"

"Because my deputy is bringing me a restraining order against your order, signed by Chief County Judge Willard Henry. Here it is now." A sheriff's deputy stepped forward and handed Carter two sheets of paper. Carter handed one to Goodwin. "This is your copy, and I've got mine. After you read it, you can take your sorry ass back to Waterton and tell your client that if he tries to fuck up my investigation again, he'll have hell to pay."

"Is that a threat, Sheriff?"

"It's whatever you want it to be, counselor."

"This isn't over yet, Sheriff. I'll be back."

"You're right. It's not over, and we'll see you again. If that happens, I'll be right here." Carter did the Seminole chop and shouted, "Go, Seminoles."

Amy smiled, and after the lawyer left, they both laughed. They could hear the deputies in the other room laughing too. Carter said that he had to get over to the morgue and speak with the medical examiner.

"If I didn't know better, John, I'd swear you got the hots for that woman."

"Well, you don't know better, because I got more than the hots for her."

They laughed, and Carter left. On the way over to the morgue, Carter thought about the lawyer's visit and wondered why Larson was hell bent on getting possession of his wife's body. There must be more to Larson than a grieving spouse. He'd have the medical examiner do a thorough check on the remains.

He decided to call Billy and have him do a more in-depth background check on the two women and the husbands. He wanted him to go as far back as possible, even high school.

CHAPTER 15

Randall County Judge Willard Henry placed a call to the medical examiner from the tenth hole of the golf course. He had just finished missing a par putt and was down four holes in the round. Marge's number was on his speed dial, and he wanted to know more about the need for the restraining order. Judge Henry was a stickler for the law and had to satisfy himself that he had done the right thing. He trusted both the sheriff and the medical examiner but always made certain that what they told him was correct. Marge was still in her car on the way to her office when she answered the judge's call.

"Marge, tell me about this evidence thing. Is the woman's body evidence, and what does the autopsy show?"

"Good morning to you, Judge." She was used to him not offering a greeting when he called her. "Judge, I haven't done the autopsy yet. I was going to do it on Monday, but now I have to do it today. When the crime-scene unit was processing the scene, one of the techs noticed what appeared to be a bullet hole in the driver's-side window. It's in the report."

Marge slowed and watched as two bicyclists turned right at the next intersection.

"Now I have to search for a bullet in the bodies, because the CSU didn't find one in the vehicle. That's one reason the body is evidence, and I have to determine the actual cause of death even though the victims were found with their heads against the windshield. That's pretty much it, Judge."

Marge gave the judge all the information she could and was sure that he would accept her opinion. He had never doubted her for as long as they'd known each other, which was a very long time. He called her by her first name, but she respected his position as judge, and that's how she always addressed him. Judge Henry had presided over the wedding ceremony of Marge and John.

"Thanks, Marge. I was sure I was doing the right thing. As always, you don't send me false information and your judgment is always correct. Don't mean to be disrespectful, but are you still sleeping with that Carter boy?"

He always asked her the same question, and it'd been an inside joke between the two of them since she married John Carter.

"He keeps chasing after me. I may need a restraining order from you one of these days to ward him off, Judge."

"Oh boy, that's too much information for me. You take care, Marge."

"You too, Judge."

Marge pulled into her assigned space at the medical examiner's office just as her assistant, Tom Morgan, arrived. They greeted each other then headed toward the examining room. Tom Morgan was in his early thirties, and had been Marge's assistant for three years. He had a lot of respect for her, and she had provided every opportunity for him to gain as much knowledge as he wanted. She hoped that one day she could appoint him the assistant medical examiner, with the official title.

Once inside the examining room, they got right down to business. Tom wheeled both bodies out, and then they began with the Larson woman, since she was of paramount importance. Marge put on her surgical gloves and turned on the magnifying lamp just above the body, and then started with the head. Carefully she searched for an entrance wound. Unfortunately, there was none. She told Tom to check the Williams woman's head for anything probative.

As Marge continued searching for signs of an entrance wound, Tom put on his surgical gloves and switched on the magnifying lamp above the Williams woman's skull. Next he carefully probed but found no entry wound, so then he checked the neck and shoulders. On the left side of her neck he found an entry wound.

"Marge, you better come look at this."

She stopped what she was doing and walked over to him. She glanced into the magnifying lamp, and sure enough, there was an entrance wound.

"Shit, Tom. Now we have a real problem. How the hell did that get there?" Marge stepped back from the lamp and said, "She was the passenger, and the bullet appears to have been fired through the driver's window."

"Maybe the driver was lucky and the bullet missed her and hit the passenger," Tom replied.

"Tom, to reach that conclusion, we have to reconstruct the scene and determine how it's possible. Sheriff Carter isn't going to be happy."

"What am I not going to be happy about?"

Sheriff Carter had just arrived and overheard the medical examiner. This was going to shed a whole new light on the matter, especially Larson's request for his wife's body.

The two examiners turned around, and Marge answered, "Sheriff Carter, I didn't know you had arrived. Good morning."

"Come on, Marge. Skip the sheriff crap and the pleasantries. You know we've already said good morning. Let's forget ceremony here and talk basics." He glanced at Tom and said, "Sorry, Tom, but I'm in no mood for politically correct bullshit. What am I going to be unhappy about?"

"No offense, Sheriff, or rather John. Why don't I let Marge tell you?"

Coward, Marge thought. Why should she have to tell him, since Tom found the entrance wound? However, she was the medical examiner.

"John, we didn't find an entry wound on the Larson woman, but we did find one on the Williams woman. The problem is that it's on the left side facing the driver's side of the vehicle." She paused, faced Tom, and then continued, "Actually, Tom found the wound. That means she took the bullet, but we haven't determined how yet, and we still have to probe for the slug. Things have changed some, don't you think?"

"Shit. That's not what I expected to hear, but it doesn't mean the Larson woman's body isn't evidence, does it? Please say I'm right."

Carter hoped that he was, because he didn't want Larson to get his way.

"For now she still is, but first let's find the slug. Tom, let's probe the shoulder."

Tom began his probe of the neck and shoulder and soon found a .38-caliber slug in Jennifer Williams's neck and placed it in an evidence bag. Then, just as a precaution, he decided to examine the rest of the remains. He rolled the body onto its side, and that's when he noticed the strange bruises. They appeared not to be as a result of the accident and were much older than those from the accident. Marge and John needed to see this.

"Marge, you and John need to look at this."

Carter and Marge were engaged in a conversation about the implications of the bullet wound when Tom called them.

"What's the problem, Tom?" asked Marge.

"Take a look. Those wounds aren't recent and certainly not from an automobile accident. See for yourself. You too, John."

Marge rolled the body over onto its stomach, and both she and Carter took a look.

"Shit, now what do we have?" Carter asked.

"Well, John, my guess is this woman has suffered some bad bruises, and I suspect spousal abuse," Marge replied. "Tom, let's check the Larson woman."

Carter stepped back, rubbed his forehead, and waited to see what the Larson woman's body had to offer. The case was starting to take on a whole new life, and not what he had expected. When Marge and Tom finished their examination of the Larson woman's body, she gave Carter the results.

"You're going to be even more unhappy, John." He leaned back against one of the tables to steady himself, expecting more bad news. Marge said, "The Larson woman has some bruises on her back and her upper arms, and I'd also say they're from someone abusing her. They appear to be more recent than the Williams woman's bruises. Maybe you should look at both of the husbands more closely."

He slapped the heels of his hands together and exclaimed, "Damn, I don't need this. That means both bodies remain in evidence until we've completed our investigation. Am I right, Marge?"

"Yes, John, and Judge Henry needs to know this. He's not going to be pleased either. You know how he feels about spousal abuse."

Tom Morgan was still examining the Larson woman's body and interrupted them.

"Marge, take a look at this wound on Larson's neck. Could it be from the bullet gazing her?"

Marge stepped toward him, leaned over, and took a close look.

"It could be, and that would explain how the Williams woman was shot."

Carter threw his hands up in frustration.

"Shit. I got to call the Orlando Sheriff's Office or Police Department. I need more on this Williams guy. Jimmy is going to have to dig deeper on that Larson character. I knew I didn't trust him. Something just didn't seem right about his hurry to get hold of his wife's body. Now we know why. Tell Judge Henry that too."

Sheriff Carter then left the morgue. On his way out, he called Billy and told him what he needed. Billy already had some info and would have it for the sheriff when he got to his office. Carter also told Billy to make sure Amy was available. He had a job for her.

CHAPTER 16

Orlando

S am Williams sat on a bar stool in the 5th Avenue Bar nursing his fourth beer. He had been coming there often since his business went to hell. He stayed late and drank too much because he no longer had a home to go to since his wife, Jennifer, threw him out. She tried her best to offer confidence, but he loved her so much and couldn't stand being a failure. Jennifer got a restraining order against him because of the one time when he took his drunken anger out on her. He didn't mean to hit her; actually he beat up on her, to be precise. Not only had she taken out a restraining order, but she also filed for divorce.

They once had a great marriage, but when his business went into the dumps, Sam lost all sense of reality and started drinking. He hoped it would make things better, but it didn't, and they only got progressively worse. Now here he was alone in a neighborhood bar, probably going to get drunk and spend the night in some cheap motel because Jennifer had changed the locks, plus there was the restraining order.

As he was drowning in his sorrows, Sam noticed two men in one of the bar's four booths. One of the men seemed familiar. Even though he was on his fourth beer, he was sure that he knew the guy. He kept looking at the two men through the mirror over the liquor bottles. It gave him a clear view of them.

"Think, Sam. I'm sure you know one of them. The guy in the suit, that's who you know, but from where?" he said to himself.

The two men in the booth were engaged in an animated conversation, with their voices low enough that none of the bar's patrons could hear them. The one in the suit seemed to be doing most of the talking. The other just listened but occasionally spoke, jabbing his finger at the one in the suit to make a point. Sam couldn't read lips, so he had no idea what they were talking about. He watched as the guy in the suit handed an envelope to the other guy.

"Wonder what that's all about?" Sam asked himself.

Sam ordered another bottle of beer. As he was paying for it, he didn't notice the other guy look his way, but the guy seemed to have noticed that Sam was watching their conversation. Not knowing if Sam overheard them, the guy told the one in the suit to glance Sam's way.

"Do you know that guy at the bar? He seems to be interested in us."

The suit took a look at Sam, but just casually enough that Sam wouldn't notice. He vaguely recognized Sam.

"He looks familiar. I think I've seen him somewhere," said the suit.

"He thinks you look familiar too, because he's checking you out." The guy leaned closer to the suit and whispered, "Could he be a PI? If he is, he isn't very good, because I picked him out rather quick. Don't let him know you're looking."

Recollection flashed on the suit's brain. He leaned forward and replied, "Wait—I think I know who he is. Yeah, now I recognize him. He married my wife's best friend. My wife was her maid of honor at their wedding. I think his name is Sam. Yeah, that's it, Sam Williams." Then the suit lifted his glass and took a sip of his drink. "Wonder why he's drinking alone. This isn't good, especially if he overheard us."

"Don't worry. I'll find out and take care of it. Let's get out of here, and don't look in his direction or make contact. Just get up and leave. If he heads your way, don't stop—I'll delay him."

The two of them got up and left, neither of them glancing Sam's way. Sam avoided contact with them. He sat there awhile and had another beer and then decided to call it a night.

Sam put a twenty on the bar, got off the stool, waved to the bartender, and said, "See you next time, Millie."

"You okay to drive, Sam? I can call you a cab if you'd like."

"I'm okay, thanks. No need."

Sam left the bar and walked to his car, entered it, backed out of the parking space, and drove to a motel. When checked in, he went to his room, unlocked the door, and realized who the guy in the suit was.

"That was Becky's husband, Peter Larson. That's who it was."

Sam hadn't noticed the truck that followed him to the motel, nor did he notice when it pulled into the motel parking lot.

CHAPTER 17

Sheriff Carter was beginning to feel the stress from the latest case and didn't need any more on his plate for now. Murder, fortunately, wasn't an everyday occurrence in Randall County, Florida. DUIs, traffic violations, and teenagers smoking pot made up the majority of cases his department had to handle. Amy Tucker and his four other deputies were capable of handling them, but this was his case. Carter hadn't called Orlando yet, as he was still deciding whether to call the sheriff or the police. He felt it might be easier to talk sheriff-to-sheriff though.

It was lunchtime, and he hadn't been to Leroy's in days, so he decided to go there for lunch. Some days the diner was quite crowded at lunchtime, but Leroy always managed to find a place for Carter to sit. When the sheriff entered the diner, Leroy motioned him to an empty booth at the far corner of the restaurant. After Carter took a seat, Leroy came over and joined him.

"Don't you have to work the kitchen or the counter, Leroy?"

"Nah, it's okay, John. I got a chef that can handle things as well as I can, and the waitresses can manage the counter and booths. You gonna eat, John?"

Carter lowered his head and rubbed the back of his neck, and then replied, "Yeah, I'm kind of hungry, and I'll eat whatever the special is as long as it's not tripe."

Leroy remembered the last time he saw Carter look so down. It was after he had thrown two interceptions. The Cougars were down 14–0. The coach yelled at Carter, and the team avoided him. Carter found a place on the bench where he could be by himself. Leroy walked over and sat next to him, put an arm around Carter, and whispered something in his ear. The fullback told Carter to pick his head up and get in the game. They still had two quarters to go. In the second half, the Cougar defense refused to give up any points. Leroy ran for two touchdowns, and Carter threw two touchdown passes. The Cougars won the state title 28–14.

"You need conversation, quarterback?"

"I could use some, Leroy, if you got time."

Leroy sat down, put both hands on the table, and leaned forward. "I always got time for you. Say, are we on for Friday night's game? It's the Cougars-Tigers game. This one is big this year."

Carter's mouth formed a forced smile. "I'm on. I'll have deputies working the game, but I'm not sure I can stay for the whole game. Don't you have to be here for after game?"

"I can stay through the third quarter; then I gotta be here. Place should be packed. Usually is after the big games."

Leroy's Diner had become a hangout for both fans and team members. Several members of the football team brought their girlfriends for an after-game meal, and some hung out in the parking lot. The diner had become sort of a tradition for everyone, especially after home games. Leroy, being an ex-Cougar, was also an attraction. Carter sometimes helped out, and his presence kept things under control.

Carter got his lunch, and Leroy got himself a Coke. When Carter finished eating, he told Leroy about the case. "Leroy, I feel like I'm in a battle and the enemy is coming at me from everywhere. It's making my head feel like a bomb is going off. I have to decide whether to call the Orlando sheriff or the police."

Leroy suggested that Carter call the Orlando sheriff because he would probably be more amenable to talking with Carter. Also, the Orlando sheriff could bridge the gap with the Orlando Police Department if necessary. Carter agreed that it was a good idea, plus he had already pretty much decided to call the sheriff. Leroy's suggestion was the clincher. It was time for Carter to get back to being a Sheriff.

"Separate cars Saturday, or do I pick you up, John?"

"Separate cars, Leroy. Just in case."

"Okay, I'll see you Friday night at the game. Can I still shout 'Go, Cougars'?"

"Go, Cougars!"

"You're still crazy, quarterback."

Carter was on his way back to the sheriff's office when he got a call from the medical examiner's office. What now? He wondered.

"This is Sheriff Carter. What's up?"

Even though he and the medical examiner were married, they stood on ceremony when it was something important.

"Sheriff, we finished most of our autopsy, and I think you best get here. I got good and bad news for you."

"Can't you tell me over the phone?"

"I could, but I don't want to. Just get the hell over here, will you?"

"Okay, I'm on my way. This had better be important."

"I wouldn't have called if it wasn't, you ass."

"Come on, Marge, don't get nasty. I'm sorry, okay?"

"Okay, but sometimes you really piss me off."

He closed his phone and hastily drove to the medical examiner's office. He parked his pickup in the space next to the one marked "Medical Examiner" and headed for the morgue. He knew that was where he would find Marge. She motioned him over to the examining table that the Larson woman was on.

"Good afternoon, Sheriff."

"Afternoon, Madame Examiner."

She was being curt, so he decided to do the same. He knew the word *madame* would rile her.

"What did I tell you about calling me madame? Do I look like a hooker to you?"

"Now that you mention it, you could if you weren't wearing that outfit. Be careful with that knife now, will ya?"

"I've a good mind to use it on you, but I'm a lady, even if you don't think so."

"Aw, Marge, I'm just razzing you. You know that. Besides, you know how I feel about you. So what have we got?"

"We have a new issue. The Larson woman was pregnant. We have enough DNA from the fetus to run it through our database. We should have a response in a few days. That's the best we can do. Hopefully we'll get a match."

"Let's hope it belongs to the husband; otherwise we have another problem. If it isn't the husband's, then we might have a motive."

"Either way, you might have a motive, John. But that begs the question as to why she was with the Williams woman."

"Shit, I'm not catching any breaks with this case. Is that the bad news? If so, what's the good news?"

"I could say I'm pregnant, but then you'd shit your brains out, but I'm not. The good news is we believe Larson was the intended target and it's possible she leaned forward just before the bullet struck the window. That's how it hit the Williams woman."

"That makes sense to me, Marge. And it means they were definitely headed north, away from Waterton, but why? I'm gonna talk to Jimmy Cochran and make sure he can confirm which direction both vehicles were traveling. It's possible the women were trying to get away from Waterton. If so, why?"

"It's all yours now, John. I have to finish both autopsies and report to Judge Henry. I think he's concerned about the judge that signed the order for Mrs. Larson's husband."

"Maybe there's more to that than we know. Thanks, Marge. I love you, wide receiver."

"Love you too, quarterback."

They both forgot that Tom Morgan was in the autopsy room, and when they finished their exchange, he gave them both a look that said, "Why don't you two get a room?" Marge blushed. Carter just waved to Morgan.

"Sorry about that, Tom," said Marge.

"I'm used to it, but why don't you two get married?"

"We are, and you know that," she replied. "Don't be a smart-ass, Tom."

They both laughed then got back to the autopsies.

Back at his office, Carter decided he couldn't put off making the call anymore. He dialed the Orlando County Sheriff's Office and asked for the sheriff. After Carter introduced himself, he was directed to the sheriff's office.

Sheriff Boyd Anders was a long-term member of law enforcement and had been sheriff of Orange County for six years. Before becoming sheriff, he was a major in the Special Operations and Investigation Division. Prior to that, he was a member of the Criminal Division of the Florida Highway Patrol. He was considered a fair and just law-enforcement officer by his staff and was well respected in the community.

"This is Sheriff Anders. How can I help you?"

"Sheriff, this is Sheriff John Carter of Randall County. I'm hoping you or your department can be of assistance to me."

"What have you got, Sheriff?"

"You think we could get on a first-name basis? I'm not one for standing on ceremony, if it's okay with you."

"Sure, John, I'm the same way. So what have you got?"

John was pleased they were now on a first-name basis. He could communicate better on a more personal basis.

"Boyd, I got what appears to be a double homicide, possibly a triple, if you include an unborn fetus. There's also the possibility of spousal abuse. The reason I'm calling you is because one of the victims was from Orlando. Her name was Jennifer Williams. I was hoping you could help me on background and find her husband. His name is Sam Williams."

Boyd Anders took the phone away from his ear, turned his head, and frowned.

"If spousal abuse is involved, I'll be more than happy to help you, especially since it's a personal matter with me. My daughter was involved in an abusive marriage. You want me to put someone on this? I've got a major in special operations and investigation that's really good. I'm sure he'd like to get hold of a wife beater too. Is that all right with you, John?"

"Perfect, Boyd. I really appreciate it, because I've also got a husband who is making it difficult for me. He got an order for his wife's body before the autopsy was completed. We quashed that with a restraining order of our own. Good thing, because later the autopsy discovered the gunshot wound, bruising on both women, and the pregnancy."

"You got a shitload to handle, John. We're glad to help. I'll talk to Major Bill Quincy and have him call you. Give me your phone number."

"Thanks again, Boyd."

After the pleasantries were over, John gave the sheriff his phone number, said good-bye, and waited for the call from Major Bill Quincy. Carter felt pleased that at least he had some help coming his way. Tonight he'd be able to relax with Marge as long as nothing new came up that his deputies couldn't handle.

Amy came into his office and said that for once things were quiet and Carter could go home and relax for one night. Carter thanked her and told her that one day they would have that talk, but for now they had a major case to deal with. Carter left for home and another scrimmage with his favorite wide receiver.

CHAPTER 18

Two days later in Bensmille, North Carolina, Deborah Worthington had just returned home from her last art class. When she entered the house and turned off the alarm, the telephone started ringing. Her husband, Charles, was away for several days on a business trip, and she thought it might be him calling. She dropped her keys on the little table by the front door, put her purse on the kitchen counter, and walked over to answer the telephone.

"This is Deborah. How can I help you?"

Deborah always answered the telephone the same way, whether at home or at her office in school. It was a habit she'd formed years ago.

A familiar voice responded. "Deborah, hi, I'm glad I got you. This is Barbara Morris from Jacksonville College. How have you been?"

"Barbara, it's so great to hear from you. What are you up to these days? Married yet?"

Deborah and Barbara first met at Jacksonville College of Art and were roommates for a couple of years. They had a close relationship, but after college they drifted apart. Deborah hadn't spoken to Barbara since she last called her for help with Jennifer Brown's application for college. Thanks to Barbara, Jennifer was accepted and given a full scholarship.

"Not yet. I'm still single and loving it. How's married life for you?"

"I love it, just like you love being single. You didn't call just to see how married life is. I'm betting you want a return favor. Am I right?"

"No, that's not why I'm calling. Deborah, I got a call from a sheriff's deputy in Randall County, Florida, about Jennifer Brown. She got married, and her last name is now Williams. Deborah, there was an accident, and Jennifer was killed. I'm sorry to have to be the bearer of bad news."

There was a prolonged silence on the other end before Deborah responded.

"Deborah, are you there? Did you hear me?"

When Deborah heard about Jennifer, she almost fainted and was now attempting to regain her composure. This isn't good, she told herself.

"I'm here, and I heard you, Barbara. It's just that I'm shocked. I loved that girl. She was my star pupil, and I was so excited when you got her into Jax College. Did the deputy say what happened?"

Barbara knew how much Deborah liked Jennifer and understood how upset she was because Barbara also liked Jennifer. Occasionally she met with her for lunch or dinner. When Barbara had heard about Jennifer, she'd reacted similar to Deborah. The three women had shared a bond.

"She said there was an automobile accident and that Jennifer was in the vehicle with another woman named Becky Larson. Do you know her?"

"Oh, my Lord, I can't believe this. Barbara, do you have the deputy's telephone number by chance?"

"Yes, I have it right here. She gave me it in case I thought of anything. She asked a lot of questions about both women. Now that I think of it, Jennifer had a friend and roommate named Becky. I'm going to check and see if I can get her full name. Maybe the deputy would like to know it. Don't know why I didn't think of that when she called me. Here's her number. Oh, I forgot that I gave the deputy your name and she said she was going to call you."

Barbara gave Deborah the number and asked what she was going to do. Barbara felt that she knew something more, but didn't want to ask.

"Thanks, Barbara. I just walked in, and now I'm going to have a drink to settle my nerves. Then I might call the deputy if she doesn't call me."

"Deborah, are you all right? Is there something you know and aren't sharing with me? We were really good friends once, and I did do you a favor with Jennifer."

Deborah wasn't about to reveal the pact she had made with Jennifer and Becky. Even though they were very close once, she couldn't trust Barbara.

"Barbara, I really can't tell you anything. Please don't press me because I really can't. I'm truly sorry, but I just can't."

"Okay, Deborah, if you insist. Because of our friendship I'll trust you. I'm glad we got to talk, even if it wasn't under pleasant circumstances. I miss you, Deborah, and I mean that."

"I know you do, and I miss you too. Take care now. My love."

"Mine too."

Deborah was still shaken, so she poured herself a tall glass of wine, hoping it would calm her nerves. But it didn't, so she had another and another. "If only Charles were here, he'd know what to do."

When Jennifer called and said she had a friend who needed help, Deborah agreed to talk to them, but it had to be done through other sources. She gave Jennifer specific instructions on what to do and made her promise not to tell anyone. Deborah told Jennifer that too much was at stake and secrecy was paramount. Jennifer agreed as Deborah requested, since she also knew what was at stake. Deborah had helped Jennifer's friend in high school, so she was well aware of the need for secrecy.

Deborah was concerned that something may have gone wrong, because Jennifer should have been in Bensmille by now. When she hadn't heard from Jennifer after three days, she started to worry. The call from Barbara really disturbed her and worried her for everyone involved. She made the call that she had hoped she would never have to make. The last time she'd had to make a similar call had been more than ten years ago.

Ten years prior, Deborah Worthington was grading papers in her classroom when Jennifer Brown, her favorite art student, approached her. Jennifer had been confiding in Mrs. Worthington for some time now, and the girl had told her about the way her parents treated her, and their strict rules, especially regarding dating boys. Jennifer had never been on a date, and because she avoided boys, she was somewhat of an outcast with many of her classmates. Teenagers could be very cruel, and they weren't the exception at this school. Mrs. Worthington anticipated that their conversation would have something to do with Jennifer's problems at school or at home.

Jennifer stepped closer and tentatively said, "Mrs. Worthington, can I talk with you?"

"Absolutely, Jennifer. What can I do for you?"

Mrs. Worthington could sense Jennifer's nervousness, and her curiosity intensified as the girl approached.

"I have this friend who needs someone to talk to. You've always been there for me, and I was hoping you would listen to her. She really needs someone to listen to her story and not be judgmental, which I know you would never be. Would you talk to her, Mrs. Worthington?"

Mrs. Worthington paused, trying to decide how to answer Jennifer's question. She'd had personal conversations with other girls, but with Jennifer they were much more personal. She decided to take a chance in this case because Jennifer seemed awfully concerned.

"Okay, Jennifer. Does she want to talk here or off school grounds? I can do it at my home, but it has to be when my husband is there. Will she agree with that, or do we talk here?"

"I've already talked to her about not meeting here, and she is willing to come to your house, but I didn't say anything about your husband being present. I'll have to ask her."

"He won't be present when we talk, he'll just be at home. Ask her if that's okay. If it's really important, I can meet with her here later this afternoon."

"Let me ask her. She's waiting in the hall, and I'll let you know."

Jennifer left the classroom and went into the hall. Just as a precaution, Mrs. Worthington called her husband, who happened to be working from home today, and alerted him to the possible meeting between her and the girl. Mr. Worthington had been party to Mrs. Worthington's frequent meetings with students at their house and knew that she was helping the girls. There hadn't been any boys so far, just teenage girls and occasionally an adult female.

Fifteen minutes later, Jennifer came back with a teenage girl named Rachel Gibson. Although she was a petite and pretty-looking teenager, Mrs. Worthington could see the sorrow and the tension in the girl's eyes and mannerisms. She knew right away that this was a troubled child.

"Mrs. Worthington, this is Rachel Gibson. She would like to talk with you. We talked about her meeting with you, and Rachel has decided she would rather do it at your house. She is okay with

Mr. Worthington being home, but she would like me to be there if it's okay with you."

Mrs. Worthington felt relieved that their discussion would be at her house and glad that she had alerted her husband. She was also worried that the situation may be more than they could handle. If help was needed, they knew who to call.

"I'm glad she decided to do it at my home, and I'm okay with you being there if that's what she prefers. I have to warn you though, if it's a situation that requires the utmost confidence, you may have to excuse yourself. Are you okay with that, Jennifer?"

Jennifer looked to Rachel for permission. Rachel nodded agreement. "Yes, and I understand and expect that may be necessary. We have already discussed the matter. What time should we be there?"

"How about four fifteen? That way you both can get home by dinnertime."

"Fine, we'll see you then. Thanks, Mrs. Worthington."

"You're welcome. Bye, Rachel."

No response from Rachel, which made Mrs. Worthington more uncomfortable, but as she left, the girl offered a little wave of the hand and a sheepish good-bye. Mrs. Worthington called her husband and told him what time they would be there and also expressed her concern. Mr. Worthington expressed his concern also.

CHAPTER 19

Randy and Richard Graebert were enjoying the success of the Outer Café on the southern edge of the city of Waterton, Florida. The two brothers purchased the restaurant three years ago from the couple that formerly owned and operated it. The Dugans were happy to help the brothers, especially since they were both veterans. Mr. Dugan was a veteran of the Korean War. The Dugans agreed to hold the mortgage on the restaurant with favorable terms since it was to be their retirement income.

The brothers had served together in Desert Storm, and after one reenlistment they decided to return to civilian life. Both worked at different jobs, eventually ending up as chefs at several restaurants in Florida before coming upon the Outer Café. The name struck them as odd, but somehow they felt that it had a nice ring for them. With the money they had saved from their reenlistment and what was left after they got out of the army, they had enough for the down payment and some working capital for the restaurant. With Dugan's financing, they took ownership and had been successful since their opening day.

Most of the menu was the same, but they added a few dishes that had proved to be popular with the locals. They also made a few changes to the interior, but the décor stayed basically the same. The major changes were on the outside. A few extra tables were added, with colorful table covers and flowers on each table. The brothers wanted it to appear like an outdoor café in a European city. Many of the locals liked the idea, and it had become a popular setting for them to enjoy a meal.

Becky Larson chose to have lunch at the restaurant and enjoy her meal at one of the outdoor tables. Randy was her waiter and noticed that she seemed a little stressed. She didn't smile and seemed to be in deep thought, as though something was bothering her. Being a people person himself, Randy tried his best to make her dining experience a pleasant one.

"Are you enjoying your meal, miss?"

"Oh yes, and I love the outdoor experience. It's so European."

Randy was glad that she made eye contact when she commented about her dining experience. Becky surprised herself when she made the comment about it being so European, but she sensed a friendly personality in Randy.

"Have you traveled to Europe, miss? I'm sorry, I don't mean to sound personal. I hope you're not offended?"

Randy worried that he may have been a little too forward. Becky actually welcomed the inquiry because she had been to Europe before. It was when she and Jennifer traveled after college. The sudden thought of Jennifer made her wonder what her friend was doing nowadays.

"Yes, as a matter of fact I have. It was right after college. My roommate and I made a trip there before going on to face the real world. It was amazing, and we often ate our meals at little outdoor cafés. I like the atmosphere you've created. Have you been to Europe, Randy? I see your name is on your nametag. My name is Becky Larson. I hope I'm not being too forward?"

Becky couldn't believe she was actually having a conversation with someone other than her husband's family. Randy felt a slight connection with her.

"Not at all, and it's nice to meet you. May I call you Becky? The answer to your question is yes. My brother and I traveled across Europe after we got out of the military. It's where we got our inspiration for the outdoor concept. I'm glad you approve."

"I definitely approve. So much that I will be back often. I would like to chat some more; however, I have a previous engagement. Maybe you'll be my waiter when I do come back,"

"I'll make certain I am, since I'm one of the owners."

"How nice. I look forward to seeing you again."

He handed her the change from her tab, and Becky felt a little tingle when their hands touched. Randy nearly blushed, but he was experienced with women and was certain that this one had a dark secret to her. Becky then left.

Three weeks later she returned, and Randy made sure he was her waiter. The two of them had a pleasant conversation discussing their trips to Europe. Becky started coming to the restaurant once a week. Three months later, they met on an old dirt road and had their first of several encounters.

She began meeting Randy at several motels upon returning from her trips to Valdosta, Jacksonville, and Thomasville, where she went to check art galleries, looking for new artists to display their works. Since the restaurant was closed on Mondays, she made her trips every other Monday. Eventually, Randy brought her to his home on the outskirts of Waterton. The meetings at his house were always hasty liaisons.

On the first occasion, Randy was all over Becky as soon as they were in the door, and she wasted no time tearing at his shirt, reaching for his belt, and unzipping his trousers. Randy pulled her blouse over her head and in record time had her bra off, exposing a pair of well-rounded breasts, which he immediately took inside his mouth.

Not wanting to waste time, they scampered to the bedroom, and in seconds were both naked and on the bed. Randy's mouth was all over her body, causing her to moan with pleasure. When he came up for air and placed his mouth on Becky's, she engulfed his tongue and went after it like a bitch in heat, which she was. Sex with her husband was no longer a pleasant experience.

They were both hungry for each other and wasted no time securing protection. Becky parted her legs and begged him to take her, all of her. She even pleaded with him to do so. Randy was surprised at her pleading, but he was lost in the aroma of her body and the lust she was offering. He plunged deep within her, and she took all he offered and screamed with pleasure.

When they were done, their bodies totally exhausted and physically incapable of any more sex, they showered together, dressed, and he walked her to her car. She left for home, and he went to the restaurant.

When Randy got back to the restaurant, his brother pulled him aside and told him to be careful with the woman, as she was married to the mayor of Waterton, and he was inviting trouble. Randy said that he knew she was married, but not to the mayor. Hereafter, he would be extra careful, not for his sake, but for Becky's.

On one of their last meetings, neither noticed the vehicle that had followed them.

CHAPTER 20

Creek City

Leroy Jones was in the diner helping Annie, his favorite waitress, clean up after the lunch crowd and prepare for dinner and the after-game crowd. He was proud of his diner, especially that it had become a popular eating spot for the locals, as well as the high school sports teams and their fans. Many came to listen to Leroy's escapades as a Cougar, his college career at UCF, and his stint with the Tampa Bay Bucs. He loved to regale them with stories about his football prowess, some a bit exaggerated. But everyone loved Leroy and enjoyed his tales.

Annie Foster had been working for Leroy since he purchased the diner. She was a single mom with a ten-year-old son named William, after his deceased father. Leroy and Annie had been seeing each other off and on for about four years. He occasionally took William to Cougar games and also fishing with him and John Carter on Sunday mornings. Carter enjoyed having the boy along, as Carter often wished that he had a son. Annie was grateful for the attention he paid her son, and appreciative that he had a role model in Leroy.

When Leroy took William to Cougar games, they only stayed through the third quarter, as Leroy had to get back to the diner and get ready for the after-game crowd. Annie always worked on those occasions, and William had his own spot in the diner where he could absorb all the fanfare. If he got tired, there was a small cot in the storeroom that he could nap on. After closing, Leroy drove them both home, tucked William in, and then tucked Annie in. He was always up and gone before William awoke, but the boy knew what was going on. In fact, he was happy with the situation and hoped that maybe one day Leroy would become his dad.

As Leroy was setting the tables, he noticed a dark-colored SUV parked across from the diner. The vehicle had been there for some time, and the driver never exited the vehicle. The SUV had exceptionally dark tinted windows, which Leroy considered were probably illegal. He was curious as to why the SUV was there. At tonight's game, he was going to mention it to John Carter.

When it was time to leave for the game and meet up with John Carter, Leroy made sure to let Annie and his cook know that he would see them later, especially Annie.

"Annie, I'm gonna take off now. Wish I could take William with me, but I'm meeting up with Sheriff Carter and have some business to discuss with him. Next game, William comes with me for certain."

"That's okay. I'm sure he'll be a little disappointed, but he'll get over it. You have fun. I'll see you when you get back. Are you coming home with us after closing?"

He gave her a wink and said, "Without a doubt. I'm looking forward to tucking William in."

"Me too, I hope."

Leroy put his finger to his lips and whispered, "Shish, woman, the boy will hear you."

He left and as he was leaving, he again took notice of the SUV. Leroy really was looking forward to tucking Annie in tonight and was glad that she'd mentioned it. He had decided he was sweet on the woman and believed that she was with him. Who knows, maybe he might get hitched someday. Lord knows he could use a good woman like Annie, and his congregation would love for him to marry up.

Leroy was the pastor for the small Primitive Baptist Church on the north side of town. When he decided to retire from football and the Tampa Bay Bucs, he chose to become a preacher. In college, he took a number of theology classes, and during his pro career he served as a deacon at several Primitive Baptist churches in Tampa. It was fitting that he would get his own church when he moved to Creek City. The congregation was in need of a pastor at the time, and Leroy happened to be at the right place at the right time. It had been a perfect fit.

When Leroy arrived at the football stadium, he found a space next to John Carter. The deputy on duty in the parking area had arranged for the two men to have good parking spaces in the event they had to leave early. Leroy asked the deputy if Carter was already in the stands and was told he was at the refreshment stand. He wandered over and found Carter scoffing down a hot dog.

"You could have at least got me one. You gonna have room for barbeque after the game, Sheriff?"

Sheriff Carter would be going back to the diner when Leroy left the game to help, and his presence there should help keep things orderly and calm, hopefully. It all depended on who won tonight. As soon as Carter finished his hot dog and cleaned the mustard off his mouth, they headed for seating in the bleachers.

Right from the start the Cougars jumped out to an early lead and kept at it the whole first half. The defense was merciless, and on offense, Jimmy Cochran was having one of his best games. By the end of the first half, he'd thrown three touchdown passes and ran for another score. The Cougars were up 28–0.

"Leroy, you seem kind of fidgety. Is something bothering you? It's not a problem with Annie, is it?"

"No, certainly not. We're fine."

Carter half believed Leroy, but he trusted his friend. If something was bothering him, eventually he would tell Carter.

"John, without making it obvious, I want you to glance across the field at the guy in the dark jacket leaning against the fence."

Carter casually glanced across the field and noticed the guy.

"I see him, Leroy, but he looks harmless. You think he's up to something? It looks like he's just watching the game. Maybe he's a college scout."

"I don't think so, John, because he hasn't been watching the game. He's been watching us. You know him? I sure don't." Leroy glanced toward the guy then said, "While I was at the diner getting ready for tonight, I noticed a dark SUV parked across the street. I couldn't see inside because the windows had a real dark tint to them. Never saw anybody get in or out of it either. What do you think?"

Carter became suspicious and wondered if it had anything to do with the Larsons and his rebuff of the request for the wife's remains.

"Don't know. Let me call my deputy who is working the parking lot and have him check for a dark SUV. If there's one, I'll have him get the license plate."

The guy in the dark jacket must have suspected they were looking at him, because he turned and headed for the parking area. Carter was on the phone with his deputy and told him the guy was heading for the parking area. He also told the deputy to act like he was doing a routine walk around but take notice of the guy.

A short time later, the deputy called Carter and told him that the guy got in a dark SUV and drove off, though not before the deputy got the license plate. Carter told him to give it to Billy in the morning and tell him to run a search on the SUV. He said good job to the deputy and hung up his phone.

"He got the plate, and by Monday we'll know who he is and maybe why he was here. Let's hope he's just a scout. We gonna stay for the third quarter or leave now? I'm ready if you are."

"Let's leave. It looks like the Cougars got this one. Besides, it will give me time to get ready for the celebration. I expect it to be rowdy. Good thing you're gonna be there, John." The two of them got up and headed for their vehicles then drove off to the diner.

Right on cue about thirty minutes after game time, the crowd started arriving. At first it was a few fans and the cheerleaders, and then most of the football team with their girlfriends arrived. That's when things started to get a little rowdy as everyone started shouting, "Go, Cougars!"

Leroy did his best to quiet the crowd but wasn't having much luck. Sheriff Carter came out of the bathroom and shouted, "Go, Cougars!" Things quieted down. His mere presence put the fear in everyone. Carter and Leroy looked at each other and gave each other a thumbs-up sign.

Just before the crowd dispersed, Carter pulled Jimmy Cochran aside and asked him if he was certain the pickup truck that left the scene of the accident headed north. He also asked which way the Toyota was heading.

"Best I can say, Sheriff, the Toyota appeared to be heading north before it was broadsided and flipped. That pickup definitely headed north."

"Why do you think they would have been heading north on 373, Jimmy?"

"Maybe they were taking a shortcut to I-75. Lots of folks do it. A lot of the pecan farmers use it, and so do some of Leroy's parishioners. You take it to White Springs, and then from there you can catch I-75 north. You have to take a number of dirt roads, but they're manageable."

The explanation made sense to Carter. After his conversation, he said good night to Leroy, Annie, and William, and then headed on home smelling of barbeque.

CHAPTER 21

Friday afternoon, Marge sat at her desk once again reviewing the autopsy report on the Larson woman. The DNA taken from the fetus had been sent out for a database search and would not be back for at least a week. As she continued to peruse the report, her stomach started to feel queasy. At first she believed she was going to be sick. However, just as suddenly as it started, the queasiness ended. Her stomach settled, but then she got an awful feeling of sadness and felt a tear coming on. She knew she wasn't going to be able to escape the emotions that were about to overwhelm her.

The death of the fetus had brought back memories of the child she'd lost when she suffered a miscarriage from an accidental fall. She had not only lost the child, but her doctor said it would be impossible for her to ever conceive again. It was a traumatic event for both her and John, and thanks to counseling they were able to overcome the loss. Marge had suffered a temporary case of PTSD. Counseling got her through it; however, she would never forget the loss of her unborn child. Today was the anniversary of that event.

Tom Morgan stepped into the doorway and noticed the expression on Marge's face. He knew immediately what was about to happen since it had happened before. She was surely overcome with grief from the autopsy results. Last time this happened, he forced her to go home and called John to alert him. Tom didn't want it to happen again, so he decided to attempt to get her to go home and away from the case.

"Marge, are you okay?" he asked.

Marge knew she wasn't and knew that Tom would be able to ascertain her problem. He'd been a very good friend, and the last time this happened he called John. This time she would take charge and be the one to call it quits for the day.

"Actually, Tom, I'm feeling a little nauseous and think it best if I take the rest of the day off. Please don't call John. He's going to the game with Leroy and has been looking forward to it tonight. I'll be all right. I just think it best if I go home and lie down. I'll see you on Monday. Maybe you should also go home."

"Okay, Marge. I'm just going to finish my report, and then I'll take your advice and go home. Maybe I'll see you at the festival tomorrow. Go on home now."

"I'm out of here right now. And thanks again, Tom."

She got up, grabbed her purse and jacket, left the office, and drove home, grateful that Tom hadn't made an issue of what happened. She'd tell John when she was ready.

When Leroy said that he had everything under control and Carter could go home, John was ready to leave. His clothes reeked of barbeque, and he would have to get out of them as soon as he got home. Marge would wash them over the weekend.

"Okay, Leroy, I'm outa here in a New York minute. Take care, Annie, and William, I'll see you early Sunday morning."

"I'll be there, Sheriff. Good night."

Carter arrived at the house and was pleased to see Marge's car in the driveway. As he entered, he removed his shirt so he could put it in the clothes hamper, and then headed toward the kitchen to find Marge. When he stepped into the kitchen, he immediately noticed the half-empty bottle of wine and the empty glass on the counter, but no Marge. They were the first things that told him something was wrong, and he instantly realized what day it was. Another year had passed, and he was sure that she was upset.

He quietly approached the bedroom and saw her lying on her side in the bed. Silently he walked over and got in bed next to her, put an arm around her waist, and said nothing.

Marge rolled over, looked him in the eyes with an eerie look on her face, and asked him to make love to her. "Now, please, John," she said.

Carter began unbuttoning her blouse and unhooking her bra. As he did so, they continued to stare into each other's eyes in silence. He put his hand on one of her breasts, fondled it, and played with the nipple, continuing to stare into her eyes. The scene was a bit macabre. Next he took the nipple in his mouth and suckled it like a newborn does when its mother is nursing the child. He never took his eyes off hers, and neither did she.

Slowly he let his tongue wander down to her midsection. He reached behind her and unzipped her skirt, and then pulled it and her underwear off. With his eyes still locked on hers, he began giving her pleasure. When her body started to twitch, he got up, unbuckled his trousers, and slid his pants and underwear down below his knees.

He was about to mount her, but with a sudden burst of strength and energy, she pushed him onto his back and proceeded to mount him. Her eyes stayed focused on his as she placed his erection inside her. When she had it in, she began pumping relentlessly, never taking her eyes off his. Furiously she pumped, and eventually he completely filled her body. She continued the routine, looked up at the ceiling, and let out a blood-curdling shriek.

Her eyes went back to staring into his as though lost in a trance. Suddenly she got off him, got on the bed beside him, and rolled over on her side with her back facing him. She then reached up and turned off the lamp on the night table. She fell into a deep sleep. Carter lay there on his back with tears in his eyes. After a while, he too drifted off into a deep sleep.

In the morning when Carter awoke, he could tell the space next to him was empty. As he lay there wondering what the morning had in store for them, he heard the silence when the shower was turned off. The bathroom door opened, and she emerged wearing a white robe and a white towel wrapped as a turban around her beautiful head. With another towel in hand, she walked over to her vanity table, placed a foot on the chair, and started putting lotion on her shapely legs.

When she finished both legs, Marge straightened up, looked at him, smiled, winked, and quipped, "There's plenty of hot water for you, quarterback. You need to get that barbeque smell washed off. You smell like Leroy's Diner at dinnertime. When you're done and dressed, I'll be in the kitchen with a hearty breakfast of bacon, pancakes, and scrambled eggs the way you like them. Don't keep me waiting, quarterback."

She dropped the robe and went immediately to her closet to begin dressing, leaving Carter with a view of the lovely body that he'd pleasured last night.

Carter started to get out of the bed, forgetting that his pants were still down around his ankles. He almost fell flat on his face; however, he managed to drop back onto the bed, avoiding an accident.

Marge noticed his near disaster and chaffed, "Careful, quarterback, the season's not over yet."

He removed his trousers and underwear, gave her a devilish smile, and headed to the bathroom for a shower. When he was done, he dressed in jeans, boots, and a long-sleeved cotton shirt.

He could smell the aroma of coffee and bacon wafting from the kitchen. Carter took one last look in the mirror then followed his nose to the kitchen.

There with her back to him, dressed in tight-fitting jeans, heels, and a halter top that exposed half her naked back, she stood flipping pancakes. He stood there and admired her beauty. When she sensed his eyes on her, she turned, and he noticed that the halter top exposed just enough cleavage to spark one's imagination. He could also see the outline of the nipples he had gently suckled last night. This wasn't the outfit of a woman in mourning, nor of the county's chief medical examiner. It was the outfit of a woman who planned to go trolling, and Carter was glad that she was his wife. Maybe everything was back to normal. He sure hoped so.

She smiled at him, put the spatula on the counter, and then walked over to him. He reached out to her, kissed her tenderly on the lips, and gathered her in his arms with her head tucked against his chest. His nostrils filled with her fragrance, and his body was enjoying her warmth. Neither of them said anything for a very long time.

Carter stepped back and asked, "You okay, wide receiver?" He was hoping for the right answer.

"Yes. Thank you, quarterback. This case brought back some memories that I thought I had buried."

It was the response he had hoped for. It meant that things were approaching normal in the Carter house.

She pulled away from his chest and joked, "That stomach of yours is making so much noise it's going to wake the neighbors. Sit down, and I'll fix you a plate."

Although he was famished and hungry for pancakes, bacon, and coffee, before he sat down he had something to say.

"You know, wide receiver, you're gonna turn a lot of heads today."

"That's what I'm hoping for, as long as one of them is yours."

"Oh, mine has already nearly spun off my spine. Damn, you are one gorgeous creature. There's not a luckier man on this planet than me."

"And there's not a luckier woman than me. Thanks, quarterback. You look like you're going hunting today too."

"It looks like we're both going hunting."

After a laugh, they sat and ate breakfast together. When they were done, Marge got a light jacket to cover her shoulders in case it was chilly out. She certainly wasn't going to use it for modesty's sake.

"You ready to go, wide receiver? We got a festival to get to."

"Then let's get the hell outa here."

As Carter drove out of town, he suddenly remembered that they would have to take County Road 373, just like Jimmy Cochran said, as a shortcut to where they were going. Damn, he didn't want to pass the accident scene. He decided that when they were close, he would engage Marge in conversation so she didn't notice.

A ways before the accident scene, they passed Leroy's church. Marge asked if he would slow down so she could read the words of wisdom under the pastor's name on the church's marquee. It usually gave Sunday's worship hours and Pastor Leroy's name. Carter slowed as Marge let the passenger window down. An elderly black woman walking toward three parked vehicles raised her hand in a friendly gesture. Marge returned the gesture.

When they were close enough, Marge read the words on the marquee.

THOSE SEEKING SHELTER ALONG HIS WAY
COME ENTER THE LORD'S HOUSE

After reading the words aloud so Carter could hear them, Marge commented that Leroy was a kind and gentle man. Carter agreed, and it became a topic of discussion that lasted until they were well past the accident scene. Carter was relieved.

CHAPTER 22

Bensmille, North Carolina—1983

Deborah and Charles Worthington waited patiently for the two girls to arrive. They weren't novices in counseling teenage girls and were prepared for whatever Rachel Gibson's situation would be. At precisely four thirty the doorbell rang, and when Mrs. Worthington opened the door, it was obvious that the teenager accompanied by Jennifer was a girl with troubles. Rachel's reticent expression said, "Help me, please."

Mrs. Worthington invited the two in and introduced Rachel to her husband. She told Rachel that he would be in his office while they talked in the living room. The Worthingtons lived in a modest three-bedroom home that had been built by Charles. He owned his own construction firm. Before moving to Bensmille, the Worthingtons lived in Tampa, where Charles worked for a commercial construction firm and Deborah was an art teacher at a small private school. They chose Bensmille because they wanted a more rural surrounding and both wanted to be near the mountains.

Mr. Worthington greeted Rachel and excused himself. Mrs. Worthington and the two girls moved into the living room. She had previously put juice and cookies on snack tables in case either of the girls wanted a snack. Jennifer took a plate of cookies and a glass of juice. She offered them to Rachel, who declined. Both girls sat down on the lovely floral-patterned sofa across from Mrs. Worthington.

There was a long silence before Mrs. Worthington said, "Rachel, I want you to know that whatever you tell me will not leave this room. You can tell as much or as little as you want. The decision is yours, and I won't press you. Whenever you're ready, I'm here to listen. Please feel comfortable."

After an awkward period of silence, Mrs. Worthington believed that the girl wouldn't speak to her; however, she was used to this. It always took a little while before the girls were comfortable talking to someone, especially a stranger. Mrs. Worthington was more than satisfied waiting for as long as needed.

Jennifer turned to Rachel, put a hand on the cushion, and said, "Rachel, it's okay. You can trust Mrs. Worthington. I promised you that she wouldn't do or say anything that could harm you, and I meant it. She's helped me a lot before. Please talk to her."

Mrs. Worthington felt uncomfortable because Jennifer seemed to be pushing the girl. The two were friends, and it was Jennifer who convinced Rachel to come here, so she said nothing, just waited.

Rachel looked around the room, avoiding eye contact with Mrs. Worthington, and then softly replied, "I'm sorry, Mrs. Worthington. It's just so personal and so awful. I don't know what I should say."

"Say whatever you want, Rachel. I'm not here to judge you." She spoke softly as she continued, "I just want to listen and be of help if I can. Take your time. Just remember, you both do have to eventually go home for dinner."

Rachel hesitated, and her voice quaked as she responded, "Mrs. Worthington, I don't want him to get in trouble, but I can't take the beatings anymore. I'm afraid he is really going to hurt me one day. It's just so awful and hurtful." She withheld the most awful part of what had happened to her.

Mrs. Worthington was afraid that something like this had happened, and now she had to go slowly and carefully, but she had to ask. It was an awful question to ask a teenage girl; however, it was necessary.

She leaned forward and asked, "Rachel, who's been beating you? Was it your father?"

The question was asked. Would Rachel respond, or would she shut down altogether?

Rachel had already decided that she could trust Mrs. Worthington, so she told her, "Yes, but I know he doesn't mean to. It's when he drinks and thinks about my mom, but the beatings seem to be getting worse. I don't know what to do, and I really don't want him to get in trouble."

It was the same response all teenage girls gave, as did the adult women. They didn't want the abuser to get in trouble, and it was not their fault. There was always an excuse.

"Rachel, there is no excuse for a parent beating their child. I'm sorry, I had to say that. I want to see your wounds. Will you show them to me? Please!"

She used the word *please* with emphasis, hoping that Rachel would show her the wounds. Mrs. Worthington just hoped that they weren't horrible to look at like the last girl's were.

Rachel got up and raised her blouse, exposing some of her back. Jennifer told her to remove her blouse so Mrs. Worthington could see all of the bruises. Mrs. Worthington gave Jennifer a look and nod that implied, "No, Jennifer, let Rachel decide." Jennifer dismissed the look and again told Rachel to remove the blouse.

Rachel dutifully obeyed Jennifer's command and removed her blouse. What Mrs. Worthington saw was horrific, and the fact that Rachel obeyed Jennifer's command made it obvious that this girl was in serious trouble. This wasn't just a parental beating; this was downright physical abuse, and maybe there was more.

The girl sunk her head to her chest in shame, and Mrs. Worthington could hear the soft cry emanating from her. She reached out to the girl and took her in her arms to console her. An abundance of tears flowed down Rachel's cheeks and into her mouth. It was as though a dam had burst, and in fact one had. It belonged to this beautiful child.

"Oh, Rachel, I'm so sorry for you. I have to ask, is there any more?"

She hoped there wasn't, but Mrs. Worthington knew better.

Rachel looked away then said, "Yes. On my legs. But they're high enough that they can't be seen even when I'm wearing shorts."

Mrs. Worthington became frightened and suspected that there was something even worse than the beatings. She felt she had to ask, but not with Jennifer in the room.

"Jennifer, would you please excuse us? Why don't you go talk with Mr. Worthington in his office?"

Jennifer knew what was about to happen, so she complied with Mrs. Worthington's request. She looked at both of them, and then excused herself. When she knocked on Mr. Worthington's office door, he told her to come in. They both remained silent. Mr. Worthington gave her a chair and a magazine to read. He also offered to turn on the television, but she said that the magazine was fine. Neither said anything more.

Mrs. Worthington delicately asked the most difficult question she had ever had to ask. Although she really didn't want to, she felt that if she didn't ask, she would never know, so she asked.

"Rachel, did your father have sex with you?"

It was a horrible question to ask any child, yet it needed to be asked, especially in this case. There was a long silence broken by Rachel's sobs and more tears. The girl's body started to shake. Mrs. Worthington feared that she might faint, so she gathered Rachel in her arms again. She held her until the sobbing ceased and Rachel was ready to talk.

"He made me do awful things to him ever since my mother died. It was disgusting, and I hated it. He's my dad, and I wanted to please him, but then it kept up. He made me do more and more." She continued to sob uncontrollably. "At first it was just touching and stroking him, but then he made me put it in my mouth. I got sick several times. Please don't tell Jennifer. She only knows about the beatings. I couldn't tell her about this."

Emotionally upset, Mrs. Worthington considered getting her husband but decided it wasn't time yet. She needed to know if there was more and sensed that there was.

"Rachel, is there anything more that happened? This is between you and me. Like I said, it goes no further."

The girl had the saddest look that Mrs. Worthington had ever seen on a child. Unfortunately there was still more to come, and Mrs. Worthington was terribly afraid of what it would be.

Rachel hesitated, looked down, dropped her arms and crossed her hands over her groin, and muttered, "He made me have sex with him. Several times, and I'm no longer a virgin."

Mrs. Worthington made the sign of the cross across her chest, looked up, and silently spoke to anyone who might be listening, *Oh my heaven. Why this beautiful child? Why, Lord, why?* Rachel couldn't hear her, and no one answered. She was all alone with the girl. She gathered Rachel in her arms to comfort her. *Could it be any worse?* she asked, and still received no answer.

Rachel covered her stomach with her hands and said, "Mrs. Worthington, I've been getting sick a few times, mostly in the morning. Could I be pregnant? I don't want to be. Please tell me

I'm not." She put her hands together as though in prayer, shut her eyes, and cried out, "I don't want to be a mother at my age, and have my father's bastard child."

This innocent child was too young to be having such thoughts, but her innocence was long gone. Her own father had taken it, and now she would have to live with that memory for the rest of her life, if she gave birth.

"I don't know, child, but there is a way to find out. We can do so right here; however, you are going to have to let my husband help. This is not our first time handling a situation like yours. It's what we do."

Rachel wasn't sure she liked the idea of Mr. Worthington knowing the situation, but Mrs. Worthington's comment about it being what they do eased her fear.

"Okay, but what about Jennifer? Does she have to know?"

"Only if you want her to. I can send her home if you'd like."

"Maybe it would be all right. She is my only friend, and I guess I can trust her. What do you think, Mrs. Worthington?"

"You need a good friend right now, and I'm positive Jennifer can be trusted. I'll leave it to you to tell her whatever you want. We may need Jennifer's help because I'm not letting you go home. You've endured enough, and if you are pregnant, it's safer if you don't. Trust me, Rachel."

"I trust you, Mrs. Worthington. I wish you were my mom, but that's not so. I'll do whatever you say, but what about my dad?"

"I'm going to have Jennifer call your father and tell him you're spending the night at her house to work on a project for school. I'll call Jennifer's mother and convince her to let you stay there for the night. I'll tell her you both are working on a very important project for my class. That okay with you?"

"But Jennifer's parents aren't very friendly people, Mrs. Worthington."

"I'm well aware of that, but I can convince them."

She was well aware of Jennifer's parents' unfriendliness—that was why Jennifer had first come to see her—but it was only going to be this one night, as she planned on getting Rachel to a safe environment. Mrs. Worthington had already alerted them to the possibility of bringing someone to them.

Mrs. Worthington told Rachel to wait there while she went to talk to her husband. She would send Jennifer out, and Rachel could decide what she wanted to tell her.

"However, Rachel, it might be best to tell her only as much as you're comfortable with, if Jennifer is going to help."

Jennifer came into the living room and asked how it had gone. Rachel decided to tell her about the rape, but not the stuff before that. Horrified, Jennifer took her friend in her arms, and the two of them cried together. That night they forged an unbreakable bond. Jennifer would do whatever she could to help Rachel.

Mrs. Worthington told her husband everything, and he was as emotionally upset as she was. He also agreed that Rachel couldn't go home. He suggested that she stay with them, but they didn't know how that would go over with the girl's father. They got the pregnancy test and joined the two girls in the living room. Mrs. Worthington could tell that Jennifer knew about the rape, but she wasn't sure about everything else. She didn't need to know. Whatever Rachel told Jennifer was their secret; she wasn't going to ask.

Rachel took the pregnancy test from Mrs. Worthington and went to the bathroom, where she followed the instructions. She waited to see what it read. When she saw the result, she took it to Mrs. Worthington. Unfortunately it was positive.

"Oh, dear Lord!" Mrs. Worthington exclaimed.

Rachel began sobbing uncontrollably and suddenly fainted. Mr. Worthington became worried that the girl might hurt herself.

"Deborah, she's not going home, and she's not going to Jennifer's either," Mr. Worthington said. "She is going to the council, where she'll be safe. They will know what to do."

Mrs. Worthington agreed. Her husband would deal with Rachel's father.

At first Rachel protested, but with Jennifer's insistence she relented and did as Mrs. Worthington requested. Jennifer said good-bye to her friend and went home.

Less than an hour later, they arrived and whisked Rachel away. At an unknown clinic, a rape kit was taken and a pregnancy examination was completed. Fortunately Rachel wasn't pregnant. The test taken at the Worthington house was a false read, and Rachel's sickness was most likely due to the trauma of the rape. The bruises on the girl's upper thighs and the tears in the vagina and anus confirmed that she was forcefully raped. A thorough psychiatric evaluation was performed, and it was determined that she was a candidate for possible suicide.

The people at the clinic had contacts with a number of influential people, including judges, lawyers, politicians, women's advocates, and members of law enforcement. With the help of everyone operating inconspicuously, Rachel was permanently removed from her father's parental rights. Nathan Gibson was convinced to give up legal guardianship as part of a plea deal to reduce his prison time. A great-aunt on Rachel's mother's side in Tennessee was happy to take custody of her.

Rachel was given extensive counseling in hopes of erasing the memories of what her father had done to her. Raised by her great-aunt in a loving environment, Rachel eventually graduated from high school. She legally changed her name with the approval of her great-aunt and became Jennifer Brooks. She took the first name out of appreciation for what her friend had done for her. Jennifer Brooks graduated from a small college in Tennessee and was now a guidance counselor at a high school in Knoxville.

Her father still lived in Bensmille as did the rest of his family. They had no idea what happened between Rachel and her father. They were told that she had a condition and was sent away to spare her embarrassment. The type of people that the Gibsons were, they accepted the explanation.

Deborah and Charles Worthington still lived in Bensmille, and Deborah was still the art teacher at the same high school.

CHAPTER 23

Duke Medical School—In the future

Jessica Carter had just finished her consultation with her faculty advisors and informed them of her decision after graduation. They were hoping that she would do her internship at the Duke medical facility, but she had other plans. Now she had to inform her parents who were visiting for her graduation from medical school. It wouldn't be the first time she'd sprung a surprise on them. The last time was when she chose Duke over Florida State. She planned on doing it tonight during dinner.

Holding the Purple Heart that her paternal grandmother had given her, she realized that it was what made her come to a final decision. The medal was tarnished a bit from age, but Jessica often polished it out of respect for what it stood for. Her grandmother gave it to her a year before she died. She said it belonged to Jessica's great-grandfather who was awarded it for an injury sustained during World War II. She also said that he used to regale Jessica's mother with stories about the war and the medal. Maybe one day Jessica's mother would tell her about her great-grandfather.

John and Emily Carter were so proud of their daughter's accomplishments and excited to be there for her graduation from medical school. They wondered where she was going to do her internship and hoped that it would be at a prestigious hospital in Florida but would be happy with whatever she chose. The three of them were having dinner at an upscale restaurant not far from the university. Since Jessica was over the age of twenty-one, they ordered a bottle of wine and glasses for each of them. John told the waiter to give them plenty of time, as they wanted to talk first.

They toasted Jessica's graduation, and then Carter asked Jessica what her plans were for an internship. Jessica hesitated before responding. They sensed that she had a surprise for them and hoped she hadn't changed her mind about becoming a doctor.

Jessica proceeded cautiously, hoping for a favorable response. "I've made a major decision and have decided to do my internship at Walter Reed in Maryland."

The look on her parents' faces told her they were shocked.

Emily asked the inevitable question, "Does that mean you're enlisting in the military, Jess?"

Carter was surprised at Emily's question and concerned that it was going to happen. His daughter was going to become a member of the US military.

She smiled and replied, "Yes, it does. I'll be commissioned a lieutenant junior grade in the navy, and after I complete my internship, I'll be commissioned a lieutenant while doing my residency. I want to become an orthopedic surgeon and work with veterans and active-duty personnel. It's what I really want to do."

Jessica got it all out and was glad. Now she hoped that her parents would be glad for her just as she was glad for herself.

"You're a big girl now, Jess," said Emily, "and capable of making your own decisions. If this is what you really want to do, then you have our love and support. Don't you agree, John?"

Carter was dumbfounded, but Emily was right. He always encouraged his daughter to make her own decisions and to take responsibility for them. Her decisions were always good ones. He had to agree with his wife.

"I agree. You have my love and full support. I'm positive you'll be a great orthopedic surgeon. In fact, I'm certain you'll be the best."

Jessica smiled, pleased that she had her father's approval.

Emily reached out and put her hand on Jessica's. She said, "Jess, your grandmother would be proud of you, and so would your great-grandfather. He was a naval pilot in World War II and actually flew a number of missions over Iwo Jima when the marines landed. Later he was injured during a Japanese aerial attack. He took a bullet in his leg trying to get to his plane. He spent three weeks in a hospital where there were a number of marines that were wounded in the battle.

"He used to regale me with stories about his missions and his stay in the hospital. Seems all the men were competing for this one nurse's attention, but she had this thing for flyboys and he got most of her attention. He told me when his hospital stay was over, she gave him her home address and told him to look her up after the war. He did, and it was love at first sight. After a month, they were married. Next came your grandmother, me, and then you.

"Your great-grandfather was awarded a Purple Heart that he would often show me. I've often wondered what happened to it. Your grandmother never mentioned it after he died. It would be nice to have it as a memento."

Jessica held the medal in her hand, and after listening to her mother's story she made a decision that would please her mother. She reached out and took her mother's hand, and with her other hand she placed the medal in her mother's palm.

"Grandma gave me this a long time ago, and it's what helped make my decision. In a way I'm honoring it and Great-Granddad. This should be yours, Mom. It's served me well, and it rightfully belongs with you."

Tears fell from both women's eyes. Even Carter shed a little tear.

"Jess, I appreciate the gesture, but your grandmother gave it to you, and you should keep it. Let it serve as your good-luck charm. I'd be happier if you kept it."

"Thanks, Mom. If that's what you want, then I'd be honored to hold onto the medal. In a way it already has been my good-luck charm."

Carter sensed things were getting a little maudlin, so he decided to interject a little humor.

"Well then, let's hoist up our glasses and make a toast. Anchors away, me boys!"

That was all it took to bring joy and laughter to them and to some of the restaurant's patrons.

"You're crazy, you know that, Dad?"

"That's what fathers are supposed to be, Lieutenant."

Both Emily and Jessica responded in unison. "And that's why we love you."

In Florida, Jessica's high school swim coach at Sinclair Academy, Jennifer Rowland, was calling Jessica's name and shouting, "Jessica, where is your head at? You're up next. Come on, girl, get with it."

Jessica apologized, got up, and walked over to the pool, ready for her event. She looked into the audience and saw her parents give her a thumbs-up. The starter fired his gun, and the swimmers were in the water. As usual, she defeated the competition. In the locker room she showered, dressed, grabbed her things, and left to meet up with her parents. In the pocket of her shorts was a small flyer from Walter Reed Medical Center. Jessica couldn't remember how it got there.

CHAPTER 24

Randall County

Amy Tucker had just finished her telephone call with Barbara Morris and was looking at her notes. She sensed tension in the woman's voice and was certain that she was holding back something. Amy had a knack for reading people's emotions, faces, and voices. When not on duty, she often served as a grief counselor and couples counselor. Amy had counseled the Carters on numerous occasions, especially Marge. Amy was a licensed therapist with a master's degree in counseling.

The Morris woman was forthcoming, but Amy had to pressure the woman to give up details. She managed to learn that Jennifer Williams had attended Jacksonville College of Art and her maiden name was Brown. Amy also learned, after much discussion, that Jennifer had a roommate named Becky. Amy recalled what the woman said.

"I know, Deputy, because Jennifer had told me about her at one of our lunches. I met occasionally with Jennifer to check on how she was doing on behalf of a very good friend."

After a lot of prying and telling the woman that this was a potential homicide, Barbara Morris gave Amy her friend's name and number in Bensmille, North Carolina. She also told Amy that Deborah Worthington had been instrumental in getting Jennifer to apply to Jacksonville College and that the woman was Jennifer's art teacher in high school.

With this information, Amy was prepared to go to John, but since he had already left for Leroy's, she decided to place a call to Bensmille in hopes of talking to Mrs. Worthington. After several rings, a female with a pleasant but hesitant voice answered the telephone.

"This is Deborah Worthington. How can I help you?"

On the other end, Deborah Worthington knew the call was from the deputy that Barbara had told her about since the Florida number appeared on the handset.

Amy could sense right away the same hesitation and emotion that Barbara Morris had when she spoke with her. She was certain that the Morris woman had called Mrs. Worthington to alert her.

"Mrs. Worthington, I'm Deputy Amy Tucker from the sheriff's office in Creek City, Florida. Do you have a few moments to talk to me? If not, I can call back another time."

Amy hoped that Mrs. Worthington would talk to her now, as she was anxious to complete this part of the investigation before the weekend. Deborah Worthington wasn't excited about answering questions but wanted to know more about Jennifer.

"It's okay, now is convenient. However, it's almost dinnertime, so can we keep it short?"

"Sure, I'll be as brief as I can. Let me explain why I'm calling. There's been an accident—" Amy didn't get the next word out because Deborah Worthington interrupted her.

"I know why you're calling, Deputy. Just tell me, is Jennifer okay?"

Amy glanced down at her notes and spoke to them, *Well, that was quick. It confirms that the Morris woman called and alerted her.*

"No, Mrs. Worthington, she's not. Unfortunately, Jennifer died in the accident and we are investigating the accident as a possible homicide. I'm sorry to be the one to tell you."

There was a ponderous silence then a scream on the other end followed by, "Oh my God, Charles."

Amy waited a very long time until finally she heard a male voice in the receiver.

"This is Charles Worthington, Deborah's husband. Who is this, and can I help you?"

The first thought Amy had was that there was more to the relationship between Jennifer and her art teacher, and she made a note of it.

"Mr. Worthington, I'm Deputy Tucker and I've just informed your wife of Jennifer Williams's death and that it's possible it was due to a homicide. I'm sorry if I upset her."

"I understand, Deputy, and thank you for your apology. Listen, can we call you back? It's a lot for my wife to absorb. Jennifer and my wife were close at one time, and right now she's in a bit of shock. I promise we'll get back to you, although it may be a few days, if that's okay?"

Amy didn't want to pressure the man and felt that there was more here than what she'd expected. She decided it could wait over the weekend.

"Sure, I understand. It can wait until Monday or Tuesday, but please understand I have an investigation to do."

She was being sympathetic; however, she did have an investigation to complete, and if they didn't call her by Tuesday, she was going to call them.

"Thank you, Deputy. We have your number, and I promise you will hear from us. Good day now."

Abruptly he hung up before Amy could say good day to him. This was an interesting turn of events, and Amy was anxious to hear back from them. Then let John know what she learned from Worthington and Morris. Maybe if she saw John at the festival tomorrow, she would alert him. Her shift would be over in two hours, and she planned on going home to enjoy a few glasses of wine. This had been a rough day, even for a grief counselor.

In Bensmille, Charles Worthington was consoling his wife. When she was calm and able to discuss the situation, they made a decision to take a trip, but not until Monday. They wanted the weekend to decide exactly what they were going to do and say. The deputy's call had them both concerned, and they also had a call to make. Something was seriously wrong.

CHAPTER 25

J ohn and Marge Carter walked the pecan festival grounds absorbing all the aromas drifting from the food vendors. John was aware of the number of heads that turned when Marge passed by. He was enjoying it, as was Marge. They gave each other a devilish smile, and John knew that everything was all right with the Carters.

They spotted Leroy, Annie, and William walking up ahead of them and decided to wander over their way. William was munching on a corn dog, his second one, and Leroy and Annie were each scoffing down a funnel cake. Sporting white mustaches and little beards from the powdery sugar, they weren't the least bit concerned what they looked like. John and Marge were pleasantly amused.

"You three look like you're really enjoying yourselves."

"Sheriff and Mrs. Carter. Man, don't you two look good, especially you, Marge. I bet you've turned a lot of heads already."

Annie gave him a stern look. "Leroy, that's not nice. Where's your manners?"

William laughed and continued munching on his corn dog.

"It's okay, Annie. It's my intention to turn some heads, including John's and Leroy's. You look pretty hot yourself, girl. What say we do some trolling and leave the boys to themselves?"

"Let me wipe my puss, and I'm right with you. How about we strut like working girls and butt wiggle for the boys?"

"I'm game."

They walked off shaking their butts. William slapped his knee and broke out in laughter while the two men scratched their heads, bewildered.

"You think we should follow them, Leroy?"

"Nah, let them be. How's Marge?"

"She's good. Had a little episode yesterday, but she's over it now."

"Maybe you two need another session with Amy?"

"Amy's been pestering me, but it's gonna be up to Marge. I'm not pressing her though. When the time is right, we'll call Amy. You made any decision about Annie yet?"

"I'm thinking I'm gonna do it. Just have to decide when the timing's right. Know what I mean?"

"There's never a right time, Leroy. You got to do it. You ain't scared, are you?"

"Yeah, I am. Hey, here comes Amy. She looks a little excited, and I got to say, for a woman her age she looks good."

"She does, doesn't she? Hey, Amy, what's up?"

"John, Leroy. William, you better slow down and enjoy that corn dog. I got something to tell you about the calls I made yesterday, John."

"Not today, Amy, and certainly not this weekend. Whatever it is will have to wait until Monday. I'm off for the weekend, and if it's anything to do with the case, I'm off-limits. Sorry, Amy."

Amy took the hint and surmised that it had something to do with Marge. She wasn't about to upset Carter's weekend.

"Okay. Now where are Marge and Annie?"

Leroy smiled and answered, "They're off trolling. The way you look, you might as well join them." He winked and asked, "Are you hunting for someone today, Amy?"

She winked back at him then replied, "Leroy, I might just be, and if you weren't tied to Annie, you might be the one."

Leroy's face turned a little reddish, and his eyebrows went up. Carter said wow as Amy wandered off to find the two women. John, Leroy, and William watched as she shook her booty at them.

William let out a giggle then asked if he could have another corn dog.

"Damn, boy, where're you putting them things?" Leroy said. "Here, get yourself another, just don't tell your mother and don't make yourself sick, else you won't be able to go fishin' tomorrow."

William took the money, laughed, and sauntered off to get another corn dog.

When he came back, the three of them wandered off with William flanked by each of them to find the best pecan pie and some roasted pecans. Carter looked at William then at Leroy. Leroy mouthed, "Don't say anything, John."

They found the women, each with a corn dog in one hand and a slice of pecan pie in the other. Neither of them offered the men a bite and told them to get their own.

Leroy asked if anyone was selling tripe stew. Carter shouted, "Not on your life."

William burst out laughing, and Carter said, "If you keep laughing, William, you ain't going fishing in the morning with us."

"Aw, man, Sheriff, come on—you just foolin' me, right?"

Carter said yes but gave William an angry stare, and the three of them promptly went and got corn dogs, roasted pecans, and pecan pie.

Meanwhile in Bensmille, Deborah and Charles were on the telephone asking what they should do and how this could have happened. As to what had happened, there was no answer, and as to what they should do, that was left up to Deborah and Charles. They were alone on this; however, they were told to be careful not to expose anyone or anything. Say as little as possible.

On Sunday morning Carter arrived at Annie's house at five thirty. Leroy and William were waiting for him, William impatiently, Leroy smiling. Leroy gave Carter a look that said the boy was excited and anxious to get going. They loaded up and headed off to the lake.

From the backseat and with a lot of excitement in his voice, William exclaimed, "Mr. Carter, I got me a new worm, and I'm gonna whip you and my dad's butt."

Carter and Leroy exchanged glances and smiled at the boy's butt remark.

"We'll see, William. You make a statement like that, you gotta back it up."

It wasn't long before Carter and Leroy learned that William would indeed back up his statement. He outfished them both. On the drive home he wasted no time rubbing it in.

"Told you I was gonna whip your butts."

All three of them laughed. When they arrived at Annie's, she was there to greet them. As soon as the vehicle came to a complete stop, William was out and running toward his mother.

"Mom, guess what?"

Before she could chance a guess, he shouted, "I whipped both their asses. Whoops! Sorry, Mom, I mean their butts."

"I'll excuse you this time, young man, because you're so excited, but next time I'll whip your butt."

"Ah, Mom."

Leroy and Carter were doing the best they could not to laugh, and Annie gave them each a "don't you dare" stare.

After William went into the house, Annie walked over to the two men, smiled, and remarked without modesty, "Whipped your asses, didn't he? I thought you two were real men. Got your asses whipped by a child. Ain't that something?"

The three of them laughed, and Carter left to go home. In the rearview mirror he saw Leroy take Annie in his arms, whisper something, and then give her a gigantic kiss on her mouth. When they finally stopped kissing, Annie was jumping up and down with a huge smile on her face.

"Guess he went and did it. Wait till Marge hears this."

When Carter arrived home, he exited the truck, got the cooler with the two small bass in it, and took it into the garage. He set it on his workbench, grabbed several sheets of paper off the roll, and set them on the table. Next he took out the two fish and commenced to clean, gut, and fillet them. He wrapped the fillets in paper, emptied the cooler, wrapped the fish remains in paper, took them to the garbage can, and tossed them in. To minimize the smell, he tossed a few mothballs in with them. In the morning, he would set the can out by the street on his way to the office.

He exited the garage through the door that led to the laundry room, where he noticed the lid up on the washing machine. It meant "throw your smelly clothes in here before coming in the house."

"She knows how bad they smell and wants me to be certain I put them in the machine," he said to the machine.

He laughed and did as instructed, and then entered the kitchen naked as a newborn baby. Marge wasn't there, so she must be on the screened porch with a cup of coffee and didn't want to see him until he had cleansed his body. Carter entered the bedroom and went right to the bathroom. On his way, he noticed that his clothes were laid out on the bed for him.

"Damn, she always knows exactly what I like to wear. Probably 'cause I always wear the same outfit after fishing. Jeans and one of my favorite T-shirts."

Carter got in the shower, turned the water to slightly more than warm, and lathered his body. While the shower rinsed him of the soap, he turned to face the shower and let the water splash onto his face, almost blinding him.

He sensed her presence as she entered the shower. The water continued to trickle over his face. She came behind him. At first he felt her breasts against his back, and then her sex against his ass. Her arms reached around him and pulled him close to her as the waterfall sprayed their bodies. She reached out with one arm, turned off the shower, and then released her hold on him. Nothing was said as she exited the shower, grabbed one of the white robes and a white towel strategically placed within reach.

She put the robe on, wiped her hair down with the towel, and exited the bathroom. Carter got out of the shower, grabbed the other robe, and put it on. With the other towel, he dried his head, and he too left the bathroom. When he entered the bedroom, he saw her on the bed lying on her back with the robe wide open exposing her in splendor. He gazed at her sex, and suddenly his erection began to protrude from the robe.

He shed the robe instantly, walked over to the bed, crawled toward her, and spread her legs farther apart. She glanced down at his large erection and then focused on his eyes. The look she gave him said, "Take me now." He placed his erection by her sex and slowly inserted it. She raised her knees and lifted her pelvis, allowing him greater ease of penetration. Their love sessions had never been a simple "wham bam, thank you, ma'am," and this morning wouldn't be any different. Marge still had remnants of Friday in her, and she wanted him to eradicate them. This time, however, their love session was to be pure carnal lust.

Later, Carter told Marge about Leroy's proposal to Annie. She smiled. "It's about time, and I'm certain it will make William a very happy boy."

Carter agreed, and they both laughed. Things were really getting better in the Carter home.

CHAPTER 26

Sunday morning, Buddy and Missy Larson sat in their usual pew shouting righteous amens along with the rest of the congregation, brought on by their self-righteous pastor. Pastor Ellison always incited the audience of congregants and labored them with comments about the virtues of a sinless life and the need to be at one with their fellow man and woman. All those self-righteous virtues and coming from a man who possessed dark secrets of his own.

Sitting in a front row pew, all alone, was his docile wife, Agnes, with her faced buried in her Bible. The congregants always commented on how devoted she was to her loving husband but also that she was a shy little thing. She rarely attended church functions, and when she did, it was always as arm candy for her husband, locked to his arm. The only words she had ever spoken were a friendly hello or good morning. She dressed in simple out-fits always with long sleeves.

To the outside world, they appeared as a loving couple, but in their home things were different. The pastor made her sleep in the guest room, and she ministered to all his wishes. The only time they shared a bed was when one of his spiritual-guidance ladies stood him up. He took pleasure in having her in his bed and seemed to enjoy it. For Agnes, it was always a degrading experience.

In Bible college in South Florida, Agnes had dreams of doing missionary work in South America. In her final year, she met her future husband. He seemed to enjoy the same things she did, and he too was planning on missionary work. After graduation, they did two years of missionary work together, and on their final night he convinced her to share his bed. Being ignorant in the ways of a man and woman, she agreed, and that night Jeremiah Ellison deflowered her.

Six weeks later, she realized that she was pregnant and informed Jeremiah. They agreed to marry and did so. Unfortunately, she miscarried when she was in her fourth month. Instead of being sympathetic, Jeremiah told her that it was because she had sinned in the eyes of the Lord when she had sex before marriage. Agnes's ego was shattered, and she never regained her confidence. The beatings started shortly after he became the pastor in Waterton. Pastor Ellison was the Larson family's personal pastor and often counseled Mrs. Larson.

At their usual Sunday dinner, the Larsons were enjoying a meal that most people would enjoy for several days. They had no shame about their gluttony.

Buddy Larson addressed his son, Peter. "You can't keep annoying that sheriff, boy." Buddy slapped the table then said, "You piss him off and he could bring trouble. Let him do his job, for Pete's sake, boy."

Peter pushed away from the table and replied, "She was my wife, and I have a right to bury her. You never approved of her, but I have to do what's right."

Both Buddy and Missy Larson had been against him marrying Becky Johnson at the time. They felt her background and upbringing were beneath their family status, but Peter insisted and eventually prevailed. The Larsons had made it difficult for Becky right from the start, and it was obvious to Becky that they didn't approve of her. It was the reason she convinced her father to leave after the wedding ceremony. She was certain they would embarrass him, and she was right, because that was exactly what they had planned.

"We told you not to marry her, but you had to be so damn foolish," Mrs. Larson shouted. "I didn't let you suck on these tits as a baby to have you end up in bed with someone like her. This family is better than what she came from."

Peter grew angrier, and if she weren't his mother, he'd get up and slap the hell out of her just as he'd done to Becky, only it was across his wife's back.

Buddy shouted, "Shut up, woman. The poor girl is dead. Let her rest in peace. Damn you."

Missy's eyes flared in anger. "Don't you damn me!" She folded her arms across her chest, glared at him, and yelled, "You're the one who should be damned."

"If I'm to be damned, then so should you," Buddy yelled back. "Now shut your mouth, you hear me?"

She threw her fork at him but missed.

They continued shouting at each other, and Peter finally had all he could stand of them. He threw his napkin on the table, got up, and walked out of the room. As he left, he shouted an expletive, "Fuck the two of you!"

"You watch your damn mouth, boy," yelled Buddy.

Peter flipped him a bird and left his parents alone with their self-righteous attitudes.

Buddy threw his napkin on the table, got up, and left Missy to herself. While his back was turned, she gave him an upward thrusting hand and middle finger. In need of counseling, she called Pastor Ellison, but her call went to voice mail.

Pastor Ellison was busy administering guidance to one of the church ladies.

Missy tried several more times, and when she finally got the pastor, she asked if he had time to counsel her in the ways of the Lord.

The pastor told her he would meet her at the rectory.

Buddy Larson was off seeking his own spiritual guidance.

CHAPTER 27

On Monday morning, Amy arrived just after Carter. She had decided that now was a good time to tell him about her Friday afternoon conversations. Amy knocked on his door, and he invited her in. She sat down and was about to launch into her spiel when Carter interrupted her.

"Amy, I want to apologize for Saturday morning. Friday, Marge had a bad day and we got through it, but I didn't want anything to spoil the weekend. That's why I cut you off so abruptly."

"It's okay, John, I understand. All's forgiven and forgotten."

"Pretty soon we're gonna have that talk. Now what do you have?"

Amy ignored his comment about the talk. When they were ready, they'd come to her. For now, the investigation was paramount.

"John, I made some calls Friday afternoon and found out some things about both women. For one, they were roommates in college, and it seems the Williams woman was being watched over by a Barbara Morris on behalf of another woman in Bensmille, North Carolina."

She was about to continue when Billy Thompston knocked on the sheriff's door.

"Excuse me, Sheriff. Amy, there's a Mr. and Mrs. Worthington here to see you. They said you would know what it's about. What should I do?"

Amy's jaw dropped. When the Worthingtons said they would get back to her, she didn't think they meant in person.

"Send them in, Billy. John, these are the people from North Carolina. I think they have a story to tell us. Let me take the lead."

"Okay, Amy, they're all yours."

The man and woman who entered the sheriff's office both had grim looks on their faces. Amy introduced them as Mr. and Mrs. Worthington and offered them each a chair. They both took a seat, but before Amy could say anything, Billy stuck his head in again and said that there was a Major Bill Quincy on the line for Carter.

Carter asked to be excused as he had to take this call. Amy bit her lip and threw angry daggers at him with her eyes. It was a look that said, "What the hell, John?"

Carter had seen that look before. He ignored her as he got up and left the office.

He went to the phone Billy held and pressed the button for the line that Quincy was holding on. "Bill, how are you doing? It's Carter, and I hope you have some good news for me."

"I'm fine, Sheriff. However, my news isn't," answered Quincy. "'Fraid I'm not going to get a chance at the Williams guy. Let me start from the beginning. We learned that his wife had a restraining order against him and had filed for divorce." He checked his notes then continued, "We got that from her attorney. It took some cajoling, but we finally convinced him to tell us everything, especially when we said she might be the victim of a homicide. He also had an address for the husband; however, he wasn't sure if it was any good."

Quincy paused to let Carter absorb what he said, and then followed with, "We sent a cruiser to the address, and it was a motel. When the deputies knocked on his door, they didn't get an answer. One of his neighbors said they hadn't seen him for days, but his vehicle was in its parking space. The deputies forced the door open and found him lying on his bed in a pool of blood. It appears he was shot with a thirty-eight caliber. Also, he's been dead awhile, so I don't think he's your shooter. Sorry, Sheriff. This doesn't make your job any easier."

Carter cursed to himself then said, "Yeah, thanks, Bill. I appreciate your help. I owe you, and anytime you need a favor, feel free to call me. I mean it."

"Thanks. I'll do that. One more thing—are you a Seminole or Gator?"

"A Seminole, of course. Why?"

"Me too. Anytime you need tickets, you call me. I'm a big time booster. The only thing is you have to share my company."

"I can handle that, but you might not enjoy mine. Thanks."

"Go, 'Noles!" yelled Quincy.

They both laughed then hung up.

Carter returned to his office, and Amy again gave him the look that said she was pissed. He ignored her, apologized, and asked her to proceed.

Amy shook her head and began with, "Sheriff, I spoke with Mr. and Mrs. Worthington on Friday afternoon and informed them about the accident and Mrs. Williams's demise."

Deborah Worthington was surprised by Amy's statement about an accident. She believed this was a homicide. She interrupted Amy and said, "Deputy, I thought Jennifer's death was a homicide. Now you're saying it was an accident. Make up your mind. Which was it?"

Carter looked toward Amy, puckered his lips, half shut his eyes, and interjected, "Mrs. Worthington, it started as an accident investigation, but now it appears to be a homicide. I don't know what you've told my deputy, but if you have anything that could help us, we would appreciate it."

Amy understood that he was annoyed at her, but his interruption made her angry. She decided to let it go temporarily. Later she would speak her mind, but she wanted to get a word in edgeways, even if Carter got pissed for her interrupting him.

"Mrs. Worthington, we're really at a loss and can use any help you can give us. Please, for Jennifer's sake," Amy said. She was playing to the woman's maternal instincts and suspected that there was a familial bond between her and the Williams woman. Carter nodded, letting Amy know that she'd done the right thing.

Mrs. Worthington remained silent and looked to her husband for guidance.

"This is difficult for my wife, so let me try and be of assistance," he told Amy. "Jennifer called us and said she needed our help. There was a woman who needed to get away from her abusive husband. She was pregnant, but not by her husband. She didn't say who the father was, but asked for our help."

He reached over and put his hand on his wife's arm and continued, "We told Jennifer to bring her to our house in Bensmille. First they had to make some stops along the way. Jennifer called us and said they were on their way after the first stop and would call us after the next one. We never got the call, and then Deborah got a call from Barbara Morris and later from your deputy."

Mr. Worthington paused to compose himself. He put his hands on Carter's desk then leaned forward. "We didn't call you back, Deputy, because we needed to decide what to do first. We decided it would be best if we came and spoke to you in person." He faced his wife then said, "We want to help as best we can; however, there are some things we can't talk about." They both looked at Carter, and he continued, "We're sorry, Sheriff, we just can't. We're glad to answer your questions, but only those that we can." Worthington removed his hands from the desk and sat back in his chair.

Carter and Amy exchanged glances. Neither knew what to do. Carter decided to venture a question, but didn't expect an honest answer.

"I'm not sure what you mean by things you can't talk about, Mr. Worthington. You realize this is a homicide investigation, and I don't want to threaten you with impeding an official investigation."

Amy gave Carter a look that said, "What the hell are you doing, John?" Again, Carter ignored her and gave Worthington a menacing look.

Mrs. Worthington relented and finally replied, "Sheriff, the reason we can't tell you things is because they have to do with a matter of life or death for people who must remain anonymous." She reached for her husband's hand and grasped it. "We need you to understand that. You seem like an honest and caring individual, but we've been fooled before and don't plan on it happening again. If you really are as you seem, you'll understand and respect our wishes."

Suddenly Carter understood, and the look on Amy's face said that she also did. He decided to avoid any questions about others.

"Can you at least tell me anything more about their trip and about their decision to go to you?" he asked. "You don't have to reveal anything more, just what you can to help us track down the responsible party or parties." Like Amy, he then chose to appeal to her sense of loyalty to the Williams woman. "Please, Mrs. Worthington, out of respect for Jennifer."

She faced her husband, he nodded, and then she replied, "When Jennifer called and told us what she wanted, we were concerned for her safety. She said it wasn't her safety she was concerned about. It was her friend Becky's. I assume she was the other woman in the vehicle."

Carter scrunched his mouth, considering her response, but Amy answered for him, "Yes, she was, and we know that the two women have a past from college and after. That's what I got from Barbara Morris, but do you have any idea who the father of Becky's child is?"

Carter appreciated Amy asking the question. She had all the information and hadn't had time to fill him in yet.

"Like my husband said, we know it's not her husband's, but he's the one who beat her," she replied. "According to Jennifer, he comes from an influential family, and Becky was afraid what he and them—those were her words—would do once they found out she was pregnant by another man. Becky was intent on having the child and also wanted to protect the father."

Carter's curiosity piqued, he decided to weigh in. "Did they give you any hint as to who the father is? We know about her husband, and now with what you've told us, it confirms our suspicions that he was the one who hurt her."

"Correction, Sheriff," she interrupted him. "Beat her is what Jennifer said. She saw the bruises on Becky's back."

Carter raised his hands, surrendering. "Sorry, Mrs. Worthington. I was just being considerate. That's all."

She nodded acceptance. "Kind of you to do so, but we're used to this sort of thing, Sheriff. Apparently, Becky met this man and had sex with him on a number of occasions. She told Jennifer she believed she was in love with him. Jennifer said she had met him but wouldn't tell us his name. Had they made it to our home, I think she would have told us. Now we will never know." Mrs. Worthington's eyes gave way to tears.

Carter reached for a tissue and handed it to her. He suddenly felt a desire to get his hands on Peter Larson and beat the daylights out of him. What he and Amy now had to do was identify the father of Becky's child. He also wanted to know if Larson owned a .38—the same caliber used in both shootings.

THE FARBER LEGACY 157

There wasn't much more that Mr. and Mrs. Worthington could tell them, so Carter and Amy thanked them and said they would let them know what they could when they knew more.

Before leaving, Mrs. Worthington asked, "What will happen to Jennifer's remains, Sheriff?"

"We don't know yet, Mrs. Worthington. It's too soon to say. We'll let you know when we finish our investigation, if you would like."

"Thank you, Sheriff. We would appreciate it."

Deborah and Charles Worthington thanked them and left. Mrs. Worthington still had tears in her eyes, and Mr. Worthington had his arm around her. They looked like parents who had just gotten the news that they had lost their child. Carter felt sympathetic toward them.

After they left, Carter asked Amy for her thoughts.

"That's two very sad people, John. They could use some counseling. I also think Mrs. Worthington had a strong attachment to Jennifer. I really would like to know who the father is. What do you suggest we do, John?"

Amy's annoyance with Carter had dissipated. She realized that Mrs. Worthington's comments had profoundly affected him, and she didn't want him to relive past memories.

"Amy, has anybody gone through the personal effects of either woman? If not, we need to do it right away. Get Billy, and the three of us can go through them."

CHAPTER 28

Tallahassee

Sarah Carter had just finished watering the plants on the balcony of her apartment at Heritage Independent Living when she heard the doorbell ring. She set her watering can on the small table near her coffee cup and went inside to answer the door. Sarah wasn't expecting company and wondered who it could be at the door. Maybe it was Ann Mathews from up the hall, who liked to visit and enjoy a cup of coffee with Sarah on the balcony.

She opened the door, and her eyes lit up and her mouth opened wide when she saw her granddaughter, Jessica, standing there.

"Surprise, Grandma! I made a special trip to Tallahassee just to see you."

"Jessica, what a nice surprise!" They hugged, and then Sarah said, "Please come in. I was just watering my plants. Come and join me on the balcony. Would you like a cup of coffee or iced tea?"

Jessica frowned and replied, "Coffee, Grandma. I'm a big girl now. I find it helps keep me awake when I've got a long study night."

Sarah grinned, stepped back, and looked her up and down. She realized the little girl she knew was now a full-grown woman, and it was no wonder she drank coffee now.

"I forgot you did. What are you doing home? Are classes over, and how is school going?"

"School is going great, Grandma, and classes are out for a while. I've great news for you. It's why I made a special trip to see you."

"Well then, let's go sit and you can tell me your great news."

Sarah went to the kitchen and poured Jessica a cup of coffee, and then the two of them went and sat on the balcony.

"Grandma, you really have a nice view from here. I bet you sit out here often."

"Oh yes, every morning. I love to watch the birds when they come to my feeders. They've gotten used to me sitting here. They just ignore me and go about their business. It's so peaceful and relaxing. Someday you'll understand how wonderful life's simplest things are. So what's your great news?"

"Grandma, I got into Duke Medical School," she announced. "I start in the fall. Isn't that great?" Jessica beamed with pride.

"Oh, Jessica, I'm so proud of you. Have you told your parents yet?"

"No. I wanted you to be the first to know."

"Thank you, Jessica. I'm sure they're going to be really surprised and very proud of you."

"Well, you were my inspiration, you know? When you told me about how you wanted to be a doctor when you were my age but unfortunately it didn't happen, I decided I would finish your dream."

Sarah was astonished that Jessica remembered their conversation about wanting to become a doctor. "But, Jessica, it has to be your own dream to make it possible."

"It is my own dream, and it always has been. You just gave me the inspiration I needed to pursue it. I'm so grateful to you, Grandma."

"Well then, I'm glad I helped. You're going to make a great doctor, of that I'm certain. How long are you home for?"

"Six weeks, and then I have to go back to Duke and get settled in before school starts, but I'll visit you some more before I go away. You can bet on that, Grandma."

"I sure hope so."

Jessica had an important question to ask her grandmother, one that was delicate to ask. She decided to just go for it and said, "Grandma, I have a question to ask you, and it's kind of delicate too."

"Whatever it is, my dear, feel free to ask."

Sarah had an inclination of what the question would be. Most likely the same question Jessica's father had once asked. It probably had to do with memory loss.

"Grandma, occasionally I find myself awakening at the weirdest times and have no memory of what happened while I was asleep. Sometimes I think that I was in another time period. Did you or my dad ever have anything like that happen?"

Sarah understood what Jessica had experienced and felt that she was old enough to know the truth, especially if she intended to become a doctor.

"Yes, Jessica, we both have. It's a long story that goes back to your great-grandfather. Let me get us another cup of coffee, and I'll tell you all about it."

Sarah refreshed their cups, sat down, and proceeded to tell Jessica the story about her great-grandfather and Sarah's father.

She told her about him getting struck by lightning and having periodic blackouts. Sarah had learned about them from her mother, after Sarah herself experienced one.

When she finished telling Jessica the story, Jessica said, "Wow, that's something. Do you think that's what's happening to me, Grandma?"

"Yes, Jessica, I believe it is, but I don't think you have to worry about it unless it interferes with your life or your studies. It hasn't, has it?"

"No, it hasn't. Not yet anyway. Since you and Dad have lived with it so long, I guess I can too."

Sarah was pleased that Jessica was being so grown up about it and taking it with the same attitude that she had when she first learned about it.

"Well, it's your father's legacy, and now it's yours also, but I guess it's my curse. Let's keep it a secret, Jessica."

"Okay, Grandma, but why do you say it's your curse?"

Sarah raised her cup to her mouth and sipped her coffee then responded, "Maybe because I inherited it and passed it on to your father and he passed it to you, or maybe it's a legacy for all of us. I don't have an answer, so that's why I say 'my curse.'"

"I prefer we call it our legacy, Grandma."

"Then we'll call it The Farber Legacy."

They sat awhile longer, enjoying each other's company, the view, and the birds. The birds didn't seem to mind Jessica's company either, because they came to the feeders to enjoy themselves. Both Sarah and Jessica seemed to have a calming effect on the birds. Later, Jessica said good-bye and left for home. Sarah went back to sitting on the balcony.

She soon dozed off with a smile on her face, dreaming of her granddaughter. Suddenly she was startled awake by the ringing of the telephone. She got up, went inside, and answered the phone. She was surprised at the sound of the caller's voice.

"Grandma, it's me, Jessica. How are you? I've got great news to tell you."

"Jessica, it's wonderful to hear from you. What's your great news?"

"Grandma, Duke University wants to offer me an academic and athletic scholarship. Isn't that great? I'm one step closer to medical school."

"Oh, that's wonderful, and I'm so proud of you. Will you be on their swimming team?"

"Yes, Grandma. They gave me one of the few scholarships they give for women's water sports. Isn't that great too?"

"Yes, it is. I'm so happy for you, and your parents must be so proud."

"I haven't told them yet. I wanted you to be the first to know. I love you, Grandma."

"I love you too, Jessica."

They said good-bye, and then Sarah went back out on the balcony with a cup of coffee. She picked up her diary and noted the date and a conversation with Jessica. Soon several cardinals came, went to the feeders, and enjoyed a meal, ignoring her presence.

CHAPTER 29

In Waterton, Randy Graebert and his brother, Richard, were cleaning up after the lunch crowd when Deputy Amy Tucker approached them. The two stopped what they were doing and questioned why she was there after lunchtime. Randy held a towel in his hand, as did Richard, who also held a bucket of dirty dishes. Richard set the bucket on a table, tossed the towel over his left shoulder, and stepped toward Amy.

"I'm sorry," he said. "Lunchtime is over. You'll have to come back tomorrow, since we're not open for dinner."

Amy wondered which of the two brothers might be the father. After Amy, Carter, and Billy went through the victims' personal effects, they found receipts from the restaurant in Jennifer's purse and some calls to the restaurant on Becky's cell phone. Amy felt certain that the calls were more than making reservations for lunch. She had a hunch that the two women had met here and one or both brothers knew them.

"I'm not here for lunch," she replied. "I'm Deputy Amy Tucker from the sheriff's office, and I'd like to talk with both of you, if you have time?"

"It's not a good time, Deputy. We're cleaning up. Can it wait? My brother Randy and I can get back to you if you leave your card."

Richard attempted to be coy and suspected this had to do with Randy and Becky Larson. He'd warned his brother, but Randy hadn't listened. Richard regretted letting the two women use their house as a place to meet.

"I'm afraid it can't wait. I'm investigating a homicide, and I think you may be able to help me."

Randy's complexion turned a shade whiter, and Amy noticed it. When he responded, she could hear the stress in his voice.

"What would we know about a homicide, Deputy?" Randy said. "Where did it happen?"

Amy could tell that something was bothering him. She looked him directly in the eyes and responded, "It happened on County Road 373. Two women were killed. We know that one of them dined here and the other placed calls to here. Either or both of you know a Becky Larson or Jennifer Williams?"

Randy looked like he had taken a mortar round, almost like he did when he was injured in Desert Storm. His knees buckled, and Richard had to grab him before he went down. Richard made him sit in a chair and got him a glass of water. Randy drank some water, and his color returned to near normal, but it was obvious to Amy that he was extremely upset.

"You want to tell me about them, or should I venture a guess?" she asked. "I think one of you was intimate with one of the women or both of you were intimate with them both. Am I close to right?"

Amy had no intention of being sympathetic. This was a homicide investigation; she wanted answers, and she wanted them now.

Randy looked calmer and answered, "I'm the one you want to speak to about Becky, Deputy. Yes, we were intimate, several times. It wasn't just sex, we were developing a relationship, but she was married and definitely afraid of her husband. The last few times she was here, we weren't together. She had lunch with the other woman, and they met twice at my home. I don't know what their meetings were about, but the last time I saw her, she said she had to leave town and would call me." His voice expressed sincere concern. "Can you tell me anything about how she died, Deputy?"

"Thanks. I appreciate your honesty. Which of the brothers are you?"

"I'm Randy, and this is my brother, Richard." He pointed toward his brother.

She jotted a brief description in her pad then said, "Thank you, Randy. From what we can tell, the two women were on their way north when they were broadsided. A shot was fired at their vehicle, and it hit the Williams woman. Becky was driving, and she must have lost control because the vehicle ended up in a ditch headfirst. Both women were slammed into the windshield. Do you know why anyone would want to kill them?"

Randy and Richard looked at each other, and Randy signaled for Richard to answer her question. Richard nervously switched the towel from his left shoulder to his right one. Amy made a mental note of it.

"You may want to talk to Peter Larson about that," Richard said, and then turned his head toward his brother. "Randy, she didn't tell you, but Jennifer told me that the reason they were leaving was because he beat Becky and she was pregnant. Jennifer said Becky showed her the bruises on her back. Sorry, Randy. Jennifer asked me not to tell you. It happened after you last had sex with her."

Randy's face turned a light shade of white, and he asked for another glass of water. Richard poured him another glass of water. He took several sips and asked the inevitable question. "Was the child mine, Deputy?"

"We haven't determined that yet, Randy. But after what you two have told me, my guess is it was yours. Sorry you have to find about it this way. Do either of you know if they were stopping anywhere after they left your home?"

Randy glanced at Richard, thinking he would know. "Jennifer said they had a stop to make but wouldn't say where, and I didn't press for an answer," Richard replied. "I don't know why, but I trusted Jennifer. She seemed like she had Becky's interest at heart."

"I think she did, Richard. Jennifer and Becky have a history together. They were roommates in college, and we believe they may have been in each other's weddings. I appreciate your help." She made a note in her pad then said, "I've got to get this information back to the sheriff. Look, don't either of you go near Larson, please. He doesn't know about the pregnancy, and he may not know about the affair. His ignorance may help us in our investigation."

Amy hoped that they would heed her warning, as Larson now had a motive. She said good-bye, gave them each her card, telling them to call if they thought of anything else, and drove back to Creek City.

Four weeks before the accident, Becky and Jennifer had met at the restaurant and then again at Randy and Richard's home. Becky had already told Jennifer about the beatings, and Jennifer tried to convince her to get away from Larson, but Becky said no. The first time they met at Randy's home, Jennifer reached for her top and started to remove it. Becky said no, not this time; it wasn't right, and she didn't want that.

Becky had misunderstood Jennifer's intentions, and Jennifer told her so. She took off her top and showed Becky the remnants of her bruises. Jennifer explained how Sam beat her up in a drunken stupor one night. She told Becky about the restraining order and about filing for a divorce. It was Jennifer's attempt to convince Becky to get away from Larson. She told her that the beatings wouldn't stop, they never did.

It was enough to convince Becky. The two decided that they would ask Richard if they could use the house again to plan their getaway. Richard agreed, and also agreed to keep it a secret from his brother. Jennifer and Becky met again, drove to a meeting place, and left Jennifer's vehicle there. Then, in Becky's car, they made their ill-fated journey.

CHAPTER 30

Marge Davids called Sheriff Carter and told him the DNA on the Larson woman's fetus was not the husband's. It belonged to a Randy Graebert. The DNA was matched to his military records, so Larson could be ruled out as the father. However, there were still the bruises, and of course the murder, which she had definitely classified the case as.

Carter thanked her, said he would see her tonight, and then went to talk to Amy and Billy to see if they had anything new for him. Both of them were talking while checking the computer. It seemed as though Billy must have found out something by the way they were acting.

Carter walked over and inquired, "What are you two up to? I hope you have something for me."

The two deputies stopped what they were doing. Amy grabbed her note pad so she could summarize the results of her visit to the Graeberts in Waterton.

"John, I visited Waterton and the restaurant where the two women visited. Two brothers, Randy and Richard Graebert, own it. They both knew the women. Randy was intimate with the Larson woman. Richard apparently shared a confidence with the Williams woman. Randy wasn't aware Becky was pregnant. However, Richard said he knew and also that they met at the restaurant, plus a few times at the Graeberts' home. He said the two women were taking a trip, and Jennifer asked Richard not to tell Randy.

She looked down at her notes and continued, "I don't think they had anything to do with the accident or the murder, but the pregnancy does give Randy a motive. That doesn't necessarily make him guilty, and I would rule him out. What they told me also confirms what the Worthington woman told us. I think we should look at Larson more closely, John."

Carter scratched his head and pursed his lips. He wasn't thrilled about Amy's assessment, but he had to admit that she made a good point. Maybe he should have another talk with Larson, only this time on Larson's turf.

"Shit," he commented. "Now I have to do something I don't really want to, and I'm not going to enjoy it. I'm going to Waterton to confront that asshole."

Amy and Billy looked at each other. Both were concerned because Carter could get mighty angry when he got something stuck in his craw, and you didn't want to be within range of his fists. They both knew this would be one of those occasions.

Amy had to do something to stop him. She grabbed his arm and said, "You want me to go with you, John?" She hoped that he would let her go with him, but Carter was one stubborn mule at times like this.

He brushed her hand away and pronounced, "No, Amy. I appreciate what you're trying to do, but I can manage on my own. Thanks anyway. You and Billy go through the two women's phones and see what else you can find."

He started to leave, but Billy stopped him. "Sheriff, I got a hit on that license plate you asked me to check on. It belongs to a Paul Schneider in Live Oak. Want me to check further?"

Carter threw his palms up. "Who the hell is he, and what the hell's in Live Oak? Damn, this is getting to be too much."

Amy, realizing the importance of Live Oak because of her discussion with Barbara Morris, interjected, "John, Becky Larson was from Live Oak. I got that much from Jacksonville."

He pointed at her. "Amy, you get on the phone with that woman in Jacksonville and find out if Becky Larson had or has any family in Live Oak." Carter pointed at Billy. "Billy, you dig deeper on this Schneider guy. See if he's got a telephone, and if he does, call him. We need a break, for crying out loud. I'm getting a headache over this case."

Carter left abruptly, and then Amy and Billy began their tasks as to Schneider and Barbara Morris.

When Carter arrived in Waterton, he went right to Larson's office and addressed his secretary. She said she would check and see if the mayor was available. When her back was to him, Carter whispered in his hand, "I'll see if the mayor's available, like he's so damn important. What bullshit."

In Mayor Larson's office, Buddy Larson and his son were having a heated conversation regarding Becky, and Peter's tangle with Sheriff Carter. Buddy wasn't happy, not in the least.

"Dammit, boy, you got to back off. You can't tangle with that sheriff." He used his hand to emphasize his comments. "You do, and you're gonna lose. Can't you just back off and let him do his job? It's in your best interest. I'm asking you, please, boy."

Peter hated when his father addressed him as *boy*. He hated it even when he was growing up. It was so demeaning to him.

"I got to do something," he replied and slammed his hand on the desk. "I told you she was my wife, and I have to at least give her a decent burial. Can't you understand for once, old man?"

He called him *old man* because he knew his father hated the term, but it was payback for *boy*.

Buddy opened his mouth to respond to Peter's remark but refrained when Peter's secretary knocked and entered. The two men looked at each other and hoped she hadn't overheard their conversation. She may not have, but Carter got a few remnants of it and was smiling.

"Mayor, there's a Sheriff Carter who would like to talk to you. Should I tell him you're busy and he should make an appointment, or do want to talk to him?"

Buddy looked at Peter and said, "Careful, boy."

"It's okay, Terry. Show him in, and thanks. Would you bring us all some iced tea, please?"

"Sure thing, Mayor." She escorted Carter into the office then left to get the iced tea.

Buddy stepped forward to offer Carter a handshake that was really a "Hey, *good old boy*, *my dick's bigger than yours*," *type shake.* When he reached out to Carter and extended his hand, Carter ignored it.

"Sheriff Carter, good to see you," Buddy said.

Carter then extended his hand to Buddy, but when their hands connected it wasn't a good-old-boy shake, it was more a limp-dick type. Buddy was annoyed, but Carter gave him a smile and said, "Nice to see you, Buddy. Too bad your candidate lost the last election. Never know what comes out of the woodwork at election time."

Buddy became visibly annoyed with Carter's remark. During the last election, Buddy backed Carter's opponent and made it a dirty campaign. The Larsons misjudged Carter's campaign abilities. When they tried a smear tactic, Carter's campaign had their own dirt on his opponent. They gave it to the media, and it helped Carter win by a landslide. The Larsons were really pissed over the results.

Peter Larson stood up but didn't offer a handshake. Instead he gestured for Carter to have a seat. Carter thanked him and took a seat.

"Sheriff, what can I do for you?" Peter asked. "I hope you have something new about Becky's case."

Carter noticed that he hadn't mentioned the murder, referring to the matter only as a case, and he was being strangely polite. Interesting, Carter considered.

"Still can't say much, as it's an ongoing investigation. Do you know any reason why your wife was traveling north on County Road 373?"

"No, Sheriff, I don't, and I don't know why she was with the Williams woman either."

"Did you know they were college roommates?"

"Yes. As a matter of fact, they were each other's maid of honor. As far as I know, Becky hadn't been in contact with Jennifer since her wedding. Why do you ask?"

Carter started to reply, but Larson's secretary entered with the iced tea and set it on a nearby table. She politely left the office and closed the door behind her. As she passed by Carter, she smiled at him without letting the Larsons see her do it. He wondered why she gave him the smile, and then waited until she was gone before responding to Larson.

"For some reason they were headed north, and we can't figure out why."

Carter knew, but he wasn't going to tell Larson. He had just a few more questions before dropping the bomb. Then he asked, "Where were you the day your wife died?"

"I was right here, and my secretary can vouch for me." Larson quickly sat up straight and said, "I don't like your questioning, Sheriff. Are you implying something?"

Before Carter could answer, Buddy added, "Look here, Sheriff. You can't be accusing my boy of anything. It ain't right."

Once again, the *boy* comment annoyed Peter, and Carter noticed the grimace by the way he squeezed his eyes shut and twisted his mouth.

Carter wasn't the least bit intimidated by Buddy's remark. He grinned and replied, "I ain't accusing him of anything, Buddy. I have to ask the question, and while I'm at it, where were you?" Carter hoped to piss him off.

"Shit, man, now you accusing me?"

"I ain't accusing anyone. Just asking questions. You both seem awfully defensive. Mind telling me why?"

Peter ignored Buddy and decided to stand up for himself. "Look, Sheriff, we're just upset over Becky's death. I told you I was here. As for Buddy, he'll have to tell you himself."

Carter made a mental note that Peter didn't use the term *father* and addressed the man as Buddy. He could tell there was friction between the two, and he just might exploit it.

He addressed Buddy and asked, "Well, Buddy, where were you?"

"I was meeting with some donors at the party's offices. You can check for yourself if you want to."

"No need, I'll take your word for it. Either of you own a thirty-eight?"

Both Larsons wrinkled their brows and bit their lips, obviously worried. "No," Buddy answered. "Why?"

"Just asking, that's all. Just to satisfy my curiosity, where was Missy at the time of the accident?"

Buddy clenched his fists in anger. "Dammit, Sheriff! You leave my wife out of this. For your information, she was at her regular spiritual-guidance session. You can ask Pastor Ellison if you don't believe me."

"I'll take your word for it. I'm done. You two take care now."

Carter got up, walked toward the door and opened it, and with his back to them, offhandedly said over his shoulder, "Did you know your wife was pregnant, Mayor?"

He exited the office with a smile on his face and closed the door. He could hear the Larsons shouting at each other. As he walked past Larson's secretary, he gave her a salute, a wink, and told her to have a good day.

She smiled, winked back, and said, "I will now, Sheriff."

As Carter exited the building, he laughed, made a Seminole chop gesture, and shouted, "Go, 'Noles!"

When Carter was in his vehicle, he made note of the dark SUV that was parked several vehicles behind him. As he drove off, he noticed the SUV pull out and follow him at a safe distance all the way back to Creek City.

Carter arrived at the sheriff's office, parked in his usual spot, and exited the vehicle. He saw the SUV pull into a parking space. Carter walked toward the building, glanced over his shoulder, and noticed that no one had exited the SUV. He decided that when he got inside, he would enlist Amy and Billy for his plan.

Amy and Billy watched as he came in and walked over to them.

Before they could say anything, Carter told them of his plan. Amy and Billy were to get their vehicles and make like they were leaving for somewhere. Instead, they were to flank the SUV and with guns pointing, have the driver exit the vehicle.

As they were about to leave to execute the plan, a man in his late fifties entered the building. He raised his hands above his head as though under arrest and said, "I think you may be looking for me, Sheriff. Should I get down on my knees, or can I come further and talk with you?"

Carter's hand slowly slid down to the butt of his revolver.

"No need for that, Sheriff. I'm unarmed. Just want to talk."

"Who are you?" Carter asked.

CHAPTER 31

Buddy Larson had been trying to get his wife, Missy, on the phone ever since Carter left his son's office. But all he got was her voice mail. He was extremely upset and concerned about Carter asking where she was when the accident occurred.

"Dammit, where the hell are you, Missy? You better not have done anything. I know you never liked Becky, but I told you to stay away from the girl. Answer your damn phone," he shouted into his phone. "You were supposed to be at one of your stupid guidance sessions with that pansy pastor. Answer your damn phone!"

The pastor raised his head and said, "Are you going to answer your phone, Mrs. Larson?"

"Let the damn thing ring," she replied. "The more he keeps calling, the more pissed off he'll get. Fuck him. He's probably calling about that bitch daughter-in-law of his."

"Oh my, Mrs. Larson. Such blasphemy, and in the presence of your spiritual advisor. Did you do something wrong?"

"You just keep advising me, or you won't get your turn, Pastor."

She pushed his head back between her legs, and he continued giving her the weekly spiritual guidance he'd been giving her for some time now. Unbeknownst to them, a third party was hiding in one of the pews and taking several pictures of Missy Larson and Pastor Ellison in some very compromising positions.

Earlier in the day, Deputy Billy Thompston had completed his check on Paul Schneider, the owner of the SUV. Schneider lived in Live Oak, and when Billy called, the man who answered said that he owned a dark SUV, but it was in the shop having major repair work and he didn't understand how it could have been in Creek City. He said he'd call the repair shop and would call Billy back, probably that afternoon.

Instead of calling the repair shop, Schneider called a friend of his, and the call wasn't pleasant. The friend said not to worry, he would handle it. He assured Schneider that nothing illegal was happening, and he would explain it all next time he saw him. Since the two had been close friends for years, Schneider said okay and also asked how he was doing. The friend said that everything was okay and his coin was still good.

At the sheriff's office, Carter noticed that the guy standing there was wearing a dark jacket, just like the guy at the Cougars game. If he'd been wearing a black hat, sunglasses, and a tie, he would look like Dan Aykroyd in *The Blues Brothers*. It was almost laughable.

"Name's Daniel Johnson, Sheriff. I'm from Live Oak. Buddy of mine called and said you were checking on his vehicle. He told your deputy it's in the repair shop and he was going to call the shop then get back to you. He's not calling you back, because I'm driving the SUV. Been doing it a couple of weeks now."

Carter and his two deputies exchanged glances and wondered what the hell this was all about. Amy and Billy didn't know about the incident at the Cougar game.

"Why all the cloak-and-dagger stuff, Mr. Johnson? If you wanted to talk to me, why didn't you just come to my office? Why follow me around, and why follow my friend from the diner?"

"'Cause I wanted to make sure your reputation was fact first."

"And what's my reputation, Mr. Johnson?"

"Please call me Daniel. I hate formality. You have a reputation for being a decent and honorable man. That's what I've been told, and I also wanted to be sure you weren't in with them Larson folk in Waterton. Look, can I put my hands down now?"

Carter found that it was amusing watching Johnson stand there with his hands up. Neither he nor his deputies had told the man to put them up. Johnson had done it himself, and Carter just obliged him.

"Never said you had to put them up. It was your idea. Yeah, you can put them down if you want. Tell me, if you were checking me out, why the stakeout at Leroy's Diner?"

Amy and Billy were surprised to hear mention about the diner. Both gasped. Neither of them knew what Carter was talking about, since he'd never mentioned anything about a stake-out at Leroy's.

"Leroy Jones, that's why. He's a friend of yours, and I'm a UCF fan. Know of his exploits there and with the Bucs. My deceased wife and I attended UCF, but that was before Jones's time. I know he's an honorable man, and I figured I might use the connection as a way to get to you. Sorry if I bungled that. I'm not used to this sort of thing."

Carter finally understood why the guy had been so deceptive and very amateurish at it. He decided to cut the guy some slack.

"Like I said, you could have just come to me even that night at the game, Mr. Johnson. What's your story anyhow, and how come my deputy didn't find any listing for you in Live Oak?"

Johnson grinned. "Becky Larson was my daughter. The reason you won't find any listing is because my phone, my car, and house are in my deceased wife's maiden name. Been that way for a long time, even before she passed, and I'd appreciate it if you let that be. Don't want any trouble with the state. I'm a recovering alcoholic, and Schneider is my sponsor and a very good friend, though I'm not so sure now. I've been sober ever since Becky's wedding.

"Sobered up for the wedding but didn't get to go to the reception. Becky warned me that the Larsons had plans to embarrass me. They weren't too keen on her marrying their son. Becky called me a while back and said she was pregnant but not by Larson. Said she was leaving him and wanted to get away to have the child. She was going to let me know where she was when she could."

Johnson looked down and then raised his head, and Carter noticed his somber expression. Johnson looked up at the ceiling as though looking for divine intervention but failed to receive anything.

"We communicated over the years but always at her office, so you won't find any calls to me. She knew my number and didn't tell anyone. It was our secret. She told me she was leaving with her friend Jennifer. Also that the father of the child didn't know about the pregnancy. Arrangements were made with his brother, and he swore to keep her secret. He didn't tell your deputy, because like me, he wasn't sure you weren't working for the Larsons."

Carter, Amy, and Billy stood motionless as though they were hypnotized listening to him. Especially Carter, who was thinking about going back to Waterton and punching Larson, but he tried to remain calm as Johnson continued.

"I talked to him after you did, and I told him I would square it with you. Sheriff, you'll have to forgive all the secretiveness, but I was protecting Becky and the two brothers. We had no choice.

Becky also said that Larson jerk had hit her numerous times. Randy was so enamored with Becky that he never noticed her bruises, 'cause he always had his eyes on the parts of her body he enjoyed. Becky said the one time he noticed a bruise on her shoulder, she told him she had a minor accident at the gallery. Poor kid believed her, but his brother didn't."

Carter reflected on Peter Larson's concern about taking possession of Becky's remains. Apparently he didn't want Carter to discover the bruises and what they represented.

Johnson waited for a response from Carter. Since he didn't get one, he continued, "Becky had to confide in the brother because she and Jennifer needed to use his house as a starting-off point. She also needed a place to call me since she couldn't go to her office. You can check her office calendar, and you'll find little notations on specific dates that I can tell you of, if you don't believe me. I was going to go to Orlando and talk to Jennifer's husband after I talked with you, Sheriff."

Carter had to tell him about Sam Williams; Johnson wasn't going to be happy, and neither was Carter. He gestured for Johnson to take a seat and said, "You'd be wasting your time, Mr. Johnson. Sam Williams is dead. He was found in his motel room, and he died before Jennifer and Becky did, so he's ruled out as a suspect."

Johnson slumped into the chair and was visibly upset. Carter could tell he was now at a complete loss. His daughter's death was still a mystery, and Johnson was now ruled out as a suspect. Carter didn't believe for one second that Johnson would have killed his only daughter.

"Shit, man, now what do I do?" Johnson said as he placed his hands on his thighs. "Can I ask if I can see my daughter, Sheriff? I'd also like to take her home to Live Oak and bury her next to her mother. Is that possible?"

Carter would really like to accommodate the man. However, Larson also wanted Becky's remains, so this was going to present

a pissing contest between the two of them. If Carter had anything
to do about it, he'd take the father's side.

"Mr. Johnson, I have to tell you, your daughter's remains are
not a pretty sight, but if you really want to, I'll arrange it with
the medical examiner. As for taking her remains, I'm afraid you're
gonna have to fight with her husband, because he wants them."

Johnson stood up and placed his palms together as though
praying. "Please, Sheriff," he pleaded. "Don't let that son of a
bitch or his family have my baby. She belongs next to her mother.
Can you help me out here?"

Carter considered Judge Henry and wondered if he had
any distaste for the Larsons. Maybe he could intercede on Mr.
Johnson's behalf. He'd ask Marge, since she had rapport with the
judge.

"I can't make any promises, but I'll see what I can do. You
stay away from the Larsons and let me and my deputies do my
job, Mr. Johnson. I need your promise—otherwise I'll have to
arrest you for obstructing an official investigation. You should go
back to Live Oak and let me take it from here."

Amy and Billy were both in disbelief. They looked at Carter,
wondering what he would do next. As far as they were concerned,
they would let Johnson take his daughter back to Live Oak, but it
wasn't their decision to make.

"You have my word, Sheriff, but I'm not going anywhere until
I at least see my daughter. Can you set it up?"

"Let me make a call. Where are you staying, Mr. Johnson?"

"I got me a room at a motel just outside town. It's not much,
but I can't afford much more."

"You mean that roach motel?" Carter asked. "You can't stay
there. My deputy will get you a room at the motel in town. She's
got a friend there who owes us a favor. Amy, why don't you make
the call and get Mr. Johnson's phone number? When I have

something for him, I'll call him. You got any belongings you have to get from that motel?"

Amy shot Carter an annoyed look, but she knew better than to argue with him. Besides, Mr. Johnson was upset about his daughter, and she didn't want him spending another night in that roach-infested motel either, so she made the call like Carter asked.

"It may take a couple of days, Amy, so get him a few nights. You okay with that, Mr. Johnson?"

"I already paid cash for tonight, Sheriff, and I can't afford more than I paid."

"Don't worry about it. Amy, put it on my tab. Once you get him settled, why don't you take his keys back to that motel and tell them he won't be staying there any longer. Mr. Johnson, if you're planning on having dinner tonight, I suggest you go by Leroy's Diner and have the barbeque. Just don't let him talk you into the tripe stew. Be sure you tell him who you are and that I sent you, and then apologize for last Friday night. You're right— Leroy is a good man."

"Thanks, Sheriff, I'll do just that. And thank you too, Deputy. I also apologize for my actions with the Graebert boys."

Amy made her call and got Mr. Johnson three nights at the Dexter Motel on behalf of Carter. She then told him to follow her. Before leaving, Mr. Johnson told Carter that he liked tripe stew. It was one of his favorites.

Carter shook his head then asked his desk, *What next with this damn case?* He would soon find out.

CHAPTER 32

Sheriff Carter called Marge and asked about Mr. Johnson being able to view his daughter's remains. He also asked about him taking possession of her. Marge said that he could view her body tomorrow morning, but as for taking possession, he would have to deal with the husband on that matter. Carter asked if she would ask her friend Judge Henry about it. She said she would, but if it ever came to a court battle, the judge would have to recuse himself. Carter reminded her that the judge had already interceded, which meant that he would have to recuse himself anyway. Marge agreed and said she would call the judge. However, it had to wait until tomorrow since it was almost quitting time.

Carter hadn't realized what time it was because of all the distractions; it was nearing dinnertime as well. But Marge was aware of it and asked him, "We eating at home tonight, or are you taking me out, quarterback?"

Damn, he loved this woman, and she was a mind reader too. "How about we go to Leroy's for some ribs? Maybe he and Annie will formally announce their engagement to us."

"That's a good idea, quarterback. What time should I meet you there?"

"Six o'clock okay for you?"

"That's good for me. I'll see you there."

They both hung up, and then Carter walked over to Amy and Billy and asked them what they thought of the day's events. Both were just as mystified as Carter.

Billy said, "Sheriff, what can we expect tomorrow?"

"Who the hell knows, Billy? I'm gonna finish up, and then I'm meeting a beautiful woman for dinner at Leroy's. You two wrap it up and go home."

Amy and Billy said that they might just go to Leroy's too, since it was rib night.

Rib night at Leroy's Diner was a popular attraction, and nearly everyone in town made a special trip to get some ribs. Most arrived around four thirty for the start of takeout. Traffic backed up for over three hours. Carter had dispatched one of his deputies to keep traffic moving as best he could. Folks didn't stay long in the diner—most ordered the ribs and left—so there was sure to be seating for Carter and Marge, and hopefully also for Amy and Billy.

To accommodate the large number of customers, Leroy had fired up two smokers earlier in the day—a ten-foot one in the rear and a six-foot one out front. The one out front handled the traffic on the street. The one out back handled the overflow plus orders from inside the diner. Leroy had it down to a science and even hired some boys from the high school to take orders and deliver them to customers. Things moved along smoothly, especially with the deputy directing traffic.

Carter met Marge at Leroy's a little before six. Right behind them were Amy and Billy. There was still a lot of traffic due to takeout, but the deputy on duty had it under control. Carter,

Marge, Amy, and Billy managed to find parking spaces within walking distance. It was like a gathering of law enforcement.

"See you two decided to have the ribs like us," said Carter.

"We wouldn't miss them, Sheriff."

"Just don't mess up that uniform, Billy."

The four of them laughed and went into Leroy's. Sitting inside and having a conversation were Leroy and Mr. Johnson. They seemed like old friends by the tone of their voices.

"Guess you found your way here okay, Mr. Johnson. You and Leroy seem like old friends. That must mean Friday night is all forgotten."

"John, this guy's got some memories of my exploits at UCF, and he even got a clipping from when I made All-American my senior year," Leroy announced. "Can you believe it?"

"Hell, Sheriff, I told you I was a big fan of this man. I even got some articles from when you two were in high school. You were a pretty good quarterback back then, Sheriff. Too bad you got hurt your freshman season at FSU. You might have made All-American too."

"Well, in high school, Mr. Johnson, I had a running back that was pretty damn good. He helped us win State. He made me look good."

"That's because you chose the run over the pass even when Coach didn't want you to, John."

"What the hell did he know? He was on the sideline. We were on the field, and good thing too."

Annie stepped out of the kitchen and yelled, "You boys gonna keep hashing high school days? We got a diner to run here, Leroy."

Annie raised her left hand in Marge's direction and wiggled it, showing off the engagement ring that Leroy gave her. Marge smiled as she admired the ring.

"Damn, Leroy," she said. "You finally grew a set of balls and made Annie an honest woman. It's about time."

"Oh, he's got a set of balls all right, and they ain't footballs."

"Damn, woman, not in front of people, especially Mr. Johnson. We just met him."

Carter looked back and forth at Marge and Annie. He was surprised by Marge's comment and Annie's retort. The two women always managed to come up with some real doozies. Their comments weren't lost on Mr. Johnson. He was actually enjoying them, but was still feeling down about his daughter.

"Don't mind me, Sheriff. Warms this old heart to see young love," replied Mr. Johnson.

Marge realized that, although he said it with amusement, the man was obviously experiencing some pain over the death of his daughter. She knew what it was like to lose an only child.

She walked over beside him and tenderly told him, "You're not an old man, sir. Why, I bet there are plenty of women in Live Oak itching to get their hands on you. If I weren't married to the sheriff, I'd make a pass at you myself."

Mr. Johnson smiled, obviously grateful for the comment and for being included in the camaraderie.

"As a matter of fact, there is this one, but she ain't as pretty as you. Last time we spoke, she told me she was tired of boring conversations and I needed to grow a pair of balls, because she has needs. Ain't that something now?"

Everyone in the diner laughed.

Marge gave Mr. Johnson a light peck on his cheek and told him to come by her office in the morning so he could see his daughter.

He smiled, wrapped his arms around her, and whispered, "Thank you." He also mouthed the same to Carter.

Carter tipped a hand to him and mouthed, "You're welcome."

When Mr. Johnson released Marge from the embrace, she turned and glanced at Carter, who smiled at her and mouthed, "Good job, wide receiver."

She smiled and pranced over next to him proud as could be.

Amy and Billy were enjoying the whole experience. For law enforcement, it was a welcome relief. Everyone ordered the rib special, and Annie and Marge engaged themselves in a conversation about William. Annie told Marge that Leroy had already gotten the adoption papers and they were planning on taking the necessary steps to proceed. Marge said she would talk to Judge Henry and see if he could speed up the process for them. Annie leaned over and kissed Marge on the cheek then thanked her.

When everyone finished dinner, they all left to go home and allow Leroy and Annie to clean up and close the diner. On the way to their vehicles, Carter told Marge that she'd done a good thing for Mr. Johnson. She said thanks. Marge also suggested that one of Carter's deputies should show him how to get to her office, but Carter said he already knew how to get there. He said the man must have been extremely busy checking out the town.

When Leroy and Annie finished cleaning up, he got William, who was sleeping, and carried him to the car. Annie locked up and then joined him. They drove to Annie's, and Leroy carried the boy into his bedroom, tucked him in, gave him a good night peck, turned out the light, and headed for the living room to say good night to Annie.

Annie had already locked the front door and turned out all but one lamp. As Leroy entered the living room, Annie wasn't there. In her place was a bronze goddess with perfectly round breasts, glorious curves, and a well-shaved triangle below her navel, with legs that didn't belong behind the counter at Leroy's Diner. Leroy stood there gazing at her from head to toe and suddenly felt a strain in his pants. She noticed the little bulge and turned, giving him a view of her perfectly shaped bronze backside.

She glanced over her shoulder at his bulge that had grown a little more, and then walked toward her bedroom. Leroy just stood there until he realized that she meant for him to follow. On his way, he turned out the last light and proceeded to begin taking his clothes off. By the time he got to her bedroom, he was down to his shorts and his erection was even larger.

There on the bed, crawling toward the center, was a sleek, panther-like creature. When she reached her destination, she rolled over on her back, lifted her left knee, and spread her right leg, exposing her sex to him. She looked at him with an expression that said, "Take me—I'm all yours."

Leroy knew that she kept a supply of condoms in her nightstand, and he approached the drawer to retrieve one, but she said, "No, there's no time. I need you now."

He removed his shorts, and she gave his huge erection another look, reached for him, and said, "Come with me. Tonight I'm all yours, and I want you to make me never forget what you do to me. I love you, Leroy Jones."

"I love you too, Mrs. Jones."

She smiled and motioned for him to get on the bed. He did, and then carefully inserted his erection into her sex. When he was sufficiently inside her, he plunged deep within her and began pumping. She moaned with each pump, reached behind him with her hands, dug her nails into his flesh, and scratched him as an angry panther would.

The piercing beat of the drums escalated, and their bodies worked in rhythm with each clashing beat. As the beat of the drums grew louder and more rapid, so did his thrusts. She wrapped her legs around him, taking him deeper into her. He took her like a wild animal, and the hungry panther relished his desire for her flesh.

When the drums finally crested then abruptly silenced, they both collapsed onto their backs like the pharaoh and his queen entombed in their pyramid. Their ferocious desire for each other was fueled by the earlier frivolities at the diner and the announcement to the public of their engagement. Tonight, their act of love was a ritualistic taking of man and beast. Leroy took the gorgeous panther and pleasured her, making certain she would never forget it, and the panther took pleasure in mating with the human.

In the morning, Annie got up to make coffee for Leroy before he left to open the diner. Leroy got out of bed and went to take a shower, dressed, and then joined Annie in the kitchen. William came out of his bedroom, entered the kitchen, and upon seeing them both, said, "Mornin', Mom. Mornin', Dad."

Both Leroy and Annie replied, "Mornin', Son."

Leroy kissed them both good-bye and left for the diner. Later, Annie took William to school and then drove to the diner for her breakfast and lunchtime shifts. In the afternoon, she would pick up William from school and either take him home to do his homework, or to a friend's house. After homework, Annie would bring him to the diner until her evening shift ended. Some days she didn't work the dinner shift, but she always did on rib night.

Whenever William visited a friend's house, the parent would drop him off at the diner and he would do his homework there. It was at a friend's house that he'd learned about adoption. The friend was adopted and told him how happy he was to have a real dad. William told his friend about Leroy and said he wished that Leroy was his real dad. What he didn't know was that soon his wish would come true.

At the Carter residence, John and Marge were finishing breakfast and getting ready to leave for their respective offices. They commented on Leroy and Annie's engagement announcement and the fun they all had at the diner. Marge told him she would call after Mr. Johnson left her office and let him know how the viewing went and also what Judge Henry said after she talked with him. Carter thanked her and they both left.

CHAPTER 33

Carter arrived at the sheriff's office and found Amy and Billy in animated conversation about last night's events at Leroy's Diner. When they realized he was there, they brought their conversation to a halt.

Carter walked over and joked, "You two don't have anything better to do than clown around?"

Knowing that he was jesting, they both replied, "Nope. We ain't got nothin' better to do, and we ain't got no cases to work on."

They all knew better, but it brought a smile and a little laughter to each of them. Which was good because things were about to change. The telephone rang, and Billy answered it and told Carter there was a Major Bill Quincy on the line for him.

Carter took the phone and answered, "Bill, it's Carter. I hope you have something for me." He was hoping for good news but when Quincy hesitated before answering, Carter was concerned it might be bad news.

"John, I've got some news for you, but you're not gonna believe what I have."

"Give me what you got."

"We've been continuing our investigation into Sam Williams's homicide, and we got a break, crazy one too. We managed to get Williams's credit card receipts and learned that he frequented a bar in a not-so-nice neighborhood here. I personally visited the bar and talked to both the bartender and the owner. You're gonna like this. The owner is a pack rat. He saves things, especially the tapes from his security system. Since the bar is in a rough neighborhood, his security cameras are set up inside and outside.

"The female bartender remembered Williams. He used to be a regular with a bunch of his friends before he got married. She remembered the last time he was in. Said there weren't that many customers in the bar that night. Besides Williams, there were a couple of regulars, a stranger who was sitting near the door, and two guys in a booth. She also remembers when Williams left, and the stranger and the two guys from the booth left right after him. Practically emptied the bar is why she remembered."

Carter made a fist, gestured it toward himself, and mouthed, "Yes."

"We got a video of them in the bar and in the parking lot. Here's the damndest thing. That night there was a working girl covering the parking lot, and she solicited the four of them. They all waved her off, but we lucked out and got to talk to her. She remembered one of them was driving a truck with North Carolina plates. We managed to print pictures from the videos. I'm gonna fax them to you. Maybe you can figure out what, if anything, the Carolina plates have to do with this case."

Quincy scratched his head and continued, "I gotta tell you, John, I've been working cases over fifteen years and never got this lucky. You couldn't script this any better for one of those television crime shows. It's the damndest thing. The pictures are on the way. Let me know when you get a chance to look at them."

Carter pumped his fist and replied, "Okay, Bill, I will. I'm with you on strange things happening in these cases. When this case up here is finished, I bet some wannabe best seller is gonna write a book about it."

That got a laugh out of both of them, but they really weren't amused with everything that'd been happening. At least they had something to work with, and maybe the pictures would help. Carter told Quincy that he would call after he and his deputies reviewed the pictures, and then both of them said good-bye.

Amy and Billy were both curious about Carter's discussion with Quincy, and they were also curious about the mention of pictures.

"John, what's this about pictures?"

"Amy, Major Quincy has some security-camera pictures taken from a bar that Williams last frequented. He's faxing them to us so we can review them. Maybe we'll get lucky. He also said that a working girl happened to be soliciting four guys in the bar's parking lot but was brushed off. You won't believe this, but she noticed two of them left in a pickup with North Carolina plates. You may need to talk with that Worthington woman again."

"Okay, John, but let's wait until we see the pictures."

A short time later, the fax machine started clicking and the first of five pictures came in from Orlando. Three were of the men in the parking lot, and the fourth and fifth showed the men in the bar. They were a little grainy but clear enough for Billy. As he was gathering them together, he recognized one of the men.

"Uh, Sheriff," he said. "We got us a little problem here. One of these guys is Larson from Waterton. You need to take a look at them."

Billy gathered all the pictures and gave them to Carter to peruse. He was not happy when he looked at them.

"Son of a bitch! What the hell was Larson doing in a seedy bar in Orlando at the same time as Williams? Shit, this case is giving me a damn headache. Excuse my language, Amy."

She waved him off and replied, "No need, John. I think we're all getting headaches over this case. Let me look at those pictures."

Carter gave them to Amy. She studied them and asked, "Which one is Williams? I can tell who Larson is, but which of the other three is Williams?"

Carter said, "The one with the *SW* in the lower right-hand corner. That was where Quincy made the mark. Aside from Larson and Williams, he had no clue as to who the other two were. But I know how we can find out."

She checked the photos again, and then Carter told her, "Amy, why don't you call that Worthington woman and ask if they have a fax machine? If they do, fax the pictures to her and ask if she recognizes anyone. Send them all to her, and don't tell her ahead of time who Larson and Williams are. Let's see if she knows them."

"Good idea, John. I'll call her right now."

Amy dialed the Worthingtons' number, and it rang for some time before the answering machine picked up. She left a message for Mrs. Worthington to call her back. The return call came an hour later, and Amy asked if they had a fax machine. When Mrs. Worthington said yes, Amy got the number and explained that she was sending five pictures to her.

"Mrs. Worthington, when you get them, please look at the pictures, and if you recognize anyone, please call me back immediately."

"Okay, Deputy, I'll let you know, but I want Charles to look at them also. He's on an estimate, and when he comes home we'll look at them together." Amy faxed the pictures to North Carolina.

When Amy finished faxing the pictures, she told Carter that it may take a little while before Mrs. Worthington or her husband called back.

"What the hell, Amy, what's a little wait? It ain't like we're going anywhere right now, especially with this case."

The telephone rang and Amy reached for it, thinking Mrs. Worthington was getting back to her real fast. However, it wasn't Mrs. Worthington, it was the medical examiner's office calling.

"Oh, hello, Marge. I thought you were someone else that we're expecting a call from about the case...You're right, a call from you could very well be about the case, but this one is coming from North Carolina. I'll let John explain. Hold on."

Amy handed Carter the phone and mouthed, "It's Marge. Be careful what you say."

Carter understood what she meant, especially what Amy told Marge about the expected call. He mouthed thanks to her and took the phone.

"Do I answer Marge or Ms. Examiner? Is it personal or business that the lovely medical examiner is calling the sheriff about?"

Amy and Billy silently laughed, and Carter smiled at both of them. Amy also gave him the thumbs-up sign, and he returned it in kind.

Marge responded in a very businesslike manner, "Both business and personal. I'll give you the business part first. As for the personal, if you go into your office, I'll give it to you then. I don't want your deputies to get any indication of what I have to tell you."

Carter figured the business part was about Mr. Johnson's visit, but what the hell was the personal part and why the secrecy?

"Okay, Marge, what have you got? Is it about Mr. Johnson's visit?"

"Yes, and it was very emotional. The poor man broke down. It took a while to get him calm. He kept saying he wanted to get his hands on Larson. I managed to restrain him, but I'm not sure what he planned to do after he left here. John, you need to put one of your deputies on him and make sure he doesn't go near Larson."

Carter didn't need this trouble, especially now with the pictures from Orlando. Marge was right; he needed to put a deputy on Johnson, and quick. Amy had to be there in case Mrs. Worthington called, so Billy got the honor.

"You're right, Marge. I'll put Billy on it right away. Is that it for the business part?"

"Yes, John. Now go into your office. Put me on hold—I'll wait."

Carter did as he was told, but he was worried that it might have something to do with that Friday when he came home and found her in the bed. He sure hoped not. He went into his office and picked up the receiver so he and Marge could speak privately.

"Okay, Marge, I'm all ears. Please don't give me any bad news."

He couldn't see that Marge was smiling. Had he been able to, he would have known she was about to play a trick on him. Something she didn't often do, but she figured he could use a little amusement. Carter didn't know that she knew he was worried about her.

"John, I just wanted to tell you how very much I love you and how glad I am that I met you on that wonderful day. You are my rock and the wind beneath my wings."

There was a prolonged silence on the other end before Carter shouted, "Shit, Marge, you scared the hell out of me. I was worried something was wrong. You got me good, wide receiver, and thanks for those words. You know how much they mean to me. I love you too, wide receiver, and you can prank me any day."

Marge laughed and was glad she had pranked him. She could tell it was a respite for him, and she knew he needed one. Marge could use one too, especially after the incident with Mr. Johnson. Her little prank, followed by Carter's reaction and loving response, served as a temporary one for her. She'd get hers tonight at home.

"We may have gotten a little break here, Marge. I'll tell you about it tonight when I get to admire those gorgeous tits of yours and that wonderful ass."

"John, what if Amy or Billy had suddenly picked up the phone?"

"I'da told them they're not getting a look-see of my wide receiver."

"You're crazy, quarterback, which is why I love you. See you tonight."

"Same here, girl."

They both hung up, and then Carter joined Amy and Billy. He promptly dispatched Billy to get eyes on Mr. Johnson and told him to call in if he lost the man.

Before Billy left, he and Amy gave Carter a shit-eatin' grin.

In Bensmille, North Carolina, Mrs. Worthington anxiously awaited the fax from Creek City. When the machine signaled that the fax was coming in, she hastened over to it to gather the pictures. She planned on waiting until Charles got home before looking at them because she wanted him there in case they happened to recognize anyone.

As she gathered the pictures together, her eyes glanced at the top one. She dropped the pictures, nearly fainted, and shrieked in horror, "Oh, dear Lord!"

CHAPTER 34

B uddy and Missy Larson were in the bedroom partaking in their rare sexual act. It had been like this for a number of years but became much less frequent after Pastor Ellison arrived in town. Many years ago, Buddy had a vasectomy at the insistence of Missy. She gave him a choice: either he got the damn thing fixed, or he'd never again get between her legs. She wasn't about to birth another child. Buddy chose the vasectomy, which actually proved to be a benefit for him, especially with some of the booster wives, some realtors, local party bosses, and the occasional whore he purchased.

During their sex act, Missy would often shout, "Oh, Buddy, you still got it." But she was just faking interest.

Buddy went at it real hard, banging the shit out of her in distaste for the woman he had come to hate. Their marriage was for the sake of convenience and appearance only. In public they were the happy sociable couple; in private they couldn't stand each other.

Missy was always her gregarious self, showering everyone with little kisses. Most of the women tolerated her, and the men found her amusing. In private, the women called her one of Buddy's "cheap tricks." The irony of it all was that a few of them were also part of Pastor Ellison's spiritual-guidance flock.

When Buddy finally went limp, he got off her. She got up and went to the bathroom to take a shower and wash away any trace of him. Buddy sat on the edge of the bed, and his phone started ringing.

He quickly answered with his typical "Gator Buddy here. What's up?"

On the other end, Peter Larson shouted, "Buddy, get down here, and hurry. I got trouble."

Buddy screamed into the receiver, "What do you mean trouble, Son? What sort of trouble?"

"Just get your ass over here, and make it quick."

Buddy's nostril flared, and he bit his lip. Peter's indignant call for help angered him. Usually it was Buddy who talked to his son in that fashion. He hung up and quickly dressed. He considered alerting his wife but instead said, "Fuck the bitch."

He drove hastily to the mayor's office and noticed two sheriff's cars and two deputies holding a man at bay. Peter was sitting on the curb holding a handkerchief to his nose. Buddy could see the blood even from his distance. He hurried over and asked his son what happened.

"That son of a bitch punched me." Peter pointed toward the man the deputies held at bay. "Thank goodness those two deputies arrived and stopped him. He was trying to beat the shit out of me."

Buddy looked at the man and asked, "Who the hell is he?"

As the deputies restrained Mr. Johnson, he yelled in anger, "I'll tell you who I am. I'm Becky's father, you son of a bitch. Your son killed my daughter, or you did, or that bitch wife of yours had something to do with it. I get my hands on either of you, I'll make you pay."

The two deputies strained to hold on to Johnson, but he was making every effort to get loose. Sheriff Carter arrived at the scene and headed over to the commotion.

When Billy called on his radio, he said that he almost missed Johnson and that the man was apparently on his way to Waterton. Billy arrived at Johnson's motel just as he pulled out of the parking lot. A minute or two later and Billy would have missed him. Billy spotted the SUV and proceeded to follow it at a safe distance. When he was sure that Johnson was on his way to Waterton, he radioed the sheriff's office.

When Carter asked Amy if they had anyone in the area, she said, "Zeke Jackson's patrolling the area. He may still be nearby."

"Good. Call him and tell him to go right over to the mayor's office, and tell Billy to stay on Johnson. I'm heading for Waterton. I'll call you when I get there. Hopefully, we all get there before Johnson does something stupid."

Amy relayed the information to Billy and Zeke and watched as Carter's vehicle shrieked out of the parking lot with its flashers on.

Zeke Jackson was twenty years old and a former offensive right tackle on the Cougar football team. His playing weight was 250 pounds, but he'd since slimmed down to 220. Zeke didn't receive any college offers, so he enrolled at North Florida Community College in Madison. After he obtained his associate's degree, he enrolled at Valdosta State University in the evenings. He was one of two black deputies on the Randall County sheriff's force. There were three, but the female deputy resigned to take a job with the state. Carter hadn't been able to find another female to replace her.

Carter hired Zeke just after he completed his associate's degree because of a recommendation from Zeke's mother. She was a deputy when Carter was first elected, but soon after, she took a job with the Florida Highway Patrol. Carter gave Zeke a six-month training course. When he completed it, he was given a sheriff's car and a gun but was told to never fire it unless absolutely necessary, for the safety of his or another's life. To date, Zeke had never used the weapon. He used his size and strength to subdue a suspect.

Billy arrived at the mayor's office shortly after Johnson. Unfortunately, when Larson exited the building, Johnson saw him and was immediately all over Larson, throwing punches and intent on severely harming him. Zeke arrived right after Billy, and they both rushed over to subdue Johnson. With Zeke's bulk and strength, they managed to get control of Johnson, and Billy shoved Larson away.

Carter was thoroughly upset with Johnson, even though he himself would have liked to do what Johnson did to Larson. However, he wasn't about to make that known. He had to control the situation and get Johnson out of Waterton and away from the Larsons.

"What the hell's the matter with you, Mr. Johnson?" Carter yelled at him. "Didn't I tell you to stay away from here and let me do my job? I understand how upset you are, but now I have to place you under arrest for your own good."

Buddy heard Carter's comment and felt that Carter cared more about Johnson's interests than his son's.

"What about my son, Carter? Shouldn't you be concerned about him?"

Carter looked down at Peter Larson and replied, "I am, Buddy, but I have to get this man out of Waterton. Your son doesn't look like he's about to lose his life. Call an ambulance and get them to patch him up." He turned toward Johnson and said, "This man is upset over the death of his only child. I'm sure you would feel the same if anything happened to Peter."

"But she was also his wife, Carter," Buddy replied.

"I'm aware of that, and I'm going to have some questions about their relationship and a trip he made to Orlando, but they can wait. Johnson first; then I'll be back to talk to your son and you. Take care of him. We're out of here." He elbowed Johnson and said, "Billy, cuff Johnson and I'll take him back with me. One of you drive his vehicle to the motel and then come back and get your own. I'll see you both back in Creek City." He pointed his fingers like two pistols and grinned, "Good job, Zeke. You too, Billy." Then Carter walked over and said a few other things to the Larsons, but not loud enough that Billy and Zeke could hear him.

Zeke was glad that the sheriff was pleased with his quick response and actions upon getting to the scene. Billy bumped fists with him, and then they went about their respective duties. Billy drove Johnson's SUV, and Zeke followed. Zeke drove Billy back to Waterton, where he retrieved his vehicle, and then they both headed back to Creek City.

On the drive back to Creek City, Johnson cursed the sheriff because the deputies had stopped him from further stomping Larson.

Carter swore at him, "Dammit, man. What part of 'stay away from Larson' didn't you understand? I told you we would handle things. You're messing up my investigation. Now you can sit in a cell and think about what you did and cool off. You're lucky if he doesn't press charges, you damn fool."

Carter felt certain that the Larsons wouldn't press charges. Before he left, he told them that he had evidence that somebody took a hand to Becky Larson, and he also had a witness who accused Larson. Carter said he would get back to them on that matter. His comment about Orlando resonated with Peter Larson.

Without elaborating, Carter told Johnson there was some new evidence, which apparently calmed him. When they got to the sheriff's office, Carter told Amy to put the man in the holding cell. Johnson protested and said that he would stay away from Larson. Carter said that he didn't believe him, and spending a day or two in a cell would make it easier for Carter and his deputies.

Amy put Johnson in the holding cell and then joined Carter.

"Amy, has Mrs. Worthington called?"

"Not yet, John."

He rubbed his forehead, let out a deep breath, and said, "Amy, I've had it for today. I'm going home and take an aspirin and maybe a nap. You can handle things here. Call if you hear from Mrs. Worthington."

"You okay, John?"

Amy worried about Carter and believed that the case was having a profound effect on him and Marge.

"Just a little headache, Amy. If Marge calls, don't tell her I went home. I don't want her worrying."

"Okay, John. You go on home, and I'll call you if I hear from Mrs. Worthington."

Carter left for home. He took an aspirin and immediately went to bed to lie down for a nap.

CHAPTER 35

In Tallahassee, John Carter dozed off while reading a case file and was startled awake when Jayne called his name. His head popped up and he apologized. He said he had dozed off and asked how long she had been calling him.

"Not long, John, but I think you've been sleeping at least thirty minutes. You getting enough sleep at night, or did you have another headache?"

"Actually I did have a slight headache and took an aspirin. I think this Whatley case is getting to me." Carter didn't want to tell her that he had another memory lapse. He rubbed his temple and asked, "Has Marge checked in yet?"

"She called and said she was doing some fieldwork and would see you later to bring you up to date. I'm glad you got her involved in this case, John. She seems to know what she is doing."

"She sure does, Jayne, and I'm glad she's with us. She has great instincts. You seem to have taken an interest in this case too."

Jayne leaned against the doorjamb and replied, "I've got two teenagers, John, and I wouldn't want anything like this to happen to my daughter. So yes, I am interested in this case, just like you."

"Well, we've got Marge, and hopefully we can get this resolved soon."

Carter cleared off his desk, grabbed his briefcase, said good-bye to Jayne, and left to go home. Before he left, he said he was having dinner with a couple of amazing women.

In Randall County, when Marge got home from the medical examiner's office, she noticed Carter's car in the driveway, which was unusual. Carter generally got home after she did, especially since this case had started. She entered the house and saw Carter's badge and holster on the dining room table. That was also strange since he never left them there. He always took them to the bedroom.

She sensed that something was wrong. Marge went to the bedroom and found him sleeping on the bed, curled up like a newborn infant. She didn't want to disturb him, so she closed the door and went to the kitchen to begin preparing dinner for the two of them. Marge knew that eventually he would awaken feeling hungry and would appreciate dinner being ready.

Marge was right, because just as she had dinner prepared and ready, Carter entered the kitchen and smiled. "You're a godsend. I'm hungry. Thanks, wide receiver, for having my back."

"You're welcome, quarterback. Rough day at the office?"

"That's putting it mildly. Johnson went to Waterton and beat up on Larson. Now I got him in a holding cell. He's gonna stay there a few days so he can't make any more trouble for me."

"You think that's the right thing to do, John?"

He threw his hands up in desperation. "I don't have any other choice. We've got some new evidence, and I don't want him bothering my deputies or me while we work it out. The sheriff's office in Orlando sent me some photos of four guys in and outside of a bar there. One of them was Jennifer Williams's deceased husband, and one was Peter Larson. The other two we have no clue yet, but we sent the photos to the woman in North Carolina to see if she can ID any of them. So far we haven't heard back. How was your day?"

She fixed their plates, put them on the kitchen counter, and then replied, "It was uneventful, except for Johnson's breakdown at the morgue. Why don't we eat, and then we can both freshen up, and maybe later have a game of touch football if you're up to it?"

"Am I on defense or offense tonight?"

"Can you go both ways, Mr. Quarterback?"

"With you, always."

Marge figured he must have had one of his headaches, especially when she saw the open bottle of aspirin in the bathroom. Since he was ready for a game of touch football, she figured he was feeling much better, but she still had some concern.

They ate their dinner and then played football.

In Dodson County, John Carter turned into the Sutter Brooke development where he lived. When he entered the house, he could tell from the aroma that Emily had dinner ready for him. She said that Jessica had made the salad and the dessert. When he asked what it was, she told him it was a surprise. Jessica finished setting the table and shouted, "Come and get it, y'all."

John and Emily laughed, and then the three of them sat down and enjoyed their meal. Jessica asked if there was anything new with Rachel's case, but John gave her a stern look that implied, "You know better than to ask."

Jessica raised her hands in defeat and chose another topic. She told her parents all about her day and how practice went. John and Emily enjoyed listening to her animated conversations, especially when she paused and said, "And guess what?" She did it repeatedly, but never gave them a chance to guess. She just kept on going and going. But they both enjoyed listening to her.

When they finished with dinner, Jessica and Emily cleared the table, and then Jessica brought out her surprise dessert.

Carter's eyes lit up, and he yelled like a little kid on Christmas morning, "Apple pie and vanilla ice cream. Yahoo!"

Emily and Jessica burst out laughing as they always did when Carter acted like that.

After dessert and when the dishes were done, Jessica retired to her room to do homework and call her friend Kristen. John and Emily retired to the family room for some adult conversation and catching the tail end of *Wheel of Fortune*, commenting on Vanna White's outfit. Later John set the recorder for one of their favorite shows and checked the Weather Channel, and then both retired to the bedroom and were in bed by ten thirty. The rest of the evening is up to your imagination.

CHAPTER 36

B uddy and Peter opted not to call an ambulance. Buddy helped Peter to his feet after Sheriff Carter and the deputies left. They decided instead to visit Doc Watkins, their family doctor, and have him treat Peter.

As they trudged their way to the car, Buddy asked, "What did Carter mean about somebody taking a hand to Becky, and what's this thing about you being in Orlando?" He shook his head and said, "You didn't hit your wife, did you? Boy, you don't ever hit a woman. You got to be stupid to do something like that."

Got to say one thing about Buddy Larson, it would never cross his mind to hit any woman, especially his wife.

"It only happened a few times after a heated argument," Peter replied. "I lost my temper and I lost control. As for Orlando, I think he's bullshittin' us on that. He's just trying to get you riled, and it looks like he succeeded." Then Peter yelled, "Now get me to Doc Watkins before somebody from the *Waterton Gazette* gets here. We don't need any newspaper coverage."

They chose not to call an ambulance because they wanted to keep a damper on the situation. The altercation was sure to make news, and an ambulance was sure to make the newspaper. They already had a small audience.

"Damn, you're a stupid asshole," Buddy replied. "What possessed you to hit your wife? This is not going to help your future. Bad enough your wife was murdered, now you're a wife beater. Shit."

Peter stopped, turned his head, pursed his mouth, and answered, "Oh, give me a break, old man. Maybe if you'd taken a hand to your wife, she would mind you. She never liked Becky, and it was her idea to embarrass her old man at the wedding reception. Johnson fooled her and left after the ceremony. Maybe you should ask if she had anything to do with what happened to Becky. Look for skeletons in your own closet, old man!"

Peter emphasized *old man*, intending to rile his father. His comment about his mother accomplished what it was supposed to, because he could tell that Buddy was pissed.

"What the hell's the matter with you? She's your mother. How can you insinuate something like that? Dammit, boy!"

Buddy emphasized *boy*, just like Peter did with *old man*. They both knew how to rile each other.

"Like I said, look for skeletons in your own closet, old man. Now get me to Doc Watkins, and hurry. I'm gonna have a black eye as it is. I just hope my nose ain't broken. I just might sue that son of a bitch."

Buddy started to say something but changed his mind, as he didn't want to make any more of a scene for the onlookers who had hung around. He got Peter in his car, and they left for the doctor's office. They didn't notice that some of the onlookers were cheering when they drove away. Larson's secretary stood in the doorway to the mayor's office sporting an enormous grin on her face and doing the Seminole chop.

Pastor Ellison was upset that no one had showed for their spiritual-guidance session. This was the first time it happened, and it left him with an emotional drain. The pastor waited until five o'clock, and still no one came. He hadn't scheduled any evening sessions, which meant he would be spending the evening with Agnes, something he dreaded. To avoid spending evenings with her, he either scheduled evening guidance sessions or worked on his sermons in the solitude of the church. He decided to go home.

Agnes was sitting out back with her eyes focused on the book in her hands. Next to her was a drink, her usual mimosa. She knew that he frowned on the use of evil spirits, and she had defied his wishes. This wasn't her first time. The last time he caught her in her sinful act, he thought he provided sufficient discipline to rid her of the evil spirits. It was apparent that she hadn't learned her lesson and found another source of supply. For this act of betrayal, she would have to pay.

The pastor quietly approached, reached for the glass, and emptied it of the wicked liquid. Startled, Agnes dropped her book, stood, and glared at her husband to let him know that he was the vilest human being on the planet. Pastor Ellison took exception to her defiant stare, raised his hand, and slapped her across the cheek, making certain it would leave a mark. He attempted to hit her again, but she raised her hands in a defensive posture, prepared to ward off his slap.

He hesitated, glared at her, and then spoke as though speaking to the congregation from the pulpit, "For this offense of the sanctity of your vows, you shall pay a heavy price. Get down on your knees, sinner."

Agnes saw the meanness in his eyes, so she did as always, and obeyed. She sank to her knees, brought her hands together as if in prayer, and asked for forgiveness. "Please don't hurt me. I will do whatever you ask, just don't hurt me."

In the past, he'd removed his belt and flogged her naked back and buttocks. She still had scars from the awful beatings from the man she once thought of as a loving husband and a man of the cloth. Agnes was certain that he would do the same this time. But the pastor had other punishment in mind.

"I shall not take my belt to you, woman, but you shall please me in the way that I taught you to."

Agnes hated what he wanted from her but was grateful that there would be no belt whipping.

Pastor Ellison undid his belt, undid his zipper, and exposed himself to her. He held his erection and ordered her to satisfy him. Agnes complied, but in her subconscious she had an inclination to bite the damn thing off. When he was satisfied and had sufficiently degraded her, he said, "Get up woman and go into the house." Agnes stood up and shielded her face in the event he slapped her. "Stay away from the bedroom. You can sleep in the den." Agnes turned and did as she was told. "And stay out of my sight," he shouted.

In the morning, after Pastor Ellison left for an early spiritual-guidance session, Agnes made the decision to no longer be a party to her husband's awful treatment. She retrieved the cell phone that Becky Larson had given her before she and Jennifer left on their ill-fated journey.

The cell phone was originally for Becky's use only, but Becky pleaded with Jennifer to allow her to give it to Agnes when she decided not to join them. She received explicit instructions that only one call could be made; after that, the number would no longer be in service and the phone would become inoperable. Once the call was made, Agnes would receive specific instructions to follow.

Agnes made the call and was told to be at the location at the precise time. If she was one minute late, she was on her own, and there would be no second chance. She was also told that she would be traveling with just the clothes she was wearing and to keep the contents of her purse to as few articles as possible, mainly her wallet and the cell phone. She would be provided with the necessary clothes and other provisions along the way. Agnes did as instructed and met the car and driver three blocks from the church where Pastor Ellison was giving spiritual guidance to Missy Larson.

She brought one extra item with her that was also given to her by Becky, a digital camera. The driver told her that he wasn't sure the camera was allowed. When she said she had incriminating pictures of her husband, the driver said he'd allow it as a special instance. At the first stop, Agnes explained what she had on the camera, and the driver agreed to send the pictures, via e-mail, to several addresses.

The first went to Buddy Larson, with copies going to Peter Larson, a reporter at the *Waterton Gazette*, and at the driver's suggestion, another prominent e-mail address. When the e-mails were sent, Agnes was driven to her next unknown location. Twelve hours later, Agnes arrived at her final destination until a permanent location could be determined.

When Peter Larson logged on to his e-mail account and opened the anonymous e-mail attachment, he shouted for his father. "Buddy, you need to look at this."

Buddy was at Peter's office to check on his condition. When he was satisfied that Peter was okay, he decided to go home but was waylaid by Peter's vociferation.

He returned to Peter's office and yelled, "What the hell you shouting about?"

"Come see this. You're not going to be happy, old man."

Buddy's belligerent look was ignored by Peter. He walked over next to Peter and glanced at the e-mail attachment. When he saw the picture of his wife and Pastor Ellison, his blood almost boiled over and the veins in his neck almost exploded from rage.

"That son of a bitch and that fucking whore. Wait till I get my hands on both of them. I just might strangle them both with my own hands." Buddy suddenly thought about the incident with Johnson and Peter's comment about skeletons in his closet. "Is this what you meant by skeletons in my closet, boy? Did you know this was happening?" He shoved most of the contents on Peter's desk onto the floor, pointed a finger at Peter's chest, and shouted, "Tell me the truth, dammit, boy!"

Peter leaned back. For the first time in his life, he was actually afraid of his father, so he decided to tell Buddy the truth.

He pushed Buddy's finger aside and asked, "If I had told you the truth about your wife, would you have believed me? I don't think you would have." Buddy stepped back and stood with hands on hips. "Yes, I knew about it, and she's not the only one he does it with. Some of the congregation's finest are also doing it with him." Buddy's eyes registered shock. "That's why I was in Orlando. I hired a PI to check up on the good pastor. We don't know where these pictures came from or who sent the e-mail. I hope I'm the only one, but you should check your e-mail. You can do it from here—just log on."

Peter's explanation about the PI in Orlando wasn't exactly the truth. However, he needed an excuse for why he was there, so he went with the falsity.

Buddy ignored the comment about the PI and used Peter's computer and logged into his own e-mail account. What he saw when he opened the attachments, was even more disgusting than what Peter showed him. The first picture was of Missy on her knees in a compromising and unflattering act. As macho as Buddy pretended to be, the picture was too much for him. He suddenly clutched his chest and dropped to the floor.

Peter rushed to Buddy's side and shouted for his secretary to call 911. An ambulance arrived, and emergency aid was administered. Buddy was rushed to the hospital in Creek City. Peter dialed his mother's cell phone several times before she finally answered.

Missy Larson was receiving a special session of spiritual guidance when her cell phone started ringing. She saw that it was

Peter calling, ignored it, and returned to her session. After a number of calls, she decided to answer.

She took several deep breaths to calm herself and said, "What is it, Peter? I'm with the pastor seeking spiritual guidance."

Peter didn't care if he disturbed them. He knew exactly what his mother and the pastor were doing. "Dammit, Missy, pull your panties up, unruffle your skirt, and get to the hospital in Creek City," he screamed at the phone. "Buddy's had a heart attack."

"Oh my, what happened?" Peter couldn't see the smirk on her face.

Oh my, my ass, Peter said to himself.

"What happened? Buddy saw some pictures of you and your pastor sharing spiritual guidance. Now get your damn ass over to the hospital, and tell that pastor that if he knows what's good for him, he'll get out of town before Buddy recovers." Peter abruptly hung up on her.

"Oh, shit," was all Missy could say.

Pastor Ellison stopped what he was doing and raised his head. "What's the matter? What was that all about?"

"Nothing—just finish what you're doing." He lowered his head between her legs.

Missy Larson had been near climax when she answered her phone, and the conversation with her son caused the experience to be delayed. She had no intention of missing out on the emotional experience she was about to have. The hospital could wait, as far as she was concerned. It wasn't like Buddy was near death, and even if he were, she had a close relationship with his attorney and knew what was in the will. Nothing could change without her knowing about it, and so far nothing had.

Missy let out several moans as she reached the height of her climax. When she was fully satisfied, she pushed the pastor away, reached for her panties, shoes, and purse, stood up, and straightened her dress. Pastor Ellison looked confused.

"Sorry, I have to go to the hospital in Creek City—there's an emergency—but first I have to pee. Which way is the bathroom?"

The pastor pointed to his right and said, "Over there."

Missy headed in the direction he pointed, saying as she went, "Guess you'll have to make do with your mousy wife tonight."

She went to the bathroom, did her business and put a drop of perfume between her legs so as not to smell of sex. Then she put on her panties and shoes, checked her makeup, and left for the hospital. She took her time as she drove and found a station on the radio that played soothing classical music. Missy Larson was in no hurry.

Pastor Ellison cussed under his breath but decided that tonight he would have to be satisfied with his mousy wife, and by golly he would make her enjoy it.

When Missy Larson arrived at the Creek City hospital, she parked her car and casually strolled toward the entrance. She walked to the information desk, said who she was, and asked for her husband's room number. After she had the necessary information, Missy stopped at the gift shop and purchased a candy bar, since she felt hungry.

She stepped out of the elevator and walked in the direction of Buddy's room. When Peter saw her, he walked up to her and shouted, "You certainly took your damn sweet time, bitch."

Missy ignored his remark, as she noticed several nurses had heard it. Instead she said, "How is he, Son?" She punctuated *son* so the nurses were sure to hear her.

Peter ordinarily would have made a comment about her remark, but he ignored it and replied, "The doctors said he eventually will be fine, but he'll be in the hospital for a few weeks. I'm sure that will make you happy."

Again Missy ignored his remark and walked over to Buddy's bedside. She glanced at the monitors and the tubes coming from his mouth and arms. The heart monitor registered a close-to-normal beat, and his blood pressure also registered close to normal. Satisfied that he was okay, she said she was going to get a cup of coffee and asked Peter if he would like her to get him one.

Peter Larson looked at his mother with dismay on his face, shook his head, and said no thanks. Missy left to get a cup of coffee.

Before leaving for the day, Pastor Ellison checked to see if his secretary was still working. When he checked her office, she had already left. Probably better that she had, he told himself. Still frustrated from Missy Larson deserting him, he left for home.

When the pastor arrived home, he noticed there were no lights on in the house and thought it strange. "Where is she?" he said, and then proceeded to enter the house and began searching for Agnes, calling out her name. He checked the kitchen but found it deserted and with no sign that she had prepared a dinner in the event he came home in time for one. The pastor became more annoyed and visibly frustrated as he received no answer to his shouts.

"Where are you, Agnes?" he yelled. "You're going to pay for ignoring me." She still didn't answer, so he decided to check the bedroom in the event she was in bed. "You had better not be sleeping. If you are, you will be sorry, woman."

When he entered the bedroom, he saw the empty bed. In place of Agnes, there was a tray positioned in the middle of the bed with a half-empty bottle and a glass bearing the imprint of her lips. Both were carefully placed on the tray so he would see them. Extremely furious now, he walked over to the bed and saw the note. He picked it up and read it.

FUCK YOU
YOU'VE GOT MAIL.

Before she left, Agnes had positioned the bottle and glass, as well as the note with her term of endearment, for him on the bed so he could see them. She put on some of the lipstick that Becky had given her and then drank from the glass, making sure he would see the lipstick imprint. Agnes was sure that it would infuriate him even more. She had also requested that an e-mail be sent to him with the pictures of the good pastor and Missy Larson.

After reading the note, Pastor Ellison threw it on the floor, lashed out at the bottle, and knocked it and the glass over, spilling wine on the sheets. He shouted several expletives that even a sailor wouldn't dare use. The pastor stormed out of the bedroom, went to his home office, turned on the computer, and opened his e-mail account. He glanced at the attachments to the anonymous e-mail and nearly keeled over from shock. The pictures of him and Missy Larson angered him even more, and he swore that he would get even with that mousy bitch if he ever found her.

Pastor Ellison froze when he noticed the notation advising that copies had been sent to Buddy and Peter Larson. Without wasting time, he hastily shut down the computer, packed a suitcase, and left the house in a hurry.

On the day Agnes Ellison left the pastor and Waterton behind for good, she came out of her shell.

CHAPTER 37

Tallahassee

Something about the Whatley case was still bothering Marge Davis, especially her last conversation with Rachel. Her instincts were telling her that the girl hadn't told her everything. She felt there was more that the girl knew, so she decided to approach John and ask for permission to speak to Rachel again. If he said no, Marge had already decided that she would do it anyway, regardless of John's decision. She knew there was something missing in Rachel's story that was important to the case.

Carter was still in his office, so she walked over and tapped on the door. He seemed like he was in deep concentration or napping like the last time, but he quickly looked up and invited her in.

"Marge, come in. How is the investigation going? Anything new yet?"

"Not anything to report just yet; however, I do have a special request, John."

"Ask away. I'm in a request-giving mood."

"John, I need to speak with Rachel again. It's really important. Something about her story just doesn't seem right. My
instincts tell me she hasn't told me everything. I want to talk
with her alone again and outside of the Whatley house." She
paused, trying to determine what his response would be. His
face registered concern, but she ignored that and asked, "Can you
arrange it? Trust me, it really is important, John."

Carter had learned to trust Marge's instincts, but this time he
wasn't sure. He was worried about what more questioning would
do to Rachel. He scratched the back of his neck and replied,
"Marge, are you really certain you need to? I don't want to trau-
matize the girl."

She stepped closer toward his desk to impress upon him the
importance of her request. "Yes, John, it is, and trust me, she
won't be traumatized. In fact, my suspicions tell me she might be
relieved after we speak."

Carter eyed her suspiciously and said, "Is there something
you're not telling me, Marge?"

"After I talk with Rachel, I'll tell you, and then you'll
understand."

"Okay, Marge, I'm going to defer to your judgment. I'll
arrange it. When do you want to do it?"

"After school tomorrow, and I'd like permission to pick her up
at school."

"Oh boy, that might be difficult." He looked down, picked
up a pen, and started tapping it on the desk as he considered her
request. "Okay, Marge, I'll ask the parents and also Rachel. In
fact, instead of calling them, I'll go by their house on my way
home tonight."

"Thanks, John."

"I'll call you after I speak with them. Will you be home this
evening?"

"Call me on my cell phone. I'll have it with me, and it will be on."

Marge had plans for dinner this evening, and she didn't want Carter to know who they were with. Things concerning her personal life were not for Carter's knowledge.

Carter drove to the Whatley house and spoke with Mrs. Whatley. He explained that Marge wanted to talk to Rachel again and preferred to do it alone with just the two of them. Carter also assured her that it was important. Mrs. Whatley conferred with her husband and daughter, and they all agreed to allow Marge to speak with Rachel. Carter arranged for Marge to pick the girl up at school. When they were done, Marge would bring the girl home. Rachel told her parents that she was okay with the arrangement.

Carter called Marge. When she answered after several rings, he told her, "Marge, the Whatleys and Rachel approved your request. You can pick the girl up at school tomorrow afternoon"

"Thanks, John."

Marge was enjoying dinner with a close friend when Carter called. Now she had to plan for her meeting with Rachel, but first she had a dinner to enjoy, followed by a pleasant evening afterward.

The next afternoon, Marge drove to Rachel's school and waited for her. She had formalized a plan that would first involve a drive by the boy's house, next a drive by the girl's house, followed by a conversation about how Rachel came to be friendly with Debbie Lakes. She wanted to find out more about the evening at the boy's house.

Unfortunately, the weather changed, and it started raining heavily. Visibility would be difficult for the planned drive-bys, but she hoped the rain would eventually stop. She wanted Rachel to identify the boy's house and the neighborhood.

Rachel arrived carrying an umbrella. When she entered Marge's vehicle, she gave Marge a pleasant greeting and asked where they were going. Marge gave her a towel to dry off. When Rachel settled into her seat with her seat belt buckled, Marge turned on the lights and wipers and pulled out from her parking space.

"Rachel, we're going to take a little ride first and talk while driving." Marge hadn't planned on asking questions until they reached the boy's neighborhood. She started with meaningless girl talk until they arrived at the boy's neighborhood.

"Rachel, do you recognize this neighborhood?"

Raindrops splattered on the windshield, but Rachel glanced out the side window and replied, "Yes. It's where I went that Saturday night."

Marge slowed down upon approaching the house, and Rachel immediately recognized it. "Oh, my gosh—that's the house, isn't it?"

"Yes, it is, Rachel. Now tell me how you really met Debbie Lakes."

"Will she get in trouble, Ms. Davis?"

"Rachel, from what you've already told me, she deserves it. Why would you want to protect her? Is there something you haven't told me?"

"It's just that I don't know if I should tell you." She looked away from Marge and watched a neighbor turn into his driveway. "Do you promise you won't tell my parents? Please, Ms. Davis."

"Rachel, everything you tell me is between you and me unless I have to tell Mr. Carter—then it's between the three of us. I promise, Rachel, and please stop calling me Ms. Davis. I thought we were on a first-name basis. It makes me feel old."

Rachel laughed. Marge hoped her comment might have put the girl at ease, because she wanted to know what Rachel was holding back from her.

"Marge, have you ever smoked pot?" Rachel asked. She looked out the window to avoid Marge's response.

Marge realized she was right. There was something more to Rachel's story. She decided to tell a little fib and admit to smoking pot.

"Yes, Rachel, I have. It was some time ago, and I haven't done it since. Is that why you didn't say anything about the girl?"

Rachel continued to look out the window. "Yes, because she's sort of a supplier to the kids in school. I've done it a few times, and that night we did it before we got to the party." She lowered her head and continued, "We did it again at Andy's house, which is why I didn't object to making out with him. But not, you know, that other thing."

Rachel's words were barely audible, but Marge heard every word.

Shit, Marge said to no one. Rachel's words were like a bomb exploding. They didn't help their case because it meant that Rachel was high at the time and a willing participant in the events. A defense attorney would insist that Rachel initiated the sex and then changed her mind at the last moment. John was not going to be happy.

"Rachel, I'm glad you're being honest with me; it's very important. Is there anything else I should know?"

Rachel bowed her head and said, "I wasn't a virgin at the time."

Again Marge could barely hear her, but she heard enough. The case just went out the window. Yet, although Rachel was a willing participant, the sex wasn't consensual and it was forced, so they still might have a case. John would have to make a decision.

"Rachel, I'm glad you told me. Why didn't you tell me the first time? Do your parents know?"

"No, they don't, and please, I don't want to tell them."

"Okay, we won't. That will be your decision."

Marge then drove to the neighborhood where Debbie Lakes lived. She asked Rachel if she had ever been to the girl's house before. Rachel said no; the night of the rape, Debbie had gone to the Whatleys' house to pick her up.

Marge had one last question to ask her, and she knew it was a difficult one; however, it needed to be asked.

"Rachel, did the boys use protection?"

Rachel hesitated, and after a long silence, turned to Marge with tears in her eyes and sobbed, "No."

Marge said thank you, and then she drove Rachel home. She then drove to Carter's office, feeling distraught and thinking about what happened to her that time when the boy also didn't use protection.

CHAPTER 38

In Randall County, Marge Davids had just finished dressing when Carter entered the bedroom. For tonight she'd chosen a tight pair of jeans and a low-neck tank top that intentionally revealed plenty of cleavage. She definitely wanted to make an impression on Carter and anyone else who noticed her. The Randall County medical examiner had some devilish ways about her, that was for sure.

When she turned around to face him, Carter's eyeballs nearly popped out of their sockets as he exclaimed, "Damn, woman, you sure are some good-looking eye candy tonight."

Satisfied with the results of her fashion statement, she responded with, "That's exactly my intention, and you're the only one who gets to taste this candy, quarterback."

Carter's head jolted back in amazement with her response. "Man, you are sure full of surprises for a medical examiner, wide receiver."

"Yes, I am, and I got lots more of them, but they'll have to wait until later. Let's get to rib night."

Her comment about more surprises left Carter wondering what was in store for him later, and he said to himself, Oh, goodie. Carter took his wife by the arm, escorted her out of the bedroom, out of the house, into his car, and off to Leroy's Diner for rib night.

When they arrived at the diner, there was a decent crowd but plenty of room for the two of them. They entered the diner, and when the men in attendance noticed Marge, they all whistled and wiped their brows as though perspiring. Marge smiled, and Carter did too, satisfied that he had the hottest-looking woman beside him. He actually enjoyed the attention she received and always did, because this eye candy was all his.

They sauntered up to the counter, and Leroy gave Carter a look that said, "You are one lucky man." Carter smiled as he and Marge sat down, ready to place their order of ribs. Before ordering, Annie came over, and she and Marge engaged themselves in a quiet conversation.

"How are you feeling, Annie?"

"Okay, except for the occasional upset stomach in the morning. How are you doing?"

"I'm good except for the same thing as you in the morning."

Both women locked eyes in surprise, and then Annie asked Marge, "Are you?"

Marge grinned and replied, "Yes."

Without realizing they were doing it, both women shouted, "We're pregnant."

Silence enveloped the diner, and everyone, including Carter and Leroy, turned toward the two women. The two men were the most surprised in the diner and also the most dumbfounded. They didn't understand the women's exclamation.

Marge and Annie said, "Woops. Guess our secret's out."

Both Carter and Leroy looked at them and together they said, "Are you kidding? We're pregnant..."

Annie said, "No, you're not pregnant; we are, fools."

Everyone in the diner laughed, pumped their fists, and shouted, "Whew, whew, whew!"

Carter and Leroy went to their wives, took them in their arms, and smothered them with kisses. Carter whispered to Marge, "You really are full of surprises, wide receiver. Are you sure it's for real?"

"Yes. My doctor assured me everything would be all right as long as I'm careful and follow his orders. Tom may have to take over more of my duties. I wish I could be there more to help with this case."

"Don't worry about the case; it's over for now. I'll tell you tonight, but not until after I've savored the mother of my child."

They locked eyes, smiled, and kissed each other on the lips tenderly.

William, who was in the back doing his homework, overheard the commotion and came out front and said, "Hey, what's all the noise about?"

Annie walked over to him and whispered, "You're going to have a little brother or sister, William. What do you think about that?"

Annie worried how he would react toward no longer being the center of attention, especially with Leroy. But she needn't have concerned herself, because William was prepared for something like this. Two of his friends at school who were adopted had become brothers too.

"Do I get to choose a brother or sister, Mom?"

"You can make a wish, William, if you want."

"Then I wish for a sister. I don't want to share Dad with a brother even though I will probably be in college by the time he becomes a pain in the butt like I was."

"You were never a pain in the butt, honey. A little annoying at times, but I wouldn't have you any other way, and neither would Leroy. We love you, Son."

"I love you guys too. I'm going back to my homework. You adults are too silly for me."

Annie smiled and went over and told Leroy about her conversation with William.

Leroy smiled and said, "I'm wishing for a sister too. Like William, I don't want to share either. But I would love to watch you play dress-up with my daughter, and I'd even have tea with her. I love you, Annie Foster Jones."

"I love you too, Leroy Jones."

Amy and Billy entered the diner and walked over to Carter and asked what all the commotion was because they could hear the shouting when they arrived at the entrance.

"Leroy and I are going to be daddies."

"No shit, John?" Amy asked.

Billy slapped the heels of his hands together and said, "Hot damn!"

Everyone in the diner turned their heads toward Amy and Billy and all shouted in unison, "Yeah, shit."

The whole crowd in the diner burst into laughter, especially Carter and Marge.

Carter leaned toward Amy and whispered, "We'll be making appointments for some sessions, Amy, real soon."

"Good, John, and they'll be pleasant ones, I can assure you."

When all the celebrating was over and rib night had come to a close, Carter and Marge left to go home. During the drive, Marge asked Carter what he meant when he said the case was over for now. Carter said to wait until they got home, as he wanted to continue to enjoy the prospect of being a daddy.

"Can I still make love to you, wide receiver?"

"For a while, yes, until my doctor says no. But I won't let you get frustrated, quarterback."

"Does that mean you're getting me a surrogate?"

"If you want to be able to continue peeing from that thing, you'll forget that idea altogether, John."

When she called him John, he knew he was in trouble, so he dropped the issue of a surrogate. Besides, the only woman he ever wanted to make love to sat next to him.

"Ouch, that hurts. You're the only woman I'll ever get in bed with, wide receiver."

"What if we have a girl? Does that mean you'll never let her fall asleep beside you?"

"Ah, Marge, you know that's not the same."

Marge laughed and so did Carter. They were sincerely in love.

When they got home and were in the bedroom, Carter carefully undressed the soon-to-be mother of his child and made love to the first pregnant woman he'd ever done it with. For Marge the experience of having an orgasm with the soon-to-be father of her child was both amazing and special.

After they were finished and were relaxing on the bed, Carter told Marge about the call he got from North Carolina that afternoon.

CHAPTER 39

In Bensmille, North Carolina, Deborah Worthington recovered from her initial reaction to the pictures and immediately made sure that all the windows and both the front and back doors were locked. She went to her purse and retrieved the phone with the special number in it. Mrs. Worthington dialed, and when her call was answered, she told the party on the other end about the pictures. He questioned her if she was certain, and she assured him she was.

She was asked where her husband was. Mrs. Worthington said he was at a client's, making an estimate. He asked for the address, told her to grab her laptop and as little else as was necessary, and to be ready to go in minutes. Within fifteen minutes, two unmarked patrol cars pulled into her driveway. Two officers, a male and a female, rang the bell. Mrs. Worthington looked through the small window in the front door and saw the two officers, and then opened the door.

The female officer said, "Mrs. Worthington, you need to come with us right now. Your husband is being picked up as we speak." Deborah's mouth opened wide, as did her eyes. "Don't worry—you both will be okay. Let's go quickly."

Deborah Worthington followed the two officers to their patrol car, and then both cars left her neighborhood. Several of her neighbors watched as they sped away, wondering what had happened.

Charles Worthington had just wrapped up his presentation feeling confident that the bid was his. He thanked the prospective client and then left to go home and give Deborah the news. As soon as he exited the prospective client's offices, two officers met him. One of them asked if he was Charles Worthington. When he said yes, they asked for identification. Not knowing what it was all about, he showed them his identification.

The officers told him he needed to come with them immediately and not to worry about his vehicle. They assured him that his wife was safe and they were taking him to her. Charles Worthington followed the two officers to their unmarked patrol car and got in the backseat. With Worthington safely in custody, the patrol car sped away with another one following.

Deborah and Charles Worthington were taken to an abandoned lake cottage. They were reunited when they exited the patrol cars and then were escorted to the cottage. Once inside, a man and a woman met them. The woman asked them to follow her. All four of them exited through the rear entrance overlooking the lake. They took the path to a small dock where a small speedboat waited. Deborah, Charles, the man, and the woman got in the boat and sped away to an unknown location. Outside the lake cottage, the two unmarked patrol cars turned around and left, leaving an older-model vehicle parked in an open shed that could easily be seen from the road.

In Tennessee, an unmarked patrol car arrived at the home of Rachel's aunt, who was greeted by two officers when she answered her door. They showed her identification and asked her to please come with them. She followed their instructions, joined them in their vehicle, and was whisked away to an unknown location.

In Knoxville, an unmarked patrol car followed Jennifer Brooks to and from her home to the school where she was employed. The patrol car stayed with her wherever she went as a matter of precaution.

With the photos in hand and the information that Deborah and Charles Worthington had given him, Colonel Edward Graham of the state's Special Investigations Unit was deciding how he would go about approaching Sheriff John Carter in Creek City, Florida. He decided to make the call, introduce himself, fax his credentials to the sheriff, and ask him to call back, so the sheriff could ascertain whom he was speaking to. When the task was completed, Colonel Graham asked Carter for the particulars of his case in Florida.

"Before I begin, Colonel, let me ask, what's your interest in my case?"

"How about we start by you calling me Ed, and if you don't mind, can I call you John? I'd prefer we be on a first-name basis with what I have to tell you."

"Okay, Ed. Now what's your interest in my case?"

Being on a first-name basis would make it easier for both of them, especially with what Colonel Graham had to say.

"We here in North Carolina have a vested interest in Mr. and Mrs. Worthington, as well as one of your victims," he said. "I believe her name was Jennifer Williams. She used to be known as Jennifer Brown. I can't go into particulars, but we are seriously interested in the men in those pictures you sent Mrs. Worthington. We know who two of them are, but there are two we're not sure of. Who's the one in the picture with *SW* in the corner? What does that stand for?" Colonel Graham waited for an answer.

Carter wanted to know who the others were, but first he answered Graham's question.

"The *SW* stands for Sam Williams, Jennifer's deceased husband. He was a potential suspect, but when we learned he had been murdered we ruled him out. One of the other men is the other victim's husband, Peter Larson. The pictures were taken from a surveillance video at a bar in Orlando. The sheriff's office there is investigating Sam Williams's murder." Carter paused. Then he asked, "Who are the other two, Ed?"

There was a definite silence on the other line before Colonel Graham responded to Carter's question, which told Carter that Graham was hedging.

"Shit!" Graham replied. "They're both from up here in North Carolina, and they're cousins. Can you tell me the caliber of gun that was used, John?"

Carter became more suspicious about the North Carolina link and wondered if there was more to it.

"It was a thirty-eight caliber, Ed. Why? What does that have to do with the two men?"

Graham considered not telling Carter, but he knew that wouldn't be the wisest thing to do. "Because there is a thirty-eight caliber registered to the father of one of the men. The father is deceased, along with his wife. They both died about two weeks ago in an automobile accident. The father was driving over the legal drinking limit and apparently must have lost control of the vehicle."

Carter scratched his forehead, unsure what that had to do with his case.

Graham continued his explanation. "The son and the cousin are missing, and now that we know they were in Florida, we believe they may have been your perpetrators, John. We've got an APB out on them. They both have served prison time, and one of them is unpredictable. What does the other husband have to do with this case?"

Carter closed his eyes and pursed his mouth, and then replied, "That's a good question, Ed. He was seen talking to one of your guys. Now I'm interested in knowing what it was about, and

I'm certain the Orlando Sheriff's Office will want to know too. Can you tell me the two guys' names, Ed, or is that going to be confidential?"

Carter wanted to know, but he really was more interested in knowing what Larson was doing talking to one of the men from North Carolina. He'd already made up his mind to let Bill Quincy talk to Larson, especially since it was Quincy's investigation.

"John, I'd like to tell you. But for now, permit me to hold off. It has to do with an older case up here, and it's not pretty." Like the Worthingtons, Graham was bound by secrecy and had the privacy of others to consider. "You married, John, and have a family?"

"I'm married, but no family. Why do you ask?"

"Because the case would turn your stomach, that's why." Graham hoped that his remark would be enough for Carter to cut him some slack. "I'd like to hold off for now. Okay with you?"

There had been enough ugliness with this case, and Carter didn't want more, especially with the way Graham was making it sound. Patience was one thing Carter had plenty of.

"Okay, Ed. I'll honor your request. Is there anything we can do here?"

"Thanks. I'll let you know, but for now I think we're going to have our hands full here. We've already taken some necessary precautions, and the Worthington couple is safe. I'll get back to you as soon as I have something, especially if I need your help in Florida. You may want to talk to the other victim's husband and see what he knows."

"I plan on it, but since we have a hate-hate relationship with each other, I'm going to let the sheriff's office in Orlando do it, and I'm going to enjoy it."

"Sounds like a good plan. I'd do the same if I were in your shoes. You take care, John."

"Yeah, you too, Ed."

They both hung up, and then Carter called Bill Quincy in Orlando and told him about his conversation with Colonel Graham. Quincy knew about Carter's relationship with the Larsons and said he would enjoy talking to the man and would do it in person. He invited Carter to join him; however, Carter declined, saying it was Quincy's case.

When Carter finished his conversation with Quincy, Amy entered his office and told him that Buddy Larson had been taken to the hospital in Creek City. She said that apparently he'd suffered a heart attack. The last word was that he was under an induced coma to stabilize him, but the prognosis was good. Larson's wife and son were there at the hospital. Amy also told Carter that she had a friend who was a nurse there, and she said that some words were had between Missy and Peter. She asked if they should visit and offer condolences. Carter said no, because Peter was going to have a visitor soon, and it had to do with the case.

Amy ignored his comment. She asked Carter if he thought that maybe she should call Mrs. Worthington in North Carolina. Carter told her no, it was no longer necessary.

"What do you mean it's not necessary, John?"

"Mrs. Worthington is out of our hands for now. North Carolina is investigating a case that involves her and her husband, and also Jennifer Williams. They've identified the men in the photos we sent. They're both from North Carolina and are related. For now, we'll let them do their thing, and if they need us, they'll call. The case may be over for us."

"Over? How do you mean over, John?"

"What I said—it's over for now. I'll explain when I can. Now I'm going home. You and Billy can do the same. You know it's rib night at Leroy's, don't you?" Then he commanded, "Go, enjoy yourselves."

"Okay, John, if you say so."

Even though Amy agreed, she wasn't happy about it. Carter had never kept anything about a case from her before, and she wondered why now. She figured she would just have to trust him, but she would really like to talk to Deborah Worthington. Since that wasn't going to happen, she decided to invite Billy to go with her to Leroy's for rib night.

CHAPTER 40

Missy Larson stood outside her husband's hospital room and wondered what she should do. Buddy was in a coma induced by the doctors to stabilize him, and his prognosis was good. She didn't see a need to hang around, but she wanted to make an impression on her son. Peter was talking on his cell phone and seemed slightly upset. She watched him say yes several times until he finally hung up and walked over to her.

"What was that all about, Peter?" she asked, although she didn't really care. "Who were you talking to?"

"It's none of your business," he snapped. "It was an officer from the Orlando Sheriff's Office. He wants to talk to me."

"You looked upset when you were on the phone."

"It's my nose." He pointed at it and said, "In case you haven't noticed, it's broken."

"Easy, boy, I was just concerned. How did that happen?"

Peter threw knives with his eyes at her because she called him *boy*, just like Buddy did.

"Don't call me boy," he shouted. "I'm not your boy. For your information, it was Becky's father who broke it. Carter's deputies restrained him before he could do worse. Carter took him away in handcuffs. He's probably in jail right now."

"Was he drunk when he did it?"

"No, he wasn't. Just forget it. When you get home, you may want to log on to Buddy's computer and check his e-mail account." His expression hardened and he said, "It's what put him here in the hospital, you lousy bitch."

"What are you talking about?" Her eyelids narrowed and her teeth clenched. "And don't speak to me like that. I'm your mother, for crying out loud!"

Peter leaned close to her and whispered, "Fuck you, Mother."

Missy's head snapped back, and then she abruptly left the hospital. When she got off the elevator, she called Pastor Ellison to see if he was up to finishing their afternoon spiritual-guidance session. His cell kept ringing and went to voice mail. She threw her phone in her car and drove home, where she went immediately to Buddy's office and turned on the computer. Missy had his password, so when the e-mail account came up, she logged in. She saw the e-mail that had been sent to Buddy via a copy from the one sent to Pastor Ellison, noticed there was an attachment, and just before she opened it, she said, "What the hell."

As soon as she saw the pictures of her and the pastor in compromising positions, she shouted, "Oh, shit." She erased the e-mail, turned off the computer, and tried the pastor again. Still she got no answer, just his voice mail. "Damn, damn, damn!" she said repeatedly.

On Interstate 10 heading west, Pastor Ellison was cruising along at seventy miles per hour. He heard his cell phone ring, checked to see who was calling, and then dropped it on the seat next to him. When it rang again, he looked to see who it was, and when he saw that it was her calling again, he turned the phone off.

Pastor Ellison had no intention of talking to Missy Larson and had no intention of ever going back to Waterton, or anywhere else in Florida, for that matter. He wished he knew where that bitch of a wife was, but he would never know.

When Carter finished telling Marge about the call from North Carolina, she had questions for him concerning the case. She thought it very strange that Carter was so calm about letting North Carolina and Orlando take over the case. It wasn't like John Carter to walk away so easily.

"John, it's not like you to walk away from a case just like that. There's got to be more that you're not telling me. I'm also your wife, remember?"

"I know that, Marge, but I really believe whatever happened in North Carolina is best left to the folks there. My gut tells me to stay away from it." He put his hand on her arm and continued, "As for Larson, that's different. I like the idea of Quincy interrogating him. Something tells me he may be complicit in what happened, although I have a feeling he hasn't a clue about it. He doesn't know the fetus wasn't his, and I can't wait to see how he reacts when he thinks he may have had something to do with the death of his unborn child. Buddy wouldn't be happy about it, that's for sure. Missy, I don't know."

"When is Quincy supposed to talk with Larson?"

"He was going to call him this afternoon or tonight. He may have already called and probably got him at the hospital."

"What do you mean at the hospital? I thought Mr. Johnson only broke his nose."

"Not Peter, Buddy. Apparently Buddy had a heart attack and was rushed to the hospital here in Creek City."

Marge waved her palms and replied, "Okay, I'm more confused now. Let's just forget about it all and enjoy the fact that we are going to be parents."

"Sounds like a great idea. You know what, wide receiver? I can't wait to spoil him."

"What if she's a girl, quarterback? Will you spoil her too?"

He laughed and said, "Hell, whichever, I'm going to spoil our child, and you can count on it."

"Just make sure we don't become helicopter parents, quarterback."

Carter's eyelids raised and his jaw dropped. "What the hell are they?"

"Parents who hover over their child all the time…"

His mouth pursed and he replied, "Don't worry about that with me, as long as we can have a dog."

Marge suppressed a smile. "A dog? What does that have to do with a boy or girl?"

"If we have a girl, she and I can walk it together, and if we have a boy, he and I can play with it and take it fishing. What do you say, Marge? Please."

Her head turned left then right. "You sound like a little kid when you say please that way. You better not teach our child to do it." Then she smiled. "Okay, but I get to name it."

"Great, Marge, and it doesn't matter whether we get a male or female, as long as we get a dog. If we get a puppy now, it will be trained by the time you have the baby—that way we'll only have one little one to train."

"You really are a little kid, quarterback. When do you want to do it?"

"Damn, I love you, wide receiver. How about this Saturday? There's always a rescue dog adoption thing at one of the parks. We'd be doing a good thing. What name do you have in mind?"

Her upper eyelids lifted, revealing white above the iris, and the corners of her mouth pulled back toward her ears. "Bailey. I've always wanted a dog named Bailey, ever since I was a little girl. It will be like a childhood wish come true. Thanks to you, quarterback."

Carter took her in his arms, kissed her passionately on the mouth, fondled her breasts, and then proceeded to make love to the mother of his soon-to-be child and an owner of their dog Bailey. The cases of the Larson and Williams murders were completely forgotten, at least for one night.

The next day, Peter Larson met with Major Bill Quincy from the Orlando Sheriff's Office. He wasn't happy about the meeting, but the way Quincy had suggested that he meet with him, Larson felt that he had no choice. Still looking like a prizefighter who'd taken a serious beating, Larson greeted Quincy when his secretary introduced him.

"Nice shiner you're getting there, Mr. Larson."

Bill Quincy purposely left off the title of mayor. After what Carter had told him about Larson, he decided he would add some salt to the wound. It was obvious that Larson didn't like not being called mayor.

"It's Mayor Larson, if you don't mind, and yes, I guess I am getting a shiner. What can I do for you, Mr. Quincy?"

Tit for tat, Larson told himself. He could play the game too and wasn't going to be intimidated.

"For starters, Mr. Larson, you can tell me what you were doing in Orlando talking with this man."

Quincy wasn't about to give Larson the courtesy he wanted and would continue the game of one-upmanship, which was why he went right to the heart of the matter. He shoved the picture of Larson and the other man in front of Larson and gave him an inquisitive smile.

Larson was taken aback and suddenly worried. "We had business, and I don't see what it has to do with anything. Why do you ask?"

Quincy decided that if Larson wanted to play cagey, he would come right out and tell him about his suspicion of the man being involved in Sam Williams's murder.

"Because we believe he may have been involved in the murder of Sam Williams. You do know who Sam Williams was, don't you, Mr. Larson?"

Larson suddenly was no longer macho, and it was obvious from the look on his face that he was concerned. "I know who he is—he's Jennifer Williams's husband. I'm not sure I understand what you're implying, Major Quincy."

Larson decided the formality was necessary because Quincy may be thinking that he was complicit in Williams's murder and possibly that of the two women.

"I'm not implying anything, but it is strange that you meet with this man at the same bar and on the same night that Sam Williams was murdered, and these two men are considered prime suspects. Care to elaborate on your meeting, Mr. Larson?"

Quincy shoved the picture of the other man in front of Larson and waited for his response.

Larson hesitated before responding. "I think I'd like to talk with my lawyer before I answer any more of your questions, Major Quincy."

"That's fine with me, but if we find you had something to do with Sam Williams's murder and possibly the murder of your wife and unborn child, Mr. Larson, then you're going to need that lawyer. Thanks for your time. I can see myself out."

Quincy turned and left Larson's office smiling. When he passed Larson's secretary, he tipped his head, gave her a slight salute, and said, "Good day, ma'am."

The secretary smiled back. "Every day just keeps getting better, and a very good day to you too, sir."

In his office, Larson slumped in his chair and buried his head in his hands. The sudden thought of possibly having something to do with Becky's murder and that of his unborn child was too much for him to believe. Although he didn't know that he wasn't the father, the thought still disturbed him. When he met with that guy in Orlando, he thought he was identifying Sam Williams and providing an address for Jennifer. Now he wondered if the guy had lied to him when he said he was investigating her. How dumb could he have been?

Major Bill Quincy was on his way back to Orlando, feeling confident that he had rattled Larson. Before long he would get him to tell him what he wanted to know. The remark about his unborn child hit home. He decided to call Carter and tell him about the meeting.

When Carter got the call from Quincy, he was happy and decided to tell him about the call from North Carolina. They both decided to let North Carolina do their thing. Maybe they would get lucky and solve both cases, but Peter Larson's involvement was something else.

Carter said, "Maybe we should let him dwell on the thought of the fetus being his. If he stews on it for a while, maybe he'll come forward out of guilt. I don't see him capable of getting involved in murder. He may have been dumb enough to think it was something else with those two guys. His mother, though, is a whole different scenario. Let's let things play out for now. What do you think, Bill?"

"I don't know anything about the mother, but I'll have to go with your instincts there. I agree, let's let things play out and see what happens. I've got a shitload of cases on my hands, and one less works for me."

"Good, because I could use some time away from this case myself. I've got some personal things to handle here. I'm gonna be a daddy, and I'm getting a puppy. How do you like that, Bill?"

"Man, that's great news. Good for you, John. I've got a dog of my own, and it's great having one. You take care, and don't forget I've got space for you and the wife come football season, so expect a call."

"I'm looking forward to it. You take care too, Bill."

They both hung up, each sporting a smile.

CHAPTER 41

Back in Bensmille, North Carolina, as Charles Worthington was being whisked away from his customer's office building, two men in a black pickup truck watched from a parking spot a hundred yards away. The passenger said, "Now what do we do, Nate?"

"Shut up, Jake. I'm trying to think." Nate rubbed his hands over his eyes. The situation had overwhelmed him. "There's probably no reason to go to the house now. I'm sure she's not there. Maybe we should follow them."

"But they may be the law, and we can't afford to be seen." Jake took out his gun and waved it. "Not after what we did in Florida. What if they know about us and are looking for us, Nate?"

"Then we either follow them or try Tennessee." Nate slammed his hand on the steering wheel. "That bitch there may know where my girl is."

"We'll be taking a risk going to Tennessee, especially if they're looking for this truck. Maybe we should follow them, Nate."

Nate nodded his head, "Yeah, let's follow and see where they go. I'd like to get my hands on that bitch Deborah Worthington."

Nate carefully pulled away from their parking space and followed at a safe distance. He made sure they couldn't be seen by one of the cars they were following. They eventually saw the two vehicles join up with two more. They were now following a convoy of unmarked cars.

Nate grinned and said, "This is too easy, Jake. Who the hell are these people?"

When the convoy of cars turned onto an unpaved road, Nate parked several hundred yards away on the side of the main road. After the convoy of unmarked cars left, Nate drove up to the dirt road and stopped. What they saw was an old lakeside cottage with a separate garage on one side. In the garage was the older-model vehicle. The cottage overlooked a serene lake, and the view was almost postcard perfect.

"Wonder what's in that lake house, Jake? Sure looks like a nice place to rest and fish."

"You want to go find out, Nate?"

"Not yet. We can wait. Besides, they may come back. Let's wait until dark and then come back. I'm hungry. Let's get something to eat at that bait-and-tackle store down the road."

"Okay by me. Maybe they'll have some pecan swirls."

"Do you ever think about anything besides pecan swirls, Jake?"

"Hell, you don't know what's good in life. If you ate pecan swirls, you might be more cheerful, cuz."

"Oh, screw you and your pecan swirls."

They drove to the bait-and-tackle store and parked. They left the truck and went in to get some lunch. The store clerk greeted them and asked if they planned on doing some fishing on the lake. Nate said they might but for now they were hungry. He asked if there were any ready-made sandwiches available. The store clerk said there were, but he could make them a fresh sandwich if they'd like. They passed on the fresh sandwich and instead paid cash for two prepackaged sandwiches, two packs of pecan swirls, and two beers, and then went and sat on the bed of the truck to eat their meal.

After sunset, when there was sufficient darkness, Nate Gibson and his cousin Jake left the bait-and-tackle store after several more bottles of beer. They told the store clerk they were going to find a spot to do a little night fishing. The store clerk said there was a pull-off spot up the road a piece that was perfect for day, morning, and night fishing. But they may have to share the spot with others. Nate told him that was okay with them. They bought two more beers and two packs of pecan swirls and drove off.

Nate turned onto the dirt road that led to the lake cottage, turned off the headlights, and drove slowly toward the cottage. He stopped fifty yards from the cottage and waited to see if anyone was inside. There were no lights on in the cottage, so Nate decided that whoever was inside was either asleep or had the curtains and shades drawn to make it appear as though no one was home.

Jake rubbed his hand over his gun and said, "Should we go on up there and break in, or do we wait?"

Nate held his hand up and replied, "We wait awhile longer. Let's be sure there is someone in there. They could be sitting out back or out on the lake. I want to be certain we're not being set up. This looks too easy."

"You sure are suspicious, Nate. I'm all for just barging in and killing them quickly, getting it over with."

"But that won't help me find my daughter. What good are they dead? I need to find out where she is first. Then we kill them, you fool."

"Don't call me a fool, Nate. Dammit." Jake pointed the gun at him. "I don't like it. Okay, we wait, but not all night."

Nate shook his head and asked himself why he brought his cousin along, but he had been helpful in Florida.

Earlier that day, at the Randall County Sheriff's Office in Florida, Sheriff Carter and his deputies Amy, Billy, and Zeke were discussing the cases they were working on. Zeke was handling a few minor cases in Waterton. One was the case that Amy had referred him to, dealing with the church secretary who reported the church's pastor as possibly missing. Zeke said he went by the church and talked with the secretary. She said Pastor Ellison hadn't shown up at the church for several days. When she called his house, no one answered. Zeke went to the pastor's house and tried knocking on the front door several times but got no answer.

Zeke mentioned that the Larsons also attended the same church, and the secretary said that Missy Larson and several other women were part of a spiritual-guidance group that met with the pastor. Several of the women had inquired about the pastor, including Missy Larson. They all were concerned, which was why the secretary called the sheriff's office.

Amy asked if he had left a message on the front door for the pastor or his wife when one of them came home. Zeke said that he had, and he'd written it in large letters that could be seen from the driveway.

Carter got up, pumped a fist, and said, "Shit—a message. That's what's been bothering me. I got to take a little drive someplace. I'll call if I need any of you. Amy, you're in charge, as usual."

"John, what's up?" asked Amy.

"I can't tell you right now, Amy. I'll be back later. It's something I have to do."

Carter left the three deputies standing there dumbfounded. He drove out to County Road 373 and went past Leroy's church. When he pulled up to the church's roadside marquee, he stopped and read the message.

DO NOT STOP ON YOUR TRAVELS
YOU STILL HAVE A LONG WAY TO GO
YOU SHALL SOON FIND HIM.

"That's it," he said to no one. He backed up and turned onto the dirt road leading to the church.

The church grounds included the church and several other buildings, including one that served as a caretaker's residence and one for visiting pastors and speakers. The remaining building was used as a kitchen for cooking when the church had monthly functions. It was also used after mass on Sundays when the parishioners gathered for coffee and baked goods. There was a covered patio used for monthly picnics and for barbeques to raise money for the church. Leroy provided the ribs and hamburgers. There were 150 members in the congregation, thanks to Leroy's presence as its pastor.

The same elderly black woman Carter and Marge had waved to on the day of the pecan festival was just coming out of the church. He pulled up close and got out of his vehicle. The woman hesitated and started to go back into the church when Carter approached her.

"Afternoon, ma'am. I'm Sheriff Carter. You mind if I ask you a question?"

She looked around for someone to help her, obviously concerned, but realized she was alone and said, "I know who you are, Sheriff. You're Leroy's friend. What is it you want to know?"

Carter didn't want to alarm the woman and knew his questions would be delicate, but he had to satisfy his curiosity.

"I'm curious about your sign out front, but what I'm mostly interested in is if you've seen any dark pickup trucks around here within the past week or so."

She seemed relieved that he hadn't asked about the marquee and its content. Then she grinned and asked, "You mean except for the occasional youngsters that use the turnoff for a romantic spot?"

Carter wondered how she knew about the make-out spot. He thought it was a teenage secret. He smiled and answered, "Yes, ma'am, except for that."

He looked away because the corners of her mouth arched down and her eyes said, Mm-hmm—I've seen you there. "Well, there was this one that passed a few times. On the day of that awful accident, I noticed it go by. Awful thing what happened to those poor girls. Are you investigating the accident, Sheriff?"

"Yes, ma'am. I'm especially interested in that pickup truck. You notice anything in particular about it? The license plate, or if there were one or two people in it?"

She rubbed her chin and answered, "Couldn't see the license plate, but I'm reasonably certain there was a passenger, and it was a white man. Noticed that when he rolled the window down one time. That help you any, Sheriff?"

"Yes, ma'am, it does. Have you seen the pickup since the accident?"

"Can't say that I have, now that you ask, Sheriff. You thinking that pickup truck had something to do with the accident?"

"Not sure, but since this is Leroy's church, I'm going to have a car patrol here for a few days. I'm going to call for one, and I'll wait until it gets here, if you don't mind, ma'am."

Her eyebrows shot straight up. "Should I be concerned, Sheriff?"

"Just want to be careful. You think you should call Leroy? I can do it for you if you'd like."

"I'd appreciate that, Sheriff, being as how you and he are friends."

Carter called Leroy and told him about the patrol car and not to panic, but Leroy said he was on his way and asked Carter not to leave until he got there.

Carter called Amy and told her to send a deputy to the church right away. "Pick one who looks like a football player, but not Zeke. Have him go to Waterton and talk to Missy Larson."

Fifteen minutes later, Leroy drove up behind Carter's car and walked over to him. Carter told him about the relevance of the pickup to his case and why the patrol car was necessary. Leroy thanked him and said that he appreciated Carter's concern, but he was going to have someone also mind the church. He told the woman to go on home and stay away from the church until Sunday's services.

Before Carter left, he told Leroy that he thought the roadside message was very interesting, same as the one the day of the pecan festival. Leroy's head turned toward the highway, back toward Carter, and then toward the church. His eyes told Carter that Leroy was worried. Carter waved his palm and said there was no need to explain. Leroy thanked him and went to talk to the man he'd called to watch the church with the deputy. Carter made a U-turn and left the church grounds.

In North Carolina, Nate Gibson and his cousin Jake were still waiting before approaching the cottage. Nate wasn't sure about the situation. The cottage had been dark for too long, and it just seemed suspicious to him. Suddenly, a light came on in the cottage, and it made Nate feel more comfortable with the situation.

"Okay, Jake, it looks like someone is in that cottage. Let's go, but slow and careful. I don't want to be walking into an ambush."

"You worry too much, cuz. You saw them cars leave. Ain't gonna be no one but them Worthington people."

"Just take it easy, Jake."

"Whatever, Nate."

They cautiously approached the cottage with their guns in hand.

Unbeknownst to Nate and his cousin, the clerk at the bait-and-tackle store was actually part of the group that had brought Deborah and Charles Worthington to the lake cottage. When the two men left, he made a call and said that they were on their way. On the roadway leading up to the cottage, an agent, watching in his car, called the cottage and said to turn on a light. The party inside the cottage turned a light on, exited the rear door, and hid behind the bushes out back.

Nate Gibson led the way, and Jake followed behind. When they reached the front porch, they started up the stairs and proceeded to the front door. Jake attempted to look in the windows, but the blinds and curtains prevented him from seeing inside. Nate tried the doorknob, but it was locked.

"It's not a problem, Nate. I have a tool that will get us in without any noise. Hold my gun."

Jake handed Nate his gun, unlocked the front door, and opened it. They carefully entered with their pistols ready. Seeing no one, they went further in and proceeded to carefully check each room. There was no one in any of the rooms. They looked out a rear window onto the deck and saw nobody there either. Then they opened the rear door and stepped out onto the deck to see if there was anyone out on the lake, saw no one, and went back inside.

"Shit. Where the hell are they, Jake?"

Jake scratched his forehead with the barrel of his gun and replied, "We saw them go inside and never saw them leave, so they have to be somewhere, cuz."

"Yeah, but where?"

They looked around again but still couldn't figure where the couple went.

"Maybe we should leave and come back again in the early morning. No sense waiting around here. Those other folk might come back."

"Yeah, let's get the hell out of here, Jake."

They opened the front door and stepped out onto the porch. Bright lights blinded them, and they had to raise a hand to shield their eyes from the lights. While they were in the cottage, ten vehicles formed a semicircle and shined their high beams at the cottage.

"What the hell, Nate. What's this?"

"Don't know, Jake, but it sure don't look good."

From within the glow of light, a voice on a bullhorn called out to them, "You're surrounded. Throw down your weapons and get on your knees with your hands held high. Do it, now."

Jake looked at his cousin. "Don't know about you, cuz, but I ain't going to jail and I ain't giving up without a fight. What say we do a Butch and Sundance?"

Nate hesitated, trying to decide what to do, as he didn't want to go to prison either. Somehow, the authorities had figured out who did the killings in Florida and were here for them, but a shootout wasn't something he wanted. They were outnumbered, and the outcome surely wouldn't result in their favor.

He put his hand out to stop his cousin from stepping forward. "Hold on, Jake, we gotta think this through. We're probably outnumbered, and it ain't gonna go our way. Maybe prison is the way to go rather than a wooden box. Think about it, Jake."

Jake shoved Nate's hand away and said, "Hell, you always was a pussy. I told you I ain't goin' to prison. Do what you have to, but I'm putting up a fight." He hit Nate in the side with his elbow and followed with, "See you in hell, cuz!"

Jake reached behind him, pulled another pistol from his belt, and jumped off the porch without warning, recklessly firing both pistols blindly at the lights in front of him.

Jake went down yelling, "Here's to you, motherfuckers!"

Nate hesitated, not knowing what to do. He decided to give up, but it was too late because whoever was out there had opened fire on both of them, spraying bullets at the cottage. Still standing on the porch, Nate was also hit with a hailstorm of bullets and went down shouting, "I surrender! I surrender!"

It was too late, both Nate Gibson and his cousin Jake died that night in front of the lake cottage. They weren't going to complete their mission. Deborah and Charles Worthington were safe, as were Nate Gibson's daughter and sister-in-law. The solution to the murders of Jennifer and Sam Williams and Becky Larson was decided at a vacant lake cottage in North Carolina.

Colonel Edward Graham made a call to Sheriff Carter in Florida and advised him of what had happened. He told Carter they would do a ballistic test on the two cousins' guns and send him the results. But he was certain that one of them would match the bullet from Jennifer Williams, and most likely it or the other would match the one from Sam Williams's murder.

"You can close out your case now, John, and so can Orlando."

"Thanks, Ed. I will. But we still have a possible coconspirator and we're checking on it. I'll let you know when and if it's resolved."

They both said good night and hung up.

CHAPTER 42

Tallahassee

After Marge's conversation with Rachel, she decided to tell Carter everything she had learned, including the girl's active participation the night of the rape. She parked her car and entered the offices of Carter and Associates, LLC. Fortunately, Carter was there and so was Jayne. When Marge approached Jayne's desk, she said, "Putting in a long day, Jayne?"

Jayne looked up and smiled. "Every day is a long day with John Carter. Did you get wet out there, Marge?"

"Actually, I never got out of my car, and it looks like I'm going to be putting in another long day. I've got a lot to talk to John about."

"How's the case going so far? Anything new?"

"Yes, there is. Wish I could talk to you about it. I could use another woman's perspective, Jayne."

Jayne pushed back from her desk. "That bad, huh? If it's okay with John, I'd be glad to help, and I can stick around awhile longer if you two need me."

"Thanks, Jayne."

Marge approached Carter's office and tapped on the door. He looked up and beckoned her in. "Marge, I didn't expect you back. You putting in a long day too?"

"Yes, John. I need to have a conversation with you, and I don't have good news."

He pushed back from his desk and turned sideways. "You're going to spoil my day, aren't you, Marge?" He waved her in. "Okay, bring it on."

"Do you think Jayne could sit in with us? You can decide what she can or can't hear. I'd like another woman's perspective on this."

Carter frowned and asked, "Is it that bad?" Marge nodded yes. "Okay, let's call Jayne in."

Jayne, on alert as usual in case she was needed, overheard John's last comment. She stood in the doorway and said, "I'm right here, John, no need to call."

"You're always efficient, Jayne. Come on in. Marge wants your opinion on something with this case. If I don't think it's something you should be privy to, I'll ask you to excuse yourself. You know the drill."

Jayne stepped in, took a seat next to Marge, and replied, "Sure, John. I understand. Marge already told me she could use another woman's view on the case. Maybe I can be of help."

Carter extended his hand toward Marge and said, "Okay, Marge, we're all yours."

Satisfied with the arrangement, Marge proceeded to tell them about Debbie Lakes, saving Rachel for last. When she finished her story about Debbie Lakes, she waited for comment from John or Jayne. Neither of them responded, but their expressions told her they were obviously surprised. Then she told them about her discussion with Rachel.

It took a while for both of them to absorb what she told them. Carter crossed his arms and shook his head. "Damn, Marge, that doesn't help our case, and it certainly puts a different light on it. I don't know what we do now, and I'm guessing you have more surprises for me."

Marge hesitated because of Jayne. But before she could respond, Jayne raised a hand and intervened. "John, I'm guessing Marge may not want me to hear what else she has to say, so if you want, I'll step out." She faced Marge but got no response, so she continued, "First let me comment on what we know so far. Somehow Rachel got herself involved with this Debbie Lakes. Rachel willingly went to the boy's house with Debbie and participated in the games as well as the make-out session. That means she isn't completely innocent in what occurred, and a defense attorney will surely use that against her. We don't know if the boys used protection, so there's a possibility of another problem." She glanced at Marge and asked, "Am I right so far, Marge?"

Marge's mouth opened wide as if to say, Wow! Jayne's analysis of the situation was spot-on, except for Rachel being a virgin at the time. She wasn't sure she should bring that issue up, but John trusted her, so she owed it to him to tell him everything.

Carter looked at Jayne and then at Marge. He said nothing and suspected more bad news was coming.

"Very intuitive, Jayne, also right on the mark," answered Marge. "Yes, there is something else, but maybe John and I should talk alone."

Carter was still in shock over everything he'd heard so far. What more did Marge have for him? There wasn't much he held back from Jayne, as he valued her judgment and confidence.

Jayne stood and was about to leave. He held his hand up and said, "Wait, Jayne." Then he looked at Marge. "Marge, whatever you have to say, Jayne might as well hear it. She's going to find out anyway."

Marge straightened in her seat, looked at Jayne then at Carter, and responded, "But, John, I gave Rachel my word."

"I understand, Marge, but we're a team here, and Jayne is a part of this team. So whatever it is, you can rest assured Jayne will keep it in the strictest of confidence."

Marge threw her hands up in defeat and replied, "John, Rachel wasn't a virgin at the time of the rape."

Carter leaned back in his chair, looked up at the ceiling and then at the two women. "Aw, damn, that's the worst thing we need now. I'm not sure what we do with this. If either of you have a suggestion, let's hear it, because this is all new for me."

Since she was now part of the team, Jayne weighed in. "John and Marge, I don't think we should get too upset with what we've learned regarding Rachel. Look, she may not be pregnant, so let's not focus on that aspect. When you two started on this case, you knew it wasn't going to be easy. Rape cases never are, so get over it and focus on what needs to be done. I believe we should focus on the other girl and what she was actually doing. Maybe we can get enough that we can get her to turn on the boys. What do you think, Marge?"

Jayne put the ball back in Marge's court, where she was sure Marge wanted it. Carter knew that Jayne was right and felt foolish about his comment. He opened his mouth and started to say something, but Marge raised her hand like a traffic cop and stopped him. He jerked his head to one side and closed his mouth. Marge and Jayne were in complete control, and he was being relegated to the position of bystander.

"I think Jayne is right, John. I'm going to start taking pictures and see what I can get that will intimidate her and maybe help us. She comes from a single-parent home, and I'm willing to bet she doesn't want her mother to know what's going on. As far as the contraband is concerned, she's the ringleader there." Marge faced Jayne and then Carter and continued, "She may also be enticing other girls to the boy's house. If I can get proof, then we have something to work on. John, are you willing to bring in the sheriff's office on this? Your friend can always pave the way."

Marge was sending the second string back into the game. He scratched his chin, rubbed the back of his head, and said, "I may not have much choice, Marge, but first let's see what you come up with. You know, I'm really glad you two are on my side. I took this case to please my daughter, but I didn't expect to get involved with something like this. Eventually, Rachel is going to have to talk to her parents." He looked at Marge and pointed a finger at her. "Marge, that's where your expertise comes in handy." Then he looked at Jayne and smiled. "Thanks, Jayne, for setting me straight. You always do."

Carter didn't want Jayne to know about Marge's background, so he concluded the meeting in respect of her privacy. If Marge wanted to tell Jayne, it was her decision.

They decided that it had been a long day, so they all went home. Fortunately for Marge, she had someone coming to visit tonight, because she needed a respite.

CHAPTER 43

The next day, Marge decided to call the attorney general and ask her to intercede on her behalf with the Dodson County Sheriff's Office. She was told that it would be taken care of and someone would call her back when the AG had a contact name. Next, Marge got her camera and left for the school and another day of tailing Debbie Lakes. Her intention was to take as many pictures as possible.

Debbie Lakes came out of school, got in her yellow car and drove off. She was unaware that she was being followed. Just like the last time, Debbie drove to Tallahassee and to the same warehouse. From her vantage point, Marge was able to take a good number of pictures using a long-range photo lens. She snapped pictures of the girl going into the building and exiting it, and also pictures of the guy who helped her put the boxes in the trunk. When Debbie drove away, Marge snapped a picture of the front of the building, making sure she got a clear shot of the address.

Just as she did the last time, Debbie drove to Andrew Zane's house, pulled into the driveway, and beeped the horn. When the two boys came out, Marge snapped a picture of both of them.

Then she took pictures of them taking a box from Debbie Lakes's trunk and the three of them going into the house.

When they exited, she took pictures of them kissing, and then she followed Debbie to her home. Marge got some very good pictures of Debbie emptying her trunk of the remaining boxes and putting them in the garage.

When Debbie went into the house, Marge decided to leave, but first she wanted to make another pass by the Zane house. She drove to his neighborhood and found an inconspicuous place to park, but decided instead to call it quits for the day and go home.

As she was about to leave, she heard a tap on the passenger-side window. She turned and saw an elderly gentleman standing there. He motioned for her to roll down the window. "Cop or PI?" he asked.

Marge was surprised by the question, but she had planned for something like this. It had happened several times on other cases. She reached into her purse and pulled out a false identification card and held it up so he could see it.

"Actually, I'm an appraiser and I'm making notes of the neighborhood. There's a house going up for sale nearby soon, and I've been hired to do an appraisal before it's listed."

He waved the card off and said, "Nice try, but I'd know if there was a house going up for sale. I know everything that goes on in this neighborhood. My guess is you're a PI and watching that Zane house. Am I right?"

Marge grinned. "You got me." She put the fake ID back in her purse. "No sense trying to fool you, is there?"

He shook his head. "Nope, not a chance. You're interested in that Zane boy, and by the looks of that camera of yours, I guess you're taking pictures too. Am I right there too?"

She raised her eyebrows. "You got me again."

"If it's pictures you want, I got a whole bunch of them you'll want to see." He tilted his head toward a house. "Come over to my house and I'll show you them."

Marge wasn't sure if the old guy was for real or making a play for her. If he was making a play for her, it was a good pickup line because she definitely wanted to see his pictures.

"Okay, you got my attention, but I ain't sleeping with you. Let me make that clear."

"Shit, woman, after my prostate cancer surgery, I couldn't get my soldier up if I wanted to. I really do have some pictures that you want to see. Pull into the driveway two houses down. If you'd feel safer, make sure your cell phone is on, but you won't need it."

Marge thought his comment about his prostate surgery was kind of amusing but also a little sad. He couldn't be more than seventy, and Marge guessed that he was probably a stud in his younger life. She felt a little sorry for the old guy, but what the heck? Maybe he could be of help, and she could sure use some.

"Okay, I'm gonna trust you, but just remember, no foolishness." She made a karate chop and said, "I've got a black belt in karate and could really hurt you."

"Young lady, I've been hurt by many a woman, so what's one more? Besides, I'm serious. Now come on."

Marge pulled into his driveway and followed him into his house. He led her to a front room, and when she entered the room she couldn't believe her eyes. It was filled with photography equipment, including a camera with a telephoto lens mounted on a tripod aimed at the Zane house.

Her eyes opened wide, and so did her mouth. "Wow, you've really got some fancy equipment here. Are you a professional photographer?" She turned to address him. "By the way, what's your name? Mine's Marge."

"Mine is Mortimer Harrison, but please call me Morty. I used to be a pro but decided to retire from the profession. Now I just do an occasional shot, but mostly I like to shoot a lot of nature scenes—keeps me occupied. I gather you like my setup, Marge?"

"This is really impressive, Morty. Have you been taking pictures of the Zane house?"

She was hoping he was and that he might share some of them with her.

Morty pursed his mouth and wrinkled his forehead. "Yep, I've been taking them for quite a while now, ever since I noticed a lot of coming and going over there."

"What do you mean by coming and going?"

"You've seen the girl in the yellow car, and I've seen you take pictures of her and of those two boys. I've got pictures of a number of girls and boys coming and going on Friday and Saturday nights. That girl is almost always there. She usually arrives with other girls in her car and leaves with them. I got a bunch of pictures if you want to look."

Marge certainly wanted to look and hoped he had a picture from the night Rachel Whatley was there.

"I'd sure like to look at them, especially on one particular night, if you by chance have them in date order, Morty. I see out the window that those boys are leaving. I was going to follow them, but you've got me more interested in your pictures."

"No need to follow them. The Zane boy is taking the other one home. He'll be back soon. Seems he brings that black kid there from school then takes him home later. As for those pictures, I got them catalogued by date. Pick a date and I'll locate the pictures."

Marge gave him the Saturday night that Rachel was raped, and he instantly found the pictures from that night.

He handed a pack of pictures to her. "That Saturday night any particular interest to you, Marge?"

She took the pack and opened it. "Yes, Morty, it is." She saw a number of pictures and asked, "How many pictures do you have of that night?" She hoped he had several, and maybe one of the two girls leaving.

"I've got a number of them. I got one of the two girls arriving in that yellow car, and I got one of them leaving. I even got a close-up of the girl who was the passenger." He gave her another pack of pictures and took one out. "Here, take a look. Looks to me like she ain't too happy. Did something happen that night?"

What Marge saw confirmed Rachel's story about leaving upset over what happened that night. "Something certainly did happen that night, Morty. I really would like a copy of these pictures, if it's okay with you."

"Sure, no problem. I may not be the smartest old geezer, but I got a feeling something wasn't right with the comings and goings. That's why I started taking pictures. Too many girls going in and out of the house, and sometimes there were too many boys too. You know what's going on over there, Marge?"

He was a smart old bird, yet Marge didn't feel that she could tell him anything specific. However, she might as well give him a little, as she would eventually need more of his pictures.

"I sure do, Morty. I can't tell you for certain, but it's not good. I'm pretty sure I'll need more of your pictures. Will that be a problem?"

He gave her a big smile. "Nope, not at all, I never did like that kid. Also, his parents are always leaving him alone while they're off for days and weeks at a time. Figured something wasn't right, especially that girl bringing other girls and those boxes she delivers. Bet they're full of drugs."

"Not sure, but wouldn't be surprised. Let's keep this between you and me, okay, Morty?"

"Okay, Marge. Guess I'm now like your assistant, huh?"

"Why not? Just don't do anything that would cause a problem for either of us, okay?"

"I gotcha."

Marge felt like kissing him because he was so cute when he said *gotcha*, but she smiled instead and felt reasonably sure that he wouldn't make any trouble, since he hadn't done anything so far. She gathered what pictures she wanted and said good-bye to Morty, telling him she would be in touch. Marge gave him her card, and he gave her his.

He looked at her card, and his mouth opened wide as he said, "Special investigator for the attorney general's office, holy shit! I see now why you want me to keep a low profile. Don't worry, because I'm a fan of the AG. Fact is, I knew her father. Did some work for him, way back."

Marge wondered if he had done some work on her case back then but didn't want to ask. She thanked him and left. Marge had a lot to tell Carter, and if the Dodson County Sheriff's Office got involved, she had some good info for them. She also had ammunition for when she confronted Debbie Lakes.

The next morning, Marge got to Carter's office early. Jayne was already there and greeted her when she entered. "Good morning, Marge. You're in early. Must have had a good day yesterday?"

"Morning, Jayne. Yes, I did, and I got a lot to tell you and John. When is he due in?"

"Not until around eleven. He had an early morning court date. Can I get you some coffee?"

"Thanks, but that's not in your job description. We girls are supposed to look out for ourselves. I'll get my own."

"Oh, Marge, that's plain bullshit. We're one big happy family around here. I don't have a job description anyway. I make it up as I go, so you sit your ass down and I'll get us both a cup of coffee. How do you take it?"

Well, that was subtle, Marge thought. She knew there was something she liked about Jayne. "Black will be fine. Thanks, Jayne. You don't mince words, do you?"

"Not when I've been around John Carter so long. Makes for a happy office."

They both laughed, and then Jayne got them both a cup of black coffee and they relaxed, waiting for Carter to arrive.

Marge decided to tell Jayne about yesterday. "You're not going to believe this, Jayne, but yesterday I drove by that boy's house hoping to get some good pictures. When the boys started to leave, this old guy tapped on my window and made out that I was an investigator. He's an amateur photographer and has been taking pictures of the things going on at the kid's house. He gave me some good pictures of Rachel the night of the rape. I also got some pictures of Debbie Lakes bringing girls to the house and leaving with them. He's got a lot more pictures that I can get anytime I'm ready. These are really going to help."

When Marge showed her the pictures, Jayne exclaimed, "Holy shit. Wait until John sees these."

"Sees what? What are you two looking at?"

The two women had been so engrossed in the pictures they hadn't noticed Carter arrive earlier than expected.

"John, you're early. How did it go in court?"

"The judge postponed the case, Jayne, so I'll be going back in a couple of weeks. I'll give you the court date and time later. Now what's so important for me to see?"

Marge showed him the pictures and explained how she got them and who took them.

He carefully perused each picture and handed them back to her. "Those are really good, Marge, but unfortunately we can't use them in court. That doesn't mean we can't use them for other purposes."

Marge took the pictures and replied, "I know, John, and I think I know how to put them to good use. I've got pictures of the Lakes girl picking up boxes at a warehouse in Tallahassee then taking a box to the Zane house and putting the rest in her garage. I've got enough to confront her and pressure her to cooperate. All we need now is the sheriff's office to get involved."

Carter grinned. "Well, that's not a problem. Patricia came through, and I got a call from the sheriff's office. You've got a meeting with the sheriff this afternoon at three o'clock." He pursed his mouth and pointed with his palm up. "You up for it?"

"Oh yes! All I have to do is arrange my notes and prepare for what I have to tell them. You want to go with me, John?"

"No, but you can take Jayne if you want. Two women are better than a man getting involved. You two will do well together. It's up to you."

"I'd like that. You up for it, Jayne?"

Jayne made like she took two guns from her holster, pointed two finger pistols, and replied, "You bet, partner! Count me in." Her face lit up in a grin. "Damn, I've always wanted to say that."

The two women went to the conference room to strategize for their meeting with the sheriff.

CHAPTER 44

Sheriff Carter arrived at the office in the morning ahead of Amy and Billy. Zeke was already waiting for him. They greeted each other and went into the building. Zeke followed behind Carter out of respect.

"Sheriff, what do you want me to do this morning?" Zeke asked. "Should I go to Waterton and interview the Larson woman?"

Carter rubbed his nose with thumb and forefinger and replied, "Yes, and don't worry about being nice. Just find out what she knows about that pastor. I'm going to Waterton myself after I call Orlando. I want to talk to Peter Larson unless he's here in Creek City. Why don't you head out now?"

"Okay, Sheriff, I'm on my way. I'll call if I find out anything. While I'm there, I'll see if anyone has seen his wife."

Zeke left just as Amy and Billy were pulling into the parking lot. They all waved, and then Zeke got into his car and drove to Waterton.

Carter went to his office, sat behind his desk, and picked up the telephone to call Bill Quincy in Orlando. When Quincy answered, Carter told him about the call from North Carolina and

about what he wanted to do with Peter Larson. Quincy agreed
with Carter's plan and asked Carter to let him know as soon as he
learned where Larson was. He'd join him, since it was his case.

Carter called Larson's office and spoke with his secretary.
She said Larson had just left the hospital and was on his way to
Waterton. Carter asked about Buddy.

"He's still in the coma but should be out of it in the next couple of days, Sheriff Carter."

"Thank you, miss. Say, I never got your name. May I ask what
it is?" Carter wanted to know who she was because of the way she
acted the last time he was at the mayor's office.

Her lips broadened in a huge smile when she answered. "It's
Betsy, Sheriff."

Carter said, "Thanks, Betsy. I'll be there after lunch and would
like time with the mayor."

She checked the mayor's appointment calendar and saw that
his afternoon was open. "Sheriff, I put you down for one thirty.
Does that work for you?"

"Yes, Betsy. Thanks."

"Hope you get to the bottom of this, Sheriff, because I'd really
like to move on."

"I hope to very soon."

"Good. See you this afternoon."

Carter thanked her again and hung up. *That was a strange com-
ment she made about moving on*, Carter said to himself. Next he called
Quincy and told him that they had an appointment with Larson in
Waterton at one thirty. Quincy said he would meet him there.

Amy asked Carter what the status was regarding the Larson
and Williams case. He told her about the call from North
Carolina and that their case was closed, except for Larson's
involvement in Orlando.

"Quincy and I are meeting with Larson this afternoon, and
we're going to question him about his involvement with those

men from North Carolina. We're not going to be nice about it, Amy."

"Good. I hope you scare the hell out of that son of a bitch, John."

"Amy, such language. Look, you're making Billy blush."

Sure enough, Billy was blushing. It made them all laugh.

Zeke found Missy Larson at home in Waterton and started questioning her about Pastor Ellison. He asked if she knew where he was.

"I haven't seen or heard from him since the day of Buddy's heart attack, Deputy."

"You have any idea where his wife might be, Mrs. Larson?"

The inner corners of her eyebrows pulled downward, and her eyes opened extra wide. "I have no idea where that mousy bitch could be, and I could care less. That fucking husband of hers can go to hell for all I care." Her nose wrinkled as though she smelled something. "You got any more questions, Deputy?"

"No, ma'am, I don't. Thanks, and you have a nice day."

"Oh, fuck you and your 'nice day' bullshit."

Zeke tipped his hat to her, and then she slammed the door shut. He walked away, got in his car, and drove to the next member of the pastor's spiritual-guidance group. "That's one angry woman there. Sounds like a woman scorned, to me," he said to no one.

At all the other women's residences, Zeke got a similar response, but none as obscene in nature as Missy Larson's comments. Zeke sensed that all the women were harboring some sort of resentment toward Ellison. He surmised that he'd met a number of scorned women.

Zeke called Carter and told him about his meetings with the women and that none of them knew where either Ellison or his wife was. Carter laughed at Zeke's comment about the women scorned and said he wouldn't be surprised if it turned out to be true. He told Zeke that he did a good job and to stay in Waterton until his shift was over.

Carter told Amy and Billy about Zeke's interviews and his comment about the women. Amy and Billy both laughed and agreed with Zeke about the women-scorned thing. Carter said he was going to Waterton to meet up with Quincy and then visit with Larson. He'd call them after the meeting, but first he was going to see Judge Henry to pick up a search warrant.

Quincy met Carter in Waterton outside the mayor's office. He had three other men with him.

"What did you do, bring a posse, Bill?"

"I got me a warrant, and these three are going to help me execute it. This is still my case, John."

"And mine too. I got me a warrant also. Let me call my deputy, and we can go in armed to the hilt. Larson's going to love it."

Love wasn't the proper word, but they all understood what he meant. Carter called Zeke and told him to get over to the mayor's office right away. Within ten minutes, Zeke arrived and the entourage entered the building. As soon as they entered, Larson's secretary was surprised to see the group.

"Sheriff Carter, I thought it was just going to be you meeting with the mayor." She smiled and followed with, "Is this some kind of tour group you're running?" Because of her beautiful smile, everyone knew she was joking.

"Not quite. Sorry for the surprise, but we've got warrants. You best ask the mayor to step out here."

"Okay. Hold on, I'll get him." She had a big grin on her face, and all the men watched as she walked into Larson's office. How could they not? She was a very attractive woman, and oh, what a figure.

Betsy opened the mayor's office door and said, "Mayor Larson, there's a group of men here to see you, and they would like you to step out here." She turned and gave the group another very pleasant smile, walked back to her desk, and sat down.

Carter whispered, "You're really enjoying this, aren't you?" She responded with a smile and a wink.

Larson stepped out from his office. When he saw the entourage, he took a step back and barked, "What the hell is this all about, Carter? You too, Quincy?"

Quincy said, "We've got warrants to search your offices, and we need to talk to you after we do, so don't leave."

The look on Larson's face said that he was obviously worried. "Let me call my lawyer before you touch anything."

"Go ahead," Carter said. "But our warrants trump your lawyer, so step aside. We're going to take your computers too. Both yours and your secretary's."

"You can't do that," shouted Larson.

"Oh, yes we can. Read it in the warrant," said Quincy as he handed Larson the warrant. "Let's go, men."

Carter and Quincy were having fun annoying Larson. Quincy went into Larson's office and seized his laptop, while Carter seized the secretary's. As he unplugged her computer, she slipped him a little note and a smile.

Larson waved both palms at them and snapped, "Go ahead, but my laptop is password protected, and I'm not giving you the password. There's some personal stuff on it, and it's none of your business."

"Sheriff, I think the mayor is mistaken, as his personal stuff is very much our business. It might take a while, but we have people who can crack a password. Thanks anyway, Mayor."

"You son of a bitch, both of you—"

"Now, now, Mayor, don't get nasty," Carter said.

"I'll show you nasty. Wait till my lawyer gets here."

"He ain't gonna get here if you don't stop talking and call him, Mayor," Quincy quipped.

Larson's secretary smiled at Carter, and her eyes secretly glanced toward the note she gave him. Carter turned his back to everyone and looked at the note. It just said "M's password."

Carter turned and smiled at her, and she winked back. She was really enjoying the situation. When they were done going through Larson's office, both Quincy and Carter called him in and closed the door.

Quincy said, "You still haven't called your attorney. Are you going to? We can wait if you want."

Larson ignored him and turned to address Carter. His expression reflected his disdain for the sheriff.

"You're enjoying this, aren't you, Carter? Yes, I'm going to call my attorney, and it will only take him fifteen minutes to get here. His offices are just up the street."

Larson called the attorney and told him to get his ass over to his office and to hurry because it was really important. He explained the situation, and his attorney said he would be right there and instructed Larson to not say a word until he got there.

"Don't worry, I don't intend to."

Within fifteen minutes the attorney arrived. Betsy ushered him into Larson's office. The attorney was maybe five feet six inches tall if he stood on tiptoes. He held his briefcase in both hands, spread his legs, and puffed his chest. Carter and his deputies, as well as Quincy and his men, were all six foot or taller. The scene resembled an NBA team on the floor surrounding their diminutive coach.

The attorney looked up at Carter and asked, "What's this all about, Sheriff? Do you have a warrant?"

Larson gave him Carter's warrant, and Quincy handed him his. After he finished reviewing them, the attorney looked up at both Carter and Quincy. "This says Mr. Larson is considered a material witness and a possible coconspirator in a homicide. We're not talking about his wife, are we, Sheriff?"

"The Orlando Sheriff's Office considers him a possible coconspirator in the death of Sam Williams, counselor," Quincy replied. "We're basing it on evidence that shows he met with the perpetrators in Orlando. It's possible he may also be involved in the death of his wife. That's the sheriff's case for now."

The attorney opened his mouth to respond, but Carter interrupted him. "The same evidence suggests your client may have been involved with two men who have been implicated in the death of Jennifer Williams and Becky Larson, counselor."

Larson started to say something, but his attorney held up a hand to stop him. "Don't say anything, Mr. Larson. As your attorney, I'm advising you not to say anything without my say-so. Do you understand me?"

Larson's eyebrows pulled downward and toward the center of his face, and his mouth formed the shape of a pout. He was obviously angry, but his attorney spoke in a manner that clearly made him understand to keep his mouth shut.

"What is this so-called evidence that you have?" asked the attorney.

Quincy grinned. "We have photographs of your client meeting with the two perpetrators on the night of Sam Williams's murder, in a bar, and in the bar's parking lot. We'll be glad to share them with you after your client explains why he was meeting with them, counselor."

Carter also grinned. "And our evidence proves those same men committed the murder of Mrs. Williams and Mrs. Larson, counselor. So, we both want to know why your client met with them."

Larson's attorney looked at him. "Mr. Larson, do you want to respond to their allegations? You don't have to. So far they haven't charged you with a crime, so it's up to you. I advise you to be cooperative, Peter. This is serious if they have the pictures."

"Oh, we have the pictures all right," Carter said. "In fact, we both have them with us. If your client is willing to explain why he met with these men, we'll be glad to show them to you."

The attorney turned to Larson. "Peter, what do you want to do?"

Larson mulled it over and decided it best that he tell them what happened. "What the hell, I didn't do anything wrong. They told me they were investigating Jennifer and her husband. They wanted me to point him out at the bar. Apparently they knew that he frequented the bar but weren't certain what he looked like, so I went there and pointed him out. I had no idea what they were up to, I swear. If I'd known what they were going to do, I wouldn't have helped them. I was just so pissed that Jennifer contacted Becky. I never liked her, and I'm sure the feeling was mutual. That's all there was."

Quincy's eyes narrowed, and the corners of his mouth pulled back toward his ears. He wasn't buying Larson's explanation. "Did they say what they were investigating Williams for, and did you ask for identification, Mr. Larson?"

Larson's expression said that he was annoyed. "No, I didn't. Call me naïve or stupid, but I just wanted to do something that would hurt Jennifer Williams. And—"

His attorney interjected, "Peter, don't say anything more. Dammit! You've said enough."

Larson's eyes pointed knives at his attorney, but he did as his attorney advised him.

Quincy took a pair of handcuffs from his belt, stepped forward, and said, "Well, Mr. Larson, you certainly did do something. Because of your comment, I'm placing you under arrest for accessory to commit murder as to Sam Williams. Turn around and place your hands behind your back."

Larson looked to his attorney for help. "What should I do?"

"Now wait a minute, Quincy," the attorney said. "My client has answered your questions honestly. You can't be serious about arresting him. Please, let's talk about this."

Carter remained silent since Quincy had the best case against Larson.

"What more is there to talk about, counselor?" Quincy asked. "Your client has admitted he wanted to do harm to Jennifer Williams, and by his actions, her husband was murdered. So was his wife by those two men. That makes him complicit in their murders. There's nothing more to talk about, unless Sheriff Carter has some questions."

The attorney practically pleaded with Carter to intercede. Carter didn't really care if Quincy arrested Larson, but he chose to respond.

"Counselor, your client seems to be pleading both ignorance and stupidity as to his involvement. But the fact remains, three people are dead because of him," Carter implied. "What more is there to talk about? Is your client pleading ignorance and stupidity as a defense?"

"Fuck you, Carter!" shouted Larson. "You're enjoying this, aren't you? You can't believe I would murder my own wife, do you?" He extended his hands palms up. "Okay, I'm stupid and ignorant. Is that what you want to hear? There, I said it, but as far as Jennifer was concerned, I thought she and her husband were in some legal trouble, that's all. Believe me, if I knew what they were up to, I really wouldn't have helped them. I'm also sorry for my cruel comment. I didn't mean it."

Carter stood silently, and then asked Quincy to step out of the office with him. They stepped out of Larson's office and closed the door behind them.

"What do you think, Bill? You really want to arrest him? I'm in favor, if that's what you want. You've got a better case than mine."

Quincy mulled it over. "Dumb son of a bitch is really freaked, isn't he? Tell you what, I'll hold off with the arrest, but I want to look at his laptop before I decide. There might be something on it that implicates him more. Then I will arrest him. What are you going to do, John?"

Carter took a moment to think about it. "I agree with you. I'd like to see what's on that laptop too. If we find something worthwhile, we can arrest him later. I'll defer to your case."

"Okay then, sounds like we got a plan, John. Let's go shake the little bastard up some more."

They both smiled and went back into Larson's office, and Quincy gave Larson's attorney their response.

"Counselor, after talking with Sheriff Carter, I've decided to hold off arresting your client for now. But I am going to look at your client's laptop, and if I find any damaging evidence, you can expect I'll be back to make an arrest. I suggest you advise your client not to leave town."

"No, you can't take my laptop!" Larson shouted. "There's personal information on it, and I don't want you to see it."

"That's exactly why we're taking it, Mr. Larson," Quincy replied. "To see if that personal information contradicts your story. Counselor, advise your client that we're within the law according to our warrant."

The attorney advised Larson that Quincy was right and to shut up. "Be glad he's not taking you into custody." Larson chose to be quiet and not protest any further.

Carter and Quincy told the attorney they would get back to him after they were done with the laptop. The attorney thanked them, and Carter and Quincy left. On their way out, Larson's secretary winked and smiled at both of them. They smiled back and left the building.

Outside, Quincy turned to Carter. "You got something going with that secretary, John? She keeps winking and smiling at you."

"Nope, she's just enjoying the circus, and I believe she's telling us there is something on that laptop we need to see. Should we take a look at it, Bill?"

"Not here. Is there someplace nearby we can go?"

"Yes, there's a restaurant that Larson's wife visited. She was involved with one of the owners. He would have been the father of their child if she wasn't murdered."

"Let's go then."

They went to Graebert's restaurant, found a place to sit, ordered iced tea and a couple of sandwiches, and then opened the laptop.

"How do we get past the password, John?"

"Thanks to that beautiful, smiling secretary, I have it right here."

Quincy entered the password, went to Larson's e-mail account, and entered the password again. It opened to Larson's e-mails, and they checked for the most recent one, which happened to be the one sent by Agnes Ellison. They opened it, as well as the attachments. What they saw was a surprise to both of them, especially Carter.

"Holy shit!" Carter said. "That's Larson's mother and her pastor. He and his wife haven't been seen since Larson's father suffered a heart attack." Carter saw who copies had been sent to. "Looks like Buddy saw these pictures, as did the pastor. My guess is he skipped town before Buddy could get a hold of him. According to who the sender was, I'd say the pastor's wife didn't leave with him. I have a feeling where she may have gone. I can close my case on their whereabouts."

"What do you want to do about the pictures, John?"

"Let's leave them. Larson will know we've seen them, and that's enough to piss him off. See if there are any e-mails relative to our cases."

They checked all the e-mails, but none of them had anything to do with their cases. A few didn't reflect favorably on Larson's integrity though. They decided the laptop provided no evidence. Quincy decided to hold on to it for several days and then return it.

"What about arresting him, Bill?"

"Oh, I think we've scared the little shit enough. Besides, we don't have enough to make a case. The killers have been taken care of, so I'll close my case. What about you?"

"I got what I wanted, which was to shake the little shit up. I'll close mine too."

They laughed, enjoyed their meal, and when they were done, left for their respective offices. A week later, they returned to Waterton. Quincy gave Larson his laptop. They told Larson's attorney they were dropping their cases for now, but Larson should consider himself lucky. The attorney thanked both of them, but first Carter wanted Larson to release his wife's remains to her father. The attorney said he would see that Larson did.

On the way out, Larson's secretary gave them both a big smile and a wink. Both Carter and Quincy winked and smiled back at her. Outside, they laughed, and then Quincy left Waterton.

Before leaving Waterton, Carter told Zeke to close his case on the missing pastor and his wife. He said that both may have taken off for greener pastures. Then he called the Randall County medical examiner and was greeted by a pleasant voice.

"Randall County medical examiner. How can I help you?"

"Sheriff Carter here. How you doing, examiner..."

"Why, Sheriff Carter, how nice of you to call. You have something for me?"

Carter felt it was time for some fun to relieve the tension from the murder case. They both could use a break from the case.

"You can close the files on the Larson and Williams murders, Marge. The case has been solved. I'll tell you all about it later when I see you. I've got one more examination for you though."

"That's good news. What's this examination and where is the body, Sheriff?"

"It will be in your bedroom when you get home. I'm going there for a little nap. When you get home, wake me. After your exam, I'll take you out to dinner. You up for that, wide receiver?"

"Why, Sheriff, how naughty of you. The county may not like me making house calls. Why don't I go by Leroy's and get us some takeout? Then I'll come home, examine you, and give you a special dessert before dinner?"

"Oh, you are a naughty medical examiner. I can't wait for that dessert. See you later, wide receiver."

"Don't be wearing anything when I get there. It will make the exam a lot easier."

"Damn, I love you."

"Same here. See you later."

They hung up, and then Carter called Amy and told her he was calling it quits for the day and going home. If she needed anything, she wasn't to call him. She was in charge.

CHAPTER 45

Marge and Jayne drove to the Dodson County Sheriff's Office together in Marge's car. Marge was able to find a parking space close by the building. Before they got out of the car, they went over their strategy one more time to be sure they had it down perfect. When they entered the sheriff's office, a female deputy walked over and greeted them. Marge told her they had a three o'clock appointment with the sheriff. She told them to wait while she got the sheriff.

Dodson County Sheriff Jim Donahue came out of his office to greet the two women. He was a good-looking man, forty-five years old, and an experienced law-enforcement officer. Sheriff Donahue had been elected to office twice, most recently two years ago. He was a no-nonsense law-enforcement officer and took his job seriously, but was also a fair man and his deputies all respected him.

"Ms. Davis, I'm Sheriff Donahue. It's good to meet you. Is this your partner?"

Jayne was immediately impressed with the man, especially since he had called her Marge's partner and not her assistant. Marge was also impressed with his polite greeting. Maybe it was because the AG's office had called him to arrange the appointment.

"It's a pleasure to meet you too, Sheriff. This is Jayne, and you can call me Marge. I'm not one for ceremony."

"Okay, Marge and Jayne, why don't you two call me Jim? I'm not one for ceremony either, unless it's necessary for political reasons. You know what I mean?"

Marge surmised that he must have been referring to the attorney general.

"Yes, and Jim it is. Can we go into your office?"

"Sure, come on in. I have an idea what you're here for based on the call I received. But why don't you tell me what you have? Deputy Miller is going to join us, if that's okay?"

Standing in the doorway to the sheriff's office was a smart, attractive-looking black female. She was an experienced deputy and also had other credentials that would prove beneficial to the case. The sheriff made the introductions.

"Deputy Anne Miller, this is Marge Davis and Jayne Burrows. Marge and Jayne, this is Deputy Anne Miller."

The three women exchanged pleasantries. "Please call me Anne."

Now that they were all on a first-name basis, they went into the sheriff's office and sat around his conference table.

Marge told the sheriff about the case, leaving out Rachel Whatley's name. She laid out the pictures for the sheriff and his deputy to look at. The sheriff and Deputy Miller took their time reviewing the pictures.

When they finished, the sheriff looked at Marge and said, "This is very interesting. We've actually started an investigation looking into the sale of marijuana and other contraband around the Dodson County High School. As of yet, we don't have any credible leads, but what you've got certainly is what we're interested in. The part about the rape and such really intrigues me, Marge."

"Why is that, Jim?"

He turned toward Deputy Miller, and she nodded okay.

"It just so happens that I got a visit from a local pastor who said a member of his congregation approached him about something similar to what you have. The girl's father approached his pastor looking for help. I happen to know the pastor; that's why he came to me." The sheriff rubbed his jaw nervously. "I told him I wasn't sure what I could do. However, now maybe there is something I can do, especially if the rape took place at that same house. Let me call the pastor and see if he can get the girl and her father to come chat with us. What do you think, Marge?"

Marge started to answer him, but Jayne intervened, "May I suggest that if they do come in, let one of us women talk to the girl and her father. Maybe even the girl alone. She may open up more to a woman versus a man. What do you think, Marge?"

Jayne was smart to ask for Marge's opinion. It put Marge in control and not Jayne.

"You're right, Jayne, that's a good idea. It worked for me, and it may very well work in this case, Jim."

The sheriff started to respond, but Deputy Miller interrupted him. "They're right, Sheriff. The girl won't respond to a man, especially you. I can sit in with Marge, or I can do it myself. It won't be the first time."

Sheriff Donahue knew he was outnumbered and decided to bow to them. "Sounds like you ladies know what you're doing. Okay, we'll do it your way. I'll make the call."

He made the call to the pastor, who called the girl's parents and explained to the girl's father what the sheriff wanted. After much persuading, both parents agreed to bring their daughter to the sheriff's office.

Thirty minutes later, the parents and their daughter arrived at the sheriff's office along with the pastor. Sheriff Donahue asked the pastor to wait outside and then escorted the parents and the girl into his office. He explained that they wanted to ask the girl a few questions and suggested that the parents let her talk to the three women alone. At first they objected, but the sheriff told them it was best if they gave the girl some privacy. The girl asked her parents to honor the sheriff's request. Reluctantly, they agreed and left the office with the sheriff.

Deputy Miller asked the girl if she would rather have one or two of the women leave also so as not to overwhelm her. The girl seemed indecisive, so Marge told her that she was also the victim of a rape and understood what the girl was going through. Marge's revelation surprised Jayne.

"I think it would be helpful if I excused myself, Marge. You don't need me here. I'll go join the others."

Marge gave Jayne a thank-you look, realizing that she was giving Marge some privacy. Jayne left the room.

"I can leave also, if you prefer?" asked Deputy Miller.

The girl glanced at both Marge and the deputy. "No. I think it would be okay if you stayed. You're with the sheriff's office and this woman isn't, so please stay."

"Okay, but I'm going to let Ms. Davis conduct the interview."

Marge placed her hands on the table and gave the girl a warm smile. "You can call me Marge. What would you like to be called?"

She bowed her head, stared at the table, and remained silent. Marge was certain that she was both ashamed and frightened, so she waited patiently.

The girl looked up and half smiled at Marge. "My name is Lettie."

"Thank you, Lettie." Marge waited to allow Lettie time to feel more comfortable. "Lettie, I'm going to ask you some questions.

You can tell me whatever you want, and if you're not comfortable answering, you don't have to."

Marge looked over at Deputy Miller, and she nodded agreement.

The two important questions that Marge wanted to ask were if the rape took place at the Zane residence and if Debbie Lakes was involved. When she asked those questions, Lettie answered yes to both. Marge showed her the pictures of the Lakes girl and the Zane boy.

"Are these them, Lettie?" She answered yes.

Marge then asked when the rape took place. The girl told her the date, and then Marge looked through the pictures that Morty Harrison had taken. She found the picture of Lettie and Debbie Lakes taken on the night of the rape. Lettie identified herself and Debbie Lakes and told Marge what had happened, including getting high from marijuana.

"Lettie, this is important. Would you mind repeating it once more, so Deputy Miller can record it? We promise your name will be kept secret." Deputy Miller assured her that it would.

Lettie nervously shifted in her seat and repeated her story as requested.

When they were done, they thanked her and asked Lettie's parents to come in. Marge told the parents they had no more questions for her and promised that something would come of the matter, but the girl's name would not be disclosed. The sheriff assured them of the same thing. Lettie's parents thanked them and took their daughter home. The pastor also thanked the sheriff and left with them.

After the girl and her parents left, the four of them gathered in the sheriff's office. He asked for a briefing. Marge decided to let Deputy Miller do the talking as a professional courtesy.

Deputy Miller told the sheriff what the girl had said and that they had her testimony on tape. She also told him that since there were two confirmed cases, the sheriff should launch an investigation and start with Debbie Lakes. Marge agreed and said that was what she had already planned on doing herself.

Sheriff Donahue leaned back in his chair, crossed his hands in front of his chest, and smiled. "I agree too. We'll make it a joint effort between my office and you, Marge. Deputy Miller will be in charge. Are you okay with that, Marge?"

"That's fine with me, Sheriff. You can also start an investigation into the marijuana issue, but you may need to enlist the Leon County Sheriff's Office."

Donahue leaned forward and tapped his hands on the desk. "That's a good idea, and it won't be a problem. The sheriff and I are good friends. I'll give him a call and a heads up. You three should be proud of yourselves. Marge, you and Anne will make a good team." He looked over at Jayne. "Will Jayne be joining the team?"

"No, Sheriff, it's not in my job description," Jayne answered. "Besides, I have enough on my plate. You're in good hands with Marge and Anne."

Jayne was happy to bow out. She appreciated the sheriff's offer to include her, but this was way beyond her pay grade.

Marge and Anne agreed to touch base in the morning. Everyone shook hands, and then Marge and Jayne left for Carter's office. Carter was slumped over his desk taking an afternoon nap.

Jayne knocked on the door and startled him awake. "Geez, you startled me. Was I napping again, Jayne?"

"Yes, you were, John, and you were moaning Marge's name. Were you dreaming about her?"

Carter couldn't remember if he was dreaming or not, and he didn't want to tell them he had a memory lapse. "Can't say. Are you sure I said Marge and not charge? I've been reading a book about a Civil War battle, and I was dreaming about a brigade charge." He wrote the name Marge on a pad. Jayne noticed but didn't say anything. She saw him do this on several occasions since the start of this case.

"Nope, I'm certain it was Marge, John."

Marge winked and smiled. "John, if you were dreaming about me, then I'm flattered."

Carter blushed and the two women laughed. He asked them to tell him about the meeting with the sheriff. Marge told him everything, including her teaming up with Deputy Miller. Carter was glad that it worked out the way it did and also glad that he sent Marge and Jayne to meet with the sheriff.

"You two did great. I'm so glad you're both on my side. I really appreciate both of you. Marge, I'm going to tell the attorney general what you did. You deserve to be recognized for this."

"Thanks, John, but maybe you should wait until this is over. We've still got a long way to go."

Carter agreed. After they left his office, he wrote the date and the name Marge in the book with his other notations. He knew it meant something from his recent memory lapse. He had been making notes about his memory lapses ever since his doctor suggested he keep a diary. The lapses were his legacy from his grandfather, Sylus Farber.

He got up from his desk and left his office. He said goodnight to Jayne and Marge then all three went home.

CHAPTER 46

Marge Davids marked the files for the Larson and Williams homicides as case closed just like Carter had told her to. One less case the Randall County Medical Examiner's Office had to deal with. But there was still the disposition of the two bodies, especially Becky Larson's. Marge would really prefer that Becky's father take the remains back to Live Oak. She'd ask Carter what she should do when she saw him that night. She said good night to Tom Morgan and told him she was going home for the day. He said he'd be right behind her and would lock up the building.

When Marge entered the diner, both Leroy and Annie greeted her. She ordered a fried chicken dinner to go for Carter and had Annie fix her a healthy salad plate without any fried food. Annie knew just what to fix her since Annie was no longer eating fried foods either. As Annie gave Marge the bag of food, she gave her a devilish smile. Marge took the package and gave the same to Annie, paid her bill, thanked her, and left for home.

Marge went right to the kitchen and set the bag of food on the counter, and then she headed for the bedroom. She saw Carter spread out on the bed in naked splendor. Careful not to awaken him, she began undressing. When she too was naked, she quietly walked over to the bed and slipped in beside him.

She reached down and took his member in her hand and began gently stroking it. He opened his eyes and gazed into hers. She mounted him and proceeded to gently slip him inside her sex. Then she gently lowered herself onto him and began to move up and down. He reached up, took her firm breasts in his hands, and gently massaged the nipples with his thumbs.

She let out several moans, and then he placed his hands on her hips and moved her body up and down, working in tandem, causing her to moan again. He moaned too as they began to reach climax together. She shouted "Yes, yes" and kept at it until he finally went limp. When he slipped out of her, she got off him and lay down beside him on her back.

Carter took her hand in his. "Damn, was that dessert or dinner? I've never experienced that with a pregnant woman ever, wide receiver."

"That was dessert. I figured I don't have many more occasions left for that, so I took advantage of the moment. Did you enjoy it? Because fairly soon you're going to have to be satisfied with just holding me, quarterback."

He squeezed her hand gently. "I'll be satisfied with holding you for the rest of my life if that's what it takes, wide receiver."

His tender comment caused her to shed a tear. She squeezed his hand in return. "I love you, quarterback."

"I love you too, wide receiver."

"We're going to be great parents, Mr. Carter."

"Yes, we are, Mrs. Carter."

They remained on the bed a bit longer, and then Carter inquired, "What did you get us for dinner?"

"I got you a fried chicken dinner and a healthy salad plate for me. No more fried foods for me. I have to eat healthy for our baby. We can shower first, or slip on robes and eat in the kitchen. If you want, I can go get it and we can have a naked picnic here on the bed—your choice."

"The naked picnic sounds good to me, but I think we better put on robes and eat in the kitchen. Afterward, we can shower together."

"Okay, but I still like the naked-picnic idea. Let's get those robes on, because I'm hungry, quarterback."

They laughed, got out of bed, slipped on robes, and went into the kitchen to enjoy their dinners. Carter told Marge what happened in Waterton and explained why the cases were closed. She asked him about the disposition of the bodies. Carter said he still had some embarrassing leverage on Larson. If she could square it with Judge Henry, he'd get Larson to release his wife's remains to her father. Marge smiled and thanked him.

When the remnants of dinner were put into the trash can, Marge turned toward the bedroom and told him to follow her. He did as instructed, and they made love again, showered together, and then retired for an early bedtime.

CHAPTER 47

The next morning in Dodson County, Marge Davis met with Deputy Anne Miller at the sheriff's office to formulate a game plan. They came up with several alternatives until they finally decided on one. Deputy Miller agreed that first they should confront Debbie Lakes with the photos and attempt to intimidate her into an admission of guilt and hopefully an implication of the two boys and maybe others. They decided that the best way to go about it was to follow the girl after school, see where she went, and then confront her at her house. With a plan in place, they went for a leisurely lunch and some pleasant conversation.

Marge decided to volunteer some of her background, including a little about her rape. Deputy Miller listened intently without interrupting or offering comment. When Marge finished, they sat in silence for what seemed like an eternity.

Deputy Miller said sincerely, "Marge, you didn't have to tell me your story. I had a feeling there was something similar in your background by the way you were at ease with the girl. I really appreciate you trusting me enough to tell me. I won't say anything to the sheriff because it's none of his business."

She then offered a piece of information about herself. "Let me tell you some of my background and why the sheriff actually picked me to work with you. I have a good friend who was raped, so I understand what you and those girls went through. I also have a master's degree in psychology from FSU. I'm working on getting licensed as a counselor to work with rape victims and victims of abuse. That's the other reason I was selected to work with you. I hope you don't mind the little ruse, Marge."

Marge had sensed that there was more to why the sheriff had picked Deputy Miller to work with her. "Anne, I had a feeling you weren't a random selection by the sheriff, and I appreciate your comments. I believe we are going to be a good team together. Thanks for sharing."

They both had said enough, so for the rest of their lunch they chatted about things unrelated to the case. Both shared a fondness for running, so they decided to get together on the weekend to run together. After lunch, Deputy Miller got an unmarked car, and then they went to the high school to wait for Debbie Lakes. Before leaving, they got a subpoena to search the girl's car and garage.

At three o'clock, Debbie Lakes emerged from the school, got in her car, and left the school parking lot.

"Anne, we may get lucky and she may go to Tallahassee."

Debbie drove to the same warehouse in Tallahassee and picked up some packages. Then she drove to the Zane house and delivered a package to the two boys. Next, she drove to her own house and parked in the driveway.

When Debbie Lakes got out of her car and went to retrieve the remaining packages from the trunk, Marge and Deputy Miller got out of their car and approached the girl.

Deputy Miller took the lead and called out to her, "Debbie Lakes?"

She was startled by the two women and started to close the trunk, but Deputy Miller walked over and put a hand on the trunk to stop her.

"Yes, I'm Debbie Lakes. Who are you?"

"Deputy Anne Miller from the Dodson County Sheriff's Office, and this is Special Investigator Marge Davis. Don't bother closing the trunk. We have a warrant to search your vehicle and your garage. Would you like to read it?"

Debbie's face registered fright, and then she answered, "Did I do something wrong, Deputy?"

"Depends on what's in those boxes and what we find in the garage," Deputy Miller replied. "You want to call your mom? You might need an attorney."

Debbie stepped back and covered her mouth. Then she said, "I think I'll call my mom. Can you wait until she gets here, please?"

Marge and Deputy Miller really didn't want to wait until Mrs. Lakes got there; however, because Debbie was a teenager, questioning the girl had to wait.

"You call your mom while we check the boxes in your trunk," Deputy Moller told her. "We'll wait until your mother gets here to look in the garage."

Debbie called her mother. She was upset by Debbie's call and didn't want to leave work early. When Debbie mentioned the sheriff's office and a search warrant, her mother said she would be right there and told her not to say anything. Debbie told Deputy Miller that her mother was on her way and she wouldn't say anything until she got there.

"Okay, Debbie, we'll wait," Deputy Miller said. Then she and Marge proceeded to open the boxes. Marge took pictures of the three boxes both before and after they were opened. In the packages they found numerous bags of marijuana and various packages of pills. Some had labels on them, and it was obvious that the pills weren't for health purposes.

They looked at Debbie, and Deputy Miller said, "You're going to have some explaining to do when your mother gets here, Debbie."

She started to respond, but Deputy Miller stopped her and told her to wait for her mother. Debbie obviously wanted to speak, but Deputy Miller kept stopping her. Finally she got the message, sat in her car, and started sobbing.

Mrs. Lakes arrived and approached the two women. "I'm Betty Lakes, Debbie's mother. What's going on here?"

"Mrs. Lakes, I'm Deputy Anne Miller from the sheriff's office, and this is Special Investigator Marge Davis. We have a search warrant to search your daughter's vehicle and your garage. We've already searched the vehicle and found some incriminating evidence, but we've been waiting for you before we search the garage. Would you like to see the search warrant?"

Mrs. Lakes's face turned red, and then she glared at her daughter. "Yes, please, let me see your search warrant. What kind of evidence did you find in my daughter's trunk, Deputy?"

Deputy Miller handed the woman the search warrant and asked her to look in the trunk for herself. When Mrs. Lakes saw what was in the boxes, she didn't bother to read the warrant. Instead she shouted, "Oh, my God. Debbie, what have you done?"

Debbie knew she was in serious trouble with her mother. "Mom, I can explain. It's not what it looks like. I don't know how that stuff got there. Honestly."

Marge and Deputy Miller exchanged looks. *Can you believe this?*

"Debbie, you can't seriously expect me to believe you don't know how those boxes got in your trunk, do you? What will they find in the garage?"

"Nothing, Mom, I swear."

"Mrs. Lakes, now that you're here, we are going to look in your garage," said Deputy Miller. "Do you have any objections?"

"Yes, I do. If my daughter says there is nothing in there, then I believe her."

"Mrs. Lakes, the search warrant authorizes us to search the garage," Deputy Miller replied. "We'll wait until you're finished reading it. However, we are going to search the garage."

Betty Lakes reviewed the warrant and told Deputy Miller to go ahead. Deputy Miller asked Debbie to open the garage door. Both Debbie and her mother stood there belligerently and did nothing. Marge reached into the girl's car to press the garage-door opener and watched as the door went up.

Inside the garage was a stack of boxes similar to those in the trunk of the girl's car. Deputy Miller and Marge stepped into the garage. Marge took several pictures of the boxes, and then they each opened a box. Inside were more packages of marijuana and containers of pills. Marge took pictures of the contents.

Deputy Miller turned toward Debbie's mother. "Mrs. Lakes, would you like to see what your daughter said was nothing?"

Betty Lakes hesitated and then stepped into the garage and looked in the boxes. She was astonished at what she saw and turned to her daughter and shouted, "Debbie, how could you? What are you, some kind of dealer?" She covered her mouth and said, "My God, this is awful. What can we do about this, Deputy?"

Marge looked at Deputy Miller and told her to go ahead and execute their plan.

"Mrs. Lakes, there's more to this, and your daughter is in serious trouble here."

"What do you mean 'more,' Deputy?"

"I don't know how to be delicate about this, but I'll put it simply. Your daughter may be involved in a series of rape incidents. We have evidence that implicates her."

"My God…No, you can't be serious. My daughter would never be involved in such a horrible thing. Tell them, Debbie."

Debbie Lakes started crying.

"Debbie, say this isn't true, please."

She continued to sob.

Marge and Deputy Miller looked at each other and felt certain the plan was working.

"Debbie, please," pleaded Mrs. Lakes.

"Mom, I can explain. It's not what you think, and it's not like they say."

"That's what you said about that stuff in your car and in the garage. What the hell have you done, Debbie?"

Marge interrupted them. "Mrs. Lakes, why don't we all calm down and go into the house and talk about this. There's no need for your neighbors to see any of this."

Mrs. Lakes looked at Marge and, realizing that she was trying to be helpful, decided to take her advice. "Okay, but can we put the garage door down and close the trunk?"

"Yes, we can. Come on, let's go inside."

They closed the garage door and the trunk of the car, and then they all went inside.

"Deputy, should I call a lawyer first?" Betty Lakes asked.

"If you want to, but why don't we do this off the record for now? Maybe we can work something out without a lawyer if Debbie is willing to cooperate."

"Mom, why don't we call a lawyer and wait until then?"

"Shut up, Debbie. I want to hear what the deputy is asking. Go ahead, Deputy, but if I don't like what you have to say, I am going to call a lawyer before Debbie says anything."

"Mom, please. Call a lawyer, that's what I'm supposed to do."

Whoops, Debbie slipped when she said that. She wasn't so innocent after all, and had been prepared for this.

"What do you mean 'supposed to do,' Debbie?"

"Mom, listen to me, please."

"No, Debbie, I won't, because now I don't trust you. You did these horrible things, didn't you?"

"Oh, fuck you, Mom."

Mrs. Lakes slapped Debbie across the face, told her to shut up, and asked Deputy Miller to proceed.

Both Marge and Deputy Miller were shocked at what had just happened.

"Mrs. Lakes, we have photos of Debbie picking up those boxes in Tallahassee and delivering them to a house here in Dodson County. We also have photos of her bringing girls to that same house. Several of those girls have said they were raped there. She's in big trouble, Mrs. Lakes, and you do need an attorney." Deputy Miller paused for effect. "If she is willing to cooperate and help us in both cases, we can possibly do something for her. It's entirely up to your daughter."

Mrs. Lakes considered the offer and turned to her daughter. "Debbie, I advise you to cooperate with these people. I'll get you a lawyer, and you'll have good legal advice. However, you have to make the decision."

Before Debbie could speak, Deputy Miller interceded. "Mrs. Lakes, I have to advise you that what we found in the trunk of the car and in the garage implicates you as well. The vehicle is registered in your name, and you own the house and garage, so that makes you complicit. You're going to need your own lawyer as well."

Mrs. Lakes's mouth and eyes opened wide from shock. "You can't be serious, Deputy. I didn't know what my daughter was doing. How can I be involved?"

"You're her mother and you should have known, Mrs. Lakes."

It wasn't part of the original plan, but it just gave them more leverage on Debbie Lakes. Her mother was sure to pressure the girl to cooperate if it got the mother off the hook.

Betty Lakes made her decision. "Deputy, we thank you for your advice; however, I've decided to call a lawyer. Neither of us will say anything until we have one. Is there anything more I can do for you?"

Deputy Miller and Marge had hoped it wouldn't come to this, but they were left with no other choice.

"Actually, I'm afraid there is, Mrs. Lakes. I'm going to call for two sheriff's cars to come here. I'm placing you both under arrest for possession of illegal contraband. Go ahead and call an attorney. He or she can meet us at the sheriff's office."

Mrs. Lakes slumped into a chair, as did Debbie. Both were in complete shock.

"Are you serious, Deputy?" asked Mrs. Lakes.

"Yes, ma'am, I'm afraid I am. You've left me with no alternative."

Deputy Miller called for the sheriff's vehicles and then called Sheriff Donahue and told him what they were doing. He asked if she was sure she was doing the right thing. She said she had no other choice. The sheriff then asked if the arrest could wait until they got an attorney. Deputy Miller said she would try, but if not, she was bringing them both in.

"Mrs. Lakes, is it possible you can call an attorney and have him or her come here? Maybe we can still work something out. If not, then I have to take you both into custody."

"I'll try, Deputy, but I only know of one attorney and I'm not sure she can help us. But I'll call her anyway."

She called and was fortunate to get the attorney on the line, because it was a one-woman law firm. The attorney was hesitant at first. Since Mrs. Lakes sounded really frightened, she agreed to come to the house, but if it became necessary for another attorney, she would contact one. Mrs. Lakes thanked her and told Deputy Miller that their attorney was on her way.

While they waited for the attorney to arrive, two sheriff's cars pulled into the Lakeses' driveway. The deputies got out of their vehicles, approached the house, and rang the doorbell. Deputy Miller let them in and told them to wait as there was an attorney on her way. The two deputies complied with Miller's request.

CHAPTER 48

The Lakeses' attorney arrived thirty minutes later and was invited in by the deputies. Amy Weisman was a slender woman, forty years old, and dressed in business attire like a typical lawyer. She introduced herself, and Deputy Miller and Marge introduced themselves. Deputy Miller and Ms. Weisman actually knew each other from the running club they both belonged to. Neither woman commented about their acquaintance.

"Deputy Miller, can you tell me exactly what my clients are being accused of?"

"Ms. Weisman, as of right now, we are only in the talking stage; however, we are prepared to charge your clients with unlawful possession of illegal substances. Debbie Lakes may also be complicit in a crime of a sexual nature."

Deputy Miller chose not to use the word *rape* at this point. When she looked at Marge, she could tell that Marge agreed.

"I'm not sure what you mean when you say a crime of a sexual nature. Are you saying rape, Deputy?"

Deputy Miller still wasn't ready to call it rape yet, so she decided to stick with her comment. "For now we'll leave it as I said, and we'll let it be up to your clients, if that's okay with you and them?" Deputy Miller gave the attorney a stern expression.

Ms. Weisman understood what Deputy Miller meant and decided not to press the issue. Deputy Miller was leaving her clients an option.

"Okay, we'll leave it at that, but what about the illegal substances? Can you tell me more?"

"We can show you if you would like."

"Show me, please."

Deputy Miller led the lawyer outside to the trunk of Debbie Lakes's car and then to the garage and let her see what was in the boxes. Ms. Weisman said for them to go inside, as she wanted to hear what her clients had to say.

As they walked away from the garage, she put a hand on Deputy Miller's arm and asked, "Okay, Anne, off the record. How bad is it?"

"It's really bad, Amy. The girl is implicated in a number of teenage rapes and distribution of illegal substances. We have physical as well as photographic evidence, along with witness testimony. Mrs. Lakes is being accused of complicity in the illegal-substance case, but we can work something out with her if the girl works with us. To be honest with you, Debbie is going to be arrested. We can't ignore what she has done."

"Is there anything you can do for her?"

"Depends on her cooperation, but there's not a lot of wiggle room, Amy. The rape thing is pretty bad."

"Okay, let's see what I can do. Thanks for being honest with me."

"Just trying to do what's right."

They went inside so the lawyer could discuss the situation with her clients in private. She asked her clients to step into another room. When they were alone in one of the bedrooms, Ms. Weisman explained the situation, making sure they understood the seriousness of it. Mrs. Lakes seemed to understand, but Debbie remained obstinate.

"Mom, I'm not doing anything. I told you all I needed was an attorney. They said I would be okay. If this woman can't help me, then let's get another one."

"Debbie, you can't be serious. What do you mean they'll protect you? Who are they?"

"Just do as I say, Mom."

Ms. Weisman tried to get her clients to understand what was about to happen.

"You don't get it, Debbie," she said. "You and your mother are going to be taken into custody and spend the night in jail, maybe longer, if I can't get you out on bail. Are these so-called people going to protect your mother too?"

Debbie hadn't thought about that, but her mother had. "Debbie, if I'm arrested and taken to jail, I will lose my job. If that happens, I will lose this house. I won't have any means of paying for a lawyer or for bail. How can you do this to me?"

Debbie still didn't grasp the seriousness of the situation and was only concerned about herself. Whatever happened to her mother was of no concern to her.

"I'm sorry, Mom, but I have to do what they told me."

Mrs. Lakes couldn't believe what she had just heard from her daughter. "You don't give a damn about me, do you, Debbie?"

Debbie turned her palms, and tilted her head, and replied, "Sorry, Mom."

"Very well then. Ms. Weisman, may I talk to you in private?"

"Sure. Let's go in the other bedroom."

Amy Weisman wasn't sure what Mrs. Lakes had in mind, but she guessed the woman had her own agenda. Who could blame her? The two of them left Debbie alone and went into the master bedroom.

"What do you have in mind, Mrs. Lakes?"

Betty Lakes was about to bring this case to a resolution, and it was not going to be in favor of her daughter. She got her checkbook out and wrote a check for five hundred dollars to Amy Weisman. It was almost all she had in her checking account.

"I'm hiring you as my attorney, and this is your retainer. If you need more, I can get it. Will you represent me?"

Ms. Weisman was confused, as she had already agreed to represent them.

"Mrs. Lakes, I'm already acting as your attorney and that of your daughter. There is no need to retain me again. As for the amount of my retainer, it's normally one thousand dollars; however, since I'm not a defense attorney, five hundred will suffice."

"No, you don't understand. I'm retaining you as my attorney, not Debbie's."

"I don't understand. What do you mean your attorney and not Debbie's?"

"You're to be my attorney only and offer no assistance to Debbie. If she wants to call whoever it is she wants to, then let her. You represent me and me only. You do not have my permission to offer any advice to Debbie. Do you understand me?"

Amy Weisman grasped what Mrs. Lakes was doing. If Debbie Lakes wanted to take the position she had held all along, then she was on her own. Maybe this would change her mind. It would certainly call the girl's bluff.

"Very well then, I will inform Deputy Miller. Let's go back in and join them. Are you prepared to let them arrest your daughter?"

"Yes. If she wants to be stubborn and doesn't care about what happens to me, then she is on her own."

"Okay then, let's go."

They went back into the other bedroom, and Ms. Weisman told Debbie to follow them. The three of them went back into the living room, so Ms. Weisman could tell Deputy Miller what their decision was.

"Deputy Miller, Mrs. Lakes has retained me as her lawyer and exclusively for her only. I'm not representing Debbie Lakes. She will have to seek other counsel. My client has expressly forbidden me to provide any assistance."

The look on Debbie Lakes's face was one of utter disbelief and shock. Deputy Miller and Marge looked at each other, and both knew instantly what Mrs. Lakes was attempting to do. She wanted her daughter to relent and cooperate with them.

Deputy Miller called the deputies in and told them to read the girl her rights and place her under arrest. Marge asked Deputy Miller if they could talk outside. She agreed and told the deputies to wait for her to return.

Marge told Deputy Miller that if they gave the girl the opportunity to make her call, they might be alerting the people involved in the illegal-substance operation. Deputy Miller agreed and called the sheriff to relay what Marge had said. The sheriff also agreed and said for them to wait until he made some calls, giving him some time to put something together.

Sheriff Donahue called the DEA, the Leon County sheriff, and the Tallahassee police chief. Everyone agreed to a joint effort with the DEA as the lead. They sent cars to the warehouse in Tallahassee to bust the operation. When they arrived, an auto-parts van was making a delivery, but not of auto parts. The bust was successful and broke up a major drug and illegal-substance operation. Sheriff Donahue alerted Deputy Miller that she could go forward with her arrest.

Deputy Miller told Debbie Lakes that she was being placed under arrest and had the right to make a call, but it would have to wait until they got to the sheriff's office. She also told Mrs. Lakes they were not going to arrest her just yet; however, they may yet still do it at another time. Mrs. Lakes was also advised that she was welcome to come to the sheriff's office in case she wanted to offer her daughter support. She said that she and her attorney would follow them, but they had her permission to question Debbie. "Deputy, I hope she comes to her senses and cooperates." She shook her head then said, "But I wouldn't bet on it."

At the sheriff's office, Debbie Lakes was permitted to make her call. When she dialed the number that she had been instructed to call, the party on the other end told her she was on her own, as things had changed and they couldn't help her. They had their own problems.

Debbie Lakes dropped the phone, looked first at her mother then at Deputy Miller. "They said I'm on my own. I don't know what to do."

Deputy Miller said they could get her a court-appointed lawyer. However, they still had to take her into custody. Debbie sobbed and gave her mother a pleading look, but Mrs. Lakes just turned her head. The girl had no one else to turn to now.

"Debbie, you can still cooperate and maybe we can work something out. It's time to do the right thing," Deputy Miller told her.

"Okay, but is there anything you can do for me?"

Sheriff Donahue told her that she was eligible to be treated as an adult, but depending on her cooperation, he would recommend that she be treated as a minor. Whatever sentence she got would be better than prison.

Debbie asked for her mother. When Mrs. Lakes joined them, she told Debbie to cooperate and make it easy on herself. Debbie Lakes made the right decision and told them the entire story about her part as a dealer and her part in the rapes.

She had befriended the girls, sold them or gave them marijuana or pills, and then enticed them to a party where they were introduced to Andrew Zane and his friend Dave. There were also other boys involved, and she named them all. When she finished, the sheriff had the names of six boys, four white and two black, and the names of other girls who had been taken advantage of.

With Debbie Lakes's sworn testimony and the pictures that Marge and Morty had taken, the sheriff's office arrested all six boys, and the county prosecutor elected to try them all as adults, with the goal of maximum sentencing for all. When the trial started, the parents of the boys all protested that their sons were being maligned and treated unfairly. They protested that the prosecutor trumped up the charges and their sons would never be part of such a heinous offense.

Andrew Zane's parents protested the loudest. They even enlisted several prominent luminaries to their cause who also championed the idea that the criminal justice system was corrupt and unjust. Their actions thoroughly annoyed Carter, but he kept calm, which was difficult for him.

Missing from the group was one set of parents. Their son, at the parents' urging, had pleaded guilty and asked to be tried as a minor in return for his testimony against the others. The prosecutor agreed to the request, and with his testimony, the pictures, and ten girls ready to testify in person, the other boys started to turn on each other. At the suggestion of their parents and their attorneys, most of them agreed to a guilty plea and the judge's sentencing requirements. Andrew Zane and David Jenks remained staunch in their defense and went to trial. They lost their case in court and were sentenced to fifteen years with no possibility of parole because of their role as the ringleaders.

Three of the boys were sentenced as adults with ten years' jail time and the possibility of parole in five years. But they would be treated as sexual offenders for the rest of their lives. Andrew Zane and David Jenks lost their case in court. They were convicted and sentenced to fifteen years with no possibility of parole because of their role as the ringleaders. The boy who first pleaded guilty was tried as a minor and sentenced to a juvenile facility until he turned twenty-one. Debbie Lakes pleaded guilty and was also tried as a juvenile and got the same sentence.

When everything was over, Marge thanked the sheriff and Deputy Miller. She left with John Carter and Jayne to celebrate at his office. They toasted with a bottle of champagne and pecan swirls.

"I guess it must be hard raising children, especially teenagers, John."

"Yes, it is, Marge, and it's even harder when you're a single parent like Jayne and Betty Lakes."

"I can't believe her daughter was ready to let the woman go to jail just to protect some lowlifes. You've been fortunate with Jessica."

"Yes, we have been. You know, you do the best you can, and then hope for the best. Those boys got what they deserved, and those parents should have paid a price too, especially for their tactics during and leading up to the trial."

"Hopefully they'll get theirs in the court of public opinion, but I wouldn't bet on it. Not the way the media covered the case. Anyway, I'm finished and could use a vacation. I'm going home now. You two take care."

"You do the same, and take that vacation. You earned it. Thanks so much, Marge."

Marge left, and Carter and Jayne left shortly after her.

Jessica was waiting in the driveway when Carter arrived home. She ran up to him and asked what had happened. After he told her the outcome, she gave him a big hug and said that she was proud of him and loved him. He thanked her and said it was all because she did the right thing then they went in to join Emily for dinner.

As they were about to sit down to dinner, the telephone rang. Emily answered it and said to John, "John, Jennifer Brooks is on the line for you."

"Oh, that must be Jessica's coach. I wonder what she wants?"

"Dad, my coach's name is Jennifer Rowland, not Brooks."

Confused, Carter took the phone and answered the call. "This is John Carter. How can I help you, Ms. Brooks?" ,,"You don't know me Mr. Carter, but I just wanted to call and say thank you for all you did. You are a kind man sir."

That was all the caller said before hanging up. Carter stood there with the phone in his hand and a look of surprise on his face. "That was the strangest call I've ever gotten. The woman said thank you, that I'm a kind man, and hung up. I honestly don't know who she was."

Together Emily and Jessica shouted, "You are a kind man, Mr. Carter."

The three of them laughed and sat down to dinner. After dinner and dessert, John and Emily decided to make it an early evening and retired to their bedroom.

After a session of lovemaking, they were lying next to each other about to fall asleep when John said, "We should get a dog."

Emily's response was a simple, "In your dreams, John Carter."

In Randall County, Sheriff John Carter and his wife, Marge, had just finished a late dinner and were cleaning up the kitchen before retiring for an early evening. The telephone rang, and Marge answered it.

She gave Carter a strange look. "John, it's Jennifer Brooks, and she wants to speak with Sheriff Carter."

Carter seemed confused. "I don't know any Jennifer Brooks. Are you sure it's for me?"

"She asked specifically for the sheriff, so here, take your call."

He took the receiver from her and answered, "This is Sheriff Carter. How can I help you, Ms. Brooks?"

"Sheriff Carter, you don't know me, but I just wanted to call and say thank you for all you did. You are a kind man, sir." That was all the caller said then hung up.

Carter stood there with the phone in his hand and a look of surprise on his face. "That was the strangest call I've ever gotten. The woman said thank you, that I'm a kind man and hung up. I honestly don't know who she was."Marge proclaimed, "You are indeed a very kind man, Sheriff Carter."

They retired to their bedroom and had a final lovemaking session, and then fell asleep with visions of a toddler playing with their dog Bailey.

CHAPTER 49

Thanksgiving at the Carter household in Sutter Brooke used to be a much bigger occasion. But with John's father and grandmother deceased and Emily's mother deceased and her father in an assisted-living facility with Alzheimer's, there were now only four of them present. John's mother always attended Thanksgiving dinner and enjoyed spending time with her son and granddaughter, Jessica. It was a bit of a drive from her home in Tallahassee-but it was one she enjoyed making.

The Sutter Brooke development was started in the midnineties, and the Carters were one of the first purchasers of a lot and home site. Their 3,500-square-foot, four-bedroom home sat on an acre and a half of property with a woodland area at the rear of the property line. When the house was first built, Emily made sure that her studio faced the woodland so she could enjoy the view as she worked on her watercolors. John's office also faced the woodland. The home featured a long, winding driveway that led to both the garage and front entryway. The lawn was well manicured, and both front and back yards were lushly landscaped. John Carter was not ashamed to show off his well-earned rewards in life.

Sarah and Emily enjoyed a good relationship, and Sarah acknowledged Emily's right as the host for the occasion. After spending some time with Jessica, she and John sat out on the screened porch by the pool, with glasses of apple cider. It was their routine every Thanksgiving, before dinner was served.

"Mom, can I ask you a question?"

Sarah Carter had an idea what the question would be. She figured sooner or later he would get around to asking and was certain it would have to do with her father and his grandmother.

"Ask away, John. You usually do, and I think I know what it's about."

John wasn't sure how he should ask, and her saying that she knew what it was about disturbed him a little. What he wanted to ask her was a little delicate, but that had never stopped him, especially since he was a lawyer. It was his job to ask the delicate questions.

"Mom, you remember after Grandma's burial I asked you a question about, for the sake of making it easy, memory loss?"

"John, let me make this easy for you. I'm certain you and your grandmother had a conversation about your grandfather and she asked you to keep it a secret. Am I correct?"

"Yes, but—"

"John, she did the same with me. She made me promise to keep it between the two of us. She told you about your grandfather being struck by lightning and experiencing occasional memory lapses. She probably wanted you to ask me if I had experienced any lapses. Is that right?"

"You told me you did, but didn't really elaborate on them. I've had a few, and I'm concerned if it's hereditary and if Jessica might inherit them. You get them, and now I get them, so it's possible Jessica might."

Sarah sensed John's concern, as she had the same concern. She too thought the memory lapses were inherited. Her doctor had no explanation, and neither did John's. She hoped John wasn't suggesting having Jessica tested.

"John, it's possible, but please don't tell Jessica, and don't put her through tests that might not reveal anything. It's very possible we've inherited it from your grandfather and it's something we both have to live with. I've lived a long life and the lapses haven't been a problem, and hopefully they haven't been for you, unless there's something more. Is there, John?"

"So far no, but I'm concerned, that's all. You know how I am. I don't like dealing with the unexplainable. One thing more—when you have your lapses, do you remember anything at all from them? Like, maybe, where you were or anything?"

Sarah hesitated before replying, not wanting to reveal too much.

"No, I've never had any memory of anything. It's like time just disappeared. Have you experienced any remembrances?"

Actually, John had occasionally experienced some things, but not much. A name or place sometimes, but they were always little bits that didn't make sense. He wasn't going to tell his mother that he had started a diary of them, as he knew she would worry.

"No, nothing at all, but it is strange, don't you think? Did Grandpa have any remembrances?"

"Mom never said he did, and Grandpa never did either. I agree it is strange, but we all have some things we have to just live with. I guess it's our curse in life. Isn't it close to dinnertime?"

Sarah didn't want to discuss the subject anymore. She was holding back things and didn't want to alarm John.

Emily suddenly shouted, "Come and get it, you two. This turkey is dying to be eaten, and Jessica and I are starved."

John and Sarah got up and joined Emily and Jessica at the table. Emily had done it again: the table looked great, with plenty of food. They offered a short grace before John carved the turkey. After they finished eating, Emily announced that this year there was pumpkin and apple pie. Emily had made the pumpkin, but Jessica had made the apple pie.

Emily, Sarah, and Jessica cleared the table, and then the three of them did the dishes together. Emily was happy they were doing it. It had become sort of a tradition. Maybe someday, but not too soon, it would become Jessica's turn to host dinner. Sarah enjoyed being part of the ritual and hoped she would be around for many more, maybe even when it was Jessica's turn. When the dishes were done, they all sat for coffee and pie. Everyone had pumpkin and apple, and the adults remarked on how great Jessica's apple pie was. Jessica was given the honor of making apple pie every Thanksgiving.

Saturday morning, the Carter family, minus Sarah, were up and getting provisions ready for their Saturday afternoon tailgating party. The Carters were responsible for the sausage, burgers, and hot dogs. They were also responsible for the television set. Others were responsible for snacks, potato salad, condiments, beer, ice, and the tent. This was a big game, and there would be at least twenty people at the tailgating party. Florida State was hosting Florida, and this just might be the Seminoles' year to stomp the Gators.

All in attendance at the tailgating party were big boosters and had consecutive parking spots in the first row across from the entrance to the stadium. Seven vehicles were parked facing each other, with space between them for the tents, grills, tables, and seating. The crowd gathered, the grills were fired up, the television was turned on, the condiment and food tables were set up, the beer was in the coolers, and the party began. Everyone was decked out in Seminole gear and doing the traditional Seminole chant.

Don Mathews asked John Carter what he thought the Seminoles chances were and what he thought about their quarterback, Jimmy Cochran. Don had been a big Seminole booster for nearly twenty-five years. He didn't play ball, but he had a passion for Seminole sports. Don was also an attorney, like John Carter, but he specialized in estate planning. The two men had been tailgate buddies for over ten years now. Don joined the group when his other tailgate group started to dwindle due to old age. What was left of them joined John's group.

"I think we got a very good chance this year, Don. That Cochran kid has good throwing mechanics, and he's proven himself a starter all season. Let's hope we get to celebrate after the game."

"Yeah, me too. I'm tired of being disappointed with fourth-quarter lapses and blowing leads."

"Amen, brother."

The game was every bit as excited as they always were. The Seminole faithful were on their feet the whole game doing the familiar chop and war chant, with the Marching Chiefs band whipping the crowd into a wild frenzy. You could barely hear anyone talk, it was so loud and exciting. The Seminoles managed to retain the lead in the fourth quarter and beat the Gators 30–14. The crowd chanted, "So long, it's been good to know ya" and "Overrated, overrated."

Back at the tailgate party, everyone was whooping and hollering and the beer was flowing. Three hours after the game was over, everybody packed up and headed for home. John, Emily, and Jessica were tired and glad when they finally got home but were still feeling the excitement. Jessica asked if she could spend the night at her friend and teammate Kristen's house. Welcoming the time alone, John and Emily wished her a good time.

That night John and Emily were like honeymooners, as they destroyed the beautifully made-up bed that Emily had very carefully arranged. Pillows were thrown all over the bedroom, and the sheets were crumpled as though a dozen animals had gotten into the bed.

After they finished making love, Emily got up, said she had to go to the bathroom, and then ran to the bathroom completely naked. John watched and enjoyed the wonderful view. When she returned, Emily noticed John staring at her and noticed his erection.

"Looks like halftime is over and we're about to start the third quarter, counselor."

"Third and fourth quarter, and hopefully I won't blow a fourth-quarter lead."

"Yes, but I may. You ready for kickoff?"

"Go, Seminoles."

They scored touchdowns in both the third and fourth quarters, and once again the Seminoles were victorious.

CHAPTER 50

Monday afternoon, Carter was wrapping up a phone conversation with a possible new client and both were beaming about the Seminoles' victory Saturday when Jayne stuck her head in.

"John, Mrs. Parker is on line two for you. She said it was important."

Carter's eyes narrowed with concern, and he told his caller that he had an emergency and had to take another call. Mary Parker was the administrator at the Heritage Independent Living complex where his mother resided. She had been the administrator there for the last ten years and was quite familiar with Carter and his mother. She often had coffee with Sarah on the balcony. When she used her last name only and said that it was important, Carter expected the worst since they had always been on a first-name basis. He knew this call would come sooner or later, but he'd hoped it would be much later.

"Thanks, Jayne. I'll take the call."

Carter answered the telephone, and when Mrs. Parker hesitated to respond, he knew it was really serious. "Mary, it's so nice to hear from you. I was just getting ready to leave and visit Mom. Is there something the matter with her?"

Mary Parker hesitated before responding. As the administrator at Heritage, she'd had to make a number of these calls, and none of them were ever easy. This one would be more difficult because of her relationship with Carter and his mother.

"Mr. Carter, I'm afraid I have bad news." She paused, considering what to say.

John realized that it was what he'd expected. He didn't want Mary to feel uncomfortable and knew that this was really hard for her, so he interrupted her. "Mary, please call me John like you always do. I believe I know what you have to say. Just tell me it was peaceful."

Mary Parker's burden became a little lighter thanks to him. "Thanks, John. Yes, she passed peacefully in her favorite rocker sitting on her balcony with a book and pen in her hand. She must have dozed off while writing and went in peace. When she didn't answer my call, I went to her apartment and found her. The paramedics are here and have pronounced her deceased." Mrs. Parker chose not to say *dead* as it wasn't the kind thing to say. "I'm so sorry, John. Will you still be coming here this afternoon?"

He was relieved about how his mother's last moments were. She passed doing what she enjoyed, and he couldn't have been any happier for her. It was the way she always said she would like to leave this world.

"Yes, Mary, I'm still coming by. I have to call Emily and Jessica and tell them. Jessica isn't going to be happy. Can I have a couple of days to empty out her apartment? I would like Jessica to be there with me when I do it."

"That's fine, John. Take a week if you need it. Just let me know what arrangements you make for Sarah."

Sarah had made arrangements for her remains to be cremated at a funeral home, so John knew what to do.

"Mom already made arrangements with Berdstom's Funeral Home. I'll see if I can contact them and have them take care of everything. I really don't want her taken to the county morgue."

"John, we have a relationship with them, and I'm familiar with the owner. Let me call him and arrange everything. Is that okay with you?"

He was relieved that Mary Parker was able to take care of matters since he wasn't really up to it.

"Thanks, Mary. I really appreciate your help. Mom would be so grateful too. Let me know what happens. Call me on my cell phone if there's a problem. You have the number. I'll see you in a little while."

" John, if you want someone to talk to, I'll be here if you need me."

They hung up, and he sat at his desk in silence before saying anything. Jayne waited quietly in the doorway.

"My mom passed away, Jayne. I have to go to her apartment and make arrangements. First I need a moment alone."

Since Jayne had known John and his mother for quite some time, she took it upon herself to offer her sincere condolences.

"John, I'm so sorry for your loss. Is there anything I can do, anything at all?"

Carter, not one to mourn for long, appreciated her offer. However, this was his situation to deal with. Telling Jessica was the really difficult part.

"Thanks, Jayne. I appreciate it, but this is something I have to deal with by myself. I'm not looking forward to calling Jessica though."

Jayne wanted to help, but he made it apparent that he had to do this by himself. She left his office and closed the door.

Alone, Carter rested his elbows on the desk, placed his head in his hands, and sobbed. After a while, he regained his composure and decided to leave for the day. He got up, grabbed his briefcase, opened the door, and stepped out. His face had a pale look, and his eyes revealed that he had cried.

"Jayne, I'm going to my mother's apartment now. I'll call Emily from there. I'm feeling kind of bummed. Why don't you go home?"

"I'll stay for a while. I feel the same. After I get things in order, I'll go home too. The traffic on Thomasville Road will probably be heavy. Drive safely, John, and don't worry about things here. I can take care of everything, so if you need the time, take Friday off too."

"Thanks, Jayne. You always have my back. I don't know what I'd do without you. I think I might take Friday off. I can use the time."

"John, if there's anything you need, let me know. If you want someone to talk to, I'm here for you."

"Thanks, Jayne, but I'll be okay. See ya."

Carter left the office, went to get his car, and drove to his mother's apartment complex located not far from his office on Meridian Avenue. When he pulled into the parking lot at Heritage Independent, he noticed that the paramedics were getting into their vehicle. Mary Parker was standing by the front entrance watching them. He parked and hurried toward the entrance, hoping he could catch the paramedics before they left.

He stepped in front of the EMT vehicle and started waving to the driver. The vehicle stopped, and the driver rolled down his window.

"Excuse me, sir, we're in kind of a hurry here."

Carted walked over to the driver's side. "I know you are. Unfortunately I believe that's my mother you have back there. Can you tell me where you're taking her? My name's John Carter."

Not sure what to do, the driver looked at the passenger, and she nodded okay.

"Is your mother Sarah Carter, sir?"

Grateful for the response, John said, "Yes."

The passenger again nodded okay to the driver.

"We're taking her to Berdstom's Funeral Home. You can make arrangements to see her there."

Relieved that his wishes were being carried out, Carter replied, "Thank you. I'll do that."

"Sorry for your loss, Mr. Carter."

"Thank you."

John walked over to meet with Mary Parker. She reached out, and the two of them embraced.

"John, again I'm so sorry for your loss, and I'm at a loss for words. Sarah was such a sweet person. I'm going to miss her."

"I am too, Mary. Can I get in her apartment now?"

"Sure. I'll go with you, if that's okay."

"I'd appreciate that, Mary. First I have to call Emily and give her the news."

Carter called her on his cell phone, and as the home phone rang, he debated about telling Emily, but when she answered he felt somewhat relieved, although he would have preferred to do it in person.

"Hello, John. Are we still going to dinner tonight?"

He was hesitant. "Emily, I have bad news."

"Is it Sarah?"

"Yes. She passed away this afternoon in her apartment. I'm here now, and they've already taken her to the funeral home. I'm going to check the apartment with Mary. I'm not looking forward to telling Jessica."

There was an ominous silence on the other end.

"Oh, John, I'm so sorry. Forget about dinner. Do what you have to, and we can tell Jess tonight together."

Her words made him feel a little relieved, but tears fell down his cheek. Carter was pleased that she would be there with him when he told Jessica.

"Thanks, Em. I'll see you later."

"Bye, John."

Carter closed his phone and put it in his jacket pocket, and then he and Mary entered the apartment building and went to the elevator. The lobby at Heritage Independent Living resembled a four-star hotel, elaborately decorated with comfortable seating spaced throughout the area and beautiful watercolors adorning the walls. A few of them were actually Emily's paintings that she had donated to the complex. Carter and Mary Parker entered the elevator and took it to the third floor. They stepped out of the elevator and walked toward Sarah's apartment. The hallway was decorated with plush carpeting and rich wallpaper. It was like walking in the hallway of a lavish hotel.

When they reached Sarah's apartment, Mary Parker opened it and let Carter enter. Sarah had elegantly decorated the apartment with the help of a design firm, but it wasn't extravagant. The furniture was simple, and nice artwork depicting scenes from Europe adorned the walls. A television sat on a table, along with a stereo and radio for her entertainment. Sarah, however, spent most of her time on the balcony reading and writing.

Mary Parker had placed the book that Sarah had been writing in on Sarah's desk. She walked over, picked it up, and handed it to John. He was lost in thought as he gazed around the apartment remembering the last time he was there to visit his mother.

"John, this is the book that Sarah was writing in when I found her."

He reached out, took the book and opened it to the first page. In Sarah's handwriting it read *"The Farber Legacy."* He turned a page and read to himself.

June 23, 1944—I had another episode and only remember something about the war. This was the first since last year that I've had one. I told Mom about it, and she said I may have inherited it from Dad.

She told me his started in 1927 after he was struck by lightning on his way home from the farm. He was out for two days and had no memory of what happened. He had others, but they didn't interfere with his way of life and the doctor said it was nothing to worry about. I decided to keep this diary in case it happened again and write down the dates and anything I could remember.

February 5, 1945—Another episode; however, I don't remember anything this time. Mom said Dad also had an episode.

April 22, 1957—Strange incident, remember something about a horse.

There were others as he continued to read, skipping over dates until he found the one in 1989.

March 27, 1989—Had a conversation with John. He spoke with Mother, and she told him about Father.

He read other pages with dates and instances on them. Carter leafed through the pages and found a notation about Jessica.

April 2001—Jessica called, said she got into Duke, and then she visited and told me again. We talked about her having incidents, also our secret and my father's legacy.

Carter was surprised to learn about Jessica's incidents. He didn't know that she was experiencing the same thing that he and his mother had experienced. Now that he knew, he would talk to Jessica about it and maybe the two could go through Sarah's diary together. The diary may tell more about his mother and the legacy.

He closed the diary and held it in his hands. Carter didn't want to leave it there because of what it contained, so he decided to take it home, so he and Jessica could go through it together.

"Mary, I'm going to take this with me. There are some private things in it, and I don't want to leave it lying around here."

"That's fine, John. Take whatever you want. It's all yours now. Is there anything else you would like to take? I can get someone to help you."

"No, thanks, Mary. This is all I want for now. I think I'm going to go home and talk with Emily, and I still have to tell Jessica. We'll probably be by Saturday to make arrangements for Mom's things."

"John, please call and let me know when you'll be coming by. I'll be sure and be here. Say hello to Emily for me."

"Thanks, I will. Take care, Mary."

"You do the same, John."

He left the apartment feeling sorrowful. Mary Parker followed him to the front entrance after locking the apartment.

Emily was waiting at home to meet him. They hugged and kissed, entered the house, and went right to the kitchen. Emily had prepared a light dinner in case he wanted to eat something.

"Jessica should be home shortly. Do you want to eat or wait for her, John?"

He shook his head and replied, "I'm really not hungry. Can we just have a glass of wine together?"

"Sure, I'll get the glasses and you get the wine."

He selected a nice chardonnay, poured them each a glass and with a heavy heart said, "These should be happy times, Em."

"They will come, John."

"I know. Just wish they were now."

They heard the garage door go up and Jessica's car pulling in, and then they heard a shout.

"I'm home. What's for dinner? I'm starved."

Jessica saw her parents in the kitchen holding glasses of wine and with somber expressions on their faces.

"What's the matter? You two look sad." Her books landed on the floor and made a sound like thunder. "Oh no!" Her mouth opened wide, and her hands covered her cheeks as she cried out, "It's Grandma, isn't it? What happened?"

Carter got up, walked toward Jessica, and held out his arms to hold her. She cuddled in his embrace.

"Jess, Grandma passed in her sleep this afternoon. She went peacefully, writing as she always does on her porch. I'm so sorry, Jess."

Jessica sobbed and looked over at her mother.

"What happens now?"

"Jess, you and Dad have to go take care of her apartment and get things in order. Dad already took care of Grandma's remains." The words left a sorrowful feeling in her heart, and she was certain it did the same to both John and Jessica, but it was all she could think of. "When you're ready, Dad will take you," she added. "It can wait awhile."

Jessica composed herself, but Carter was still sobbing.

"Dad, can we get it over soon, before the funeral?"

Emily walked over, embraced Carter, wiped his eyes with a tissue, and offered a smile. Carter regained some of his composure and managed a smile back.

"It's probably better we did, Jess. How about we do it Wednesday?"

"Okay, Dad."

Carter thought of the diary. "Jess, there is something I want you to read with me, but we'll do it tomorrow. We're all feeling down, so we'll just let the rest of the day go on without any more sad talk. Maybe it will help us feel better."

Carter, Emily, and Jessica embraced and held it for a full ten minutes.

The next day Carter and Jessica went through the diary. Both learned a lot more about Sarah and the legacy. Carter asked Jessica about her incidents.

"They come once in a while, and I don't remember anything. What about you, Dad?"

"Mine seem to come when I'm under stressful situations like Rachel's case. I get bits and pieces, and I'm keeping a diary. You should do the same if you remember anything, Jess."

"I will. Can we go for a walk?"

"Sure. Mom, too?"

"No. Just you and me."

"Okay, let's go."

As they walked, Carter held Jessica's hand.

Several days later, Sarah Carter was laid to rest. A brief memorial was held at Heritage Independent.

After returning home from the memorial service, John and Jessica went into his office and he gave Sarah's diary to her.

"This is yours, Jessica. I'd rather you keep it. Your grandmother may have wanted you to have it."

"Thanks, Dad. I'll go through it starting from the beginning. Maybe I'll add my own comments."

EPILOGUE

Five months later, John Carter, Leroy Jones, and William were fishing on a beautiful Sunday morning. So far all three had been fortunate to have caught something. They were really enjoying themselves, especially William, who caught the most fish. It was a fishermen's day; even the weather was cooperating. Suddenly both Carter and Leroy's phones rang. They each answered and then closed their phones, looked at each other, and bumped shoulders like in high school after scoring a touchdown.

"What's the matter, Dad? You look surprised."

Leroy slapped his forehead and shouted, "You're about to be a brother, Son!"

"And I'm about to become a daddy," screamed Carter.

Leroy turned his palms up and asked, "What do we do, John?"

Carter started reeling in his line and answered, "We do what we were told, that's what, and we get our asses to the hospital." He started dialing his cell phone and added, "First, I'll call and arrange for deputies to get both women there. We should get there in time. Let's get going."

They packed up their gear, piled into Carter's truck, and sped off to the Randall County Hospital. When they arrived, the deputies had already delivered the women there. The three of them rushed inside and asked where the maternity floor was. After getting directions, they headed for their respective wives' rooms. Each man walked into his wife's room only to be told that it was about time. Thirty minutes later, the two women were taken to their individual birthing rooms. Shortly thereafter, both delivered healthy baby girls.

Carter asked Marge what they should name the little one.

"We are going to name her Sarah, after my grandmother, Sarah Riddling Farber. She was someone special and an important influence in my life. In honor of her, our little girl's name is Sarah. You okay with that, quarterback?"

Carter's mouth formed a huge smile. "It's fine by me. I believe there was a Sarah in my family too. If she has our good looks and my charm and wit, then it will be a legacy we give to her. Sarah it is, wide receiver. I love you both."

"You're crazy, quarterback, but we love you too."

Leroy stepped into the room and introduced them to his daughter, Anne, named partly after Annie and partly after his maternal grandmother. Everyone was excited and happy, including William, who wouldn't have to share his dad with a brother.

Several months earlier, Marge had released the body of Becky Larson to her father, who took her back to Live Oak and buried her next to her mother. Peter Larson had signed a release, and Judge Henry authorized the release of the remains. Deborah and Charles Worthington took possession of Jennifer Williams's body and had it delivered to Bensmille, North Carolina, where she was buried alongside her mother.

Pastor Jeremiah Ellison ended up preaching out of a tent in small midwestern towns. At his last location, he disappeared after he was discovered giving spiritual guidance to the wife of a local farmer. The farmer and his two sons took matters into their own hands and hung him from a tree behind the tent. Then they buried his body in an undisclosed location. Eventually the tent was taken down and no questions were ever asked about what happened to the pastor.

Agnes Ellison found her calling as a pastor at a small, rural church in eastern Tennessee. She had a brand-new identity as Abigail Waverly and also worked with abused women and children. The marquee in front of her church read:

COME REST YOUR GENTLE SOUL
ALONG YOUR JOURNEY TO THE LORD

Buddy Larson recovered from his heart attack and was released from the hospital after a two-week stay. He didn't divorce Missy, but instead made her life a living nightmare. He told her that if she wanted spending money, she had to get a job and earn it. If she refused, he would divorce her, and according to the prenuptial agreement, she would get nothing due to her infidelity.

Whenever Buddy went to UF football games, he left her at home and took Peter instead. The folks in the booster box were happy she wasn't there. Buddy also resigned his position as the Democratic Party's state party chairman.

When Peter Larson came up for reelection, he had a difficult time and lost to a relatively unknown candidate, Richard Graebert. With his brother, Randy, as his campaign manager, he ran a formidable campaign using the restaurant as campaign headquarters. He soundly defeated Peter Larson. Buddy and Peter attempted to use smear tactics, but when the subject of incriminating pictures was brought up, they backed down. Richard's popularity came from the patrons at the restaurant who spread the word. Larson's secretary had resigned and joined the Graebert team.

In Dodson County, Deputy Anne Miller completed her licensing requirements. With the help of the sheriff, she started a counseling program for women and girls who were victims of rape and abuse. Rachel Whatley was one of the first girls to join the group. Several of the other girls who were part of the case against the six boys also joined. Marge Davis was a frequent guest speaker, and her presence attracted some adult participants. Marge frequently attended the meetings as a participant.

John Carter increased the size of his practice with the addition of Amy Weisman, who agreed to take on some pro bono cases as well as her own cases. He changed the name of the firm to Carter and Weisman, LLC. Jayne Burrows was now the legal assistant for both attorneys and periodically received help from a few law students who desired to do an internship.

Rachel Whatley changed high schools. With a recommendation from Carter, she enrolled at Sinclair Academy and joined the girls' swim team. She was also enjoying her newfound friends, Jessica Carter and Kristen English.

During her senior year, Jessica announced her intentions to accept a scholarship to Duke University. Carter was disappointed that she hadn't chosen FSU, but he was proud of his daughter and would support her wherever she went. He was also happy that she'd made her choice because she planned on enrolling in medical school after graduation and not law school. Emily glowed with so much pride that she couldn't stop congratulating her. Jessica eventually had to lovingly tell her to cease and desist. It became a family joke.

Marge Davis, Annie Miller, and Amy Weisman became good friends, and the three of them get together on Saturday mornings for a five-mile run.

AUTHOR'S COMMENTS

As previously stated at the outset, this book is a novel, a work of fiction. Though several of the cities mentioned do exist, as do the Orlando Sheriff's Office and the North Carolina Special Investigation Unit, people and events in this book are fictitious. Any resemblance to actual events, locales, or persons, living or dead, is entirely coincidental. The events that took place in this book are a product of my imagination.

Unfortunately, acts of rape and abuse of women and girls are facts of life in today's society. These were purely fictitious cases. To say the writing of the heinous nature of these acts didn't have an emotional impact on me would be an enormous misconception.

There are cases where women who have experienced a miscarriage or even an abortion have been told that they can no longer conceive but have been fortunate enough to experience the miracle of birth. With all the evil in this world, God has still found time to perform this miracle, along with the gifting of the joy and the trials and tribulations of parenting a child.

In doing my research, I relied on a number of Internet search engines and numerous websites for background information. My thanks to the wealth of information they provided. It's truly amazing what you can do sitting at your desk nowadays. I would have had to do a bit of traveling, but instead I let my fingers do the work.

Made in the USA
Middletown, DE
12 June 2016